D0016372

PRAISE FOR *THE RESCUE*

"Steven Konkoly's new Ryan Decker series is a triumph—an action-thriller master class in spy craft, tension, and suspense. An absolute must-read for fans of Tom Clancy, Vince Flynn, and Brad Thor."

—Blake Crouch, *New York Times* bestselling author

"*The Rescue* by Steven Konkoly has everything I love in a thriller—betrayal, murder, a badass investigator, and a man fueled by revenge."

—T.R. Ragan, *New York Times* bestselling author

"*The Rescue* grabs you like a bear trap and never lets go. No one writes action sequences any better than Steve Konkoly—he drops his heroes into impossible situations and leaves you no option but to keep your head down, follow where they lead, and hope you make it out alive."

—Matthew Fitzsimmons, *Wall Street Journal* bestselling author

"Breakneck twists, political conspiracy, bristling action—*The Rescue* has it all! Steven Konkoly has created a dynamic and powerful character in Ryan Decker."

—Joe Hart, *Wall Street Journal* bestselling author

"If you are a fan of characters like Scot Harvath and Mitch Rapp, this new series is a must read. Steven Konkoly delivers a refreshingly unique blend of action, espionage, and well-researched realism."

—Andrew Watts, *USA Today* bestselling author

"An excellent source for your daily dose of action, conspiracy, and intrigue."

—Tim Tigner, author of *Betrayal*

"Fans of Mark Greaney and Brad Taylor, take notice: *The Rescue* has kicked off a stunning new series that deserves a place on your reading list. Ryan Decker is a must-read character."

—Jason Kasper, author of *Greatest Enemy*

"*The Rescue* immediately drops the reader into a well-drawn world of betrayal, revenge, and redemption. Ryan Decker is a flawed, relatable hero, unstoppable in his quest for justice."

—Tom Abrahams, author of *Sedition*

THE RESCUE

Also by Steven Konkoly

The Fractured State Series

Fractured State
Rogue State

The Perseid Collapse Series

The Jakarta Pandemic
The Perseid Collapse
Event Horizon
Point of Crisis
Dispatches

The Black Flagged Series

Alpha
Redux
Apex
Vektor
Omega

The Zulu Virus Chronicles

Hot Zone
Kill Box
Fire Storm

THE
RESCUE

STEVEN KONKOLY

THOMAS & MERCER

This is a work of fiction. Names, characters, organizations, places, events, and incidents are either products of the author's imagination or are used fictitiously. Any resemblance to actual persons, living or dead, or actual events is purely coincidental.

Text copyright © 2019 by Steven Konkoly
All rights reserved.

No part of this book may be reproduced, or stored in a retrieval system, or transmitted in any form or by any means, electronic, mechanical, photocopying, recording, or otherwise, without express written permission of the publisher.

Published by Thomas & Mercer, Seattle

www.apub.com

Amazon, the Amazon logo, and Thomas & Mercer are trademarks of Amazon.com, Inc., or its affiliates.

ISBN-13: 9781542042246 (hardcover)
ISBN-10: 1542042240 (hardcover)
ISBN-13: 9781542040273 (paperback)
ISBN-10: 1542040272 (paperback)

Cover design by Rex Bonomelli

Printed in the United States of America

First edition

To Kosia, Matthew, and Sophia—the heart and soul of my writing.

PART ONE

CHAPTER ONE

Ryan Decker wiped the perspiration from his face with a damp, thread-bare hand towel. A futile gesture he'd repeat again in a few moments. The temperature inside the dank motel room pushed ninety degrees, the rattling air conditioner unable to keep up with the extra demand imposed by his teammates and a table packed with overtaxed computer towers.

Luckily for him, the two-day stay at La Jacinta Inn was rapidly approaching an end. Barring any unforeseen difficulties, they should be packing up within ten minutes. Gone in less than twenty.

"Ghost just crossed phase line Charlie," said Brad Pierce, the team's second-in-command.

"Tell them they need to pick up the pace," said Decker. "Specter crossed Charlie a minute ago."

"They know what they're doing."

"I know," said Decker, confirming Ghost's position on the flat-screen monitor.

Ghost, a five-man team of seasoned hostage-rescue operators, had the tougher approach, crossing several hills and ravines from their drop-off point north of the target house. The thicker scrub and occasional tree in the hills would camouflage their approach and allow them to nestle in closer to the Bratva "distribution center" than Specter, which would have to cross nearly a hundred yards of flat, sandy ground to reach the house.

SPECTER was the direct-action assault team, assigned to clear a path immediately outside and then inside the target structure for GHOST. Comprised of six former SWAT and Special Forces operators, they would arrive from the south and split into two groups of three, to enter the house from opposite sides. GHOST would closely follow whichever team encountered the least resistance and execute the hostage-rescue phase of the operation.

Decker had outsourced the hostage-rescue team from an exclusive word-of-mouth-only group that specialized in "actively opposed asset recoveries." His in-house hostage-rescue team was top-notch, but the men and women he'd hired for this mission were the absolute best in the business. You didn't cut corners with the life of an influential US senator's daughter on the line.

Deborah Payne, his lead tactical operations coordinator, spoke without moving her eyes from the screen. "SPECTER reports no obvious movement in the house. All dark."

"Thermal imaging?" said Decker.

"Nothing."

He didn't like that. A few guards would be active, even at two in the morning, especially given what the long-range surveillance team had confirmed earlier in the day. Fifteen children and teenagers had been moved into the house during the morning. Decker had planned to move on the location last night—but when he learned that more kids were on the way, he delayed the mission by twenty-four hours. He couldn't leave these children in the hands of the Russian mob.

The isolated Riverside County compound served as a Bratva collection point for children abducted from the greater Los Angeles area. Abductees were inspected and evaluated over the span of a few days, then assigned to various categories for distribution into the Bratva's human-trafficking network.

The senator's daughter could endure one more day of captivity to save this newly arrived "crop."

"Dammit," muttered Pierce. "I told you it was a bad idea to wait. If the place is empty, we're screwed."

"It's not empty," said Decker. "We've had a team watching the place for three days. She's there."

"What if she's not?"

"Then our intelligence is wrong, and she was never there."

"The intel is good," said Pierce.

"Then we have nothing to worry about. Only the driver and escort crew left with the delivery van. Just like they always do."

"As far as we could tell."

"They've never concealed a transfer at a location like this before," said Decker. "Hell. They barely disguise what they're doing in the middle of the city—in broad daylight."

"I'm just saying we have a lot riding on this one."

"We always have a lot riding on these," said Decker.

"You know what I mean."

Decker nodded. "I do. Everything will be fine."

Pierce didn't look convinced, and Decker started to have his own doubts. He shook his head. No. The kids were there. The guards were there. Senator Steele's daughter was there, and if she wasn't, the Bratva had moved her long before Decker received the information asserting her presence at the house.

He'd been entirely frank with Senator Steele and Jacob Harcourt from the start: too much time had elapsed since the girl's disappearance, the FBI had produced no physical evidence, and no ransom note had been delivered. The likelihood of finding Meghan Steele was nearly nonexistent. Nearly.

Decker's World Recovery Group got extremely lucky after a long month and a half of searching. Needle-in-a-haystack lucky. The odds of finding this needle twice would be nonexistent once the Bratva learned what happened here. This would be Decker's last shot at finding the senator's daughter.

"Ghost is in final position," said Payne.

Decker took a deep breath, releasing it slowly. "Give them the green light."

"Specter. This is Tombstone. You have a green light to breach the house. Ghost, advise when you start the hostage-rescue phase."

Decker watched the Specter team leader's bouncing feed as the operative reached the back door. The other half of his team was on the other side of the house. Several seconds passed as the team prepped small explosive charges that would blow the door off its hinges.

"Specter Two ready for breach," announced a gravelly voice.

"Copy that. Specter One ready. Stand by to breach," said the team leader. "Two. One. Breach."

The simultaneous flash of the door charges was followed by rapid, confusing camera movement. A few seconds later, the video feed stabilized. A tightly clustered, night vision–equipped group of operatives appeared in the far left corner of the feed, panning their rifles around a large common area featuring a combined kitchen and living room. The team leader's camera pointed at a padlocked door leading to the other half of the house.

"Something's off," said Payne. "No guards."

His teams must have been detected on the way in. That was the only explanation. Decker had a bad feeling about what they'd find on the other side of that door. Pierce muttered an obscenity, shaking his head.

"Bring Ghost up and breach the padlocked door immediately," said Decker.

Payne relayed the orders, and the body armor–clad operatives swarmed forward to attach the explosive charges. Ghost team stacked up along the wall next to the door, waiting for Specter to finish their job.

Pierce tapped his shoulder. "We have company," he said. "FRONT DOOR has a tight convoy of Suburbans and Town Cars turning onto Florida from Santa Fe. Heading in our direction."

FRONT DOOR was a two-person surveillance team situated on the roof of a realty business across the street from the motel. They had a commanding view of Florida Street and the front entrance. Another team sat on the roof of a two-story building behind the motel, ensuring nobody could sneak up on Decker's command center undetected.

"Do you want me to delay the breach?" said Payne.

"Hold on, Deb," said Decker, turning to Pierce. "How long until the vehicles reach the motel entrance?"

"Ten seconds max. They're moving fast."

The time would feel like an eternity for the teams at the target house, but Decker needed to know what they were up against from the vehicles outside the motel before making a final decision.

"Any sign of similar activity near the target house?"

"Negative," replied the operations technician seated next to Payne. "GRAVEYARD reports all clear."

It had to be the FBI. Agent Reeves, the special agent in charge of the Steele case, had protested WRG's involvement from the start, embarking on an immediate campaign of harassment that had required the senator's intervention. Reeves had picked the worst possible moment to renew his vendetta.

"Tell them to breach in twenty seconds unless they hear otherwise," said Decker.

"Are you sure that's a good idea?" said Pierce.

"If a bunch of Russians jump out of those vehicles, I'll assume the worst about the house and withdraw the team."

"You haven't already assumed the—" Pierce began. "Hold that. BACK DOOR reports heavily armed teams on foot approaching the back of the motel. *FBI* stenciled in bold letters on their ballistic shields."

"Has to be Reeves. The senator will have his badge for this," muttered Decker.

"What are we doing?" said Payne.

"The operations center stands down. Only the operations center," said Decker. "Tell GHOST to breach the door now and rescue the hostages. Then transfer command of the operation to GRAVEYARD. Let them know we're compromised."

"Copy that," said Payne before transmitting the orders.

Red strobe lights flashed through the thin cracks between the window shades as tires screeched in the distance.

"FRONT DOOR reports heavily armed personnel exiting the vehicles and heading for the motor court entrance. FBI stencils confirmed," said Pierce. "What now?"

"We disarm and walk out with our hands up. Immediately," said Decker, removing his pistol from a concealed hip holster and tossing it on the bed.

"What about the surveillance teams?" said Pierce.

"My guess is they've already been made. Probably under sniper cover. Tell them to raise their hands and stand very still. Wait for the FBI."

Pierce relayed instructions and threw his pistol on the bed next to Decker's. "None of this makes sense," he said. "The house—and now this?"

He was right. It didn't add up, but there was nothing they could do about it right now. The best they could hope for was a miracle at the target house.

"Any word from GHOST?" said Decker, his hand on the doorknob.

"Breaching in a few seconds," said Payne.

He wanted to wait, but they needed to beat the FBI into the motor court or things would get complicated. "It's in their hands now," he said. "Everyone disarm and walk out behind me."

"I'll switch the feed over to a wireless earpiece," said Payne, standing up. "They might not notice."

"Good thinking."

Satisfied that everyone was disarmed and ready, Decker opened the door and raised his hands, scanning the empty, weed-infested parking lot. Red strobe lights from a dark SUV penetrated the arched motor court entrance, reflecting off the ground-floor windows. He took several steps into cooler night air, turning his head far enough to see that everyone on the command team had followed. Doors on both sides of the motor court creaked open, and his internal security teams streamed into the parking lot.

All of his people stood in the middle of the lot, hands held high above their heads. A few seconds later, the courtyard swarmed with heavily armed, body armor–encased FBI agents barking orders. Decker followed their instructions, ending up facedown—with his hands zip-tied behind his back. He turned his head to the side, scraping his cheek on crumbled asphalt. A rifle barrel gently poked the other cheek.

"Don't move," said the agent, activating the flashlight attached to his rifle.

Decker closed his eyes, unable to keep them open in the blinding light.

A nearby agent yelled, "Over here," and more light penetrated his eyelids.

"Ryan," Payne whispered next to him. "The feed went dead."

He turned his head. "What do you mean?"

The rifle barrel pressed against the top of his head. "Stop talking and stop moving. That's your last warning."

"The feed just flatlined," said Payne.

"What part of *shut up* don't you understand?" The agent standing above Payne pushed her head down with his rifle barrel.

"Where's Decker?" said a familiar voice. Special Agent Reeves.

Before anyone answered, the pavement shuddered once, the word *earthquake* thrown around the motor court by the agents.

"Isn't that ironic!" said Reeves, his voice nearby. "An earthquake at the very moment Ryan Decker is shut down for good."

"I think the word you're looking for is *coincidence*," said Decker, the rifle barrel pressing hard into his cheekbone.

Reeves squatted between Decker and Payne, a victorious grin plastered on his face. "What's going on here, Mr. Decker?"

"We're completely legit."

"We'll see about that," said Reeves. "I imagine I'll find some non-California-compliant firearms in these rooms. This looks like the kind of operation you'd want to protect with some serious firepower, given the people you're bound to piss off."

"Sounds like you're the only one pissed around here. Everything is California compliant."

"Well. I'm not interested in this half of the equation," said Reeves. "I want the other half."

"This is it. We're conducting routine surveillance related to Meghan Steele's kidnapping."

"You're doing more than following up worthless leads. Something big is going on nearby."

One of the agents spoke up. "The woman here was saying something about a feed going dead."

"Feed to who?" said Reeves.

A deep, window-rattling crunch cut off Payne's smart-ass reply.

Reeves looked around the parking lot. "That better not be any of your handiwork, Decker. High explosives are pretty freaking far from California compliant."

It all came together for Decker in the blink of an eye. *No guards at the target house. Ground waves traveled faster than sound.* The parking lot vibration, then, thirty seconds later, a massive, distant explosion. The house had been rigged with explosives. The Russians had known they were coming—well before Decker's team arrived in Hemet.

It was the only explanation. But why didn't they drive a truck bomb into the motor court at the same time and simply cut the rest of the operation down? All of this was related. It had to be. But how? The Russians must have tipped off the FBI, which brought him back to one of his previous questions: Why not vaporize everyone at once?

Decker's vision narrowed with the realization that the command team had been spared for a reason. *The Russians weren't done with them.*

CHAPTER TWO

Two years later

Decker dragged the flimsy disposable razor over the thick stubble on the side of his chin before swishing it in lukewarm water. He repeated the process until the thin layer of gel was gone and his face was smooth. The moment he set the razor down on the side of the sink, a rap against the cell door reminded him the rules still applied, regardless of why he had been transferred. He walked the plastic razor to the door and put it in the small stainless steel bin, which quickly closed.

"Get dressed," said the guard through the intercom. "Marshals are waiting for you."

Decker nodded and returned to the sink to wipe the rest of the gel from his face. Pausing in front of the mirror, he took a long look at the hard face staring back at him. *Same face. Same man.* At least that's what he told himself every time he could bear to look. In truth, nothing was the same—and never would be again. Life as he'd once known it had come to a sudden, unceremonious end two years ago, at a rat-trap motel in Hemet, California.

Overnight, Ryan Decker, decorated Marine veteran and savior of the innocent, had become Prisoner 6581, criminally negligent mercenary and killer of children. Even worse, the loving husband and caring father of two had turned into a disgraced widower and father of one. The newspapers had been merciless from the beginning. The prosecutors—ruthless to the bitter end.

Even his surviving daughter, Riley, blamed him for what happened and wanted nothing to do with him, or so he'd been told. His wife's sister had assumed custody immediately after his arrest and hidden her from the world—and him. Unceremoniously ripped from his life, like his wife and son.

He'd give anything to see her again, or even hear her voice. He'd sent her dozens of letters through his parents, so her aunt wouldn't intercept them, but he'd never received a reply. Decker had no idea if she read them. His parents passed them along during the regular visits they were allowed, but she never opened the letters in front of them. It didn't matter. He'd keep writing. At some point she might change her mind, and he wanted her to know he'd never given up on her.

He rubbed his smooth chin and looked away from the mirror toward the stack of loosely folded civilian clothes on the bed. Khaki pants, long-sleeved blue button-down shirt, black socks, and a pair of brown loafers. He lifted the shirt, frowning at the wrinkles. Seriously? This was the best the FBI could do for a court appearance? Whatever. It beat the orange jumpsuit—barely.

Normally he wouldn't care, but today wasn't about Ryan Decker. It was about something bigger. Something he cared passionately enough about to put aside his distaste for Special Agent Reeves, the man who had made it his personal mission to put Decker behind bars. The very thing that landed him here in the first place—a compulsive sense of duty to protect the innocent.

At some point today, he would testify against the Solntsevskaya Bratva, in a trial focused on the mob organization's human-trafficking operation—or at least that's what he assumed. The Department of Justice had moved him without prior notice from the United States penitentiary in Victorville, California, to the Los Angeles Metropolitan Detention Center, a few blocks from the US District Courthouse. He was familiar with the facility, having spent several months here awaiting his own trial. Inmates returned only to testify in federal cases.

The secretive nature of his transfer further supported the theory. The federal case against the Bratva had kicked into full gear six months after the Hemet disaster—partly due to a wealth of detailed information collected by Decker over the years. Information not subject to Fourth Amendment evidentiary standards, but dependent on his testimony. Hard-earned testimony.

In just over two years of federal custody, Decker had survived eight attempts on his life—a new record, according to the warden at Victorville. Someone *really* wanted to bury that testimony, and Decker's money was on the Russians. The Bratva had a vested interest in deep-sixing him, and the feds had no intention of fumbling the case this close to victory. Hence, the pains they had undertaken to keep the transfer a secret.

He'd been placed in protective confinement at Victorville three days before US marshals arrived unannounced and drove him straight to Los Angeles. He'd been in this solitary holding cell since his arrival around four o'clock in the morning. No visitors. No fanfare. Marshals stationed nearby. Factory-sealed MRE for breakfast. The US attorney's office wasn't taking any chances today.

Decker removed his jumpsuit, catching a glimpse of a tightly mus-cled upper body in the mirror. Several finger-length scars wove across his body, each representing a different chapter in the near-death story that had defined his life. Only one other person knew the full story, taking it to her grave because of him. As far as he was concerned, that story would never be told again.

He finished dressing and checked his appearance. *Business casual in federal court—after sleeping in the same clothes for a week.*

"Could be worse," he muttered before knocking on the door. "I'm ready."

The door opened without the usual series of strict verbal instructions, causing Decker to tense, then move to the opposite wall and place his palms against the painted cinder block. He kept his head turned toward the door to get a jump on attempt number nine, should it materialize.

The same guard he'd seen upon arrival appeared in the doorway. "No need for that," he said, motioning for Decker to step into the corridor.

Decker didn't like the change in strict routine that had become his way of life for the past two years. The informality felt wrong.

"Are you sure?" said Decker, lowering his hands and turning around.

"I was given those instructions directly by my section leader," said the guard. "You won't be any trouble, will you?"

He shook his head.

"How about you cover some ground and make your way out of the cell, then?"

Decker complied, stepping into the wide, brightly lit hallway. A furtive look past the guard confirmed they were alone. Five sets of opposing doors ran the length of the hallway, which ended in a featureless door in both directions. A dome camera was attached to the ceiling above the hallway exit doors.

"We're headed that way," said the guard, pointing toward the door to Decker's left.

The door buzzed for a long second, followed by a series of clicks. It automatically opened to a tight room, where a matching pair of US marshals in suits—easily identifiable by the distinctive five-pointed-star lapel badges—stood waiting.

"We'll take him from here," said one of the marshals.

"He's all yours," said the guard before disappearing into the small cellblock.

When the door closed and sealed behind him, the door beyond the marshals buzzed.

"You ready, Mr. Decker?" said the lead marshal, nodding respectfully.

Mr. Decker? He hadn't been formally called anything but "prisoner" or "inmate" since his conviction. Informally, he'd been called every pejorative in the book, plus a few he'd never heard before. Something was off.

"I think so," said Decker. "Where are we headed?"

"Processing," said the marshal. "This way."

He followed the marshal through the door, into the section's control station. Three detention-center guards dressed in olive-drab, military-style uniforms sat behind thick ballistic glass inside the fully enclosed floor-to-ceiling structure. Situated in the middle of the octagonal room, guards inside the impregnable station controlled the comings and goings of prisoners placed in solitary or protective confinement. He imagined it was one of the quietest jobs in the building.

"Processing for trial?" said Decker. "To go over my testimony?"

The marshals cast him a confused look.

"No. Outprocessing," said the marshal.

Decker froze in place on the shiny concrete floor. "I don't understand."

The federal officer shrugged. "That's all I know. Sounds to me like you'll be a free man within the hour."

"Unless you want to go back to a cell," said his partner, chuckling softly at his own joke.

"This must be a mistake. I was supposed to testify in a US District Court case against members of the Solntsevskaya Bratva," said Decker. "I assumed that's why I was brought here."

"That case was dismissed three days ago," said the marshal.

"What? Wait. How the hell did that happen?"

"Something was wrong with the evidence."

A bored intercom voice interrupted the conversation.

"I need you gentlemen to clear the space," said one of the control station guards.

"Busy day?" said the lead marshal, flashing a grin.

"Funny man," said the guard. "Don't let the door hit you."

The door on the other side of the station buzzed, opening a few seconds later. Decker remained in place, running what he knew through his head. It didn't take him long to reach a conclusion. His release was neither a mistake nor a coincidence. Somehow, the long arm of the Bratva had pulled enough levers to get him released—in downtown Los Angeles.

"You heard the man," said the marshal.

"This doesn't make any sense," said Decker. "Why would they bring me to Los Angeles?"

"No idea," said the marshal, losing patience. "I need you to keep moving, Mr. Decker. My orders are to deliver you to processing."

More like deliver him to an execution. He'd be lucky to last thirty minutes on the streets.

CHAPTER THREE

Decker stood in the blazing noontime sun next to the detention center, contemplating the unexpected turn of events. Faking a Bureau of Prisons release must have cost the Russians a tremendous amount of money. An investment they'd be eager to recoup. He thoroughly scanned the street below him, not detecting anything suspicious. No surprise there. The Russians could be crazy and arrogant, but they weren't stupid.

They'd track him from a distance and wait for a less conspicuous time and place to make a move. Decker planned to use that against them. He'd head a few blocks south to a part of Los Angeles called Skid Row, where he'd disappear among several city blocks of makeshift tents and homeless people. On the way, if circumstances allowed it, he'd duck into a coffee shop recommended by one of the marshals. He could really use a good coffee, especially if it might be his last.

Satisfied that the Russians didn't plan on gunning him down in front of the detention center, he descended the steps to Alameda Street and walked south. He'd been told to follow Alameda until East First Street, where he'd see a Japanese-looking tower. Directions got even hazier after that. The café was tucked into an open-air shopping plaza on the edge of Little Tokyo.

Long rows of bleak warehouses gave way to lively shops as he approached the intersection of First and Alameda. He glanced back over his shoulder at the lifeless blocks he'd just walked. A perfect shooting gallery for the Bratva: No witnesses. Nowhere to run. A missed oppor-. tunity. He turned right at the intersection and spotted the red tower. Their loss. He was getting that coffee.

Pedestrian traffic picked up on First Street, bringing ample opportunity to better his situation. Choosing his victim carefully, he lifted a promisingly fat wallet from an entirely oblivious tourist before crossing the street. Two hundred dollars and three credit cards richer, he stuffed the wallet into an overflowing trash bin at the entrance to the Japanese Village Plaza and plunged into the noontime mall crowd, looking for a cell phone he could use to arrange a more permanent vanishing act later.

A glance over his shoulder confirmed that the gray Suburban that had been ghosting him since the intersection had stopped on the far side of street, in front of the northern plaza entrance. The windows were heavily tinted, but he knew what was inside. Bratva soldiers. Coffee would have to wait. He walked briskly through the crowded outdoor mall, his focus on reaching Skid Row.

He'd just passed the café recommended by the marshals when a windowless white van crept into view on Second Street, effectively blocking his escape from the busy shopping plaza. Time for a new plan. Decker turned and headed for the coffee shop, where he'd presumably be safe—for now.

Decker opened the heavy door to the Sweetspot Café, taking in the rich aroma of freshly ground coffee beans. He'd grab a coffee and assess the situation. Possibly pick up a weapon he could use to surprise one of the men sent to kill him.

He separated a twenty from the small wad of cash in his pocket and settled in behind a pair of young women with toddler daughters. One of the girls peeked around her mom's tanned leg at him. He smiled, the little girl's blonde hair and blue eyes reminding him of his own daughter. His smile faded just as quickly, and for the same reason.

He couldn't afford to think about her right now. Decker's only chance of seeing his daughter again hinged on getting out of here alive, and it was going to take all his focus to pull that off.

Glancing through the café window, he checked on the van. The front passenger seat was empty. One of the Russians was on the plaza. He craned his head a little farther but couldn't spot him among the shoppers and tourists. *Damn.* That was an epic fail. Then again, he'd never found it particularly difficult to pick them out of a crowd before. Bad haircuts. Distinctively out-of-place clothing choices. Neck and arm tattoos. Turtlenecks in the middle of August—to cover said tattoos. He'd take a seat at the counter and scan the crowd. It shouldn't take him long.

The van rolled away, immediately replaced by a black SUV. Maybe they did plan to cut him down right here. He looked again at the little girl, who hid her face behind her mom. *What the hell was he thinking?* Decker stepped out of the line. He had to get out of here. If the Bratva wanted him dead more than they cared about a public relations mess, he was putting a lot of people at risk by being here.

CHAPTER FOUR

Harlow Mackenzie accelerated into the intersection, the yellow light changing to red before she started the turn. When her car straightened on Second, she drove as fast as possible without hitting the careless jaywalkers popping out of nowhere. Like the gaggle of business types stepping into the street right now. She hit her brakes in time to glide to a precarious stop a few feet shy of them.

"What don't these idiots get about crosswalks?" she muttered.

She refrained from laying on the horn as they debated whether to continue across the street. Decker had two vehicles working him. A gray SUV and a white cargo van. There were bound to be more that she hadn't spotted. Instead of drawing undue attention to herself, she impatiently waved the group across, keeping her eyes on the road beyond them. The cargo van turned onto Second Street from Alameda, heading in her direction.

"Dammit!" she said, pounding the steering wheel.

If Decker was careless enough to approach the street, he could stumble right into a curbside ambush. She sped up, running a few quick plans through her head. Her creaky sedan arrived at the southern entrance to the open-air shopping plaza several seconds ahead of the van, giving her a chance to scan the plaza without making it too obvious. Not that her crappy little sedan would draw a second look.

Harlow immediately spotted Decker, headed toward one of the shops lining the plaza. Looked like a coffee shop. *What the hell was he thinking?* This was not the time to sit in one spot. She'd have to intervene sooner than expected. The white van rolled in front of the plaza entrance as she furiously typed a text message to her assistant. When she looked up, the tall vehicle mostly obscured her view of the coffee shop. A serious-looking driver wearing an earpiece gave her a passing glance before scanning the street ahead.

She squeezed her vehicle through the pedestrian traffic at the crosswalk ahead and parked along a red curb. The car was one of her throwaways, so she didn't care if it got towed, though she hoped her assistant could move it before the tow truck arrived. It all depended on what happened in the next ten minutes.

Her feet hit the street seconds later, carrying her swiftly between the slowed traffic toward the other side. Pretending to be absorbed by her phone, she reached the sidewalk and merged with the eclectic mix of Little Tokyo tourists and locals headed toward the plaza.

Harlow was invisible to them now, dressed in Southern California's patented "might be working out or might be running errands" outfit—purple backpack, black yoga pants, tight midriff top covered by an unbuttoned, long-sleeve studio wrap. Olive-drab ball cap with jet-black ponytail pulled through the back.

A fit-looking man wearing hiking boots, cargo shorts, and an untucked navy polo shirt got out of the van's front passenger door and blended into the plaza's foot traffic. Not a bad disguise, except for the boots. She turned into the plaza and headed for the café, keeping her eye on the possible shooter. He drifted out of the crowd and took a seat next to an elderly Asian woman on a bench across the plaza from the café.

She scanned the people approaching the café from the other direction. She presumed that the gray SUV had dropped off a few operatives to make sure Decker didn't double back. Nobody in the throng passing underneath the strings of red and white Japanese lanterns looked out of place, which further complicated an already problematic situation. She turned toward the café and spotted Decker in line.

"Had to get that coffee," she mumbled. "Didn't you?"

By the time she reached the door, he had stepped out of the line, a worried look on his face. He was bailing on the coffee. Not the best idea at this point, with multiple unidentified bad guys floating around the plaza. Decker was good, but he wasn't that good. He'd definitely need her help to get out of this. She opened the door and placed a firm hand on his sternum, careful to position her body so that nobody approaching from the gray van could see she was touching him.

He reacted instantly, gripping her wrist and applying a frightening amount of pressure.

"Do not break my wrist, Decker," she said firmly. "I'm one of the few friends you have left."

"You don't look familiar. At all," said Decker, his eyes locked onto hers.

Harlow hesitated, a wave of disappointment washing over her. Decker couldn't possibly know who she was or how they were connected, but she couldn't help it. She knew Decker's face better than her own brother's at this point. His dismissive statement cut a little deeper than she'd have thought possible coming from someone she'd never met before. She shook it off.

"The café is under surveillance. Possibly surrounded. You're going to need my help," she said. "Get back in line before they notice something is off."

The pressure eased, but his piercing glare remained. "How many?" he asked.

"One that I'm sure you spotted, across from the café sitting next to the old Asian lady," said Harlow. "My guess is that two more followed you through the mall, from the gray Suburban parked on First Street."

Decker released her wrist and got back in line. Harlow took her place behind him.

"What's your angle here?" Decker said over his shoulder.

"My name is Harlow Mackenzie. I've been watching you for a long time."

"Hardly creepy at all."

"Let me try again. I'm a private investigator," she said. "That's probably not what you want to hear, either."

"Strike two. One more strike and—you don't want to know what happens after strike three."

"World Recovery Group got me off the streets thirteen years ago," said Harlow. "Your work on behalf of Recovery Street saved my life."

Decker ran a hand over his buzz cut. "That's right when we started. Was it the McNulty group?"

"Yep," she said. "I was strung out in Van Nuys, waiting for an *audition* that would never come. Sounded like a great idea at the time."

"Always does," said Decker. "They had quite a racket going. We took down six apartments that night and seized information leading to thirty more across greater Los Angeles."

"I was in an apartment on Kittridge."

"Small world. Crazy," said Decker, shaking his head. "So now what?"

"You're going to get a coffee. I'm going to get a coffee," said Harlow. "By the time we've finished, I'll have a plan to get us out of this."

"How did you know I'd be released? Just over an hour ago, I thought I was getting dressed to testify in court."

"I have a friend at Victorville," said Harlow. "I got the call at nine this morning, when my friend's shift began. I just guessed the marshals were taking you here. Lots of guesswork in this business. I got lucky."

"Or not. The Bratva won't hesitate to kill you—or worse," said Decker. "You should just walk out of here right now."

"This isn't the Bratva."

He turned his body and looked past her at the plaza outside the shop.

"What are you doing?" she said.

"Looking for the people that want to kill me," said Decker. "I'd look more suspicious if I didn't."

"Good point," she said, pretending to stare ahead.

Instead, she gave him a covert once-over—finally free from his intense scrutiny. The buzz cut wasn't exactly flattering. The blue dress shirt was a few sizes too large, hiding a rock-solid physique underneath, judging by the sculpted neck muscles. This close, his face looked a little starker than in the pictures. Ruggedly handsome with signs of battle wear—namely, a one-inch scar across his left cheek and a slightly longer one on his right temple. Once again, she found herself mesmerized standing in front of someone she'd admired from a distance for so long.

"Doesn't look like a Russian. I'll give you that," said Decker, turning back to face the counter.

"I need to show you something," said Harlow. "I did some digging after your arrest. Deep digging."

"I just want to see my daughter again," said Decker. "That's all I care about right now. How do we get out of here?"

"There's more to Hemet than the Russians."

"Look. I appreciate whatever you're doing here, but—"

"I think you were set up by whoever hired you to find Senator Steele's daughter."

He visibly tightened in front of her. The two women and their daughters moved aside, but Decker remained in place.

"You have proof?"

"I have a good start," said Harlow. "Grab two seats somewhere. Try not to make it obvious."

"Not my first rodeo."

"Just making sure," she said.

Decker stepped up to the cashier, speaking over his shoulder.

"I hope you understand what you're getting into here. Russians or not, they look serious."

"Not my first rodeo, either."

Chapter Five

Decker took his cappuccino to the wall-facing counter next to the bathroom, snagging a free local magazine from a display stand on the way. He set the magazine on the low-back stool next to him and took a seat. A glance at the vacant leather lounge chairs near the front window left him craving their well-worn luxury. No reason to get greedy. He had what he wanted right in front of him.

The first sip burned the inside of his mouth. Rookie mistake. Coffee on the inside was served warm to lukewarm so you couldn't throw it in someone's face and put them in the infirmary. Now he'd have to wait a minute or two before he could taste again. Not a problem.

Decker was in no hurry to get out of here. His executioners had taken up positions surrounding the café, and from what he could tell, there was no back door. He hoped Ms. Mackenzie had a solid plan to get him out of the shop.

Motion in the far reaches of his peripheral vision announced her arrival.

"Is this seat taken?" she said.

He shook his head and moved the magazine, placing it next to his coffee. She set her frozen drink on the ledge and dropped into the seat, keeping the purple backpack in her lap. Neither of them said a word for close to a minute, each going about their business. Decker savoring his cappuccino. The woman slurping her slushy drink and texting away on her phone.

"Are you actually using the phone?" he said. "Or is that part of the act?"

"I'm adjusting the plan," she said without appearing to move her lips.

"About that," he said. "What's the plan?"

"Working on it. I didn't expect you to stop for coffee," she said, pretending to nod at her phone. "Based on your route, I figured you were headed for Skid Row. Easy to disappear in there."

"That was the plan. The white van changed my mind."

"Well. *That* is no longer an option," she said, checking her phone. "We'll have to go with a more direct approach, which will take a few minutes to arrange."

"I like the sound of that," said Decker before taking a long sip of his drink. "So. What's this proof you were telling me about?"

"Now you're interested?"

"What can I say, Ms. Mackenzie? You've given me hope I'll see my daughter again."

"Call me Harlow," she said, taking a sheet of paper out of her backpack.

Harlow leaned close to him, pretending to adjust her shoe. She slid the sheet under the magazine and sat upright, taking a sip of her drink. He waited a moment before returning to the flimsy magazine. Using the magazine to shield it from view, he removed the document and placed it directly in front of him, scanning it from top to bottom.

"Airspace waiver request for unmanned aircraft systems," said Decker. "I'm very familiar with these. We did everything by the book. Looks like a class-C airspace waiver for Riverside Municipal Airport, but I can't make sense of these coordinates without a map."

"Filed by Ares Aviation's office in Riverside. Coordinates line up with the southeastern fringe of RMA's restricted airspace, just west of

Hemet. You're not the only one that does things by the book," she said. "The waiver codes granted by the FAA gave the operator permission to conduct night operations over populated areas, out of line of sight of the unmanned aerial vehicle—above four hundred feet."

Decker frowned at the request form. "Over four hundred feet? Out of line of sight?"

"That's what you're focused on?" she said. "Not the location?"

He took a slow sip of the strong espresso drink and nodded slowly. "The location is obviously important," he said. "But the combination of requested waivers tells a more interesting story."

"More interesting than the fact that someone requested a sur-veillance drone waiver over the Bratva distribution center your team raided?"

"Right. First—it tells me that Ares Aviation wasn't flying a drone you can order off the internet."

"I kind of already guessed that," she said.

"Nighttime and out of line of sight kind of go together. Can't see the drone at night regardless. The two are always filed together."

"Makes sense, which doesn't sound very interesting," she said. "We don't have a lot of time, Decker. The drone isn't run-of-the-mill. So what?"

"For night surveillance at that distance, you'd need a sophisticated night-vision sensor with significant magnification and clarity, which gets really expensive. At over four hundred feet, I'd also guess we're talking about some kind of thermal-imaging component."

"An expensive drone, then."

"A high-tech drone. Military grade. Raven or latest generation. And the Bratva isn't into drones. They're decidedly low-tech," he said, pondering the implications. "Ares Aviation? I assume you dug a little further?"

She nodded and held her phone up, pretending to laugh at a text. "Parent company is Aegis Global. More like a second-cousin company. The connection is obfuscated, but it's definitely one of their holdings."

"Aegis Global," said Decker. "The top military contracting company in Iraq and Afghanistan."

"The *only* company providing military and logistical support to the ongoing wars in Iraq and Afghanistan," she said. "Things have changed while you were away."

Decker shook his head again, draining his cup before crushing it against the brown painted wall in front of him. He didn't care if his observers saw it. Partly because it was a logical thing for him to do as a hopeless ex-con. Mostly because he didn't give a crap. Or did he care? The single sheet of paper presented by Harlow Mackenzie, stalker extraordinaire, provided an enticing spin on everything he'd come to believe over the past two years.

The Russians were involved somehow. The Solntsevskaya Bratva had owned the house in Hemet, and some very scary-looking men with extensive Bratva ink had perpetrated most of the attacks against him in prison. They were indisputably linked to this mess; he just wasn't sure how anymore. If the paperwork Harlow had produced was real, a third party was involved—which changed everything.

"You okay?" she said.

"Not even close," he said, squeezing the crumpled cup in his hand. "So where do we go from here?"

"That depends on you," she said. "How far do you want to take this?"

"All the way."

"I was hoping you'd say that. The first thing we need to do is get you out of here alive."

"Sounds like you already have a plan."

"I wouldn't call it a plan." Harlow removed a black nylon kit from her backpack. "I haven't ironed out many of the details." She pushed the football-size kit into his lap. "Keep that out of sight and grab a stall in the bathroom after I leave. The contents should be self-explanatory. Put on the gloves first, for obvious reasons."

"Where are you headed?"

"Out there," she said. "To even the odds."

"You don't have to do this for me," said Decker. "Seriously."

"Can I be really honest with you for a second?"

"Shoot."

"I want you to see your daughter again," she said. "But I also want these monsters to pay for what they did, and what they'll keep on doing unless someone stops them. I'm going to need your help with that."

"Sounds like our goals are aligned—for now," said Decker.

"Don't linger in the bathroom," she said before leaving.

Decker waited another minute before heading into the bathroom. Miraculously, the single stall was unoccupied. He locked the door and quickly took a seat on the toilet, unzipping the kit she'd given him. The contents made him smile.

The first thing he removed was a pair of tight, skin-colored gloves, which he slipped over his hands, followed by a well-worn Glock nine-millimeter pistol with a threaded barrel. Not believing the threaded barrel was a coincidence, he reached into the bag and retrieved a six-inch cylindrical suppressor.

"Harlow Mackenzie. Who *are* you?" he mumbled before screwing the suppressor onto the barrel.

Further digging revealed five magazines for the pistol and a wireless communications kit. He inserted one of the magazines in the pistol, chambering a round by pulling the slide back and letting it slam forward. The other magazines disappeared into his pockets. A quick look at the communications rig revealed that it was ready for immediate use. Decker pushed the translucent earpiece into his ear and clipped the microphone to his collar. The compact transceiver went in his front trouser pocket. She'd thought of everything.

"Mackenzie. You there?" he said, assuming the rig was voice activated.

"I'm here," she said. "Along with another member of my firm, so don't freak out if you hear another voice."

"I'm not prone to freaking out," he said. "I assume the pistol is a throwaway?"

"It's clean if you need to toss it," she said. "But I don't anticipate you using it."

"I guess that depends on what we're up against. What are we looking at?"

A long pause ensued. "It's going to take a miracle to get you out of here."

CHAPTER SIX

Harlow walked inside a sandal shop two doors down from the café and opened her backpack, removing a pair of pants and a hat.

"Can I help you?" said a middle-aged woman behind the counter.

"Quick wardrobe change," she said. "Trying to ditch my boyfriend. I just broke up with him."

"Okaaaay," said the woman, stepping out from behind the counter. "Just keep the merchandise out of your backpack, please."

"Feel free to keep an eye on me," said Harlow, pulling a pair of baggy tan drawstring pants over her tight yoga outfit.

"Don't worry," said the woman, stopping several feet away and crossing her arms. "I will."

"How are we doing, Katie?" said Harlow.

"Excuse me?" said the shop owner.

"Talking to someone else," said Harlow.

The woman looked around before raising her eyebrows. "Maybe it's time for you to move along."

"I'll be out of here in ten seconds," said Harlow. "Katie?"

"Who's Katie?"

"Imaginary friend of mine," said Harlow, swapping her olive-drab baseball hat for a pink Dodgers cap.

She took off her studio wrap, stuffing it in the backpack along with the hat. A quick change to throw off surveillance, just in case she had attracted any attention. Her plan depended on the element of surprise—and Katie, who was more than capable of delivering.

"I'm all set," said her assistant. "Primary vehicle is in the parking garage. Second level. Take an immediate left out of the stairwell. You'll see it."

"All right. Stay sharp. We're working with a really small margin of error here," said Harlow.

"That's what you always say."

"This time I actually mean it."

"I guarantee there will be no margin," interrupted Decker.

"Just be careful," said Harlow. "I have a really bad feeling about this crew."

"They'll never know I was there," said Katie.

"I'm heading out," said Harlow.

She reached for the door handle, pausing for a second.

"Decker. It's time. Head for the door. Once you get outside, take a right. Your sole mission is to get to the parking garage door two stores down."

"Harlow?"

"Yeah?"

"If things go sideways, I want you to walk away," said Decker. "This isn't your fight."

He had no idea how personal this fight was to her, or how closely he was connected to it. Ten years earlier, she'd been a mere day or two, possibly just hours, away from being "offered a chance" to repay the "enormous debt" she had incurred over the past two months. The cost of a drug-fueled, luxury apartment life—specifically designed to entice and ensnare young women who had flocked to Los Angeles to make it big in Hollywood. Decker had unknowingly snatched her from the jaws of a machine that devoured thousands of young lives every year.

"That's not exactly true," she said, pushing the door open.

CHAPTER SEVEN

Decker scanned the mall's concrete courtyard through the café's windows, quickly identifying three of the neatly dressed men sent to kill him. The man seated across from the café slowly stood, pretending not to focus on him. The other two flanked the coffee shop at cautious distances—one on each side. Their stationary presence amid the constant ebb and flow of tourists and lunchtime locals made them easy to spot. Almost too easy. He had no doubt that more of them were on the move, timing their approach. They'd be the real threat.

"I have three of them," he said, his hand feeling the invisible tug of the suppressed pistol. "Forming a triangle around my exit."

"They've left you enough room to move," said Harlow.

"More like enough rope to hang myself."

"Hold on. I have a fourth coming from the north. Passing me now," she said. "I'm following him in. Time to move."

"Stepping outside," said Decker, opening the door.

"I'm wearing a pink Dodgers cap," she said. "I see you coming out."

He glanced to the right, immediately spotting her—and the linebacker headed directly for him. The guy's untucked, light-blue oxford shirt bulged at the seams, no doubt concealing a weapon along his muscular frame. The other three men remained in place, waiting for Decker to make a move.

"Don't worry about the guy in front of me," said Harlow. "Turn in my direction and start walking."

"Harlow. I have two moving in from the south. That's six," said Katie.

"Decker. Start moving," said Harlow.

Decker walked toward Harlow, now completely convinced she had misread the situation. She had him walking directly into a brick wall of a man, who was undoubtedly armed and well trained, while five more men converged on him across a 180-degree arc. This would be over in less than ten seconds, and he couldn't envision a scenario that didn't involve the gun tucked into his waistband. A sudden flurry of movement in his peripheral vision suggested a far more compacted timeline. This was it. His right hand started to drift along his side, headed for the pistol.

"I'm going active," said Katie, momentarily keeping him from drawing the weapon.

"Do it," said Harlow. "Decker. You keep walking."

"I don't think that's a good—"

A police siren pierced the air, startling Decker and stopping the oncoming man in his tracks. A quick glance over his left shoulder showed that the entire crowd had stopped, everyone searching for the source of the shrill sound. A crackling noise drew his attention back to the linebacker less than twenty feet away—just in time to see him drop to the concrete like a sack of stones. Harlow stood over him, a Taser in her hand—the coiled wires from the device bridging the gap between them.

Two low-pitched thumps echoed through the courtyard, immediately followed by a loud hissing sound. He didn't have to look behind him to figure out what was happening. Harlow threw the Taser onto the ground next to the twitching man and pulled a black hood out of her backpack, wrestling it over his head. Before Decker could nod his approval, she produced a cylindrical gray canister from the pack and pulled the pin. She was out of her mind—and he kind of liked it.

"Get to the parking garage and stay out of sight," she barked before underhanding the smoke grenade into the crowd to his left.

Decker took off at a dead sprint, pandemonium erupting behind him as screaming shoppers and panicky tourists scrambled to get away from the canister. Almost simultaneously, a string of firecrackers erupted on the other side of the courtyard, pushing the already frightened crowd into a frenzy. He ignored the stampede, plunging into a short, dimly lit hallway marked by a **PARKING GARAGE** sign. A green metal door with a thin vertical window greeted him. He stopped for a moment and looked over his shoulder, expecting to see Harlow following him.

"Where are you?" said Decker.

"Don't stop. I'll be up shortly. I need to make sure nobody followed."

"I can't imagine any of them sticking around for the inevitable police response," said Decker, opening the door and stepping into the stairwell. "Well done."

"It's not over yet," said Harlow, the sound of terrified screams nearly rendering her radio feed incoherent. "Katie. Get out of here."

"Already on the way out," said her assistant. "These guys don't look eager to stick around, either. I'm hearing a lot of sirens."

"I have one of them on the ground right here," said Harlow. "I don't see any others."

"Don't spend too long down there," said Decker. "If the police block the parking garage exit, we're kind of screwed."

"I got this," said Harlow.

"Of course you do," he mumbled before bolting up the stairs.

When he reached the second level, screams filled the stairwell below for a moment before the space went silent.

"Harlow. Are you in the stairwell?" he whispered.

"No."

"I think someone got past you," he said, drawing the suppressed pistol.

"Nobody got past me."

Rapid footsteps echoed off the gray concrete walls, casting serious doubt on her stubborn proclamation.

"Somebody got past you."

"I'm on my way," she said.

"Be really careful," he said.

Decker considered his options. He could open the door and position himself in the garage, but his pursuer would most likely hear the door. If the thug relayed that information back to his buddies in the van, Decker would have an entirely new series of problems on his hands. No. He had to take the man out quickly, before he could react or warn the others. Decker lay flat on the rough concrete landing, his pistol aimed just above the top of the stairs leading up from level one.

The sound of the steps below intensified for a moment before going quiet. The man was close, proceeding cautiously up the stairs. The opposite of what he had hoped. His impromptu tactic worked a lot better against a rushed opponent, who would be focused on the doors and upper reaches of the next flight of stairs. Decker lay in the middle of the landing, the last place anyone should expect him. *Should* being the operative term.

He kept the pistol level with the floor and waited. A few seconds later, clothing rustled below, followed by soft footsteps. A mop of brown hair came into view, and Decker applied pressure to the trigger. Before he could fire, a door slammed open below, causing the man to duck.

"Decker. I'm coming up," whispered Harlow, her voice just barely audible in the stairwell. "What's your status?"

Before the man could report what he'd heard or reposition to engage Harlow, Decker pushed off the concrete and fired twice. The bullets struck the man's right temple in a tight pattern, spraying the concrete behind him with bright-red, speckled gore. The operative instantly dropped out of sight, his central nervous system switched off like a light. Decker stood up slowly, his eyes following a thick red streak down the wall to the man's crumpled body.

"Decker. Please tell me you didn't"—started Harlow over the radio, continuing out loud when she swung into view on the landing below— "blow someone's brains out."

Decker put his index finger to his mouth and shook his head. She nodded her understanding of the situation, frowning at the grisly sight. Decker moved quickly, finding a wireless voice-activated microphone inside the man's collar. He removed the translucent device and placed it on the step, crushing it under his shoe.

"This is bad," she said.

"He didn't leave me much choice," said Decker.

"Now we're dealing with a murder investigation under really unusual circumstances. The cops will be all over this."

He wanted to lay into her for letting this guy sneak by but didn't think it would be productive. Plus, she'd saved his life. He stuffed the pistol into his waistband and knelt next to the twisted corpse.

"Don't touch the body," she said. "You'll get—"

Decker turned the man's head, revealing the mostly exploded side. He pulled the earpiece out of the man's half-missing ear and wiped it on his pants.

"—blood all over you. And the car. Great."

The piece looked intact, so he pushed it into his ear, catching part of a conversation.

"He said something about the parking garage," said a male voice. "I saw him bolt north through the smoke."

"We can't stay here any longer," said another man. "The first LAPD units are moments from arriving, and every cop within five miles is sure to follow. Whoever orchestrated that little stunt knew exactly what they were doing. I want all teams moving away from the scene immediately, and switch radio frequencies—in case Rich gets nabbed."

"Copy that," said the first voice, followed by two more acknowledgments from different men.

He took the earpiece out and stuffed it in his pants.

"Did you hear anything?"

"Get the car and pick me up at the door," said Decker. "LAPD is seconds away."

"Where are you going?" she said, starting up the stairs.

"Nowhere. I need to search this guy," he said, turning the body over. "I'll be right up."

"We don't have time for this," she said, passing him.

"The guys talking on the radio weren't Russians," he said, digging through the man's pants for some kind of ID.

Harlow continued up the stairs. "I could have told you that."

He fished a slim wallet out of the man's pocket.

"There. Let's go," said Harlow, reaching for the door on the landing above him.

"I need to check one more thing," said Decker, pocketing the wallet. "Do you have a phone?"

"What?"

"For a picture," he said. "So we can ID this guy."

Harlow tossed him her phone. "Five seconds. That's as long as I wait," she said, stepping through the doorway into the garage.

Decker grabbed the man's blue polo-style shirt by the bottom and pulled it up to his armpits. Finding nothing, he yanked the shirt over the man's shattered head, tossing the blood-soaked garment to the landing below. Still nothing. He rolled the man onto his chest, exposing his muscular back. Bingo. A familiar tattoo lay across his left shoulder. A frog skeleton with one of the bony feet crafted to vaguely resemble the business end of a trident. He took a picture of the tattoo, followed by a few shots of the man's face.

A minute later, they were headed north on Alameda Street, passing police cars headed in the opposite direction.

"Well?" she said.

"Uh . . . thank you?"

"Did you find anything?"

"The guy had a bone frog tattoo. Ex-SEAL," he said, watching the Los Angeles Metropolitan Detention Center pass to their left. "Definitely not a Russian."

"Maybe we should start digging into Aegis Global," she said. "Start with Ares Aviation."

He glanced at her with a raised eyebrow. "Aegis isn't going anywhere," he said. "But when word hits the street that I'm still alive, someone critical to our understanding of this is guaranteed to disappear for a while."

"Who?"

"You're not going to like this."

A few moments passed before she took her eyes off the road to meet his glance.

"You're out of your mind," she said.

"Do you know where I can find him?"

"I don't think that's a good idea—at all."

"You don't have to come along," said Decker. "In fact, I'd prefer you didn't."

"Because you've done such a great job keeping yourself alive so far?"

Once again, he didn't feel like arguing the finer points of who saved whom back at the shopping plaza. She'd orchestrated a clever escape from a nearly hopeless situation, but she'd nearly gotten herself killed in the stairwell. They each had their limitations right now, and their strengths. He'd keep working with her—not that he had other viable options.

"Do you know where he is?"

She hesitated, finally nodding. "Of course I do. I keep a close eye on them. I have to. Despite all of the very negative attention lately, human trafficking is still big business for them."

"You'd think they'd have the sense to lie low."

"I suspect they were never worried about losing business. The federal case against them was dismissed a few days before you were released."

"I still can't make sense of that," said Decker.

"Money talks," said Harlow.

"All the more reason to pay Viktor Penkin a visit first."

CHAPTER EIGHT

Gunther Ross leaned forward and put his elbows on his knees, staring over a row of stucco-tile rooftops at the distant downtown Los Angeles skyline. He sat alone on a park bench, gathering his thoughts about the failed attempt to erase Ryan Decker from the planet. He couldn't get past the most obvious observation. A skilled crew had helped Decker out of that jam. But who?

Decker didn't have a friend left in the world. They'd made sure of that. And even if he'd somehow managed to keep a friend under the radar, he or she wouldn't be the type to pull off that kind of counterassassination operation. Ross had completely severed his last links to that world over the past year.

The Russians? They could be self-destructive from time to time, but a stunt like this had the potential to deliver a fatal blow to their operations on the West Coast. And what would they possibly gain by snatching Decker?

Who was left after the Bratva? Some enterprising prison guard at Victorville? Something didn't add up here, which was why he hadn't called Harcourt with the bad news. He was waiting for any shred of evidence that might point him in the right direction. Unfortunately, he couldn't postpone the call much longer.

"Anything?" he said, turning his head toward the man standing several feet to his right.

"Hold on," said the man, pressing buttons on his cell phone.

Gunther returned to the expansive hilltop view of Los Angeles. Low-rise housing surrounded the small bump of skyscrapers, extending in every direction. He'd never found the city appealing, but over thirteen million people chose to call the Los Angeles metropolitan area home, the vast majority of them packed like sardines in tiny, overpriced houses, which were likewise jammed side by side into crowded neighborhoods. He couldn't imagine living here.

A rapid-fire conversation erupted next to him, the gist of it hanging in the air. He'd have to make that call empty-handed. Gunther took a deep breath and glanced at Jay Reid, who ended the conversation and shook his head.

"Rich is dead," he said.

"I gathered that much."

"He was shot in the parking garage stairwell. Two bullets to the right temple. Spaced less than an inch apart," said Jay, raising an eyebrow.

"Professional."

"His wallet is missing, and his communications rig was found smashed on the steps next to his head."

"The wallet's a dead end," said Gunther. "Fake driver's license and a few preloaded credit cards."

"I'm more concerned about the earpiece."

"If Decker heard any of our chatter, it's fair to say he knows we're not Russian," said Gunther. "Beyond that, I'm not worried."

"He's probably narrowed things down a lot further," said Jay. "They found Rich facedown on the stairs—shirtless."

"Shirtless?"

"His shirt had been removed and thrown down the stairs," said Jay. "Our LAPD contact reported an upper-shoulder tattoo."

"Let me guess," said Gunther. "SEAL trident or bone frog."

"The latter."

"Decker would recognize that right away. It's a fair assumption that he's having serious doubts about the root cause of his spectacular fall from grace. We need to find him before he starts digging around on his own."

"We can activate the full surveillance and detection network available to us in the greater Los Angeles metro area," said Jay. "Shake all of the trees."

"It's probably going to take more than that. I'll request additional assets," said Gunther. "Why don't you take a short walk while I make the call."

"Good luck."

"Better me than you, right?"

"Something like that," Jay said before walking toward the parking lot.

Gunther pulled out his phone and stared at the touch screen for a moment before pressing a series of numbers known only to him. Things were about to get complicated.

CHAPTER NINE

Jacob Harcourt disconnected the call and walked over to the cocktail cabinet built into the cherry wall next to his desk. He poured a sorely needed early-afternoon bourbon. The news from Gunther Ross was disturbing on many levels. Decker's stubborn insistence on not dying represented a clear and present danger to the scheme he had meticulously cultivated for close to a decade.

He never should have let Frist talk him out of the idea of driving a truck filled with explosives into the La Jacinta Inn motor court, vaporizing Decker and his team instantly. Then again, nobody could have predicted that Decker would survive multiple professionally executed attempts on his life. The man had proven to be unstoppable, which scared Harcourt.

If Decker had caught even the faintest whiff of something rotten, like the circumstances suggested, he'd keep sniffing until he found the source. The sooner they found and killed him, the better.

Harcourt would immediately deploy a second black-ops team to Los Angeles to help with the Decker situation, in addition to diverting every electronic surveillance asset available in the country to support them. Combined with Aegis's local surveillance network of law enforcement and private entities, they'd have the city electronically locked down within twelve hours.

Facial-recognition software would scour LAPD surveillance cameras, traffic feeds, and private security cameras linked to security firms. Digital eavesdroppers would filter internet keyword searches. A very expensive cell phone surveillance package provided by an unnamed alphabet agency would sift through millions of conversations, listening for trigger words. They'd wait for Decker to make a mistake—and he would. Decker wasn't the type to sit still for very long.

All the more reason to move on him quickly. Harcourt was little more than a week away from seeing his life's work come to fruition. One lousy week—and the Solntsevskaya Bratva screwed up again. He shouldn't have involved the Russians any further. Their first mistake had been bad enough.

He'd spoken at length with the Bratva's legal team, going over the plan, and they still screwed it up. The US attorney's key evidence against the Russians would be dismissed during the trial. Harcourt had seen to that. Decker was the last remaining witness who could testify about the veracity of the documents collected by World Recovery Group. The rest of his team had been eliminated or effectively silenced.

The judge would grant the defense's motion to dismiss the case based on a lack of evidence. Decker's testimony would be too biased to be credible, leaving the case without merit. A life-changing sum of money had been deposited in an account owned by the judge to ensure that dismissal.

Instead, the Bratva's attorney jumps the gun and convinces the US attorney to drop the case before it goes to trial, forcing Harcourt to take drastic and possibly traceable measures to once again deal with Decker. A hastily arranged operation that ended in a temporary setback. One he now had to explain to a very nervous politician.

He dialed a private number, barely getting the cell phone to his ear before Senator Gerald Frist's impatient voice broke through.

"Is it done?"

"We hit a small snag," said Harcourt. "Apparently our friend still has a fan or two there. We were moving on him at a mall in Little Tokyo when all hell broke loose. One of my operatives was killed, and Decker vanished. I had no choice but to pull my teams out before the police arrived."

"I don't like the sound of that—at all."

"Neither do I, but I have everything under control," said Harcourt.

"How the hell did this go sideways on you?"

Harcourt took a deep breath and exhaled. "I don't know," he said. "Someone from Decker's past slipped through the cracks."

"Have you contacted the Russians?"

"It isn't the Russians," said Harcourt, taking an oversize gulp of bourbon.

"Get in touch with them," said Frist. "Just to make sure. They've proven to be thoroughly unreliable from the beginning. We don't need them getting any strange ideas."

"There's no way this can come back to you. I've made sure of it."

"Just like you've taken care of Decker?" A long pause ensued. "Sorry. We have a lot at stake in the upcoming week. Decker makes me nervous."

"Your concern isn't unfounded. Decker can be resourceful, which is why I've been trying to get rid of him for the better part of a year. That said, I don't see how he could bring anything crashing down on us."

"I'm more concerned about whoever rescued him," said Frist. "Any ideas?"

"We conducted exhaustive research into his previous contacts and determined no threat of interference. He's essentially a pariah. We're going back over the list."

"You might want to make a new one," said Frist. "My guess is that someone has made a dangerous connection between what happened to Decker and our little enterprise."

Harcourt took another sip from his glass, then said, "I'll start with the Russians. I don't think they're involved, but they have their own network of informants—and they've been known to sit on information before."

"Should we try to get ahead of this, in case word gets out that Decker is loose? If Senator Steele discovers that he's on the streets, she's going to raise hell, drawing a lot of attention to his miraculous, and frankly suspicious, release. I don't need to point out how that could backfire on us."

He didn't. Harcourt had outsourced the Bureau of Prisons hack through a cutout, but nothing was untraceable these days, particularly if a powerful and influential senator demanded that the cyberbreach be aggressively investigated. Then there was the judge, who would no doubt come under scrutiny.

"I can take care of the judge," said Harcourt, "but I don't see how we can manage Steele's reaction."

"I can offer certain off-the-books services, free of charge, to make the situation right," said Frist. "The good senator might find that idea appealing, given how unsatisfied she was with Decker's sentencing. She wanted him locked up for life."

"You have a knack for sniffing out opportunities," said Harcourt.

"I've built a career on it."

"If I can't get the Decker situation back on track within twenty-four hours, I think we should proceed with your idea."

"Keep me in the loop," said Frist. "One week. That's all we need."

"One week," said Harcourt, disconnecting the call.

Harcourt finished his drink and briefly considered another. Later. He needed a clear head right now, and the bourbon had hit him surprisingly hard.

CHAPTER TEN

Viktor Penkin pounded a tall shot of Russian Standard vodka, his third in a row, and settled into the leather booth. He tried to focus on the two women dancing on the stage in front of him, but he kept returning to the implications of the call he'd just received from the man that had orchestrated the Steele fiasco. He wondered if he might be better off taking the extended vacation his boss suggested—and sooner than later.

This Decker guy had already caused enough trouble, landing half of his crew in prison with the evidence he had collected on their operation. Evidence seized by the FBI when Decker took the fall for the crap the American mercenaries had pulled. Crap that nearly burned Penkin's West Coast business to the ground. All the more reason not to trust these Americans. His boss had been smart to jump the gun on tanking the US attorney's case.

"Get them out of here," he said, pouring another shot.

The two women grabbed the scant clothing piled on the side of the stage and scurried away, their handler pushing them through a sparkling bead curtain that covered the entrance to a stairwell. The "women," clearly teenagers, were kept upstairs with at least a dozen other girls until the club opened for customers. He glanced at his watch and shook his head. Sergei, his security chief, materialized from the dark hallway leading to the back of the club. The man took up most of the hallway when he appeared, a beast squeezed into a custom-fit suit.

"We're leaving town until this Decker business settles," said Penkin. "I want to be on the road in five minutes."

"You got it, boss," said the man. "How many are coming with us?"

"Two. Alexei and Vlad. I'll let Alexei know."

"Can you say where we're headed?"

"I'm thinking the Caribbean," said Penkin. "A nice, isolated villa."

"I'll start making calls," said Sergei. "Does it matter what airport?"

"Whichever can get me out of the country fastest."

Sergei cocked his colossal head. "That bad?"

"I don't know," said Penkin, downing the vodka. "And I'm not sticking around to find out. Alexei!" he bellowed.

Sergei lumbered away. Penkin filled the four shot glasses on the table, spilling the vodka as he moved from glass to glass. When his second in command walked into the room from the front lobby, Penkin pushed one of the glasses toward him, waiting impatiently for him to take it.

"What's the occasion?" said Alexei.

"We're taking a vacation from here," said Penkin. "Until this Decker thing is resolved."

"I'll drink to that," said Alexei, clinking Penkin's glass. "He's been nothing but trouble from the start."

The dark-haired former Spetsnaz captain finished his shot in a single gulp and slammed the glass down on the table. Penkin did the same before pushing another shot toward Alexei.

"I want to get out of here immediately. Our American friend sounded nervous."

"I need to run across the street and tell Misha that he's in charge of the place," Alexei said before downing the last shot. "The bar is starting to fill up with customers."

"Make it quick," said Penkin, sliding out of the booth.

Penkin contemplated another drink after Alexei had left, but decided against it. He'd felt a little woozy when he stood up. Six generous shots of vodka within a short span of time tended to do that. He glanced around the squalid room that passed for one of his clubs. Dingy lighting hid the cracked wood-panel walls, stained ceiling tiles, and scuffed linoleum floor—not that any of his customers cared. They weren't here for the ambience. They were here for the girls, and Penkin was here to take their money.

The setup was diabolically simple, repeated in dozens of locations throughout the East San Fernando Valley, most of them concentrated in North Hollywood and Van Nuys. A dive bar served to collect and funnel customers into the clubs, which were situated within easy walking distance to Bratva-owned fronts, usually near a condemned apartment building or failed business.

Customers would get liquored up in the bars, where Penkin's people vetted them for trouble. Undercover cops and private detectives from trafficking-rescue organizations frequently showed up, temporarily bringing operations at that location to a halt. He always ran a few dozen clubs at the same time to counter their efforts and keep the cash flow steady.

The number of active clubs fluctuated daily, the ebb and flow of law enforcement activity dictating the final count. The average location lasted two weeks, requiring him to actively seek new real estate for the business. He had a dedicated crew working that problem, and they'd so far managed to keep the numbers from shrinking. A small miracle—given the targeted interest in his business over the past year—but more importantly, a profitable one.

With twenty or so active clubs, he had around three hundred girls making money for him on any given night. It didn't sound like a lot, but each girl brought in more than a thousand dollars per night, the younger ones even more. Working seven days a week, the average prostitute in one of his clubs represented a street value of more than half a million dollars. His total gross for the year topped a hundred million, and that didn't include the money made on booze and "membership" fees in the feeder bars.

For a moment, the sheer weight of the numbers emboldened him. A Bratva *avtoritet* wielding this kind of power and making this kind of money shouldn't feel compelled to run from trouble. He had plenty of muscle available to handle threats, but something about Decker unnerved him. The man had accomplished the impossible, locating Senator Steele's daughter at one of their distribution centers. Penkin should have melted her in a tub of lye as soon as he discovered her identity. He'd foolishly held on to her for future leverage, a decision that cost him close to a year in prison. No. He'd get the hell out of town. He had no intention of getting caught up in whatever mess Decker currently represented. That psychopath American could deal with it while he sipped mojitos on the beach.

Chapter Eleven

Harlow had no doubt she'd been made by the Bratva lookouts, but she wasn't in any danger—yet. The Russians expected surveillance. Part of doing business when you ran a prostitution ring in plain sight. This particular club had been in business longer than usual, close to six weeks, leading her to believe that the location's longevity had been secured with a payoff. The police would eventually shut it down, after someone gave the Russians ample warning. The lookouts would keep an eye on her, and that was about it, until Decker jumped into action.

"I still think this is a bad idea," she said over the radio net.

"You should see it from my end," replied Decker. "Still nothing?"

"Nothing," she said. "I told you this was a long shot."

"A bad idea and a long shot. Great combo," said Decker. "Are you sure he's here?"

"He's here. My sources confirmed it."

"How reliable are your sources?"

"Very," said Harlow.

The lookout seated in the car parked directly in front of the shuttered hardware store spoke into a handheld radio.

"Hold on," she said, raising a night-vision scope. "Something's up."

"I'm not going anywhere," said Decker. "And neither is this smell."

"Hey. You insisted on authenticity."

"Remind me to cut some corners next time."

Harlow failed to stifle a quick laugh. Decker had traded his clothes and the contents of a stolen wallet, along with a prepaid motel room, for a homeless man's clothes a few hours ago. The man had been so excited, he'd stripped half-naked on the street before they could get him into her car and bring him to the motel—a decision she'd instantly regretted when the stench hit her. Decker had been wearing that reek for the better part of ninety minutes.

She steadied the scope on the front door to the business and was rewarded several seconds later when Alexei Kuznetsov stepped onto the street. She recognized him immediately. Kuznetsov was Penkin's right hand, head of security for the Bratva's Los Angeles prostitution ring. He'd spent the last several months with Penkin in the Metropolitan Detention Center, awaiting the trial that never happened. His presence absolutely confirmed her source's information.

Kuznetsov leaned into the front passenger-side window and spoke briefly with the lookout. Both of them glanced momentarily in her direction before he crossed the street and disappeared into a windowless bar. She had definitely been made.

"I just watched Kuznetsov cross the street and head into their feeder bar."

"Both of them in one place?"

"Thick black hairline almost down to his eyebrows. He's unmistakable," said Harlow, lowering the scope. "It makes sense."

"Which one will know more?" said Decker. "I doubt I can take both of them."

"Penkin. Definitely Penkin. He'll have someone spying on Kuznetsov. That's how their organization works."

"I don't know about this. I'm seeing a lot of shiny new SUVs back here. I'm guessing he has some serious security," said Decker. "Couldn't we do this at Penkin's house?"

"In Bel Air?" she said. "I don't think so. This is our best bet, and it's a—"

"Long shot. I think you might have mentioned it before."

She detected movement on the dimly lit sidewalk in front of the bar. Kuznetsov crossing the street, moving fast.

"Interesting," she said.

"What's interesting?"

"Kuznetsov just bolted back across the street. We might be in business," said Harlow. "Looks like they're in a hurry to do something."

"I guess we'll know shortly," said Decker, pausing. "There's no going back from this, Harlow."

"You keep saying that."

He was starting to sound like a broken record—and just a little more than patronizing. Harlow might not have the kind of black-ops background and training he'd acquired in the Marine Corps and CIA, but she'd worked the gritty, unpredictable streets of Los Angeles for close to a decade as a private investigator, honing her skills from scratch—on her own.

"This time there's really no going back. These people have long memories. Painfully long," said Decker. "Are you sure I can't convince you to drop the car off near the alley and walk away?"

Relentless. He truly didn't get it. Harlow had witnessed this crew's depravity and cruelty firsthand more times than she could stomach recalling. They treated the kids dragged into their trafficking network like disposable commodities, selling them to overseas slavers or body-part harvesters when the customers started to lose interest. It got worse, but she didn't want to think about that right now. She couldn't afford to cloud her judgment any further. Decker's life depended on it—not to mention hers.

"Not a chance," she said.

Chapter Twelve

Decker raised the whiskey bottle, taking a clumsy swig while scanning the alley. He'd emptied the cheap booze and replaced it with tea, but could still taste traces of whiskey. Part of him wished he'd left the booze in the bottle. He could use a nip or two right about now. His plan to take Penkin alive was a stretch. *Hardly a plan* might be a better description.

He'd wandered up and down the side street leading into the alley for the better part of an hour, talking to himself the whole time. When the lookout posted next to the club's back door quit paying attention to him, he stumbled into the dark alleyway and collapsed against the tall concrete wall separating the alley from the neighborhood behind it. The lone Russian guarding the exit made his way over to investigate, finding a homeless drunk who had spilled his guts on the crumbled asphalt.

Decker wasn't sure if the kimchi–clam chowder mixture or the powerful stench radiating from his clothes did the trick, but the lookout left without giving him a second glance. After the guard left, he had sat against the wall sipping from his bottle. Observing. And that was the extent of his so-called plan. Act like a drunk to get close enough to exploit any opportunity that presented itself. So far so good. What came next was anybody's guess.

The lookout posted next to the club's back door raised a handheld radio to the side of his head, exposing the barrel of a submachine gun under his loose-fitting Starter jacket. The guard nodded once and responded with a few clipped words before scanning the alley.

"Stand by," said Decker. "Looks like something's up."

"Ready," responded Harlow.

He set the bottle down next to him and drew the suppressed Glock from one of the deep coat pockets. When the Russian started moving across the alley toward the row of SUVs, Decker assumed a two-hand grip and centered the pistol's illuminated tritium sights on the guard's torso, pressing the trigger twice. The man stumbled, dropping to a knee while Decker aligned the pistol's centermost green dot with his head and fired again.

"I need you in the alley, right now," said Decker.

"On the way."

The Russian remained upright for a moment before collapsing forward, his head striking the pavement with a thud. Decker scrambled to his feet and sprinted toward him, hoping to drag him out of sight before Penkin's entourage emerged. He reached down and grabbed the dead man's jacket collar on the way by, pulling him to an adjacent dumpster. The club's heavy metal door creaked open before he could drag the guard any farther, leaving him with one option if he wanted to take Penkin alive. He sat on the Russian's sprawled legs and started singing like a drunk.

Two men stepped into the alley, drawing their pistols, and headed straight in his direction, yelling in Russian while he sang. Decker understood some of what they were saying; his three semesters of Russian were not completely wasted. They wanted to know where Dmitry had gone. In the alley's darkness, they obviously couldn't tell that he was sitting on their friend. With his left hand, Decker pointed to the side-street alley entrance.

"He went that way! I think," said Decker, breaking into drunken song again.

"Shut *up*!" yelled one of them.

The other turned toward the door and spoke sharply in Russian, pointing where Decker had just indicated. A heated debate broke out inside the doorway, ending when the nearest SUV chirped, its taillights blinking at the same time. Two men emerged from the club arguing, one of them instantly recognizable in the sparse light from Harlow's surveillance pictures and her recent description. Kuznetsov. Penkin's right hand.

When the guard standing in front of him glanced over his shoulder at the argument, Decker quickly extended his hand and fired a single bullet through the side of his head. Two more suppressed shots dropped the next guard, leaving Penkin and his associate stranded in the middle of the alley. Neither one of them seemed to know what to do when Decker rose from the ground beyond the two recently fallen Russians, pointing a pistol at them.

"Don't do it," said Decker.

"Fuck you," said Kuznetsov, reaching for his weapon.

Decker shot him in the chest twice, then shifted his aim to the other Russian.

"Viktor Penkin?" said Decker as Kuznetsov fell to his knees clutching his boss's arm.

"Decker," muttered Penkin, trying to shake Kuznetsov loose.

"Surprised?"

"You're a dead man," hissed Penkin.

"A dead man walking—nothing more dangerous," said Decker, firing a single shot into the dying Russian hanging from Penkin's arm.

Kuznetsov slid down Penkin's right leg, his head coming to rest on the Bratva boss's shoes.

"I guess this is it, then," said Penkin.

"Not yet," said Decker, closing the distance to him.

"You'll have to kill me," said Penkin, slowly reaching into his jacket.

Decker pocketed the pistol, continuing to move forward. "The police have picked you up twenty-three times for one thing or another. Never a weapon."

Penkin bolted for the back door, screaming for help, but Decker had already pulled one of Harlow's compact Tasers from the other pocket. The Russian flopped to the pavement, unable to make a sound, as Harlow's nondescript gray sedan raced into the alley, its headlights illuminating the ghastly scene.

"We need to make this quick," said Decker.

"I know. Three Russians ran out of the bar while I was turning on the side street."

"Hell."

Decker switched the Taser into his left hand and drew the pistol with his right. He crossed the pistol over his left forearm, keeping it aimed at the door as he approached Penkin. The Russian twitched on the ground, his body locked in an electrical paralysis. Harlow pulled the car as close to the back of the club as possible without running over Kuznetsov's lifeless body.

"Can you get Penkin in the car?" Decker said quietly into his radio mic. "I might need to take a more proactive approach to keeping us alive here."

"It hasn't been proactive so far?"

"We're running out of time. I can hear voices inside—headed this way."

"I can deal with Penkin," said Harlow, opening her car door.

"He's all yours," said Decker, tossing the Taser to the ground. He scrambled for the dumpster, catching a glimpse of a human silhouette deep inside the club. Yelling had erupted from the hallway by the time he reached the dead lookout's body.

"Decker. I'm a little exposed out here."

"Hang in there."

Decker knelt next to the body, surprised to find a Russian PP-2000 submachine gun. A nasty little weapon designed to fire even nastier ammunition. He disconnected the PP-2000 from its one-point sling and searched the guard's pockets, finding a spare magazine and a compact pistol. He pocketed both and crouched next to the dumpster, studying the weapon. He'd seen these before but never fired one.

"Can't be too hard," he muttered.

While he fumbled with the oddly designed weapon, someone turned off the light deep inside the club, which meant one thing. He was about to have company. A man barreled out of the building, turning and firing in Decker's direction. Bullets sparked off the dumpster as a second man emerged, aiming his pistol in the same direction. The second man paused before firing, turning his attention to Harlow, who had Penkin on his feet—a black bag over his head.

Decker flipped the only switch that resembled a safety and touched off a long burst of automatic fire. The bullets ripped through the two men, knocking them flat on the concrete. Decker placed the next burst in the doorway, yielding a high-pitched scream from inside the club.

While Harlow strong-armed Penkin into the car, Decker emptied the PP-2000's magazine, burst by burst, into the building. Before loading the second magazine, he lobbed a flash-bang grenade into the doorway. A hollow metal rattle echoed in the dark hallway, immediately followed by panicked voices.

"Flash bang out," he said, covering his ears and looking away.

The explosion lit the alley like a flash of lightning, the multiple high-decibel detonations penetrating his hands like gunshots. Decker didn't stick around for the inevitable counterattack. Most of these men would be former Russian Special Forces, not likely to be dissuaded for long by a little gunfire and a flash bang. He ran for the car, drawing return fire when he passed in front of the doorway. The bullets passed behind him, thumping into the side of one of the SUVs.

"You're driving!" Harlow yelled out of the rear passenger window.

Decker changed course in midstride, leaping up to slide across the sedan's hood. The homeless guy's sticky clothes brought him to an abrupt stop on the metal, forcing him to roll the rest of the way. He hit the ground behind the car an instant before a string of bullets struck the windshield and hood. Rising to his knees, Decker stuck the submachine gun into his shoulder and fired the entire magazine through the doorway.

"Countermeasures!" he yelled, tossing the weapon and jumping into the car.

Staying low in the seat, he put the car in drive and hit the gas while Harlow tossed a few surprises out of her window. Bullets punched the trunk and shattered the rear windshield as the car picked up speed. Several earsplitting detonations interrupted the gunfire, the alley once again flashing white. A quick look in the rearview mirror revealed several men standing in the middle of the alley, in various states of disorientation and pain—a thick cloud of smoke rising to obscure them.

Decker raced the car down the alley, slowing just enough to make the tire-squealing turn onto an empty side street.

He glanced over his shoulder, seeing that Harlow had everything under control. She pressed a stun gun against Penkin's hood, right under his neck. Her other hand held a compact semiautomatic pistol, which she rested on her thigh, pointed at the Russian. Decker started to say something, but Harlow cut him off.

"Just drive."

"Drive me back, and I'll let both of you live," said Penkin.

She jammed the pistol into the Russian's crotch, causing him to inhale sharply.

"Give me a reason," she said.

Five very quiet minutes later, Decker merged the sedan into light northbound traffic on Interstate 405—headed toward a reckoning.

Chapter Thirteen

Harlow reluctantly guided Penkin through the charred skeleton of a structure that had once been a house, terrified by the prospect of what was about to unfold. Mostly terrified. A part of her wanted this to happen. The really dark part she couldn't yet embrace. Wouldn't embrace—she hoped.

Decker walked several feet ahead of them, directing his flashlight at the debris-littered floor. He carried a metal folding chair in one hand and a red plastic gasoline container in the other. The sight of the container sickened her. It was one thing to think or dream about burning this piece of human garbage alive, but something completely different to be delivering him to this gruesome fate.

"I smell an old campfire," said Penkin, his voice muted under the black hood. "But stronger."

She'd started taking shallow breaths as soon as they reached the incinerated house, unable to shake the feeling that she was inhaling more than charred wood. Harlow couldn't believe he had brought them here. Life as Decker knew it had come to an end because of this place. It would be the last thing she'd ever want to see again—but Decker didn't appear to be on a healing journey. Quite the opposite. He seemed hell-bent on destroying himself. The moment she finished that thought, Decker unfolded the chair and slammed it down, turning it to face Penkin.

"Sit him down," he said in a tone that sounded a lot like an order. She pushed Penkin toward him. "This is your show."

Decker twisted the Russian's arm and forced him to sit down. When Penkin leaned against the seat back, Decker ripped the hood off his head and directed the flashlight beam at his face. The Russian squinted, raising a hand to block the light.

"Do you know where you are?" said Decker, panning the light over the burned-out, three-quarters-missing structure.

Penkin followed the light for a few seconds before taking in his surroundings at his own, slower pace. As the top-ranking member of the Bratva in Los Angeles, it was highly unlikely he'd ever been here. On top of that, there was no way for him to geographically determine his location. The house had been strategically situated on a rolling patch of high desert land, well out of sight of the distant neighbors. The perfect location to keep prying eyes away from a grim business.

Penkin turned his gaze to the gas container and chuckled. "You really brought me here?"

"I couldn't think of a more fitting place," said Decker, unscrewing the top of the container. "To make things right."

"I recognize her," said Penkin, out of nowhere. "A troublemaker on the rise. Miss . . . uhhhh . . . Mackenzie. How the hell did the two of you end up together?"

"Actually, your organization indirectly facilitated that," said Harlow. "Several years ago."

Decker's foot hit Penkin in the solar plexus. While the Russian groaned, bent over in the chair, Decker dumped a long stream of gasoline over his head. When Penkin finally sat up, he poured the rest of the can in his lap, tossing the container aside.

"Good," hissed Penkin. "Finally that piss smell is gone."

Decker squatted in front of him. "So. You get to choose."

"Choose what?"

"How this ends."

"Let me guess. I get to choose between flames or a bullet to the back of my head?"

"Front of your head," said Decker. "I don't have a problem looking people in the eye when I kill them."

"You might be a tough son of a bitch, Decker. But you're not a killer," said Penkin, pausing for a moment. "Not this kind of a killer."

"I'm looking to try new things before I cash out," said Decker. "Dead man walking."

"There's only one dead man walking here, and it's not you—or Miss Mackenzie back there. You signed my death warrant the moment you showed up at the club. And believe me when I tell you, the two options you offer are far better than what I'd get from my own people."

"Why would they kill you?"

"They don't like attention, and I've attracted more than my fair share over the past year—thanks to you."

"I'm the gift that keeps on giving," said Decker.

"Yes. You are. Snatching me right out of one of my clubs, in front of my soldiers—that was the end," said Penkin. "A real shame, too. The US attorney dropped the case against me a few days ago. Things were back on track."

"You can't outrun karma."

"Who's karma?" said Penkin. "What is that?"

"He's stalling. Trying to talk his way out of this," said Harlow. "Not a word out of him for two hours. Now he's chatty Kathy."

Penkin's face flattened. "I know I'm not leaving here alive."

"I'm glad we're on the same page," said Decker.

"Then why all of the theatrics? You know I don't care if I go up in flames. Dead is dead. It doesn't matter how you get there. Burning me alive will hurt you more than me."

"Now you're a philosopher?" said Decker. "Trust me. Burning a sex slaver won't bother me in the least."

"I meant *her*," said Penkin. "I've burned more people alive than I can remember. Never bothered me, either. But Miss Mackenzie—badass heroine of the streets—this will ruin her forever. I could use a cigarette. Did anyone bring a condemned man a last smoke?"

Penkin laughed hysterically, clapping his hands against his gasoline-soaked thighs. The part of Harlow that wanted this sadistic maniac to go up in flames grew rapidly, threatening to tip the scales. She started to move forward, but Decker seemed to sense her anger. He glanced over his shoulder at her and shook his head.

"This is on me," he whispered.

"So," said Penkin. "What do you want with me, Ryan Decker?"

"The truth."

"I'll give you the truth. If Miss Mackenzie returns my flask. I could use a drink."

"You have a lot of bad habits," said Decker.

"I never expected to live a long life."

"At least you're realistic," said Decker, turning to Harlow and nodding. "You have his flask?"

"Really? You're going to give this asshole a drink?"

"Can't hurt," said Decker. "Maybe it'll loosen his tongue."

"It's back in the car."

Decker shrugged.

"Why don't I pick up a pizza, too, while I'm at it," Harlow said before turning around in the dark and yelling over her shoulder, "Any other requests?"

"Extra pepperoni," said Penkin, laughing again.

Harlow gave them the finger and set off carefully through the wreckage, the light from her phone shining the way. She couldn't believe Decker was indulging him. Penkin was a calculating, merciless animal. A flask of booze wasn't going to influence what he planned on telling him. Nothing the man said could be trusted.

"Dead man walking, my ass," she muttered.

Halfway to the car, she breathed deep, purging her lungs with the crisp desert air. The smoky ruins of the house clung to her nose the rest of the way, gradually fading by the time she reached the car. They'd parked her shot-up sedan behind a stand of tall bushes growing behind a hill, a few hundred yards away from the house—just in case. She opened the back door and grabbed the metal flask from the passenger-side seat back, closing the door quietly behind her.

A distant gunshot stopped Harlow in her tracks. She tossed the flask back in the car and drew her pistol, fairly certain that the gunfire hadn't been directed at her. She hadn't heard the telltale snap of a passing supersonic bullet.

She considered calling Decker's phone but didn't want to risk giving away her position. It was nearly impossible to conceal the phone's light while talking or sending a text. Not to mention the loss of situational awareness. No. She'd watch and wait. A single gunshot meant one thing. One of them was dead—and the survivor was headed in this direction.

Given this fact, Harlow decided to move off the direct path between the house and the car. She settled against a slight rise in the ground, about thirty steps to the left, and waited. A darkened figure appeared in the distance, walking at a normal pace toward the general vicinity of the car. She raised her pistol, thinking that Decker would be using his flashlight, before remembering that he'd first turned it on only when they reached the house. On the other hand, Penkin wouldn't be stupid enough to use it and give himself away. Keeping the pistol aimed at the approaching figure, she crouched lower, presenting as little of a target as possible.

"Harlow! It's Decker! I can see you hiding over there, next to that little hill. I saw you move off the path."

She pocketed the pistol and headed toward the car, both angry that he'd sent her away like a child and relieved that he'd spared her the sight of an execution. Harlow couldn't help wondering if she'd made a mistake saving Decker earlier today. His hell-bent focus on revenge would get them both killed long before either of them could shed a steady light on the shadowy group behind Meghan Steele's kidnapping and death. She might be better off on her own at this point.

Decker met her in front of the car.

"He killed himself with a pistol I took off one of the Russians," said Decker. "I gave him the option, and he accepted. I figured he would. He knew it beat the alternative."

"Alternative?"

"I could have let him go," said Decker. "The Bratva would catch up with him eventually, wanting to know who kidnapped him and why. Of course, that conversation wouldn't happen over drinks and dinner. It would happen over a bathtub of sulfuric acid, while they dipped him feetfirst, a centimeter at a time."

"You actually trusted him to put a gun to his head and not shoot you?"

"I'm not completely crazy," said Decker. "I took cover and threw him the pistol, with one bullet."

"And he just shot himself."

"They say that people feel absolved from their sins right before they take their own life. I'm not sure how *they* know that, but I have to admit—Penkin looked relieved right before he pulled the trigger. It almost felt wrong giving him that kind of peace."

Harlow's knees buckled, the day's gravity finally catching up to her. She steadied herself against the bullet-riddled hood.

Decker moved close to her. "You okay?"

She wanted to punch him. Even better, kick him in the groin. Knock a little sense into him. Of course she wasn't *okay*!

"What do you think?" she said. "You've killed what—eight people within the past twelve hours?"

"I didn't have a choice at the mall, or the club," Decker said before pointing in the direction of the burned-out house. "And Penkin? I can live with that decision."

They stood there silently, staring at each other. He was either deep in thought or about to explode. After a few tense moments, Decker walked around the car and opened the rear passenger door. He returned with Penkin's flask and took a seat on the hood.

"I need a drink," he said.

"Right now?"

"Why not?"

Decker unscrewed the cap and raised the flask to his nose.

"Vodka?" said Harlow.

"What else?" he said, and tipped the flask back. "Yikes. I haven't had a drink in a while."

He offered her the flask, which she accepted reluctantly before leaning against the front of the car. She took a small drink of the smooth vodka and stared at the star-filled sky.

"I'm sorry to put you through this, Harlow. I want to burn the entire world to the ground right now."

After a few deep, cleansing breaths, she handed the flask back to Decker.

"I'll never know what you've been through," she said. "But you can't kill your way to the end of this. I understand it could happen again. We're up against some really bad people. I get it. But violence has to be our last resort. I won't work with you unless that's crystal clear."

"Clear enough," said Decker, taking another long drink. "We do this your way from now on, holding my skill set in reserve."

"Close-quarter gun battles aren't your only skill set," said Harlow. "You ran a very successful human-recovery operation for years. How many times did your operators utilize the set of skills you leaned on today?"

"Rarely," he allowed. "It was bad for business."

"A last resort."

"Exactly," he said, offering her the flask.

She shook her head. "I'm driving."

"Good idea. This stuff is going straight to my head," said Decker, emptying the flask onto the ground.

"So where do we go from here?" said Harlow.

Decker looked at her, his face mostly a shadow. "Don't you want to know what he told me?"

She shrugged. "Can you really trust anything he said?"

"He had nothing to lose by coming clean."

"Except his loyalty to the brotherhood."

"I don't know," said Decker. "I get the feeling he was telling the truth."

"What did he say?"

"He insists they had nothing to do with Meghan Steele's kidnapping. They knew something was odd when she was delivered, but they didn't discover her identity until after the transaction was complete."

"Transaction?"

"They were paid to make her disappear—permanently," said Decker. "But when they suspected there was more to the girl than met the eye, they did a little digging. Didn't take long to discover the truth. They kept her here, as a domestic slave, thinking she might be useful at some point."

"These people are animals."

"Animals don't do this to each other," said Decker, continuing with Penkin's confession. "He claims the same crew that delivered Steele showed up at one of his clubs a few months after they handed off Meghan, infuriated that she was still alive. Claimed they had a complication that required a drastic solution."

"Blowing up the house and setting you up?"

"Way more than that," said Decker, his voice trailing off.

She didn't want to push the conversation any further, knowing where it would end. Instead, she completely shifted topics.

"What now?" she said.

He took a while to answer.

"We go with your first idea and visit Ares Aviation in Riverside—tomorrow," he said. "Right now, I need some sleep. A lot of sleep."

"Sounds like a plan," she said, pushing herself away from the car. "Keys?"

Decker handed them over and hopped off the hood.

"I'm not driving you back smelling like that," she said. "It was bad enough on the way over. Your clothes are in the trunk." She handed him the keys back.

Decker retrieved his clothes and walked over the small rise between the car and house. She waited for what felt like an excessively long time for a man to change. Harlow drew her pistol and set off looking for him.

She found him just over the hill, seated with his arms crossed over his knees on the hardscrabble ground—face buried. Harlow quietly backtracked until he was out of sight again. Tears streamed down her cheeks. She truly couldn't imagine what he was feeling out here.

CHAPTER FOURTEEN

A sharp knock jolted Decker awake. Despite having no recollection of where he had just awoken, his hand shot to the nightstand to grab the pistol he vaguely remembered placing there before falling asleep. All he found on the nightstand was a full glass of water. Eyes fluttering, he tried to make sense it all. The pounding on the door continued as the information rushed back into place.

He was somewhere Harlow Mackenzie had brought him after their trip to San Bernardino County—to interrogate Viktor Penkin. A hotel? Her apartment? Light peeked through the edges of the floor-to-ceiling shades in front of the bed, exposing enough of the room to confirm that he wasn't in a jail cell. It hadn't been a dream. He was free!

"Hold on!" he said, checking to see if he was wearing clothes. Somehow he was in tight-fitting gray UCLA sweatpants and a light-blue V-neck T-shirt.

"Okay," he said, swinging himself to the side of the bed. "Come in."

The door cracked open a few inches.

"Decent?" said Harlow.

"Yeah. If you consider a man dressed in women's clothing decent."

She opened the door and walked toward the front of the bedroom. "I wasn't expecting guests. Sorry."

"I'm not complaining," said Decker. "As long as you don't expect me to set foot out of the building like this."

"We'll get you squared away with some clothes before we head out."

Harlow pressed the digital controller next to the rightmost shade, sending all of the shades into a slow, controlled ascent.

"Thank you," he said, before glancing toward the nightstand. "The gun?"

"What gun?"

"The Glock."

"You mean the one traceable to several homicides committed yesterday? I'm pretty sure it's going on a fishing trip today—and not coming back."

"Can I get a replacement?"

"I have coffee and bagels waiting in the kitchen. Good coffee," she said. "We can discuss it then."

He took his eyes off the rising blinds to follow her as she walked back to the door. She was barefoot, dressed in pressed gray slacks and a light-blue blouse.

"Are we headed in to the office?" he said.

"No," she said, turning in the doorway. "You and I are headed back out to San Bernardino County to speak with the gentleman at Ares Aviation who submitted that waiver."

"Well, all right then."

"Glad you approve," she said and then was gone.

He turned his attention to the view unfolding beyond the windows, once again momentarily transfixed by what he saw. The downtown Los Angeles skyline filled the floor-to-ceiling glass, the first skyscrapers seemingly less than a block away. Decker got up and walked to the windows, guessing the room was at least twenty stories above the ground. Judging by the position of the skyscrapers to the east, he guessed this building was on the far edge of Westlake. Extremely expensive real estate given its proximity to downtown.

He glanced around the room again, taking in its simple but elegant decor and the dark, meticulously smooth hardwood floors. It didn't look like the kind of place a private investigator could afford, and it was devoid of any personal touches or knickknacks. Had he missed something?

Admittedly, he'd fallen asleep on the ride back from Hemet and woken up in a parking garage—but he'd just assumed they were closer to the coast. He remembered getting in an elevator and stepping into the apartment, but that was about it. Was it a hotel? If it was, it was a very expensive hotel. He made his way to the bathroom to wash his face, noting the immaculate dark-gray tile and shiny black granite counter-top. All very high-end.

Decker rinsed his face in the sink and took a long look at the tired man staring back. He could use another twenty-four hours of sleep in that luxurious bed, possibly longer, but he knew their window of oppor-tunity would be shut by then. Getting to the bottom of what had really transpired with Senator Steele's daughter would rely on maintaining a quick tempo.

They had to stay as many steps ahead of their adversaries as possible to keep them guessing. Hopefully, they could sustain the pace of their investigation long enough to find the next piece in the puzzle—before the Russians or this Aegis group shut them down.

Decker dried his face and examined the luxurious towel, looking for a hotel monogram. Nothing. Could she possibly own this place? He couldn't stop thinking about it. On the way out of the bedroom, he glanced out the windows again. The Metropolitan Detention Center couldn't be more than a mile or so beyond the small cluster of skyscrap-ers. The Japanese Village Plaza where he had shot the former SEAL was even closer. Nice as it was, he didn't want to spend another night here if he didn't have to.

When he opened the bedroom door, Decker stepped into a spa-cious central living area, which shared the same view of the city. Stainless steel appliances, more granite countertops, and a sea of gleam-ing hardwood served as the background for an apartment filled with

Scandinavian-style furniture—most of it oriented to take advantage of the view.

Harlow sat at a light-finished wood table separating the kitchen from the glass-enclosed living room. He continued to study the apartment, not finding any framed photographs or items of a personal nature. Either the place was a last-minute rental or Harlow Mackenzie didn't have much of a private life. At least not the kind she cared to display. His scan ended with a closed door next to the kitchen.

"Another bedroom?" he said.

"Office," she said. "The master bedroom is next to the laundry room. Kind of sucks that it doesn't have a view, but trust me, the lights and sounds of the city can keep you up at night. Always something going on downtown."

Decker laughed uncomfortably, making his way over to the table. "Sorry. This is maybe going to sound a little assholish, but is this your place?"

She put down her coffee as he took a seat. "Huh. I see. You just assumed I was some struggling, do-gooder PI, torn between making a little scratch in the LA trafficking scene or paying the bills?"

"I don't know what I thought, but this is a crazy serious place."

"Brace yourself," she said. "Yes. I own this apartment and a few others around LA. I've done pretty well for myself in this business. Nothing on the scale of World Recovery Group, but I've found a profitable and satisfying niche."

"I'll say you have," he said, nodding at the coffee. "Can I?"

She passed the carafe.

"We can get an espresso on the outside, if that's your thing. It's still good coffee, though."

He poured a cup and savored the smell. Really good.

"Kona blend?"

"Yes. I broke out the good stuff for you."

"Thank you," he said, lifting the mug toward her. "And thank you for—everything."

"Don't mention it," she said before pointing to the bagels on the counter next to the toaster. "Self-service this morning."

"This is fantastic. I haven't had a bagel in a long time," he said, happy not to be eating off a plastic tray.

"Can I ask you a question?" she said.

"Sure."

"Last night you told me they did way more than blow up the house and set you up. What did you mean? I assume it had to do with what happened—" She stopped, a pained look on her face. "Sorry. You don't have to talk about it. I shouldn't have done that."

He sat down with his bagel and took another sip of coffee. "It's fine. It happened. Out of my control now," he said, not even coming close to believing the words he'd just uttered. "Penkin said the crew that came into the club was pissed, and rightly so. The Russians were supposed to make Meghan Steele disappear for good, but they didn't."

"And you found her," she said.

He nodded. "The group that delivered her, which Penkin simply refers to as the Americans, demanded that the Russians fix the problem."

"Did he give any identifying details about the group?"

"Nothing we didn't already know. Penkin said they were ex-military, like his own people. Special Forces or the equivalent."

"Contractor types," she said.

"Right. But here's the kicker. Penkin claims the group orchestrated the house trap, from start to finish. Penkin's people were gone five days before the doomed raid."

"Wait. That was before you started surveillance of the house," said Harlow, squinting. "I thought the FBI traced parts of four adult males back to the Bratva organization?"

She'd figured it out faster than he had.

"They supposedly did, which makes zero sense if this mystery group took over the house five days before the raid," said Decker. "Why would the Russians still be there?"

"Penkin is lying?"

"I don't think so," said Decker. "There's more. He said these Americans also wanted the Bratva to do the other thing." For a moment, he was unable to get more descriptive. "When Penkin refused, they offered a very significant sum of money for the job."

"Those animals would sell their own mothers into slavery for the right amount," she said.

"Apparently it wasn't the right amount, or even the Bratva has its limits," said Decker. "Penkin swears they turned down the offer."

"The Bratva has no limits. Trust me."

"Then they passed on the job because of the potential fallout."

"They got blamed anyway," said Harlow.

"But they got to show exactly what happens to anyone that messes with the Bratva, secure in the knowledge that they couldn't actually be tied to the murders," said Decker. "Free advertising."

"It's sick," said Harlow, pushing her plate away.

For a fleeting moment, the images of his wife and son flashed through his head, nearly breaking him down. He hadn't burst into spontaneous tears for several months. The memories hadn't faded; he'd just learned to compartmentalize them, only letting them out briefly to cherish before putting them away where they wouldn't cripple him. Harlow looked like she was about to cry, which meant he hadn't locked them away fast enough.

"It's a disgusting revelation," said Decker. "But it gives us a solid focus. The man I killed in the parking garage is undoubtedly connected to the group that handed Meghan Steele over to the Russians. Then there's Ares Aviation. If we play this right, we might draw out the original crew."

"I can have my SCIF team try to ID him with the pictures you took on my phone."

"You have a SCIF?"

A dedicated sensitive compartmented information facility like the one he'd set up to support World Recovery Group operations was expensive, and resource intensive.

"Not in the traditional sense," said Harlow. "I don't keep a fixed space for intelligence gathering. Too risky. Especially with the Russians, FBI, and possibly the cartels breathing down my neck."

"Damn. You're big-time if you have the FBI watching you."

"Don't worry. They're not watching me," she said. "But my computer people are convinced they've tried to hack my team. That's why I move them around."

"How many do you have on the payroll?"

"That's my little secret," said Harlow, sipping her coffee.

He got the distinct impression that she'd had a small retinue of support staff following them yesterday. They'd changed cars twice in the afternoon, and once on the way back from Hemet, late last night. The process was always the same. Harlow would unexpectedly turn onto a side street, where they would switch cars. Any required supplies or gear would be found in the new vehicle. It was a simple but effective process, adding a necessary degree of separation between Harlow and her operation.

"And Katie?" said Decker. "She did some impressive work at the mall."

Harlow acted like he hadn't asked the question. Even more secrets.

Chapter Fifteen

Supervisory Special Agent Joseph Reeves lowered his phone. Unbelievable. He pushed his black-framed glasses tight up against his face and turned to Special Agent Kincaid.

"Matt. You're not going to believe what I just learned."

"I'm not sure you can top this," said Kincaid, nodding toward the cluster of bodies drawing flies behind the Bratva club.

A joint team of a dozen or so LAPD and FBI crime-scene investigators snapped pictures and documented evidence at the murder scene. Actually, it looked more like the site of a small battle. A very one-sided battle. The Russians had taken a beating here. Nine dead. Two wounded, their bodies destroyed by the armor-piercing ammunition presumably fired by the PP-2000 submachine gun found underneath one of the SUVs.

The weapon had been designed specifically for Russian Special Forces to fire the latest generation of armor-piercing bullets, and it was at the top of the ATF's import ban list. Reeves's ATF colleagues wouldn't be happy to learn they'd found two more inside, along with several dozen magazines of armor-piercing ammunition. Reeves would let them worry about it. The presence of a few banned weapons paled in comparison to what he had on his hands now.

"Remember what I said when we arrived here last night?" said Reeves.

"Couldn't have happened to a nicer guy?" said Kincaid.

"After that."

Kincaid shook his head. "I'm too low on coffee for guessing games."

"I said that there's only one person on the planet I could think of who would have the motivation and the skills to do this."

"I think you said 'balls' instead of 'motivation.'"

"Probably. It's been a long night," said Reeves, putting a hand on the agent's shoulder. "But I dismissed that crazy thought, because that person is locked away in a federal penitentiary—five years from the earliest possible parole."

"Decker?"

"Decker," repeated Reeves. "I couldn't shake the odd feeling that he did this, so I gave Victorville a call." He paused, surveying the bloody mess before them. "Decker is free."

"He escaped from prison?" said Kincaid. "Why the hell didn't they tell us?"

"Oh no. He didn't escape from prison. He was released from federal custody yesterday morning."

"Stop. What?" said Kincaid, holding up a hand.

"You heard me. Decker was moved to the detention center downtown in the wee hours of the morning and set free around ten a.m. Just released. Like that."

"How is that even possible?"

"Your guess is as good as mine," said Reeves. "MDC is forwarding the paperwork. Apparently, the Bureau of Prisons felt Mr. Decker deserved a reduction in sentence based on a compassionate release motion."

"On what basis?"

"That's the million-dollar question, to which there are no apparent answers right now."

"So. Decker is somehow freed," said Kincaid, "and the guy responsible for ruining his life and murdering his family is kidnapped less than twelve hours later."

"Not exactly hard to connect those dots."

"Hard to feel bad about what happened here."

"Agreed. But his release is problematic. The warden at Victorville swears he never advocated for Decker's compassionate release or signed any paperwork. The entire process would have originated from his office. He was under the impression that Decker's transfer related to the trial."

"The case was dismissed three days before Decker's release," said Kincaid.

"Decker's release papers are obviously bogus, as well as his transfer order. But how? That would take some serious computer ninja action."

"Not to mention this spot-on intelligence regarding Penkin's whereabouts."

"Exactly. I couldn't have told you where to find Penkin last night, and I run the LA field office's Russian organized-crime division," said Reeves, shaking his head.

"The easy explanation is a leak inside the LAPD."

"Possible," said Reeves. "It's not like this place was a secret within certain circles of the North Hollywood division. But that little arrangement has gone on for years, and nobody has been able to crack the code. Like you said, it would still require some targeted intelligence."

"I don't mean to be the master of the obvious right now," said Kincaid, "but we need to find Penkin. Alive or dead, he'll lead us to Decker."

"We're not technically looking for Decker. Not until the Bureau of Prisons posts an escape warrant or a mistaken release document. I wouldn't expect one of those until tomorrow at the earliest. They have a lot of digging to do."

"So if we somehow come across Decker, we let him walk?"

"I highly doubt we'll find Decker, but if we do, we sit on him," said Reeves. "It's only a matter of time before his clock runs out, and I intend to be there when it does."

They didn't have much to go on. One of the Russians had told a paramedic that the building had been under police surveillance right before the attack. They had supposedly identified a woman in a gray sedan parked farther south on Sepulveda Boulevard. LAPD couldn't confirm the report, but it was something to keep in mind. Possibly a part of whatever network had sprung Decker.

Besides that, crime scene investigators found a discarded whiskey bottle set against the alley retention wall. Tests were still pending, but the light-brown liquid inside the bottle smelled more like sweetened iced tea than hard liquor. He didn't expect to find fingerprints. Decker had probably disguised himself as a drunk homeless person to get close enough to the club's back door to neutralize the alleyway guards. There was certainly no shortage of homeless people stashed into the nooks and crannies of this neighborhood. LAPD and FBI investigators would comb through nearby homeless shelters and tent cities for possible leads.

"Matt," said Reeves. "Get with LAPD and see if anything unusual took place yesterday from the time Decker walked out of the detention center until now. Focus on murders and missing-persons reports. I have a hard time believing Decker didn't break a few eggs getting to Penkin."

"Will do," Kincaid said before looking around at the carnage. "I have to admit, Decker did a solid here."

"Decker got lucky. Correction—ten kids got lucky," said Reeves. "Decker had no idea what he was up against here, or how the Russians would react. They could have blown the kids up, like last time. Bury the evidence."

"The violence looks pretty contained."

"Tell that to the families of the kids Decker got killed a couple years ago," said Reeves. "You better not be going soft on me, right?"

"I'm not. Just glad it worked out the way it did."

"Me, too. I can't imagine my next phone call if the Russians had turned that room into teenage spaghetti," said Reeves. "This is gonna be bad enough."

"Senator Steele?"

"I'm going to take a walk for this one. She's not going to like what I have to say."

"Stop it. You're one of her favorites," said Kincaid.

"Not after this call."

CHAPTER SIXTEEN

Senator Margaret Steele's grip on the telephone handset tightened to the point she felt the plastic start to crackle.

"I need to put you on speakerphone," she said, not entirely sure that was going to prevent her from damaging government property. "Give me a minute. I'm a little challenged with this thing."

"I'll call you right back if we get disconnected, ma'am," said Reeves, the tension in his voice unmistakable.

She took a few deep breaths with her eyes closed before switching the call over and replacing the handset. It took every bit of restraint she could muster to keep from glancing at the picture on the wall next to her. She knew that would crack the facade of composure she'd built since her world had been turned upside down.

The past few days—watching the beasts behind her daughter's ordeal walk free—had been hard enough. The power and influence she had spent nearly twenty years amassing had amounted to nothing. The Department of Justice couldn't risk taking Viktor Penkin and his associates to trial given new revelations about the source and validity of the evidence.

If the US attorney's office had lost the trial, the repercussions would be felt for years, jeopardizing future cases. Better to build a new case from the ground up, based on untainted evidence. One that'd stick. Whatever. These people had ruined her life. She wanted the same for them, times a thousand. Her fitness band vibrated, indicating that her heart rate had topped 110. Several deep, slow breaths later, she had her heart rate under a hundred. Back in control—sort of.

"Joe? You still there?"

"Yes, ma'am," said Reeves, his voice filling the senator's office.

"Thank you. I needed a few moments to compose myself."

"I understand, ma'am," said Reeves. "It's been a, uh . . . not a good week."

"A shitty week, Joe. A very shitty one."

"Yes, ma'am."

"I'm just going to come out and say it, Joe. How the fuck did this happen?" said Steele. "Pardon my language, by the way."

"I don't have that answer, ma'am, and I suspect the Bureau of Prisons won't have an answer right away, either," said Reeves. "The warden at Victorville was unaware that Decker had been released. He learned it from me."

"Wait. Why are you in the middle of this?"

"Technically, I'm not," he said. "I don't know how to explain this, ma'am, but I was checking up on Decker. I have some more big news to share with you."

"Joe, I can't take any more bad news today," said Steele.

A long pause ensued. "I'm sorry, ma'am. It's been a long night, and I lost track of the date. Sorry. I just wanted you to hear this from me, instead of seeing it on the news."

"I appreciate that, Joe. You've been a good friend and a dependable ally through all of this," she said. "What's the other news? May as well get it over with."

"It's not exactly bad news," said Reeves. "Penkin was kidnapped from one of his clubs last night. I'm at the scene right now. We have nine dead Russians. Two seriously wounded. One of the dead is Kuznetsov. Ten kids escaped unharmed."

"This sounds like wonderful news," said Steele. "What's the catch? Wait. You think Decker had something to do with this?"

"I do. That's why I called Victorville. When I saw the carnage, and we determined Penkin had been taken, he was the first name that came to mind. A lot of people want Penkin dead, but Decker is at the top of that list. It can't be a coincidence."

"No. It can't. Do you have any leads on Decker?"

"Nothing from the kidnap scene, but he obviously had a lot of help pulling this off," said Reeves. "And I'm guessing that he's not finished. He'll surface again, and we'll be there to grab him."

"Do you think he'd come after me?"

"I can't imagine it, ma'am. But if you'd asked me last week if I thought Decker might orchestrate his own release so he could torture and kill Viktor Penkin, I would have said the same thing."

"I can't say I would have agreed with you on that, Joe. I think Decker would like nothing more in the world than to torture and kill that animal," said Steele. "I say that from personal experience."

"I get it, ma'am," said Reeves. "To the degree I can."

"As much as I'd like to hope Decker won't come after me, I can't afford to operate under that assumption. I was instrumental in getting him locked up."

"You and me both."

"Then you better watch your back, too, Joe."

"I honestly hadn't thought of that."

"I need you to find Decker and return him to prison—where he belongs," said Steele. "I won't be able to sleep until I know he's locked up again."

"I'm already working on it."

"Keep me posted, and let me know if you run into any bureaucratic wrinkles. I'll do whatever I can to iron them out for you."

"Hold on, ma'am. I think we might have something."

Her fitness tracker buzzed again. She waited as long as she could stand. "Joe. What's going on?"

"Apparently, there was a murder at the Japanese Village Plaza yesterday morning, less than an hour after Decker was released from the Municipal Detention Center downtown. The plaza is two blocks from the detention center."

"Are you one hundred percent sure it's related?"

"No. But there was some kind of public scare right at the same time as the murder. Someone tossed several smoke grenades and police-grade flash bangs into the lunchtime crowd, creating a panic. The victim was found in an adjacent parking garage stairwell. Two bullets to the head. LAPD said the guy was wearing a wireless communication device, which they found smashed next to him. They also found a pistol in the stairwell with the victim's fingerprints. He had a tattoo typically found on Navy SEALs. LAPD thinks he was a contract military type, but they haven't found him in any database."

"I don't know what to make of that. What does your gut instinct tell you?"

"First impression? Either Decker has nothing to do with the murder and it's just an amazing coincidence, or he was somehow involved. If he was involved, that's when things get a little murky. If the guy was there to help Decker, someone else was there to kill him. If the guy was there to kill Decker, well—he failed. Either Decker somehow killed him or Decker's accomplices did it."

"Either way, Decker's in the middle of it."

"It looks that way, unless it's a coincidence."

"You don't believe that, do you?"

"No," said Reeves. "Something bigger might be in play."

"Keep me in the loop, Joe. You can call me at any hour," said the senator, pressing a button to disconnect the call.

Her hand trembled when she withdrew it from the phone console, her wrist still buzzing from the fitness tracker. She removed the watch and set it on the desk. There was no point to wearing it for the rest of the day. Probably the rest of the week.

Would Decker really try to hurt or kill her? Why would he hold that kind of a grudge against her? Of all people, Decker should fully understand why she held him responsible for destroying her life—and why she'd gone after him so relentlessly.

He'd gambled with Meghan's life and lost, killing both her daughter and her husband in the process. David had committed suicide a year ago today, the final casualty of Decker's hubris. He'd crawled under their deck and ended twenty-four years of a wonderful friendship with a shotgun. She could forgive David for leaving her with this mess—he'd struggled with severe depression for years and absolutely adored Meghan—but she could never forgive Ryan Decker.

Senator Steele grabbed her purse and buzzed her executive assistant. She needed to make a phone call that shouldn't be placed from her office.

"Scott. I need to get some fresh air," she said. "I'm going for a walk."

"Do you want anyone to accompany you?"

"No. I need some time alone."

"Of course," he said. "Just don't wander or stay away too long, please. Everyone is concerned about you."

"I'm fine," she said. "Just need to clear my head, away from this place."

"I'll have someone follow you," he said. "At a very discreet distance."

She was about to protest, but then she thought about Decker. Maybe it wasn't such a bad idea.

Chapter Seventeen

Gunther Ross craned his neck to get a better look at the commotion on the side street next to the Bratva club. He didn't catch anything new or interesting before a police officer waved his driver into a slow right turn off Sepulveda Boulevard. A dozen or more LAPD cruisers and SUVs formed a tight perimeter around the club, diverting traffic onto side streets. Several unmarked cars sat parked at odd angles within the perimeter, men and women in suits and blue FBI windbreakers. A shiny black truck with **Bomb Squad** emblazoned on the side blocked his view of the club's entrance.

The trip out here had been a waste of time, not that he'd expected to catch Decker slithering out of a backyard or climbing out of a window. He'd pretty much learned everything he needed to know from Aegis's LAPD and FBI contacts. An unknown number of assailants had hit the Bratva club around 10:00 p.m., killing most of the Russians in the building and grabbing Penkin.

Penkin's kidnapping was assumed, since neither of the two surviving Bratva soldiers would confirm that he'd been present at any time that night. A few of the teenage kids rescued from the club reported seeing someone matching his description sitting in one of the booths shortly before the attack, but half of the Bratva roster had dark hair, dark eyes, and neck tattoos. For all anyone knew, this could have been an internal conflict. Penkin's position had weakened during his incarceration.

Maybe the Solntsevskaya Bratva's highest leadership had decided he was more of a liability than an asset at this point. It wouldn't be the first time they'd cleaned house.

No. As much as Gunther wanted to press the easy button on this, he knew better. Penkin's disappearance was connected to Decker, which meant he had to assume that Penkin had talked, and the suspicions stoked by Rich's SEAL tattoo had been confirmed: that there was far more to Decker's failed raid than vengeful Russians.

"Dammit," he muttered.

"What?" said Jay, straightening their vehicle on a cramped neighborhood road.

"Penkin represents a real liability for us."

"*If* he talks," said Jay. "These *mafiya* types are pretty hard-core."

"True. But as much as I'd like to imagine Viktor Penkin spitting in Decker's face while his ear is being cut off, I get paid to assume the worst."

"Penkin can't identify Aegis. From what I've read in the files, the original contact team followed the strictest protocols. No money changed hands. Surveillance came back clean. The best he could do is say a group of American ex-military types tried to negotiate Meghan Steele's release and it all went south. What's Decker going to do with that?"

Gunther was pleased to hear Jay repeat the cover story with conviction. He truly believed what he had been told, which would be critical in the unlikely event that Aegis's involvement in Meghan Steele's kidnapping ever saw the light of day. It was a carefully crafted lie, told to a select few who held leadership roles in the current operation. The truth no longer existed outside of Gunther, Harcourt, and presumably Senator Frist. He had long ago buried it, along with the operatives directly involved. Jay and the two operational team leaders in Los Angeles had been fed a highly sanitized version of the truth. One that established the critical importance to Aegis's future of quickly and discreetly neutralizing Decker.

"Don't underestimate Decker," said Gunther. "He managed to escape from a maximum-security penitentiary, elude our team, and kidnap one of the West Coast's top Bratva bosses inside of twelve hours. Frankly, I'm a little worried about what he might have planned for today."

"I'm just saying he doesn't have any solid leads to pursue," said Jay. "There's not much he can do with the information he gets from Penkin. He can't go to the police or FBI. They'll throw his ass right back in jail. He certainly can't take his thin findings to Senator Steele. She'll have him arrested on the spot. I don't see where he can go with this."

"He's surprisingly resourceful. That's all I'm saying," said Gunther. "We need to get ahead of him. Start working a list of potential opportunities he might pursue. Even if they're dead ends for him, we might be able to catch him out in the open."

Gunther's phone buzzed in the vehicle's center console. He answered it immediately.

"Mr. Harcourt. I was about to call you," said Gunther. "I'm with Mr. Reid. We just drove by the North Hollywood location. I'm afraid there's not much to report."

"You didn't find Decker dressed up like a homeless guy, watching the scene from a distance?" said Harcourt.

Jay shrugged, rolling his eyes.

"No. The place is crawling with cops—and the FBI."

"What's your next step?" said Harcourt. "And before you answer, Senator Steele has been made aware of the current situation."

"How current?"

"Up to the minute, compliments of Supervisory Special Agent Reeves," said Harcourt. "She knows Decker is on the loose and that Penkin has been kidnapped."

"How did the FBI figure the Decker thing out that fast?"

"Reeves," said Harcourt. "You need to watch your ass with him around. I guarantee he'll be looking for Decker. We need you to avoid any FBI run-ins."

"Understood. This complicates things," said Gunther.

"I don't pay you what I pay you to solve simple matters. What's the plan?"

"We get ahead of Decker, working under the assumption that Penkin confirmed that another organization had a hand in the botched raid out in Hemet. I'm coming up with a list of angles he might pursue with this information. When he surfaces, we'll nail him."

"That's a very theoretical plan. A little light on details."

"I have no hits on the citywide surveillance network," said Gunther. "He materialized like a ghost last night to grab Penkin, then vanished again. It's like finding a needle in a haystack until we start getting some hits."

"You know how you find a needle in a haystack?"

"Not really," said Gunther, shaking his head.

"You stomp on the hay barefoot until you step on the needle," said Harcourt. "Start stomping on LA. We need to find this guy. There's too much at stake here."

"Copy that," said Gunther, not sure what Harcourt meant by that.

"I'm going to send some paperwork to your operations center. You are now authorized by Senator Steele to make inquiries into Decker. Be very careful how you do this."

"I can work with that," said Gunther.

"Good. She's just as eager as the rest of us to tie up loose ends," said Harcourt, disconnecting the call.

Gunther turned to Jay, who wore a mildly annoyed face.

"My guess is that Senator Steele's idea of a loose end in this case vastly differs from Harcourt's," said Jay.

"Just slightly," said Gunther.

"Hey. I had an idea while you were on the phone. You mentioned Hemet. This might be a long shot, but what if Decker took Penkin out to the scene of the original crime?"

"Huh. It's isolated, that's for sure," said Gunther. "Perfect place for something like that. Probably the last place anyone would think to look."

"Or want to look."

"That, too," said Gunther, thinking it over. "It's not like we have any other leads."

Chapter Eighteen

Decker scanned the half-empty parking lot, seeing nothing that raised any alarms. Ares Aviation sat tucked away in the corner of a quiet, L-shaped strip mall adjacent to Riverside Municipal Airport. The strip mall was part of the airport's business park, almost every sign or logo indicating that the company housed inside catered to the airport or airport customers.

He gave Harlow a once-over, shaking his head. "You know that can get you arrested, right?"

She adjusted the plastic badge holder attached to her jacket lapel, moving it uncomfortably closer to her effectively exposed cleavage. He shifted his view back to the Ares Aviation office.

"Nowhere on the badge does it say 'FAA.' The background logo is for the Department of Homeland Security. Not my fault if they can't take their eyes off the goods long enough to figure that out."

"And you've done this before," he stated.

"In this very office," she said. "Trust me."

"What if you're dealing with a woman?"

"Don't worry. One of the guys will take over before she has a chance to figure it out," said Harlow. "And if that doesn't work, I'll send you in. Let you work some of your magic on the ladies."

"Funny," he said. "I'm sure my prison vibes will mesmerize."

"Anyway, I don't need to be convincing. I just need to raise a few alarms. Enough for someone to place a call. I have to imagine someone inside that office has been alerted to your presence."

"Our presence," he said. "They know I had help."

"Even better. We need to pique their interest."

"You're made if they have video surveillance. Life could get very difficult for you in this city after that."

"Now you're not even making sense," she said. "I'm harboring a fugitive from contract killers and the police. Probably the FBI at this point. How much more difficult for me could it get?"

"Seriously. Watch yourself in there. For all we know, they've anticipated this move."

She got serious for a moment. "I'll be careful. You'll be able to listen to everything through my phone. If you see anything out here, honk the horn."

"Old-school works for me," said Decker.

"Last check. How do I look?" she said, turning in the seat.

His eyes went right to her chest.

"See? Nothing to worry about."

"Don't get too smug," he said. "I did just get out of prison."

"See you in a few minutes," said Harlow.

She walked across the parking lot, disappearing into Ares Aviation. He raised the volume on the phone and set it on the dashboard, listening to her conversation as he casually scanned the parking lot for threats. Eight minutes later, she returned, having acquired none of the information she requested—but that had been expected. She tossed the folder over her shoulder and shrugged.

"I think that went well," said Harlow. "I have no doubt they're calling this in as we speak."

"I didn't exactly get that from your conversation."

"I did," said Harlow, removing the fake badge and tossing that onto the folder. "The same guy I talked to last time was at the reception desk. He didn't look at my badge once."

"I'm sure he didn't."

"He didn't look at that, either," she said. "He focused on my face, avoiding my eyes. The guy was terrified. His eyes kept darting toward the back. Freaked me out a little. I think he was just nervous about one of his colleagues overhearing our conversation. He wasn't like this last time."

"I guess we'll know soon enough. Nice work," said Decker. "Video surveillance?"

"Unfortunately."

"We can't go back to your apartment, or any place easily traceable to you."

"I have plenty of safe options."

"Good. We'll need them," said Decker. "Now what?"

"We park across the street and wait for these Americans to show up," said Harlow, mimicking Penkin's thick Russian accent.

"That's good," he said immediately.

"Really?"

"Not really. You sounded like Natasha Fatale."

"She sounds like fun," said Harlow, starting the car.

"She's from a cartoon. An old one."

"You're dating yourself, Decker."

"This is like a Cold War cartoon. I'm not that old."

She smiled, starting to turn her head to say something but stopping before any words formed—like she had thought better of it. She put the car in gear and drove them out of the lot, turning south on Airport Drive. A few blocks away, she cut a U-turn and brought them back to the business park, where she eased the car into the parking lot across the street from the strip mall housing Ares Aviation. They settled into the least obvious spot possible, keeping a clear view of the company's entrance and adjacent lot.

"Want to take bets on how long?" she said.

"I don't have any money."

"I wasn't serious."

He shrugged. "Everyone bets on everything in prison."

"Cigarettes. Gum. Commissary credits."

"You've watched *Shawshank Redemption* one too many times," said Decker. "Ramen noodles. Stamps. Condoms filled with drug-free urine. Condoms for other reasons."

"Yuck. Sorry I brought it up," she said. "So. What did you bet on?"

"Do you really want to know?"

"Not really," she said unconvincingly.

Several seconds passed before he answered.

"I bet on my own life. After the second serious attempt to kill me in prison, I was a long-shot bet," said Decker. "Six failed attempts later, I owned most of the ramen noodles in my cellblock and nobody would bet against me."

"That's pretty grim."

"Not if you like ramen noodles."

CHAPTER NINETEEN

Gunther trudged uphill, the sand giving way under his boots with every step. He wiped the sweat off his forehead with a hand and grumbled. A few hundred yards of sunbaked desert still stood between them and the site of the doomed raid. Ironically, one of Decker's assault teams had taken the same path to the house on that fateful day. He'd watched them snake through the hills on the drone operator's thermal imaging feed, patiently waiting for all of the teams to disappear into the house—before triggering the blast that would consume them.

He'd chosen the same approach because it would give them an opportunity to scan the property for any other interested parties. If Supervisory Special Agent Reeves was sharp enough to discover Decker's prison trick on his own, he had to assume the FBI agent would visit the Hemet location at some point, looking for Penkin. From one of the boulder-strewn rises south of the house, Gunther would decide whether it was safe to proceed.

The last thing he needed right now was a run-in with the FBI. He could talk his way out of it, especially with Senator Steele's get-out-of-jail-free card, but it would undoubtedly put him on Reeves's shit list. The agent wasn't a big fan of freelancers. Gunther preferred to save his free pass for a much stickier situation.

He stopped and turned to Jay, who trailed him by several feet. "Not too much farther."

"You keep saying that," said Jay, continuing to climb the hill.

"It's the safest approach."

Jay stopped next to him, setting his small olive-drab backpack on the ground. He dug through the main pouch, removing two perspiring bottles of Evian.

"Water?"

"Sure," said Gunther.

They drank greedily for a few seconds, each of them draining at least half of the bottle. Before they set off again, Jay scanned the nearly empty landscape around them.

"How the hell did Decker find this place? Seriously. I don't think I could drive us back out here without your help."

"Aegis hired Decker for several difficult human-recovery cases. He'd developed a vast human intelligence network across the world. He knew everything there was to know about the various human-trafficking networks and organized kidnapping rings."

"Yeah. But how the hell did he find someone out *here?*"

"Steele was high profile, so he figured she'd either be ransomed back or sold. When she wasn't ransomed, he assumed she had been sold off. A fifteen-year-old girl would be sold into the sex-trafficking industry, so he focused his efforts there. It took a little while, but he got a hit from a rescue house contact in San Bernardino. A thirteen-year-old had escaped one of the Bratva truck stop operations and reported being held at a house in a quiet, isolated area in the desert. She described a girl at the house that matched Meghan Steele's description. She also said the girl appeared to be part of the operation. The Russians didn't sexually abuse her like the others, and she didn't try to run away."

"Stockholm syndrome?" said Jay.

"Right. They assumed she had been there awhile based on that. The girl also reported frequent aircraft passes. Big aircraft. Decker started searching rural areas near any airports that landed commercial airliners.

Took them three weeks, but they found it. None of this was in the file?" said Gunther.

"The file was pretty thin."

"Intentionally thin," said Gunther. "This was a colossal screwup for Aegis. My screwup."

"It wasn't your—Aegis's fault."

"Not intentionally," said Gunther, repeating the lie. "But we tipped them off when we approached Penkin to negotiate Meghan Steele's release. He played us long enough to set a trap that would vaporize most of the evidence and send a brutal message to anyone that crossed the Bratva."

"And Decker walked right into it."

"Nobody could have predicted what Penkin's organization had in mind," said Gunther. "Decker is an unfortunate victim of circumstance. Our job is to close the loop on his misfortune. Aegis's national defense mission around the globe is too important to be squandered on a scandal like this. Senator Steele is a vital ally, and we intend to keep it that way."

They proceeded cautiously up the hill, cresting it slowly. The burned remains of the house appeared in the distance beyond several clumps of thick, twisty bushes. They pulled out binoculars and studied the area around the house, making sure nobody else had beaten them to the idea. The rough vehicle path leading to the house looked clear all the way to the hard-packed dirt road that connected the property to civilization. From this vantage point, they could visually sweep the entire property, with the exception of a few spots hidden by bushes or shallow ravines.

"Looks like we're alone," said Gunther.

Jay lowered his binoculars and nodded toward the house. "Except for the dead Russian."

Gunther focused his binoculars on the burned-away structure, immediately spotting a body slumped on a folding chair in the middle of the charred ruins.

"I need to take a closer look," he said. "He looks mostly intact from here, except for the head wound. If Decker worked him over, I'd expect him to be stripped down and bloodied."

"I can't believe this place hasn't been leveled," said Jay. "Given what happened here."

"Out of sight. Out of mind. Nobody can see it from the surrounding properties."

"The Russians don't play around. That's for sure," said Jay. "Seeing this kind of hits you in the gut."

"Don't think about it," said Gunther. "What's done is done here. Penkin got what he deserved in the end."

"Have to give Decker credit. Dragging Penkin out here was a nice touch."

"Decker's a piece of work, that's for sure."

He stood up and brushed the sand and dirt off his clothes.

"Keep a close eye out for visitors. Don't forget to check your six. Decker is lethal. Don't ever forget that."

"Understood," said Jay, pointing the binoculars in the direction they had just come.

Gunther descended the shallow slope, using the bushes to cover his approach, just like Decker's assault team. At the edge of the brush, he stopped to listen for a minute, just in case. He'd learned long ago never to trust a single input source. Senses played predisposed tricks on the mind. Intelligence sources produced information confirmed by their own biases. The list went on. His brain, and its close connection to his eyes, had very likely assumed that the house was safe after his initial look through the binoculars.

Hearing nothing unusual, he emerged from the scrub and crossed the burned threshold. Quiet, deliberate footsteps took him through the exposed ruins of the room that once had been packed with explosives—and freshly slain bodies. Twenty-two, including four aspiring and unwitting members of the Solntsevskaya Bratva that Penkin had supplied.

He stepped over a scorched piece of timber and approached Penkin's corpse, stopping when he smelled gasoline. A quick look around revealed a red gasoline container tossed behind a pile of rubble, and a pistol lying a few feet away from the chair. Interesting. Decker had doused him with gas but didn't follow through. Burning a man alive was the ultimate revenge, especially if you could stick around to watch. For some inexplicable reason, Decker had held back, ending Penkin's life mercifully with a single bullet to the head.

Gunther crouched next to the body, examining the head wound. It almost looked like Penkin had committed suicide. The bullet had penetrated his right temple—the same side as the discarded pistol. Decker would have shot him in the face or forehead. At least that's how Gunther would have carried out the execution. Why the hell would he risk giving Penkin a gun?

A closer look at Penkin's face revealed no signs of damage beyond the entry and exit holes. No discoloration or bruising on his hands or arms. Had he come clean to Decker in exchange for a quick death? Gunther could only assume that Penkin had told him everything, which meant Decker would go into deep hiding with his new allies, until they were ready to strike. Harcourt would go ballistic when he learned this.

His phone buzzed, giving him a quick jolt of adrenaline. Either Jay had spotted someone approaching or Harcourt had read his mind from three thousand miles away. A glance at his phone indicated it was neither. The number belonged to one of several relays sending calls to his phone from various sources across the greater Los Angeles metro area.

"Hello. Who am I speaking to?" said Gunther, holding the phone to his ear.

"Hi. This is Justin Peters with Ares Aviation at the Riverside airport. I was told to call this number if anyone came by asking questions about flight waivers submitted by our office."

"Do you have something to report?" said Gunther.

"Yes. An FAA investigator came in about five minutes ago, with a copy of a class-C airspace waiver for Riverside Municipal Airport that we submitted close to two years ago. She wanted information about the type of drone used. We don't have that information."

"Did you check her credentials?"

"She's been in before," said Justin. "Specializes in airspace waivers. She was in about four months ago auditing our waiver database."

That would have been nice to know. Must have slipped Justin's feeble mind.

"Did you verify her credentials four months ago?"

"I'm pretty sure I inspected her badge," said Justin. "I didn't sense anything off. Is there a problem?"

"Not from you. I work with the Ares legal department, and we've had a few fake inspectors and auditors hit Ares locations in the southeast United States. Florida up the East Coast to North Carolina. We're pretty sure one of Ares's competitors is behind it."

"Wow. That's crazy. Why would they want to do that?" said Justin. "All it takes is a quick call to the FAA to ask about the waivers."

"Exactly. We're not really worried about it, but I do need to follow up," said Gunther. "I'm going to swing by in about forty minutes to review video and take a close look at the waiver. Maybe there's a pattern."

"Perfect. Most of the techs are out on calls, and that's right in the middle of lunch. I'll stick around, and we'll have the place to ourselves. So we don't spook anyone."

"Even better. Any chance the agent is still around?"

"No. She took off. I watched them leave."

"Them?"

"There was another agent in the car," said Justin. "He didn't come in."

Gunther disconnected the call and immediately dialed one of the preset numbers on his phone.

"All clear up here," said Jay.

"Haul ass to the vehicle and drive it as far up the path we followed as possible," said Gunther. "I think Decker was in Riverside, at Ares Aviation."

"I'm on my way out," said Jay. "Is he still there?"

"No. But this might be the freshest his trail will ever get for us. Penkin wasn't tortured. In fact, I think Decker let him commit suicide."

"That's not good," said Jay.

You have no idea.

CHAPTER TWENTY

Harlow cracked open a Diet Coke and took a long drink, stopping when she hiccuped. Then she plunged her hand into the cylinder of Pringles, straining at the fingertips to reach the depleted stack of sour cream and onion chips. Decker watched her curiously.

"What?" she said, finally lifting several chips free.

"You're like a junk food monster."

"Based on what? A few hours observing me in the car?" she said, chomping down on the Pringles.

"My guess is that you spend a lot of time in your car on stakeouts," he said, pulling an empty Skittles bag from between the seat and center console. "Munching on garbage."

"One man's garbage is another woman's treasure," she said, snatching the bag out of his hand and stuffing it into the door cup holder. "There's more Diet Coke in the cooler."

He glanced toward the back seat, then shook his head. "Any water?"

"Just Diet Coke," she said. "Sorry. You should have said something."

"When you told me you filled a cooler with drinks, I just assumed."

She honestly couldn't tell if he was joking or serious. Was he really complaining about the drink selection?

"You really won't drink Diet Coke?"

"I gave up soda."

She was about to say something sarcastic when he continued.

"About nineteen months ago."

"That's a conversation stopper," she said before taking another sip.

"Maybe I'll give one a try. I never got into the diet soda, honestly."

As he reached between the seat backs for the cooler, a silver SUV pulled into view on Airport Drive.

"Forget the Coke. We might have company," she said, putting the can down and swiping her cell phone from the dashboard.

Decker remained motionless, twisted in his seat. Even the slightest movements attracted the eye. Sitting up in the seat while the SUV pulled even with them could have easily betrayed their position.

"Tell me when I can move," said Decker.

She waited a few seconds, until the SUV had pulled into the strip mall parking lot across the street.

"You're good," she said, putting together a quick text.

Decker glanced at her with a thin frown before lifting a telephoto lens–equipped digital camera from the case between his feet. "Who are you texting?"

"None of your business."

"Did one of your people follow us out here?"

She sent the text and grabbed the camera. "What do you care?" she said. "I have this covered."

"I don't like surprises."

"Good. Keep a close eye on our surroundings," she said, readying the camera. "I don't like surprises, either."

Harlow focused the camera's viewfinder on the SUV, following it into a reserved parking space right in front of Ares Aviation. She zoomed in and looked for a clear picture. The vehicle next to them mostly obscured the two men in the front seat. She'd have to wait until they stepped out of the SUV, which wouldn't provide much opportunity to capture their faces.

"Anything good?" said Decker.

"Not yet," she said, pressing the shutter release. "I might get one of them on the way in—if I'm lucky."

The two men got out of the SUV at the same time, the driver pausing for a moment before closing his door. She snapped a series of pictures, catching his face perfectly when he looked over his shoulder. By the time she switched to the passenger, the opportunity had passed. The black-haired man had already started walking toward Ares Aviation.

"Missed the passenger," she said. "Have to get him on the way out."

"The passenger was probably the important one."

"The chances of the passenger looking over the SUV, in this direction, were minimal. I could have bet next month's paycheck that the driver would give me a nice picture. Now I can focus on one person coming out. Surveillance one oh one."

"Surveillance one oh one," mimicked Decker.

She kept the camera focused on the passenger, just in case he decided to turn around for a look at the parking lot. No such luck. He didn't pause for the door. The driver held it open for him.

"Now for the hard part," said Harlow. "Keeping this camera on the door until they come out."

"Better you than me," said Decker, reaching for the cooler.

Staring through the viewfinder, she heard the crack of a freshly opened can, followed by gulping.

"Not bad," said Decker. "Not good, but not bad."

"It grows on you," said Harlow, already uncomfortable holding the camera still.

She shifted to the left of her seat and rested the telephoto lens against the outer steering wheel, wedging her elbow lightly against the interior.

"Careful with the horn," he said. "I've warned off a few skips before."

"Skips?" she said.

"What?" said Decker. "I worked my way up in this business just like everyone else."

"WRG had a rather exclusive client list," said Harlow. "*Skips* is more of a street term."

"You make it sound like I managed World Recovery Group from a fancy office."

"Your offices were pretty fancy."

"I didn't realize you stopped by to check on us."

"You were too busy to meet with me," said Harlow.

"Sorry," said Decker, sounding genuine. "We had a lot going on and an unending list of requests for help. Expensive requests."

"No apology needed. WRG got me off the streets. You guys did a lot of good work," she said. "It's just that no matter how hard we work on the trafficking problem, we barely make a dent. I feel like there's no end in sight."

Decker grunted. "It grows every year, here and abroad, like a pandemic. Except pandemics eventually get some institution or another stepping in to at least help slow the problem. This just gets an uncoordinated, local law enforcement fight, with individuals like you and antitrafficking organizations pitching in to help. I could have dedicated the entire weight of WRG to the fight, and I'm not sure we would have made a dent, either."

"I think you made a small dent in it last night."

"Yeah, but you know the Bratva's operation won't skip a beat. A few clubs might close down as new arrangements are made, but overall, the show will go on."

"I hate it."

"We have that in common, too," said Decker.

"What else do we have in common?"

"Diet Coke, I guess."

"Can you hand me mine?" she said, continuing to stare at Ares Aviation's front door.

Decker raised his binoculars instead of answering her question.

"What is it?" she said.

"I could have sworn I caught something in my peripheral vision, on the far left side of the strip mall near the street. Like someone peeking around the corner of the building. They were gone when I checked."

"There's no way those two made us on their way in," said Harlow.

Decker shifted the binoculars. "Shades are shut on the front windows and door. My guess is you would have noticed if they had been peeking between shades."

"Most likely," she said. "I can see the entire office front through my lens."

"Motherfuhhhh . . . ," said Decker. "There's a security camera above the door, tucked against the overhang."

"What? I didn't—" She spotted the concealed camera. "Hell. I screwed that up."

"I didn't see it, either—until I was looking for it," said Decker. "I guess we need to ask ourselves how badly we want a picture of the other guy."

"Pretty badly."

"Then the next question is, How good is your secret backup plan?" He nodded at her phone.

"Pretty good."

"Can I assume this plan would warn us if a second team showed up?"

"You can assume that."

"Then I say we get that picture," said Decker. "We won't have to wait very long. In fact, I have an idea. Give me the camera."

"Do you know how to work one of these?"

"I was in prison for nineteen months. Not nineteen years," said Decker, taking the camera. "Pull through the parking space in front of us and stop. Lunch is on me if they don't come barreling out."

"I thought you didn't have any money left after the clothes."

"I'm not worried about losing this bet," he said, adjusting the tele-photo lens.

"Ready?" she said.

"Do it."

She eased the car through the empty space, turning toward the street.

"Stop!" said Decker, and she hit the brakes.

Two men burst out of Ares Aviation, heading for the silver SUV. Decker snapped two pictures, then lowered the camera. "Get us out of here."

"That's it for the pictures?" she said, her foot still on the brake. "We're going to need more than that to run through the facial recogni-tion program."

"We can skip that step," said Decker. "I know the face."

"Seriously?"

"Without a doubt," said Decker. "Can we leave now? This guy is bad news."

She accelerated out of the parking lot. Decker sounded more con-cerned about the guy in the SUV than he had about snatching Penkin away from a dozen heavily armed Bratva soldiers. The stark difference frightened her.

With her eyes fixed on the rearview mirror, Harlow floored the accelerator, rocketing the car away from Ares Aviation. A few seconds later, the silver SUV careened onto the road behind them. Decker twisted in his seat, positioning himself to watch their pursuers.

"I need your pistol," said Decker.

"No, you don't."

"They're closing. We're about ten seconds away from a gunfight."

"Trust me," said Harlow, turning her attention back to the road ahead of them.

"Is this car bulletproof?"

"Funny. Just keep watching."

"Dammit, Harlow. This is serious!" said Decker.

"You don't think I know that?"

"I don't—" he started. "Holy crap. What was that?"

She glanced in the rearview mirror in time to see the SUV swerve into a light post. The remote-controlled spike strip had already retracted to the base station Katie had placed next to the road.

"A very expensive piece of gear," she said. "That I won't get back."

"I've never seen one of those used live. Impressive."

"Me, neither," said Harlow. "Never needed it before."

A minivan pulled out of a lot ahead of them, Katie's face momentarily visible through the driver's window. Harlow smirked, not wanting to tip off Decker. The less he knew about her tight network of assistants, the better. Harlow would sooner die than betray any of their identities. They were all victims, directly or indirectly, of the sex-trafficking industry—drawn to her agency by a single, focused desire to make a difference.

"We need to go off the grid in Los Angeles or get out of the city altogether," said Decker.

"That bad?"

"Worse," said Decker. "I don't know the guy's real name. I knew him from the CIA. Gunther Ross. A pure sociopath. I bumped heads with him at a few of the black sites I was assigned to protect. Some really dark stuff went down on his watch. I heard he went to work for Aegis. Figured it was a match made in heaven."

"How deep can Aegis look into my business and life?"

"All the way through it," said Decker.

"I know how to disappear in this city."

"As long as it doesn't involve living under a tarp in Skid Row."

She checked the rearview mirror. Two swiftly receding men stood in the middle of the street next to the crippled SUV, one of them holding binoculars.

"It's a few steps up from Skid Row," she said. "And you'll appreciate the irony of your surroundings."

"I can't wait," he said.

Chapter Twenty-One

Gunther entered Ares Aviation's air-conditioned office, barely containing the homicidal rage brewing behind his fake smile. He needed to clean this place out quickly, before someone reported the damaged and obviously stranded SUV, linking it to their visit to Ares Aviation.

"Justin?" he said impatiently.

Justin stepped into the doorway leading to the back of the office. "You're back," he said. "Did you catch them?"

"Yes. We couldn't have done it without you," said Gunther, placing a leather satchel on the counter. "Are the camera feeds stored here or transmitted to a remote location?"

"It's all kept here. In back. The hard drive stores thirty days of continuous video."

"Can you show me?" said Gunther. "I'll need to submit that as evidence. We'll get a replacement hard drive here within the hour."

"Sure. It's in the same room as the security monitor."

"I can take care of it," said Gunther. "Unfortunately, I'm going to need you, too. You're not in trouble, but I need to conduct a quick search of your vehicle."

"Why would you need to do that?"

"Either we do it or the FAA does it. Standard procedure in a case like this. Trust me. You don't want the FAA involved. It'll eat up a vacation day."

"I guess," said Justin. "Sounds kind of odd."

"They bring in the dogs, unzip cushions, take apart the engine. The full bureaucratic treatment. I just give the car a quick look and write that up in my initial report. Satisfies their protocol every time."

Gunther stepped into the cramped server room. He quickly identified the hard drive connected to the video feeds, detaching the unit and slipping it in the satchel next to a pistol. A second look at the basic security system convinced him that he hadn't missed any additional memory storage.

"Ready?" he said, stepping out of the server room.

Justin jingled a set of keys. "Yeah. Let's get this over with. Will I have to make an official statement?"

"Unfortunately, we have to do the paperwork drill, but it won't take long. I'll have you write a statement, then I'll see if I need any more information. Not a big deal. You did the right thing calling as quickly as you did."

Justin looked relieved. "I'm just glad you guys were able to get over here that fast."

"Me, too," said Gunther. "Shall we?"

He followed Justin to a red, four-door sedan parked at the back of the parking lot. Jay remained out of sight, watching the road for signs of a police response.

"Where's your partner?" said Justin.

"He's down the street a little, waiting for the police. We kind of bumped those two off the road."

"Really? That's pretty cool. Wish I could have seen the looks on their faces."

"They weren't happy. I'll tell you that," said Gunther. "Let's start with the trunk."

"I bet they weren't," said Justin, pressing a button on his remote.

The trunk opened a few inches, Justin helping it the rest of the way. The young man stepped back and motioned for Gunther to take a look.

"Looks empty to me," said Gunther.

When Justin's hands started for the trunk, Gunther craned his head forward, like he was examining something deeper inside the dark space. "I need you to open the spare-tire compartment really quick," he said. "That's a favorite hiding spot, and I like to put that in my report. Keeps them happy."

"Sure," said Justin, beginning to move the keys to his pocket.

"I can hold on to those for you."

Justin handed him the keys before reaching into the trunk. "I've never actually done this before, so . . ."

"There's usually a pull handle in the back of the trunk, near the seat backs."

He slid the keys quietly into his pocket before removing a suppressed pistol from the satchel at his side. With Justin halfway in the trunk, struggling to find the latch that didn't exist, he pressed the end of the suppressor against the nape of his neck and pressed the trigger. The man's body collapsed, the bulk of his weight falling neatly inside the trunk. Gunther returned the pistol to the satchel, then lifted Justin's limp legs up and over the tail of the car.

"Were you going to tell me about this?" said Jay, startling him.

"What are you doing off the street?"

"I was starting to get worried. It shouldn't take that long to hot-wire a car," said Jay, glancing from Gunther to the trunk. "Obviously you had more in mind than stealing Justin's car. What are we doing here, Gunther?"

"Our jobs," he said. "We're authorized to use any and all means necessary to contain this situation. What did you think we were going to do with Decker?"

"Decker is different."

"Really? How?" said Gunther, glancing around to make sure nobody had taken an interest in them.

"He's . . . I don't know. He's in the game. I just thought he was the only liability we'd have to remove from the equation."

"You mean kill," said Gunther.

"Right. I didn't expect the killing to expand beyond Decker."

"We don't have the time to get into this right now. Grab the keys out of his pocket."

When Jay leaned over the trunk to dig through the man's pockets, Gunther drew the pistol from the satchel again and fired a bullet into the back of his head. He hadn't been kidding when he said he didn't have time for this. The last thing he needed from any of his operatives was hesitation, regardless of the cause. He particularly couldn't afford to be second-guessed by his assistant operations lead. The stakes were simply too high at this point with Decker sniffing out the truth about Hemet.

PART TWO

Chapter
Twenty-Two

Jacob Harcourt cracked his knuckles, drawing the secretary's attention away from her computer monitor for a moment. He'd been waiting to see Gerald Frist for just over thirty minutes, the trip from his Georgetown brownstone to the Russell Senate Office Building adding another hour to the total, thanks to lunchtime traffic. He knew what Frist wanted, which annoyed him even more. More assurances that the Decker situation was under control.

A simple phone call should have sufficed, but the closer they got to clearing that final hurdle, the more Frist exhibited signs of deepstate paranoia. Ironic, given the fact that his upcoming vote would support an agenda that made the deep-state believers sound rational. The thought almost made him laugh. He couldn't wait to end this charade with Frist. The guy was barely tolerable under the best circumstances, but he was necessary and irreplaceable at this point. It had taken Harcourt years to find someone like Frist to exploit.

Wealth and power came with the territory in the Senate. There was nothing special about it in those circles, and Frist had plenty of both, but he had another quality that had taken some close inspection to uncover. Senator Gerald Frist, with all of his power and accomplishment, suffered from an inferiority complex. Unlike most individuals who identify with this psychological condition, Frist used it to fuel his ambition and achievement, incapable of understanding that he could never satisfy the deeply buried feelings of inadequacy and failure.

After earning Frist's confidence and trust over a number of years, Harcourt encountered no resistance when he eventually confided in the senator about a plan to tap into unchecked power and unlimited wealth. Two political currencies Frist could never turn down. Harcourt's sole job right now was to keep him from panicking, which was why he'd driven down here to meet in person. By this time next week, he could finally take a break from these incessant meetings. They needed to put some distance between each other anyway, in preparation for the next phase of the plan.

His phone beeped, drawing the secretary's momentary, noncommittal glance. He feigned a smile and answered the call.

"Can I call you back in a few minutes?" he said. "I can't talk here. Everything okay?"

"We've had a few developments," said Gunther.

"Good or bad?"

"Both. It's important."

"I'll call you back shortly," he said, ending the call.

He waited several excruciating minutes before the door finally opened, disgorging a pack of middle-aged men in dark suits, each stabbing their hands through the tangle of arms and shoulders to shake Frist's hand. When the last of the jackals had cleared the office, Frist ushered him inside.

"Hungry?" said Frist. "I appreciate you coming by during lunch-time. I can have Tanya order from the canteen. Be here in ten minutes."

He had no intention of being here that long.

"Thank you. I had a late breakfast," said Harcourt. "I actually need to call my tactical operations lead, if you don't mind. He had an update on Decker."

"I can't believe he had the balls to grab the Russian. That's not good. I'm a little concerned about my own security. I mean—if he can grab a Russian mob boss right off the—"

"Gerry. There's no link between you and Decker, or the Steele thing. None," said Harcourt. "Right now I'm doing everything I can to erase the last trace of a link between Aegis and Decker. Once he's gone, the slate is officially clear."

"I know, but if Aegis takes a hit—that affects me, too," said Frist. "I've invested a considerable amount of money in the company, not to mention the rest of what I've done—and what I'm about to do."

"I have my best people and resources dedicated to this," said Harcourt. "We'll get it resolved."

"I'm just a little nervous with the vote coming up."

"There's no connection between your bill and Aegis, either. We've mapped this out, Gerry. It's a slam dunk."

"I hope so," said Frist. He motioned to the leather couch next to his desk. "Sorry. Grab a seat. Make your call. I'm eager to hear the status update."

Harcourt sank into the luxurious leather cushions, adjusting his posture while Frist sat gingerly on the opposite side of the couch.

"Gunther doesn't know anything beyond Aegis," said Harcourt. "So try your best not to jump into the conversation. You'll be tempted."

"I would never."

"I've known you a long time, Gerry," said Harcourt, pressing "Send" on his phone. "You're never at a loss for words."

"My lips are sealed."

He put the call on speakerphone when Gunther answered.

"Gunther. What's up?"

"Decker and some woman posing as an FAA investigator showed up at Ares Aviation in Riverside this morning," said Gunther. "I called that office yesterday, requesting they contact me if anyone inquired about local airspace waivers. Covering all bases."

Frist mouthed, "Airspace waivers?" and Harcourt waved him off.

"Did they get a copy of the waiver?" said Harcourt.

"They already had a copy."

"What?"

Frist was becoming frantic trying to get his attention.

"The woman showed up with it, asking questions about the type of drone used," said Gunther. "Apparently, she had shown up a number of months earlier to audit their airspace waiver database."

"Please tell me you have her face on video," said Harcourt.

"Affirmative. I have her on the office security feed. Close up. We'll get her ID'd right away," said Gunther. "Ready for the bad news?"

"I didn't hear any good news."

"It's all relative at this point."

"What's the bad news?"

"I strongly suspect the same woman had a hand in the mall fiasco," said Gunther. "She disabled our SUV with a remote-controlled spike strip, a few hundred feet from Ares Aviation."

"She was still there?"

"Decker was there, too. They had Ares Aviation under observation from a parking lot across the street," said Gunther. "She's a pro. No doubt about that. She wasn't the least bit worried about sticking around, knowing that spike strip would stop us cold."

"So it's fair to say that Decker ID'd you?"

"If he didn't recognize me in the parking lot, he'll certainly recognize me when they go over the pictures. One of them was using a telephoto lens–equipped camera."

"Son of a bitch," hissed Harcourt. "Decker has been two steps ahead of you the entire time."

"We have a solid lead."

"The woman? You think she's going to head back to her apartment, order some takeout, and sit around waiting for you to show up? She's gone. He's gone. You need to get into Decker's mind and figure out where they're going next."

"Oh God," whispered Frist, raising his hands. "They'll be headed here."

What didn't this idiot get about the complete lack of nexus between him and Decker? Harcourt shook his head vigorously and focused on the call.

"Gunther?"

"I heard you, sir," said Gunther. "But if the woman turns out to be a dead end, I'm fresh out of leads unless Decker pops up on the grid."

"You can't expect him to make that kind of mistake, especially if he has highly competent help."

"Then I need to know everything."

"What do you mean?" said Harcourt. "You have the file."

"No. The real file. All of it," said Gunther. "I know there's more. I gave Jay a sanitized file, knowing damn well I had received one, too. I know Aegis had another group working the job. A group separate from mine. The intel you fed me about Decker's rescue operation could have only come from an informant deep inside Decker's group. Someone more than likely present at the very moment of the Hemet raid. If you want me to think like Decker, I need a complete picture of Aegis's involvement in this. That's the only chance we have to find him."

"I'll send it to you," said Harcourt, pausing for a moment. "It goes without saying that Jay is not cleared for this information."

"You don't have to worry about that," said Gunther. "Jay is dead, along with the guy at Ares Aviation. They're in the trunk of the car I'm driving."

"Jesus," whispered Frist.

"I trust your judgment on that," said Harcourt. "Do you need me to make a call regarding the bodies?"

"Negative. I'm ten minutes away from a car swap," said Gunther. "I'll pore through the file and come up with a game plan to get ahead of Decker. Please don't leave anything out."

"I won't," said Harcourt. "Keep me posted."

"Copy that, sir," said Gunther, and the call ended.

He turned to Frist, who looked like he was in the middle of a myocardial infarction.

"Nothing to worry about," said Harcourt, glad he wasn't connected to a polygraph machine.

"Are you kidding me?" said Frist. "What's in the rest of this file?"

"Nothing connected to you. We had a mole inside Decker's team, who provided us with real-time intelligence regarding Meghan Steele's rescue operation."

"Please tell me he or she is not still alive."

"*He* was paid a lot of money up front for his cooperation," said Harcourt. "And apparently made good use of that money to vanish immediately after the failed rescue attempt."

"So there's another liability out there. Wonderful."

"He's stayed off the grid for close to two years," said Harcourt. "We have no idea where he went. Probably living in some banana republic right now, surrounded by well-paid locals. He hasn't resurfaced for a reason."

"Anything else I need to know?" said Frist, standing up and studying the stocked liquor cart in the far corner of his office.

"That's it. If Decker stays in LA, they'll find him. He won't get lucky twice."

"Three times."

"Point taken," said Harcourt. "If he ranges out of LA, we should be able to anticipate his next move."

"But your mole went missing," said Frist. "How the hell can you beat him to a place you can't find?"

"I have a few ideas."

"I'd like to hear them," said Frist.

"Then maybe I should take you up on the lunch offer," said Harcourt, resigning himself to the misery of an extended visit.

"I'll let Tanya know," said Frist, looking oddly upbeat given what had just transpired. "Crab cakes?"

"Same recipe?"

"Same recipe for twenty years," said Frist. "If it ain't broke, don't fix it—right?"

"Right." Incredible how this fool's outlook could turn on a crab cake.

Emboldened by Frist's sudden change of demeanor—a hallmark inferiority complex symptom—Harcourt decided the moment was ripe to float a bold idea.

"Gerry. I wonder if you could try to move up the vote? Just to give us some breathing room. I don't know if that's possible, but I'd feel better if we got it out of the way sooner than later. Steele's support is critical."

"I was thinking the same thing," said Frist. "I'll start walking the idea around this afternoon. The earliest we could pull this off is Monday."

"Better than Thursday. Three days could make all the difference. Keep in mind, I'm fully confident that we'll have the situation under control long before Monday."

"Maybe we should skip lunch," said Frist. "This is going to take every available moment from here on forward."

Frist's words were music to his ears. He couldn't wait to get out of this office, and the entire building.

CHAPTER
TWENTY-THREE

Decker followed Harlow into the third-floor apartment, hauling two paper grocery bags by their strained handles. As he carefully lifted the bags onto the kitchen counter, Harlow left two carry-on–size backpacks on the tile floor next to a distressed-wood dining room set and disappeared into a dark hallway to clear the bedrooms.

Beyond the spacious wood table sat a leather sectional couch; two comfortable-looking, cushioned basket chairs; and a rustic, square coffee table. The furniture faced wide slider doors, which opened to wavering palm fronds and occasional glimpses of sparkling water. Not a bad place to hide out for a few days.

Returning to the front door, he engaged the dead bolt and swung both of the door guards into place, one at eye level, the other a foot below the doorknob. He studied the door for a moment, thinking the doorframe would splinter inward after a few well-placed kicks or a single strike from a handheld battering ram.

"You'll find an industrial-strength security doorjamb in the closet next to the door," said Harlow, who had reappeared in the dining room. "And one in each bedroom and bathroom. The idea is for the front door to hold long enough for the occupants to retreat into one of the bedrooms and deploy the next set of locks. The bedroom door should slow down an intruder long enough to barricade the bathroom door, where they hide until the police arrive."

"LAPD knows about this place?" said Decker, heading back to the kitchen to unload the groceries.

"No. But the apartment's security system is equipped with a panic button linked to the LAPD dispatch system. Dispatchers get the location when the panic button is triggered, and the call gets priority handling. The organization that runs this network of safe houses has a nice arrangement with the LAPD."

"And deep pockets, I'm guessing," said Decker, digging through one of the bags for the beer. "I was expecting something a little more tucked away."

"And cheap?"

"I wasn't expecting three blocks from the beach with a partial ocean view."

"It's an apartment in LA," said Harlow. "Just happens to be more expensive than most. The organization's benefactors have been very generous. They own dozens of less impressive safe locations, but they wanted a few places to be special."

"I wasn't implying that the apartment is excessive. Just surprised. God knows the women they help deserve something like this."

"They're just relieved to be somewhere safe. Doesn't matter where it is," said Harlow. "But yeah, this is a nice treat when you've hit rock bottom."

"Please tell me they didn't move anybody on my account."

"No. We got lucky. They transitioned the woman staying here into her own apartment yesterday," said Harlow. "But don't get comfortable. We'll more than likely have to relocate tomorrow."

"The more we move around, the better." He lifted a cold bottle of craft beer from the six-pack. "Beer?"

"Please," she said, taking off her Dodgers ball cap and tossing it on the table.

"Bottle opener?"

"Somewhere," she said, shrugging.

He searched the drawers while she unloaded the rest of the groceries. They'd bought mostly breakfast food, a few snacks, fresh fruits, and beer. Dozens of restaurants sat within easy walking distance of the apartment building, most of them offering delivery or takeout, so they hadn't overbought. Keeping his hands on the shopping cart hadn't been easy. Decker could have filled several bags with the snacks and foods he'd missed over the last nineteen months.

"No opener?" she said.

"I really can't find one."

"Follow me," she said, grabbing both beers.

Harlow led him onto the small private balcony, handing him one of the beers. She placed the bottle cap against the thick wood balcony railing and hit the top of the bottle, loosening the cap enough to twist away. He handed her the second beer and watched her repeat the process.

"Impressive," he said.

She grinned and had just lifted her bottle to his when a sharp knock at the apartment door set her in motion. She rushed inside, setting her bottle down on the coffee table before drawing her pistol from a concealed holster on her right hip.

Decker set his beer next to hers and brushed past her to get a knife from the kitchen.

"What are you doing?" she said.

"Grabbing a knife," he whispered. "Unless you have another gun."

"I don't," she said. "And you won't find anything sharp in the kitchen. Part of the rules."

"Rolling pin?"

"Not a lot of baking goes on here," she said, stopping at the touch-screen alarm panel just inside the hallway.

She pressed the screen, activating the interface and displaying the peephole camera feed. Decker moved next to her in the hallway, taking a close look at the image. He recognized the razor-bald black man immediately.

"Unbelievable," muttered Harlow, apparently recognizing him, too. "What do we do?"

"He's not holding up his badge," said Decker. "I've dealt with him a lot in the past, and he'd flash the damn thing at a dog if he thought it might be involved in one of his cases. And then there's the fact that he hasn't brought a SWAT team down on our heads. My head."

"Dammit," said Harlow, activating the intercom. "How can I help you, Special Agent Reeves?"

"Good evening, Ms. Mackenzie. I was hoping to have a word with you and Mr. Decker."

"The name sounds kind of familiar," she said. "Maybe I've heard it in the news?"

"Or you just drank a beer with him on your balcony," said Reeves. "I'm not here to arrest either one of you, yet. I just want to have a friendly chat. If I wanted to arrest you, I'd go about it in a drastically less friendly manner."

Harlow holstered her pistol and proceeded to the door, disabling all of the locks before opening it. Decker stood several feet behind her, a neutral look on his face.

"Decker," Reeves said, nodding in his direction.

"What can we do for you?" said Harlow.

"May I come in?"

"I don't consent to a search," she said, backing up a few steps.

"This is strictly a courtesy call."

"Nothing courteous about you, Reeves," said Decker.

"I'm not here to trade barbs."

"Then what are you here for? If you're not here to arrest me."

"Can I come in? I imagine the last thing you want to do is draw attention to this apartment."

"Is that a threat?"

Reeves sighed, turning to Harlow. "I would never purposefully jeopardize one of Second Chance's safe houses. You and I are doing the same work."

"He's on the same side, too," said Harlow, looking back at Decker.

"I'll respectfully disagree, and leave it at that."

Harlow stepped aside, letting the agent pass. Reeves motioned toward the dining room table.

"Can we sit?"

"Why not," said Harlow. "Beer?"

"It's a courtesy call, not a social call," said Reeves, sitting down.

Decker remained standing while Harlow took a seat across from the FBI agent.

"So. What's this about, Reeves?"

"Isn't it obvious?"

"You're not here to take me back to prison?" said Decker.

"I'd love nothing more than to escort you back to your prison cell, but by all accounts, you're a free man," said Reeves. "That could change at any second, but it appears that all of your paperwork is in order. The warden at Victorville has no recollection of petitioning the Bureau of Prisons for a compassionate release in your case, but it's kind of hard to walk this kind of thing back."

"Well. If it's any consolation, I have no idea—"

Harlow caught his attention before he could complete the sentence, shaking her head. *Damn.* Reeves almost got him to admit that he hadn't initiated the compassionate-release paperwork. Maybe it hadn't been a good idea to invite him inside.

"I'm not trying to trick you into admitting anything," said Reeves. "Unless you want to make this easier on everyone and come clean. I'd have to Mirandize you first, so please let me know if you plan on confessing anything."

Decker decided it would probably be in his best interest to remain mostly quiet for the rest of this bizarre meeting.

"I don't think we should say any more," said Harlow. "I just need to know how you found us so I can assess its future viability as a safe house."

"Fair enough," said Reeves. "Did you hear what happened to Viktor Penkin?"

Harlow cocked her head. "The Viktor Penkin? Russian mob boss?"

"Suspected head of the Solntsevskaya Bratva's Southern California crime syndicate," said Reeves. "Runs one of the biggest human-trafficking networks in the United States, but you already knew that."

She shrugged. "What happened?"

"You really didn't hear?"

She shook her head.

"The two of you must have been really busy today," said Reeves. "Someone shot up one of his clubs last night, killing nine of his associates. Not only that, they grabbed Penkin."

"I was supposed to testify against Penkin and Kuznetsov, but the case went away somehow," said Decker.

"We're still scratching our heads about that, but it doesn't really matter anymore," said Reeves. "On a wild hunch, I sent a few agents out to Hemet this afternoon. Apparently, Viktor Penkin shot himself in the head after dumping gasoline on himself."

"That's some hunch," said Decker.

"Well, when we heard about Penkin and examined the scene of the kidnapping, I couldn't help thinking you had something to do with it. Sounded crazy to me, too. How could a man locked away in prison kill nine Russians and kidnap a high-profile Russian mobster? Impossible. Right?"

He waited a few seconds for a response before continuing.

"I know. It's the kind of story that leaves you speechless," said Reeves. "But it gets better. I decided to call Victorville, to verify that you couldn't possibly have exacted vengeance on Penkin, only to find that you'd been transferred to the Metropolitan Detention Center to testify in a case that was dismissed three days earlier. Crazy, right? No need to answer.

"So here's where the story takes the dark turn, leading me to Penkin's oddly located body. I call MDC, and they tell me you've been released yesterday morning. Free as a bird. I think I mentioned that the warden at Victorville had no knowledge of your release, right?"

Decker nodded. "I believe so."

"Now I'm starting to wonder. Is there a connection between Penkin's disappearance and Decker's release? Not likely. I mean, how is Decker going to locate Penkin on his own? I can't even find Penkin, and I run the LA field office's Russian organized crime division! So it had to be a coincidence, right? Just like the ex–Navy SEAL who was shot twice in the head, in a mall parking garage stairwell, two blocks away from where you were released. Also less than an hour after federal marshals pointed you in the direction of a good coffee shop in the same mall."

"Good thing I headed north to Chinatown," said Decker.

"Really good. They had quite a scare at that same mall at precisely the time the ex-SEAL was killed. Someone tossed a bunch of firecrackers, flash bangs, and smoke bombs into the crowd on the plaza. A lot of people got hurt. It was total mayhem."

"Sounds like every other day in LA," said Harlow. "So. How did you end up here?"

"Sorry. I got sidetracked. I'll give you the short version. I made kind of a crazy assumption and ran with it. I assumed you had something to do with the mall killing and the Penkin massacre. I don't normally go out on a limb like that without evidence, but it was purely an academic exercise. The only thing I couldn't figure out was how you located Penkin so quickly, so I assumed you had help."

"Lot of assumptions," said Decker.

"Exactly. The road to hell is paved with bad assumptions. That's my spin on a classic phrase."

"I like it," said Harlow, feigning a smile.

"Unfortunately, you won't like this part," said Reeves. "I asked myself, and my division's intelligence analysts, who in the greater Los Angeles metropolitan area had the resources to find Penkin? Your name was at the top of the list."

"My name?" said Harlow.

"You've provided my division with some spot-on intelligence regarding the Bratva operation in the past. Before I took over," said Reeves, "I was told they leaned on you pretty heavily for street-level information. They haven't done it recently, so maybe you forgot."

Harlow remained expressionless, listening to Reeves lay out his theory.

"We cross-referenced you with the agencies and rescue groups that have provided us with information in the past, finding you closely linked to one rescue organization in particular, through fund-raiser announcements, public appearances, and social media posts."

"The location of this safe house, and the others, is a well-guarded secret," said Harlow. "You'd need a sealed search warrant to get that information. I don't think you have one."

Reeves raised his hands. "I rode in here on a wave of assumptions, and look what I found."

"Congratulations," said Decker. "You get to keep your FBI badge for another day."

"Always cracking jokes, Decker," said Reeves.

"It's about all I have left," said Decker. "Are we done here?"

Reeves stood up slowly and considered him for a few moments.

"I don't blame you for what you did to Penkin. A part of me is glad you did it. What they did to you and your family was unconscionable," said Reeves. "But I can't let you continue running amok out there. This is over. I'm going to sit on you until the Bureau of Prisons unscrews itself. Then I'm taking you in. Enjoy the beer. Enjoy the comfortable bed. Enjoy the female company. Because it'll probably be the last time you have any of this again for a really long time."

"Get out," said Harlow.

"I didn't mean anything inappropriate by the female-company comment."

"Just get out of here," said Harlow, standing up.

"I'll be right outside if you need me," said Reeves, heading to the door. "And Ms. Mackenzie?"

"What?"

"I don't know what he has over you, or why you're so emotionally wrapped up in this, but I suggest you take a few steps back and reevaluate your continued involvement."

She pointed at the door. "I'll take it under advisement."

Reeves studied her face for a moment. "You don't know, do you?"

"Know what?"

"When did you put together those backpacks?" said Reeves.

Harlow stayed quiet, not wanting to give Reeves any sense of a timeline of their movements today. They'd gone straight to an apartment she owned in Pasadena after ditching Gunther Ross in Riverside, assuming that Gunther would eventually ID Harlow and unravel her widespread nest of residences. She owned four apartments throughout the greater LA metro area, all in expensive neighborhoods.

"I'm going to assume you put them together before your apartments were torn apart."

"I think I'd know if I had a break-in," said Harlow.

"I didn't see your places in Pasadena and Manhattan Beach firsthand, but I've been to that swank pad of yours in the sky on Wilshire Boulevard. Someone tore it apart," said Reeves. "I was on my way to your place up by Palisades Park when my agents spotted the two of you here. I hear someone did a number on that place, too."

"That's what insurance is for."

"You're going to need more than property insurance with the Russians involved," said Reeves. "This might be a good time to bid Mr. Decker adieu and book a one-way flight to Thailand. Hang out in a beach bungalow for a month until this settles. I'd hate to see you burn up in this man's orbit. A lot of people count on the work you do here. I mean that."

Decker sensed an opportunity to start Reeves down a path that might help them in the long run. "It's not the Russians," he said.

"Really?" said Reeves. "Kind of hard not to connect those dots."

"What do you know about Aegis Global?"

Harlow gave him a puzzled look, which he ignored.

"Is that a rhetorical question, or do you want a detailed answer?" said Reeves.

"I saw someone connected to Aegis this morning, out in Riverside."

"You were in Riverside?" said Reeves. "That's awfully close to the dead Russian in Hemet. The coincidences keep piling up. What brought you to Riverside?"

"Ares Aviation."

"Ares Aviation? You looking to take flying lessons?" Reeves pretended to check his watch. "I don't think you're going to have time to check that off your bucket list."

"It's an Aegis-owned corporation."

"Let me get this straight before I run it up to the director of the FBI. You saw someone connected to Aegis at an Aegis-owned company."

"I saw an old colleague of mine. Gunther Ross. I heard he's running some serious stuff for Aegis these days. Off-the-books stuff. My bet is that you're going to find a lot of interesting connections to Aegis around town. They keep popping up around me."

"Along with a lot of corpses."

"There's more to the Steele kidnapping than the Russians."

Reeves shook his head. "Decker. Again, I'm truly sorry about what happened to your family. To everyone. But you pissed off the wrong people and they rained hellfire down on you. It's as brutally simple as that. And now it's over. Revenge has been served. Time to stand down."

"I'm the only one left that can make this right."

Something crossed the agent's face, vanishing just as quickly. Decker recognized it immediately. A momentary flash of smugness. A secret self-satisfaction triggered by Decker's comment.

"See you tomorrow, or maybe later tonight."

"Can't wait," he said.

"I'll show myself out," said the agent, shutting the door behind him.

"I might need something a little stronger than beer," said Harlow, her hands trembling slightly.

"Meet you on the balcony," said Decker. "I'm not letting him spoil my first beer in nineteen months."

"Maybe we should pound them all," she said. "Might be our last for a while."

While Harlow headed for the balcony, he locked and secured the door, checking the image still displayed on the security panel. Reeves stood in front of the door for a minute, appearing to argue with himself. They'd need to leave the apartment quickly before Reeves changed his mind. When the FBI agent walked away, Decker joined Harlow on the balcony, taking in the cool saltwater breeze. She handed him one of the beers and clinked his bottle.

"Do you think they're listening to us?" she said.

"Probably not. But we should head inside after finishing these beers. Just in case. Sorry about your apartments."

"It's not the first time this job has lashed back at me."

"This isn't your typical backlash," Decker said before sucking down half of his beer.

"I knew this would be a rough ride," she said. "I'm a big girl."

Harlow produced her phone and started tapping the screen.

"Instagram?" he said.

"Like you know what Instagram is," she said. "No. I'm making arrangements for dinner."

"Immediate arrangements, I hope," he said. "Reeves looked like he was having second thoughts about my incarceration status."

"Actually, this is going to work out nicely," said Harlow, furiously texting.

Chapter Twenty-Four

Reeves walked out of the apartment building and approached the group of agents standing on the sidewalk next to the street, under a canopy of palm trees. Special Agent Kincaid broke away and approached him on the walkway.

"Anything?" said Kincaid.

"He said they were out in Riverside this morning, at Ares Aviation."

"You gotta be kidding me. That wasn't enough to grab him?"

"I don't want to jump the gun on this," said Reeves. "Technically, we don't have any evidence linking him to a crime. For all we know, the Bureau of Prisons will never figure out what happened. If I grab him now, without something solid, a good lawyer could tie this up for months."

"The warden said he never endorsed a compassionate-release waiver, and the US attorney's office canceled the request to transfer Decker to the Metropolitan Detention Center. That's enough to sit him in an interrogation room for forty-eight hours. Long enough for BOP to unscrew themselves."

Kincaid was right. The dead ex-SEAL at the mall. The shootout at Penkin's club followed shortly by the Russian's curious death. And now a missing-person report for a sales representative working out of Ares Aviation's Riverside office.

Justin Peters had left the office around lunchtime and hadn't been seen since. His wife contacted the police when he failed to pick up their daughter from day care and didn't answer his phone. Reeves spoke with the office manager, who said Justin had volunteered to stay behind during lunch and answer calls, something he'd never done before.

It was probably more than enough to grab Decker, but Reeves still couldn't shake the odd feeling that he was missing a bigger connection. He'd felt that way since this morning, when he learned about the murder and commotion at the Japanese Village Plaza, but he couldn't put his finger on it until Decker started rambling about Aegis a few minutes ago. There was more to the past days' murders than a simple revenge plot. There had to be, and he was willing to sit on Decker a little longer to let it all shake out. If there was more to the Meghan Steele tragedy than the Russians, he owed it to the senator to find out.

"Let's triple the number of agents assigned to watch Decker and Mackenzie. Call in the teams working Mackenzie's other apartments. Something is off."

"If something is off, we should bring him in. It's safer for everyone that way, especially with a bunch of pissed-off Russians running amok."

"Not that kind of off," said Reeves. "I want to look into a few things."

"You can't do that with him in custody?"

"I'll explain it a little later. I want those agents here now," said Reeves.

"Got it. Do I need to bring a tactical team in?"

He shook his head. "I just don't want to lose Decker. Remember who we're dealing with here. Mackenzie, too. She's worked every nook and cranny of this city for a decade. Don't underestimate her."

While Kincaid briefed the other agents, Reeves called the FBI watch desk at the Los Angeles Joint Regional Intelligence Center.

"JRIC. FBI division. Special Agent Carl Webb speaking. How may I direct your call?"

"Carl. This is Supervisory Special Agent Joseph Reeves, authorization code five-niner-six. Standing by to authenticate."

"Switching you over to authentication," said Webb.

A series of clicks and a few seconds of dead air preceded an automated voice that requested a second code. He spoke the eight-digit combination slowly and waited.

"Supervisory Special Agent Joseph Reeves. You have been authenticated by code and voice. What can I do for you tonight?"

"I need you to send me everything we have on Gunther Ross. Possibly an employee of Aegis Global or one of its affiliates. Also suspect he may have been in the United States Marine Corps or Central Intelligence Agency. Some kind of lettered intelligence agency. Current location Los Angeles."

"I have that typed in. We'll run it through the database. Anything else?"

"There was a murder yesterday at the Japanese Village Plaza. LAPD suspects the victim was a former Navy SEAL. They didn't have a name when I spoke with them. ID turned out to be fake. I need everything you have on the victim when he's identified. And one more thing, when you're ready."

"I'm ready," said Webb.

Gut instinct told Reeves to scrap his final request. If Aegis or one of its affiliates was indeed up to something in Los Angeles, triggering a citywide data and surveillance crawl for Aegis operatives would only serve to give them a heads-up. He had no doubt that Aegis, which ran the world's premiere private intelligence-gathering services, had contacts in every local, state, and federal law enforcement division and department in the city—if they hadn't outright hacked all of the systems.

"I'll hold off on that until I see what you produce for the other two requests," said Reeves. "No sense in getting ahead of myself."

Reeves ended the call and took a deep breath, praying he didn't come to seriously regret setting this in motion.

CHAPTER

TWENTY-FIVE

Decker glanced over his shoulder and shook his head.

"At this point, I honestly can't tell if the car right behind us is FBI," he said. "Either way, you're not going to lose them in this traffic—or anywhere. They're just sitting on us."

"We talked about this," said Harlow. "Everything is fine."

"Six vehicles followed us from the safe house. I'm sure more joined them."

"The car right next to us is probably FBI," she said, smiling.

"I don't think the FBI drives minivans."

"That would be a pretty solid cover, though," said Harlow. "Who would suspect a minivan?"

"Seriously, I'm starting to get a little worried here. You're heading toward the airport, which normally isn't a bad place to shake a tail, but it won't work with this many agents following us."

"They've gotten wise to the airport trick. Even if you manage to gain some distance after taking the terminal off-ramp, they call ahead and notify Los Angeles airport police. Between LAXPD, LAPD, and the LA County sheriff, Los Angeles airport is probably the worst place to try to shake police surveillance. Still works great against private-sector or criminal-sponsored tails, though."

"Then why are we headed toward LAX on one of the busiest roads in the city? I assume they know that you should know the airport isn't a viable option."

"I want them to second-guess themselves," said Harlow. "Maybe think I've come up with a workaround."

"Listen. What's the plan?" said Decker. "Whatever you've cooked up has to be one hundred percent. We only get one shot at this."

The light ahead of them turned green, and southbound traffic starting moving again—slowly picking up speed. Just as they passed under the yellow light at the Superba Avenue intersection, a cascade of brake lights started to appear in the distance. The next traffic light, several hundred feet away, had turned red. She eased the car forward until traffic came to a complete halt.

"Dumping me on the street isn't going to work," Decker said without even looking at her.

"Do you trust me?"

"I just don't see how you're going to pull off a vanishing act."

"Do you trust me?"

Decker nodded. "Yes. I trust you."

"Then you have nothing to worry about."

"You're really not going to let me in on your plan?"

She shook her head, smirking. "There's really not much to it. Don't worry. I'll say goodbye before you go."

"Wait. You're not coming?"

"Like you said, it's going to take a miracle to escape them," said Harlow. "And I can only miracle one of us out of here right now."

"I don't want this to come down on you," said Decker. "You've done enough for me already."

"I'll be fine. Once they figure out you're gone, they'll haul me in for a talk and that'll be it. If Reeves had anything tangible on either of us, we wouldn't be having this chat," she said. "Plus, I have a full network of support available to me here. I can research and feed you information from a distance. It'll make it that much harder for anyone to track you."

"Can I assume it goes without saying that you need to pull a disappearing act as soon as possible? The same people will be looking for you."

"Already working on that," she said. "I'm shuffling everyone around. New SCIF locations. New everything. Nothing connected to anything I've done before."

"First sign of trouble and you bail out of this. Understand?" he said. "I'm serious. Hide out and let this all blow over."

She pursed her lips and stared into the traffic snaking south on Lincoln Boulevard. "I'm not that kid you rescued from the streets anymore," she muttered.

Decker cocked his head to the side and squinted at her.

"I gathered that much over the past few days. You can take care of yourself," he said. "But I really need you to listen and take my words seriously. I'd give the same advice to anyone under these circumstances. Gunther Ross isn't someone you cross lightly, especially with the full weight of Aegis Global behind him. And you know the Russians will be tearing the city apart trying to figure out what happened. Not to mention the little FBI problem we have. Sorry if I came across as patronizing. I just don't want to add another ruined life to my scorecard."

She shook her head slowly. It was impossible to fully wrap her head around the full scope of the nightmare he'd endured, and she had no intention of trying. Harlow wanted to help him find his way again. To rekindle the vision and purpose that had driven him to save all the lives he'd saved.

His scorecard could never be muddied as far as she was concerned. She'd read the court transcripts and scoured the articles. Ryan Decker had been crucified for delaying Meghan Steele's rescue in order to save fifteen kids from short, brutal lives in the sex-slave industry, or possibly worse. Some kids were sold right away for body parts, a fate worse than death. Tragically, the raid ended unforeseeably in the deaths of not only the kids but also the eleven members of his hostage-rescue team.

He went from savior to destroyer in a single high-explosive blast. While sizzling fragments of wood and body parts rained down on the burning wreckage of the house, an even more insidious nightmare was in progress around the country. The systematic rape and butchering of World Recovery Group's primary stakeholders' families. A brutal and unforgiving message sent by the Solntsevskaya Bratva to any organization or group standing in their way.

"You're not looking at the entire scorecard," she said.

"I'm looking at the part that matters the most to me." She started to reply, but he cut her off. "We can talk about this later. You asked if I had any last-minute requests?"

The traffic light several hundred feet away, at the intersection of Venice Boulevard and Lincoln, turned green. She knew from experience that this light was short, due to the volume of traffic on Venice Boulevard, a bustling three-lane road. This would be as good a chance as any they'd get tonight.

"Hurry up," she said.

"My daughter. Riley? I have no idea where to find her, but we need to warn her somehow. Get her into hiding until I get to the bottom of this. All I know is that she's with—"

"Your sister-in-law. I know where to find her. I'll take care of it," said Harlow. "Same with your parents. You don't have to worry about any of them."

Decker looked stunned. "You know where they are? Why didn't you say something earlier?"

"I needed you to stay focused," she said.

"Seriously? That's a little cold."

"What else? We're running out of time."

The distant brake lights started to disappear in a chain reaction, as two lanes of vehicles accelerated through the intersection. She pressed "Send" on a prepared text message as Decker spoke.

"Something Reeves said—actually, it wasn't something he said, it was his reaction to something I said. I told him I was the only one that could set this right, and I swear the strangest look flashed across his face. Like he knew something I didn't."

"I need you to talk faster," she said, guessing that they'd be on the move soon.

"I think someone from World Recovery Group survived the Russian purge," said Decker.

From what her people could tell, all of the company's principal members and everyone present in Hemet had either committed suicide or had been murdered, in or out of prison. Decker had been the sole survivor, having somehow thwarted multiple attempts on his life.

"We didn't find any survivors, but I'll have my team look into it again," said Harlow.

"I don't know if you have this capability, but I'd check into the federal witness protection program."

"I might. Are you sure you want to dig into that?"

"I don't have a choice," said Decker. "Whoever sold us out to the Russians had to be inside WRG. I didn't share detailed information about the operation with Harcourt. I learned early in this line of work that the less a client's proxies know about the specifics, the better."

"But Penkin denied being involved in the explosion and murders," she said, easing her foot off the brake. "And he'd have no interest in bringing the FBI into the equation."

The car edged forward, the traffic barely crawling toward the intersection.

"Then the mole played both sides, giving the location of our tactical operations center to the FBI—for a deal."

"That's a stretch, Decker."

"Is it? Everything happened simultaneously. I'd always wondered, but with everyone supposedly dead—I quit torturing myself with it. Reeves got me thinking about it again."

"I'll look into it," she said. "And take care of the other stuff. You about ready?"

Decker looked around. "Here?"

"Almost," she said. "Disengage your seat belt but hold it in place."

"I can't escape on foot. It won't happen. There's too many of them," said Decker, pressing the orange button on the seat belt.

"Just do exactly what I say, when I say, and you'll be off the grid in a few minutes."

"This makes no sense," he said, shaking his head.

"You said you trust me."

"Do I have a choice?"

"Not really," she said, accelerating to fill the gap that had formed in front of her car.

CHAPTER
TWENTY-SIX

Reeves scanned the road ahead of them with binoculars, keeping Decker and Mackenzie in sight. He wasn't worried about losing them, since his agents had placed two nearly undetectable GPS trackers on the vehicle. He also had a total of ten vehicles on the job. Four tailing, four working the side roads, and two more merged into the traffic ahead.

And just in case that wasn't enough, he had access to the nearest LAPD helicopter, which he'd been assured could arrive within five minutes. Mackenzie knew the city, but she couldn't run this gauntlet. Not tonight. He lowered the binoculars and raised his handheld radio.

"We have a busy intersection coming up. Stay frosty," he said.

Agent Kincaid eased them forward as the traffic started moving. "What's their game?"

"I guarantee it's not dinner and a movie."

"Sounded reasonable," said Kincaid. "It is his last night out on town."

He glanced at Kincaid, who was smiling. "I should have grabbed him when they left the apartment. This is a waste of time and resources."

"You know he's going to make a run for it. He has nothing to lose," said Kincaid. "When he does, we take him out for pizza and beer to thank him for Penkin, then put him in an interrogation room until BOP comes through."

"He certainly did us a favor with Penkin," said Reeves. "But don't *ever* let anyone hear you say something like that. That stays between you and me."

His radio squawked. "This is Tail One. I got a delivery truck trying to cross over to the northbound lanes. Dammit! The car just let him in. I lost sight of the target."

Reeves raised his binoculars. An organic-grocery delivery truck had indeed pulled across the southbound lanes, right behind Decker's vehicle, edging into northbound traffic. *What the hell?*

"Anything from the lead units?" said Reeves, hoping the vehicles in front of Decker had been closely monitoring the situation behind them.

"This is Lead One. Negative," reported the vehicle in the outside lane.

"Lead Two. Nothing. Everything looks the same."

The truck pulled into the slow-moving traffic, causing a discordance of horns and tire squeals.

"I don't like it," said Reeves. "Tail Three and Four, break off and stop that truck."

The two vehicles behind Reeves's vehicle swerved into the northbound lanes, scattering traffic. He peered through his binoculars at Mackenzie's sedan, just as the passenger glanced back through the rear window. Decker was still there.

"This is Lead Two. I still have Decker and Mackenzie in the vehicle."

"That's what I'm seeing," said Reeves. "Tail One. I want you right behind Decker from now on. Nothing gets between you and that car. Understand?"

"Understand," said the agent. "Next chance I get, I'll slip in behind them."

"This is Tail Three. You still want us to stop the truck?"

He didn't see any reason to pursue the truck, with both of his surveillance targets still in the car.

"Negative. Break off and work your way back into position," said Reeves. "Use your emergency lights if you have to. It's no secret we're here."

They picked up speed as the two lanes of traffic ahead of them poured through the intersection, but he knew it would be short-lived. It had taken nearly a minute for the packed cars to start moving when the light turned green. Seconds later, the lights facing them turned yellow. Presumably in response to the agonizingly short light, vehicles started turning onto the side roads, hoping to skip the busy intersection.

"This is Lead One. I'm moving into position right behind the target. We had some vehicles clear out."

He briefly considered moving the car directly next to Decker, to prevent Mackenzie from turning them onto a side road, but decided against it. There was no feasible way to constantly maintain a direct lateral position in this kind of traffic. Tailgating Decker was the better option. Plus, Reeves had plenty of support on the side streets if Mackenzie decided to pull a drastic maneuver.

"Copy. Hold that position," said Reeves.

A flood of brake lights streamed toward them, quickly bringing them to a stop. By his calculation, it would take them three more cycles to get through this intersection. If Mackenzie brought them all the way to the airport, they'd be stuck in this for another hour.

Kincaid let out an audible sigh. "It's going to be a long night."

"Tell me about it," said Reeves.

CHAPTER TWENTY-SEVEN

Reeves could barely believe what he had just witnessed. Without warning, Mackenzie had veered off Lincoln Boulevard onto LAX's **ALL TERMINALS** off-ramp. Decker was actually going to try to vanish in the airport. The two FBI vehicles directly ahead of Reeves's sedan slid into place behind Mackenzie's sedan. Kincaid eased them into the far-right lane, under the off-ramp sign.

"All units. The target just turned into the airport," said Reeves. "Lead One and Two, circle back at Century Boulevard and take Ninety-Sixth Street to airport terminals. You'll see the signs."

Immediately after the two units responded, he got back on the radio.

"Tail One and Two, I'm going to move into position directly behind Decker. The off-ramp opens into several lanes. I'll pass you there."

"You really think he's going to try something here?" said Kincaid.

"We can't underestimate this guy," said Reeves. "I don't see how he can pull it off, but the guy managed to fake his own prison release. I'm not taking any chances. If he takes one step out of that vehicle, I'm hauling him in."

Reeves redialed a number he'd contacted a half hour ago, reaching the LAXPD duty sergeant.

"Sergeant Powell."

"Sergeant. This is Supervisory Special Agent Reeves again. My surveillance target just turned off Lincoln into the airport. I don't know if he's going for departures or arrivals yet, but I could use a few of your officers on each level to keep an eye on him, in case he gets too far ahead of us."

"Not a problem. I have a few dozen officers on each level," said Powell. "We can't grab him without a warrant or probable cause, so this will be strictly surveillance—unless you can provide either of those."

"If he gets out of the car, I'm taking him in for questioning on multiple murders."

"You didn't mention that earlier," said Powell. "Dammit. This changes things."

"I just need your officers to watch him. He's not a public danger. I honestly believe the last thing he'd do is harm a civilian or a law enforcement officer. We'll be all over him if he gets out of the car."

"All right. What's the description?"

"He's in the front passenger seat of a silver Toyota Camry. Caucasian male. Short brown hair. Buzz cut. He's wearing khaki pants and a light-blue oxford shirt. Untucked. Brown hiking boots."

His radio squawked, but he missed the transmission.

"What was that?" said Reeves, elbowing Kincaid.

"He just put a ball cap on. They can't tell what color."

"Sergeant Powell? Sorry. I was just told he donned a ball cap."

"I got it," said Powell. "I'll pass this along to all of my officers in all of the terminals and hold this line until you determine if he's going for the departure or arrival level."

"Thank you, Sergeant. I'll keep you posted," he said, setting the phone on his lap. "I muted the phone."

"Good. I was going to ask you if you really believed he wasn't dangerous," said Kincaid.

"I truly don't think he's a danger to anyone, but he's obviously desperate. Given the right circumstances, who knows what he's capable of."

Traffic was thin beyond the off-ramp, and Kincaid managed to speed ahead of the two FBI vehicles, sliding right behind Decker before the road split into the departure and arrival lanes. The target vehicle kept to the right as the split approached, convincing Reeves that Decker would try for the arrivals zone.

"Tail Three and Four. I want you in the leftmost lanes, in case they pull a wild maneuver and go for departures," said Reeves. "Everyone else hold your position."

"Arrivals makes the most sense," said Kincaid. "It's chaotic as hell in the pickup lanes. Baggage claim is even worse. If he gets inside, it'll get crazy."

"I figure he'll go for that and try to disappear long enough to reemerge upstairs or on the same level. Grab a taxi or even hijack a car. All he has to do is get in another vehicle unobserved, and we've lost him."

"I'll stay right on his ass," said Kincaid, closing the distance to the sedan.

Reeves watched the sedan closely as they approached the split, looking for any indication it might swerve left and go for departures on the upper deck. Several seconds later, the target vehicle passed the concrete divider separating the two approaches. The wide, three-foot-high barrier opened to a section of curb thirty feet later, giving Mackenzie one more chance to break for the other lanes. She kept the sedan in the rightmost lane as the road rapidly descended toward the arrivals loop.

"That's it," said Reeves, picking up the phone and unmuting it. "Sergeant Powell?"

"I'm here."

"He's headed for arrivals. And I'm right on his tail."

"I'll move the officers in the arrivals terminals onto the sidewalks. You call out your position in real time and I'll pass it right along so they'll be ready to assist you with surveillance if your target gets out of the car. Who's your target, by the way? I forgot to ask."

"Ryan Decker," said Reeves, hoping the sergeant didn't recognize the name.

"Ryan Decker from the trial with the kids blowing up?"

"That's him."

"Damn. I thought he got ten years," said Powell. "Kind of a messed-up case, actually."

Reeves wasn't entirely sure what to make of the sergeant's last statement. Public opinion about the case had been somewhat mixed, despite the gruesome outcome of Decker's negligence, but the law enforcement response had been nearly unanimous against Decker. Reeves's hadn't been the only police department or agency bypassed or trampled on by World Recovery Group. Powell's comment could be interpreted either way, so he decided to deflect it.

"We're turning into the underpass. This is definitely going down in the pickup zone," said Reeves. "I'll turn on my hazard lights and start flashing high beams so your officers will have a live visual cue."

"I'm passing that along," said Powell.

Kincaid rode the Toyota's bumper all the way to the second terminal, where Mackenzie deftly maneuvered the sedan between two vans and stopped next to the curb.

"Target stopped at terminal two. In front of door four," said Reeves, not waiting for a response.

He placed the cell phone in the center console and unbuckled his seat belt as Kincaid turned abruptly behind the second van and sped into place right behind Mackenzie's sedan. He flashed the high beams a few times and put the car into park, disengaging his seat belt. On the sidewalk under the bright fluorescent lighting, several police officers formed a dispersed perimeter, keeping their distance. Reeves and Kincaid sat there for close to a minute.

"What the hell is he doing?" said Kincaid.

"Assessing the situation."

"There's not much to assess here," said Kincaid. "Decker isn't going anywhere."

"He's got something cooking."

"Heads up," said Kincaid. "You've got an officer approaching your door."

Reeves glanced to his right, catching a nod from a portly officer with sergeant's stripes. He rolled down the window and nodded back.

"Sergeant Powell. Joe Reeves. FBI."

The police officer stopped a few feet from the car and bent down, putting his hands on his knees.

"We need to resolve this situation quickly. My officers are getting nervous, and we're backing up traffic here," said Powell. "Normally, my officer would move them along by now, but obviously we don't want to escalate the situation."

"He should have left by now. There's nowhere to go," said Reeves, suddenly remembering the detailed report from the Japanese Village Plaza. "Hell."

"What?" said Powell, standing up.

"Nothing," said Reeves, turning to Kincaid. "We should probably just take him in now. This is ridiculous."

"I'm good with that. We have him boxed in."

"Sergeant, I'm putting an end to his little game here," said Reeves, reaching for the door handle.

The moment Reeves pushed the door open, Decker bolted out of the Toyota, heading for the revolving door that led to baggage claim. Reeves scrambled out of the car, nearly knocking the sergeant over as he sprinted toward Decker.

"He's running for baggage claim!" said Reeves, drawing his pistol with his free hand. "Blue ball cap. Everyone out of the cars!"

Decker continued running for the door as a dozen FBI agents jumped out of their cars, guns drawn, and sprinted across the walkway in pursuit, scattering the crowd of travel-weary passengers. Amid screams and fleeing civilians, Reeves barreled toward his target, realizing he wouldn't reach Decker before he piled into the baggage claim area. *Enough of this,* he thought, bringing his gun up.

Before Reeves could bark out a command, Decker collided with a long-haired woman—but oddly didn't knock her down. Decker had the woman in an embrace, kissing her passionately, when Reeves skidded to a halt next to them.

"Decker! That's it for—" he started, finishing with a hiss. "What the hell?"

A sturdy, buzz-cut woman dressed exactly like Decker pulled away from the kiss and glared at him. "The hell? You gotta problem with two women kissing?"

The other woman, a stunningly attractive brunette, gave him the same look.

Reeves grunted and pointed at them. "I'm not buying this, ladies," he said, glancing over his shoulder at Kincaid. "Keep these two right here."

"Where's Decker?" said Kincaid, as Reeves took off for the silver Toyota.

"Who's Decker?" said the brunette, loud enough for Reeves to hear.

Reeves wheeled around. "You know exactly who Decker is!"

"Exactly who are *you*?" said the buzz-cut woman.

"Supervisory Special Agent Joseph Reeves," he said, fumbling for his badge. He stuffed the radio in his pants pocket and drew the badge holder out of his suit-coat pocket, opening it in her face. "And you're an accessory!"

"To what?" said the woman.

Reeves paused for a moment, not coming up with a good answer. "Hold that thought," he said, turning toward the Toyota.

He froze in place, briefly unable to move. The driver was gone.

"Dammit!" he muttered, frantically searching the crowds. "Sergeant Powell!"

The police officer jogged over, an exasperated look on his face. "What's going on here?"

"I don't know yet. Decker seems to be missing," said Reeves, approaching the empty Toyota. "I need you to shut down vehicle traffic going in and out of the arrivals level."

"That's not gonna happen. Sorry. I'm not going to lock down one of the busiest airports in the world without a warrant for Decker's arrest or rock-solid proof he committed a very recent crime. I'm getting the distinct impression you have neither."

"I'm not asking you to lock down the airport," said Reeves, looking inside the sedan's windows. "Just the roads leading out of departures. She probably hopped in a car that was following us."

"She? How many people are you following?"

"Decker may not have been in the car at all." Reeves motioned to the two women surrounded by FBI agents. "The woman there, with the ball cap, must have swapped with him somewhere."

Powell looked unconvinced. "Do you plan on arresting either of these women?"

"I don't know yet," said Reeves. "I need to search the car."

"Do you have a warrant to search the car? Probable cause?"

"I don't have a warrant."

"Or probable cause," added Powell, sighing. "Sorry. I'm going to need you to move your agents out of the pickup zone. You can continue this circus anywhere but here. I have an airport to secure."

"You don't have to be disrespectful about it."

"My apologies," said Powell, quite unapologetically. "I just put every officer at the airport on alert for a guy that's not here. I need this area clear of your vehicles immediately. No hard feelings."

"None at all," said Reeves, grumbling as he dug the radio out of his pocket.

There was no point to pressing the issue, or attempting to find Mackenzie. She was as gone as Decker at this point. "All units. Let's pack this up. All vehicles on the move in thirty seconds." He looked at Powell. "Is that good enough for you?"

"Perfect. Better luck next time."

Reeves feigned a smile and left the sergeant standing next to the Toyota. He passed several agents on the way to Kincaid, who clearly had his hands full with the two women.

"There he is," said the brunette. "Can I go home now? I've been traveling all day."

"I'm sure you have," said Reeves, before focusing his attention on Buzz Cut. "So. When did you switch with Decker?"

"Sorry?"

"Just cut the crap," said Reeves. "I know you switched out with him somewhere on the drive here. Was it the grocery delivery truck by Venice Boulevard?"

"I've been in that car all night," said the woman.

"Sure you have, and I suppose Ms. Mackenzie just went for a walk right now. Should be back any time."

"How should I know? She just handed me the keys and got out of the car. I assumed she was going to help with Jess's luggage."

"And you're not concerned that she just vanished," said Reeves, smiling at the ridiculousness of their conversation.

"Hey. I'm not her mother," said the woman. "And it's my car. If she doesn't want a ride back from the airport, she can get an Uber. I don't give a crap. I was doing her a favor."

"She's been driving your car for the past few hours," said Reeves. "I know you weren't in the car when I talked to them in the apartment at Santa Monica Beach."

"She borrowed my car for the night. That's called a favor," she said. "And I walked right past you in front of that apartment building."

"No way. I would have known—"

"Excuse me! Sorry to break this up," said Sergeant Powell, appearing next to Kincaid. "I need their car moved, too."

"Am I under arrest?" said Buzz Cut.

"I can't be under arrest," said the brunette. "I just got here."

"You have an airline ticket?" said Reeves.

"Gentlemen?" said Powell, impatiently.

The brunette dug through her designer handbag and produced a ticket jacket, with the ticket stub and printed itinerary tucked conveniently inside. Reeves snatched it out of her hand and gave it a look.

"Jessica Arnay," he said. "You flew in from Minneapolis?"

"Yes," she said. "Would you like to see my ID?"

He shook his head. "What was your business in Minneapolis?"

"None of your business," she said, flashing a cold look that told him everything he needed to know about her. She was part of this scheme, whatever it was, her fluffy, chic exterior nothing more than camouflage. Buzz Cut was the same deal. Seasoned operators in Mackenzie's circle of friends.

"Then I guess I shouldn't hold you up any longer," said Reeves, motioning for them to pass.

"That's it?" said Kincaid.

"That's it."

Kincaid drove them slowly past the Toyota, Reeves staring at the two women through his open window. Sergeant Powell stood on the curb next to the sedan, waiting to help them load their luggage into the trunk.

"Maybe he's in the trunk," said Kincaid.

"Nope. She swapped with him either at the apartment or on the road," said Reeves. "They wouldn't have asked the good sergeant to help with their luggage if Decker was curled up in the trunk."

"True," said Kincaid. "Obviously the two of them were lying through their teeth."

"Yes and no."

"No?"

"Buzz Cut was lying, but the other one?" said Reeves. "I have no doubt she traveled to Minneapolis."

"She could have picked up that ticket in the trash," said Kincaid. "You never checked her ID."

"I didn't have to. Decker's parents live in Minneapolis," said Reeves. "And that's just too much of a coincidence for me to ignore."

Kincaid didn't look convinced.

"Did you see her entire itinerary?" said Reeves. "Ms. Arnay didn't leave for Minnesota until late yesterday afternoon."

"Before Penkin was grabbed?"

Reeves nodded. "Nearly six hours before."

"I don't know," said Kincaid. "It's a whole lot of circumstantial speculation."

"Or Penkin was just the beginning," said Reeves. "And Mackenzie is thick as thieves with Decker."

"The stuff about Aegis?"

"If it's real," said Reeves.

"Sounded a little contrived to me. A little too convenient."

"Normally, I would agree, but for some reason I can't shake the distinct feeling that there's something much bigger at play here."

"Are we going to follow these two?" said Kincaid.

Reeves reached into the back seat and retrieved a ruggedized digital tablet, placing it on his thighs. A few moments later, the screen came to life, illuminating the passenger compartment with a full-color street map centered on Los Angeles International Airport. He dimmed the screen and checked the data feed. Both tracking devices pinged with strong signals.

"Of course we are."

CHAPTER TWENTY-EIGHT

Harlow sprawled across the back seat of the SUV that had moments ago whisked her away from Supervisory Special Agent Reeves's dragnet, watching the streetlights pass above her. Reeves had swallowed the entire bait in the pickup zone, presenting her with the irresistible opportunity to vanish far sooner than she'd expected. She truly hadn't expected to get any sort of a break from Reeves at the airport, but she'd arranged the pickup vehicle just in case. When every FBI agent in sight dashed after Pam, she slipped out of Pam's Toyota and into the adjacent SUV.

"That was almost too easy," said Sophie, her top skip tracer.

"You're positive they didn't make you?"

"No way. Not in this traffic. Not at night," she said. "They were focused on you. I watched the two tailing units work their way back through traffic after chasing the diversion back at Venice Boulevard. Never looked anywhere but ahead of them."

"Wow. I thought we'd have to pull some pure fucking magic on them later tonight," said Harlow.

"I think you maxed out your PFM credit line already."

"Yep. Time to lie low and analyze."

"I got you covered," said Sophie. "Full operations center in a sick Hollywood Hills rental. Gated community. No way the FBI is going to sniff this place out, and if they did, they can't get eyes or ears on it."

"How much did that cost?"

"You really don't want to know. But I think it's necessary in this case."

Harlow couldn't help but wince at the additional expense. Not for her own sake, but her partners'. She'd gladly spend every dime she had on Decker's cause. Her mission in life was perfectly aligned right now. Uncovering the conspiracy behind Decker's fall could do more to expose the institutional rot responsible for the unhampered growth of the human-trafficking industry than she could ever hope to accomplish with her firm.

If they could connect Aegis Global to the Meghan Steele tragedy, along with the Bratva's trafficking network, the government would be forced to act. Senator Steele would undoubtedly make that her sole focus.

Her partners had felt the same way, agreeing to devote their full attention and the firm's considerable resources to the "Decker situation," but the cost and potential liability to the firm had grown exponentially in a very compact span of time.

"Are you okay with that?" she said.

"Come again?" said Sophie, glancing back at her between the seats.

"It's just that the Decker situation is expanding, and the stakes are getting higher," said Harlow. "I'm just . . . I don't know."

"We're all one hundred percent in on the Decker situation."

"I'm just saying. This could implode on us," said Harlow. "Severely."

"I don't care. I'll gladly go to jail for this. Or worse."

"Worse is where this is headed," said Harlow. "I think we need to get everyone together and check the commitment level, given today's developments."

"You don't have to worry about me," said Sophie. "I'm in this to the end."

"I'm not *worried* about anyone," said Harlow. "I just want to be fair. We've worked our asses off to get the firm to this point. Pushing this any further could wreck all of that. We may have already done irreparable damage. The FBI isn't going to give us a pass on this. Neither will the Solntsevskaya Bratva. They'll figure out we were involved somehow. Then there's Aegis. They've already tossed my apartments. It's only a matter of time before they toss everyone else's places."

"We can always get new apartments," said Sophie. "We'll never get a chance like this again. A real shot at making a real difference in the war against these traffickers."

"We make a difference every day. That's real."

"I know, but think about this. Some sick fucker out there kidnapped the teenage daughter of a US senator and handed her to the Russians, expecting them to melt her in a barrel of lye. Then they threw a fit when they found out these unscrupulous Russians kept her alive for leverage and executed a mass murder across several states to cover it all up."

"It's insane," said Harlow, thinking about the murdered families.

"That's the really troubling aspect of all this. It didn't sound insane to someone. Someone considered this to be the best solution to a problem—which must have been one hell of a problem."

"Funny you say that," said Harlow. "I've spent most of my time focused on what happened in Hemet—at the very end of the Steele tragedy. But Penkin's claim that the Bratva didn't kidnap her, assuming I believe him, sent me back to the beginning. If the Russians didn't kidnap her, who the hell did? And why? We answer those questions and we unravel everything, taking every sick bastard involved in this nightmare down."

"I like the sound of that," said Sophie.

"Me, too."

"Then we'll work on the bigger picture while we steer Decker," said Sophie. "We have the tools and the talent to dig pretty deep. May as well put it to good use."

"After we get everyone's consensus."

"That, too," said Sophie, adjusting the rearview mirror. "You can sit up now. We're about to merge onto Century Boulevard. There's an In-N-Out Burger just past the casino, if you're interested."

She sat up and peered through the lift-gate window, not seeing anything that piqued her suspicion.

"I'm very interested."

CHAPTER
TWENTY-NINE

Decker sat in the second row of the tinted-windowed minivan, replaying the transfer in his head. He once again had to hand it to Harlow. The move had been perfectly executed. One moment he sat in the front passenger seat of Harlow's car, the next he had been yanked out of his seat onto the street. An identically dressed man with a buzz cut told him to get in the van before hopping into Mackenzie's car.

The minivan's automatic sliding door had already started to close, giving him no choice but to dive into the floor space between the middle row and the front seats. His total time in between vehicles couldn't have been more than two seconds, a grocery delivery truck blocking his view of the FBI vehicles behind them. The truck's sudden appearance clearly hadn't been a coincidence.

"Do I have to sit back here like a child the entire trip?"

"We need to get out of the greater LA metro area," said the driver. "Unless you'd like your face picked up by a traffic camera."

"Fair enough," said Decker, recognizing her from the near miss at Ares Aviation. "Katie. Right?"

When she didn't respond, he continued, knowing she'd likely shut him down. "How far are you taking me?"

"Harlow told me you're on a need-to-know basis."

"And I suppose she also said I don't need to know anything?"

"Since I'm feeling generous, all you need to know right now is that I'm going to drive you to Las Vegas and check you into an out-of-the-way, fleabag motel for the night," she said. "That'll hopefully be the last we see of each other."

Decker laughed.

"Having fun back there?"

"No. I promise I'm not," he said, but he was having a tough time stifling more laughter.

He had a presumably silent four-hour drive ahead of him, followed by an overnight stay in a fleabag motel.

"I was just overwhelmed by your concept of being generous," he said.

"This isn't exactly my idea of a funfest, either," she said.

"I understand," he said. "Sorry. For some reason that just hit me funny. It's been a long couple of days."

The van slowed to a stop at a traffic light. When it accelerated a few moments later, the orange light from the intersection streetlamps momentarily filled the vehicle and he caught the side of her face in the muted glow. A deep scar ran across the length of her right cheek.

He wondered if she was a victim of trafficking like Harlow. It really didn't make a difference. She was clearly just as committed and competent as Harlow. Another perfect stranger willing to risk everything for him.

"I truly appreciate what you're doing for me. For Harlow. I'll leave it at that if you don't want to talk."

"I can give you like two minutes every hour," she said drily.

So she did have a sense of humor.

"How about two for the first hour, then two additional minutes each hour after that? It's going to be a long ride."

"Longer with you talking my ear off," she said.

"I won't bother you. Promise."

"We'll see."

"When do you think I'll be able to sit with the grown-ups?"

"Not until we reach Angeles National Forest—about an hour and a half with traffic."

"Fine," he said. "Do you have a phone I can use to call Harlow, to pass the time when my two minutes are up?"

"She's busy at the airport."

"They'll grab her if she heads toward the terminals."

"They won't touch her, especially when they discover you're missing."

"Why doesn't she just drive them around town for a while, until they decide enough is enough?"

"First: she's taking the feds away from us. Second: she really has to pick someone up at the airport."

"Seriously. She's making an airport run?"

"Yeah. She's picking up one of our associates from a trip to Minneapolis."

"Minneapolis," he repeated dully, something heavy settling in his gut.

"What about it?"

He shook his head to clear it. "My parents live outside Minneapolis. I'm worried about them. They're targets if—"

"They're in Canada now."

"What?"

"One of our teams escorted them over the border to a very secluded property on Lake Superior," she said. "Your daughter and sister-in-law's family will join them shortly. It's a big place."

"Wait. What? Harlow set this up already?"

"She set the plan in motion as soon as you were transferred to the LA Metropolitan Detention Center."

Like that, the heaviness in his gut was gone. Harlow was just full of surprises.

"You know where my daughter is?"

He'd wanted to press the issue with Harlow a few minutes ago in the car, but they'd run out of time. He needed to get in touch with Riley. To let her know he was sorry and that none of this was his fault. That he was going to make the people responsible pay with their lives.

"Forget I asked that," said Decker. "I know you won't tell me."

"I don't know where she's going, anyway," said Katie. "The person Harlow will pick up at the airport is the only one that knows the location. We compartmentalize that kind of information. Less risk and exposure to our clients that way. But even if I did, I wouldn't tell you."

"I'd ditch you in a heartbeat," said Decker.

"That's what I figured."

"Still might ditch you."

"I doubt it," she said.

"It's nice that you're bringing them to the same place. Thank you," said Decker. "They're going to be freaked out by this. Probably hating me even more, if that's possible."

"I'm sure they don't hate you."

"Not my parents, but Riley and my wife's family?" said Decker, pausing. "My wife's sister told me she wished I had been killed with everyone else."

"Sorry," she said. "Will they get along with your parents? We can find two places."

"I never told them she said that," said Decker. "And despite her hating me, she brings Riley to visit them pretty frequently. There's no bad blood there."

The van slowed and pulled in behind a seemingly endless line of cars. There was a lot to like about LA, but the traffic erased almost all of it.

He noticed a small blue cooler tucked between the front seats. "What's in the cooler? Anything good?"

"Diet Coke," she said.

"Great," he mumbled.

"Just kidding. It's all water. I don't drink those chemical concoctions," said Katie. "Harlow told me to say that."

"She's hilarious," he muttered.

CHAPTER THIRTY

Decker's eyes fluttered, opening to see a partially lit neon sign for a motel chain he'd never heard of. A seemingly endless parade of dingy hotel signs and grimy car dealership billboards lined the expansive boulevard. Despite all the cheap light from the signs and sodium-vapor streetlights, the eight-lane street felt dead. Even worse—like the kind of place that sucked the life out of everything and had nothing to show for it. Not liking the view, he shut his eyes. An elbow to his shoulder let him know he wouldn't get off that easy.

"Rise and shine, Decker," said Katie, not sounding one bit tired. "Your luxury accommodations await."

He rubbed his face. "Nobody will find me here. That's for sure."

"That's kind of the point. The room is paid for in cash for a week."

"Pool?" said Decker.

"Sorry. No pool. This is the kind of place that rents rooms weekly or hourly. Not a lot of vacationers out this way."

"Where exactly are we?"

"Fremont Street," she said before easing the minivan into a U-turn.

After the turn, they drove a short distance before she pulled into the barely lit parking lot of the Lucky Sass Motel. Except the *L* and *S* were unlit.

"The Ucky Ass?" said Decker.

Finally, a full-blown laugh from Katie.

"Aptly named," he said.

"Beats prison."

"I'm not so sure."

Three cars sat parked in the lot, a newer-looking SUV and two beat-up sedans that didn't look like they'd start without a mechanic. Katie parked next to the SUV and sent a text; the door to the room directly in front of the SUV opened a few seconds later. A pale-green light spilled into the parking lot, partially blocked by a tall, sharply dressed woman with curly, shoulder-length blonde hair who couldn't have looked more out of place at this motel if she tried.

"Out we go," said Katie.

Decker opened the door and stepped onto the crumbly asphalt, which instantly brought to mind the motor-lodge parking lot in Hemet, but worse. Somehow, Katie had managed to find a motel seedier than the one that had been the staging ground for his demise.

Just when he thought it couldn't be that bad, the faint smell of Pine-Sol mixed with stale cigarettes hit his nostrils, killing the notion. While Katie opened the rear lift gate, he surveyed the motel, his eyes never passing the one-foot-tall weed sprouting through the crack in the cement at the woman's feet.

"It's not as bad as it looks. No cockroaches from what I can tell," said the woman in the doorway. "I'm Sandra. It's a pleasure to meet you, Decker."

He met her at the door and shook her hand. "Likewise, but I don't buy your no-cockroach assessment."

"I guess you'll know in the morning," she said.

"Let's get this over with," said Katie. "It's gonna be a long drive back to LA."

"You're not spending the night at the Ucky Ass?" said Decker, looking over his shoulder at Katie.

"Sorry. Duty calls elsewhere," she said. "Come on. Move."

Sandra chuckled and withdrew into the dank room. Decker followed, immediately scrunching his nose.

"This smells," he said.

"They all smell," said Katie, brushing past him and tossing a black duffel bag on one of the dimpled beds. "Most of them reek. This isn't half-bad, Sandy baby."

"Thank you, Katie dear," said Sandra, giving Katie a quick hug before shutting the door.

Katie unzipped the duffel bag and started unloading its contents on the bed. She started with two sets of clothing to complement his "Gap dad" look and a pair of gray hiking shoes. He'd swap the shoes for his clunky boots the next time he left the room. A few pairs of gray briefs, gray socks, and matching undershirts followed. A small toiletry kit and a set of white towels joined the pile. Very thoughtful.

"No towels here?" he said.

"None that you'll want to use," said Sandra.

"I added a set of cheap sheets, too," said Katie. "You might want to put those over the—uh—existing linens."

Decker grimaced, glancing uneasily at the beds. He'd slept in some dives before, but this one actually had him nervous.

"Now for the good stuff," said Katie, removing a concealable holster and a sturdy brown belt.

"Is that for the cockroaches?" he said.

She drew the pistol from the holster and racked the slide, leaving it locked back.

"Sig P320 compact. Nine millimeter. Right out of the box. Untraceable."

"That was nice of Harlow," said Decker.

"Harlow doesn't know about this," said Katie, glancing at Sandra. "Let's keep it that way."

Sandra shrugged. "I didn't see anything."

Katie tossed the empty pistol on the towels, along with five loaded pistol magazines and two knives—a fixed blade in a hard plastic scabbard and an easily concealed foldable knife.

"Just in case," said Katie.

"There's always a case to be made for their use," said Decker.

"Don't make me second-guess my judgment. Harlow said no weapons."

"Well, she's no fun, is she?"

"I think she's just trying to keep the number of 'accessory to a homicide' charges against her to under a dozen at this point."

"Funny," said Decker. "What else is in the goody bag?"

"Money," she said, tossing him a thick envelope.

A quick thumb through the stack of twenty-dollar bills left him uncomfortable with the bounty. "This is a lot of money. You don't have to—"

"Five thousand dollars."

"I can't take that much money."

"I'm not taking it back with me. We can charge you a high interest rate if that makes you feel better."

"I can't see how I'm going to pay this back," said Decker. "This is more than likely a one-way trip for me."

Katie stood there staring at him for several uncomfortable seconds while Sandra studied the room.

"I'm not going to tell Harlow you said that," said Katie, dumping the rest of the contents on the bed. "We don't expect you to pay any of this back."

A wallet with ID and credit cards, a US passport, and a satellite phone sat in a tight pile on the stained comforter. Decker didn't bother to ask why they hadn't given him a cell phone. With Aegis and the FBI looking for him, there existed a better-than-even chance that serious domestic spying muscle would be flexed to find him.

"You'll want to buy a laptop and a data transfer connection for the sat phone," said Katie. "I didn't know what kind of system you like to use."

"Happen to notice a Best Buy within walking distance?"

Sandra tossed a set of keys at him, which he plucked from the air a few inches from his face. "The SUV outside is rented for three weeks. You're not listed as a driver, so watch yourself on the road."

"Who exactly am I?" he said, reaching for the wallet.

"Raymond James," said Katie. "Longtime Nevada resident. American citizen. The IDs are top-notch. Credit cards give you twenty thousand dollars of additional spending power. Use them when it makes sense. You know the drill."

"What did you mean by 'we don't expect you to pay any of this back'?" said Decker. "And the other part."

She looked at him puzzled for a moment before nodding slowly, an understanding smirk appearing on her face.

"We're partners with Harlow," said Katie.

"Full partners?"

Up until now, he'd just assumed they were on Harlow's payroll.

"Me. Sandy. Harlow. A few others," she said. "We form the core partnership. Each with our own areas of expertise."

"Huh," said Decker. "What's your specialty?"

"Can't you tell?" said Katie.

He shrugged his shoulders. "Saving my ass?"

Katie broke out in laughter.

"I was going to add 'does all the dirty work,' but I get the feeling all of you are highly capable of that," said Decker.

"Covert field operations. Behind-the-scenes stuff," she said. "You'd be surprised how invisible this scar makes me."

"Shrapnel?" he said, thinking she was ex-military.

"One of Penkin's thugs," said Katie. "I left college and came out to LA nine years ago looking for my little sister. They put me in the hospital for a month. I was pretty naive back then."

Katie's face didn't betray her emotions, but he sensed them. In fact, he was very familiar with their heaviness.

"Did you ever find her?" he said, knowing the answer.

"Like I said, I was pretty naive back then," she said, turning to Sandra. "We need to get on the road."

Sandra nodded and opened the door.

"What's your specialty?" said Decker.

"Hiding people," said Sandra, stepping into the night with a devilish grin.

"Wait. Did she help with my—"

"Your daughter is safe, Decker," said Katie. "We put one of our most trusted outside teams on the job."

"Thank you," he said. "For all of this. I don't know how I can repay it."

"For starters—don't get yourself killed," she said.

"I'll see what I can do about that," said Decker, sitting on the edge of the empty bed.

"Keep that phone on at all times. We'll be in touch," said Katie.

"Don't call us. We'll call you," he said.

"See you around, Decker," she said, closing the door behind her.

"Can't wait," he muttered, plopping backward.

Decker lay on his back for a few minutes, the comforter's odor completely permeating his nose. A not-so-subtle combination of mildew and dumpster that he'd probably take with him wherever he traveled over the next day or so. He got up and secured the door, throwing the dead bolt and swinging the bar lock shut. It didn't escape his notice that the door locks looked like the only part of the room that had been updated in the last thirty years.

A quick check of the windows showed recently installed security bars. Great. Not only should he levitate above the bed to avoid infection, he'd apparently need to sleep with one eye open to avoid being robbed for meth money in the middle of the night. At least the air-conditioning worked. Sort of. The rattling unit didn't inspire a lot of hope.

He debated taking a shower, concluding it wasn't a good idea at this time of the night, despite the robust system of locks. Sleeping probably wasn't the best idea, either, but that wasn't really up for debate. Eyeballing the two beds, he selected the one farthest from the window and door. Decker repacked the duffel bag with everything except the satellite phone, loaded pistol, and sheet set.

Five minutes later, he set the pistol and activated satellite phone on the nightstand and turned off the light, listening to the late-night traffic speed by on Fremont Street. The sunbaked dumpster odor still leached through the sheets, but it was fainter, and he felt reasonably assured that he wouldn't wake up with bedbug bites on his hands and face. Reasonably.

CHAPTER

THIRTY-ONE

Reeves gently lifted the blankets and eased out of bed, trying not to wake his wife, Claire. It was 5:16 a.m. and she didn't normally wake up until six, when the kids started moving around the house. He'd woken her last night after midnight when he tried to quietly navigate the bedroom, failing miserably thanks to the Barbie Dream Camper left in the middle of the floor. After twenty-three years of chasing bank robbers, domestic terrorists, and mobsters for the FBI, his daughters' toys continued to pose the greatest threat to his safety.

His wife stirred under the covers as he rose from the squeaky mattress. She turned her head on the pillow, like she might say something, before sinking back into a solid sleep. He admired her placid face for a few moments, wishing he could lie here with her a little longer, but he'd been wide-awake for close to an hour at this point, his mind racing back and forth over the Decker case.

Relying on the faint glow of a night-light in the hallway, Reeves shuffled his bare feet across the carpeting, painfully aware that he hadn't cleared all of the sharp plastic hazards strewn across the room. Arriving safely at the bedroom door, he stepped into the hallway and eased the door shut.

Armed with a glass of water and the knowledge that a pot of freshly brewed coffee would be ready in five minutes, he made his way to the home office. Claire's home office. He'd only managed to stake out enough space in her graphic-design studio to charge his laptop. Once inside the studio, he turned on a desk lamp and retrieved his computer from the edge of her desk before settling into the cozy leather club chair she relied on to spawn ideas. Maybe some of the chair's magic would rub off on him this morning.

A minute later, he'd negotiated a secure connection with the remote-access server specifically configured for his use, confirming his identity using the fingerprint scanner built into laptop. He dived right into his email inbox, finding a message from the FBI's JRIC Liaison Office.

"Let's see what we have," said Reeves, clicking on the link embedded in the email.

He started with Rich Hyde, currently employed by Constellation Security, an Aegis Global subsidiary. Left the SEALs as a second-class petty officer after ten years of service. Three combat deployments to Iraq. Two to Afghanistan. Two Bronze Stars, each with the combat "V" designation. A dozen other military decorations. Honorable discharge. Hyde had been no slouch during his naval career, which made his murder in an obscure parking garage stairwell even more bizarre.

Beyond the two tightly spaced bullet holes in his right temple and the gaping exit wounds on the other side of his head, Hyde had been found with an untraceable pistol. The kind of loadout he'd expect to find on a Bratva hit man. The discovery of a sophisticated wireless communications rig suggested he hadn't been working alone, and whatever had happened didn't give his team enough time to sanitize the scene.

Had he been freelancing outside Constellation Security? Reeves couldn't imagine any reason why Constellation Security would be running an operation on US soil, unless it had something to do with Decker. But why would Constellation or Aegis be interested in Decker?

Reeves shook his head. He wasn't going to let Decker sidetrack him. For all he knew, Decker had hired these guys to spring him from prison and then double-crossed them at the mall, with the help of Harlow Mackenzie. But why would she help Decker and continue to run interference for him despite the FBI's involvement? No. Things got too messy too quickly at the Japanese Village Plaza. He sifted through Hyde's file for another minute or two, not finding anything useful.

Gunther Ross's file didn't shed any light on the situation, either, beyond confirming some of what Decker had told him. His profile summary didn't say Central Intelligence Agency, but Reeves had seen enough files like his to sniff it out. Ross certainly hadn't spent fifteen years working as an international sales manager for a pharmaceutical company that the FBI classified as a "nonentity." Reeves didn't need to research Arco Pharmaceuticals to know he wouldn't get any further than a functional website and phone system that would forward his messages to a phone bank in Virginia.

Ross's career got even murkier after Arco Pharmaceuticals. No known addresses. No tax filings. Nothing to indicate he'd grown roots anywhere in the United States or had any current connections to his home country other than a US passport.

If Reeves had to guess, Ross had probably used his network of shady overseas connections to acquire a few more passports so he could establish banking credentials in tax-haven countries and move his money around without attracting the IRS's attention.

No amount of digging was likely to unearth anything useful on the former CIA employee, but Reeves knew everything he needed to know about him. His presence in Los Angeles at the same time as Decker's bogus release was not a coincidence. He just wasn't sure how much time and energy he wanted to devote to figuring out how the two were connected.

He glanced up from the laptop screen to find his wife in the office doorway, holding two cups of steaming coffee.

"Figured you'd be out the door early today, so I thought I'd spend some time with you before the kids got rolling," said Claire. "But I don't want to break your chain of thought. You looked pretty disturbed there for a moment."

"No. I'm good," he said, waving her in. "I just woke up and couldn't shake a few thoughts. Figured I may as well get up."

She handed Reeves one of the mugs and sat in her office chair, turning it to face him. The room was so small their toes touched.

"Penkin?" she said.

"Penkin and a few loosely connected issues." He took a cautious sip of the hot brew. "Maybe not so loose. Decker was released the other day."

"I thought he was at least four years from possible parole."

"Somehow, he walked out of the Metropolitan Detention Center a free man two days ago," said Reeves. "I'm keeping an eye on him until the Bureau of Prisons figures out how he was released."

"They don't know how he was released?"

"They know how, they just can't seem to find a flaw in the paperwork and digital trail," said Reeves. "I think the warden and the BOP director are too busy pointing fingers at each other. They'd both have to sign off on an early release."

"It sounds almost comical."

"Trust me. It isn't," said Reeves, before taking a longer sip of the strong coffee.

"I understand your history with Decker, but isn't keeping track of prisoners BOP's job? Or the US marshals'?"

"Normally. Unless a certain US senator has a direct interest in that prisoner—and your career."

"You went above and beyond the call of duty for Senator Steele during the kidnapping investigation and Decker's trial," said Claire. "She can't possibly hold anything over your head."

"I know," he said. "But I called her the moment I discovered that Decker had been released. I just felt compelled to let her know, since he was released in LA, among other things."

Claire nodded. "Then pick him up and drive him back to Victorville. Let them figure out what to do with him."

Reeves rubbed his unshaven chin. "Decker disappeared. After I had a little chat with him."

"You found him and didn't haul him in?"

"Technically, I didn't have a reason to bring him in."

"Well. Then that's that. Not your problem. Time to move on," she said. "You probably have your hands full with the Russians, anyway. Especially with Penkin missing."

Reeves took a long sip of his coffee before responding. "Penkin isn't missing. He's dead, and if I had to guess, I'd say Decker was responsible. This is obviously not for public consumption."

"Of course," she said. "But once again, none of this is really your problem."

"I know. I'm just keeping an eye on some loose ends, and if I can find Decker, all the better."

"You look worried," she said. "I saw it on your face last night, too. This is a new look for you, Joseph, so don't try to deny it or say you're exhausted. What's really going on with Decker?"

"I'm not sure I know anymore," said Reeves. "And that's what has me worried. I can't shake something Decker said yesterday."

"Is it a game changer?"

"It could be—if it's true," he said.

"Does it cost you anything to check into what he said?"

"No."

"There's your answer," she said.

He leaned forward in the chair and kissed her hand, feeling a little better about the day ahead of him.

CHAPTER THIRTY-TWO

Harlow sipped a hot cup of coffee and stared at the neat latticework of distant rooftops and trees beyond the sparkling blue infinity pool. Located high in the Hollywood Hills, a few blocks north of Mulholland Drive, the house had expansive views of San Fernando Valley. If the property had been situated on the opposite side of the road, they would have been looking down on West Hollywood and Beverly Hills.

She still hadn't asked Sophie what the house had set them back. Regardless, she had to admit it felt great up here. Breezy and light. The direct opposite of the valley below, where the traffic, crowds, and stifling temperatures felt oppressive. The rarefied air up here came with a hefty price tag, but it also came with privacy and security, which they desperately needed with three well-funded, serious-as-hell organizations trying to find them.

As long as the firm's known partners kept their trips out of the hills to a minimum, and employed both active and passive countersurveillance techniques when doing so, they could run operations out of this exclusive enclave indefinitely, or until the money ran out. Her partners had unanimously agreed to continue helping Decker during a quick meeting this morning, but she suspected that their enthusiasm would wane if this dragged on for too long.

They'd put most of their active cases on the back burner at the start of this. For the next few days, or however long the Decker situation lasted, not only would they be digging into their cash reserves, they wouldn't be generating anything close to their normal levels of income. Stuck in this house, there was only so much they could do on behalf of their regular clients. Harlow gave it one week before her partners started to pull away, which put them on a compressed timeline.

Sophie sat down next to her, pushing her jewel-bedazzled, black-rimmed glasses back on her nose before sipping a fresh orange juice. "I could get used to this view."

"It's a little out of our price range," said Harlow, raising an eyebrow.

"If this thing drags out past a week, we can think about changing locations. It's always a good thing to stay on the move, anyway."

"I'm worried about Jess," said Harlow. "She has a full schedule of court appearances, and the FBI no doubt has her tagged."

"She's a silent partner, so there's no exposure beyond the FBI's interest in her timely arrival at the airport," said Sophie. "Which any investigator will conclude was completely coincidental. That's actually true, by the way. Her return ticket was purchased nearly two days ago."

"I'm more concerned with the Russians and this Gunther Ross guy," said Harlow. "It's no secret that she does a lot of legal work for us. If the wrong people find out about the little stunt at the airport, they'll connect the dots. I'd feel better if we put some security on her. Something obvious, so anyone interested in grabbing her will know she's a hard target."

"I'll make the call right away," said Sophie. "What else?"

"We wait and see what our surveillance teams report from the city and hope the operations crew can dig up some actionable intelligence for Decker."

"Finding someone who went off the grid that long ago is going to take a miracle."

"That's *if* someone went off the grid," said Harlow. "A big *if*. My money is on the investigation in LA. If we can identify and track Gunther Ross's people, we can link them to Aegis and whoever is pulling Aegis's strings. Once we identify the source, I strongly suspect the entire picture will become clear."

"Steele's abduction still baffles me," said Sophie. "If she was never meant to be found, what was the point of it?"

"Revenge? That's the only reason I can imagine."

"Someone wanted to send Senator Steele the unmistakable message that nobody is untouchable."

"If so, they got their point across."

"Then there's Aegis, if Gunther Ross is still working for them," said Sophie. "Did Decker ever mention Aegis being involved in the Steele kidnapping?"

"No. As far as he knew, the only other group actively searching for Meghan Steele was the FBI."

"And you think Penkin was telling the truth? Everything ties back to the Russians very neatly. They'd be at the top of my suspect list."

"Too neatly," said Harlow. "I don't know if Penkin was completely truthful, but given the attempt on Decker's life at the mall and Gunther Ross's appearance at Ares Aviation, an Aegis-owned company, I think it's fair to say that a second group played some kind of a role in the Meghan Steele tragedy."

"If it's Aegis, this is going to be huge."

"It's going to be a huge mess," said Harlow. "For all of us. Even if the truth comes to light and Decker is vindicated—we could all get buried under the fallout."

"Everyone is fully aware of the risks."

"I know. I just feel responsible for bringing this down on our heads."

"Harlow. We'll survive. No matter how big of a bomb we set off."

"It's going to be a big one," said Harlow.

"The bigger the better," said Sophie, nodding at the view. "That's what it takes to truly change things out there."

Harlow scanned the horizon, seeing it differently for a few moments. Nearly a million people lived within view of her seat. From people barely making ends meet to multimillionaires. Every race. Every religion. Every walk of life. Every conceivable vice to feed the population's ravenous appetite, right alongside the inconceivable. This was where Harlow and her associates fought an exhausting war against the traffickers. A seemingly never-ending and unwinnable war—until now.

She knew Sophie was right. They all knew it. Business as usual for their firm made a difference to hundreds of women and children every year, but the Decker situation represented an opportunity to instigate change that could help thousands. Possibly tens of thousands. If they exposed Aegis's dirty connection to the Solntsevskaya Bratva, the government would be forced to take real action. Nearly every lawmaker in the country had ties to Aegis money, and none of them would be able to escape the fallout without bolstering their stand against the traffickers. It was a chance she was willing to take, and it sounded like she wasn't alone.

"I hope we burn it all down," said Harlow, focused on the valley below.

"There's the Harlow beast I love and adore."

She turned to her best friend and colleague with a grin. "Did you just call me a beast?"

"In a good way."

"That's what I thought," said Harlow, raising her glass.

The sliding door behind them swished along its track. Joshua Keller, their lead operations center tech, stepped onto the slate patio. He had an enhanced team set up inside the house, taking up most of the spacious master bedroom with multiple workstations, stand-alone monitors, independent computer servers, and assorted technology equipment. The king-size bed had been pushed into one of the corners and served as a landing zone for all of their boxes and junk. They'd chosen the master bedroom for its massive size and privacy from the outside world.

"Miss Mackenzie?"

She stood up. "What's up, Josh?"

"I'm a little embarrassed to admit this, but I think Decker may be right," he said. "I can't find a verified death certificate for one of World Recovery Group's plank owners, or for any members of his family."

Harlow gave him a puzzled look. "Didn't we look into this?"

"That's why I'm embarrassed. I previously scoured publicly available sources and even dipped into some classified sources for data on every member of WRG in a position to turn witness or compromise the operation."

"Right. And you didn't find anything," said Harlow. "I went through your summary and even dug a little deeper with you into some of the outliers. Nothing stood out."

"Come inside. I need to show you what I've assembled."

She and Sophie followed him through the window-enclosed great room to the hallway leading to the master suite. When they reached the bedroom suite, the tenor changed. Six SCIF techs chatted away inside the cavernous space, typing furiously at their keyboards and sporadically yelling across the room. Upon the entrance of Joshua, Harlow, and Sophie, none of them looked up from their work.

All of the bandwidth required to keep them in business streamed back and forth from six satellite dishes placed in discreet locations around the property and connected to the routers serving each station. Joshua wirelessly pulled data from whichever station he piggybacked on to guide their efforts.

Harlow made her way over to the seventy-five-inch flat-screen LED TV, which stood behind the workstations, mounted to a sturdy mobile stand. While Harlow and Sophie approached the oddly positioned screen, Joshua pulled a chair with an attached mouse tray over to the side of the screen. Before sitting down, he grabbed his keyboard.

"I put together a comparative analysis sheet including every key employee at WRG, in addition to any employees or contractors directly involved in the Hemet operations, and ran the old parameters, in addition to a few new. One being verified death certificates. Take a look."

The screen activated, showing a database of names and data points that spanned the entire width of the TV. Joshua scrolled to the line containing one of the most prominent last names on the list and stopped it in the middle of the screen.

Harlow said, "He served a year and disappeared with his family on a camping trip in Idaho. Foul play suspected. Their campsite was ransacked. Signs of struggle. SUV left abandoned. The worst was assumed. I checked it off the list as soon as the news broke."

"Right," said Joshua. "The worst was assumed because it was a familiar scene. A repeat of what happened to nearly every other principal at WRG, just delayed due to his jail sentence. But I think it was staged."

"Because no bodies were found?" Without a body or compelling evidence, like blood or gore at the suspected crime scene, the coroner's office in charge of the jurisdiction typically withheld issuing a death certificate until a significant period of time elapsed. Sometimes years.

"The crime scene and the prison sentence. I couldn't find any prison-release documents in the public domain," said Joshua.

"In a sensitive case like this, the Bureau of Prisons might seal that kind of information," she said.

He shook his head. "I may or may not have accessed their sealed database, very briefly. No sign of Brad Pierce in the BOP system outside of his initial detention at MDC, awaiting a trial that never happened."

"Interesting," she said.

Harlow ran the most likely scenario given this information. Brad Pierce, one of WRG's principal members and Decker's lead tactical operations officer, turned into a federal witness against Decker and WRG in exchange for a sealed deal. She shook her head. No. Pierce had never appeared at Decker's trial to testify against him. It had to be something else. Whatever he agreed to, the feds had sealed everything and thrown away the key, letting him walk. Pierce vanished and spent the next year or so planning his fake death. The Department of Justice wouldn't play any role in that, so it would be totally up to him to put the finishing touches on his disappearance.

"What about DOJ records?" said Harlow. "Any way to see what kind of arrangement he had with the feds?"

"BOP information security was more or less a joke," said Joshua. "I can't say the same for the DOJ. Hacking into their system carries some risk."

"We're already pretty exposed on this one," said Harlow, turning to Sophie. "I don't think it's necessary. Just knowing that something is wrong with Pierce's story is enough for now. I'll pass this along to Decker and see what he thinks. Any chance of finding Pierce?"

"We can try," said Joshua. "But my guess is we'll come up with goose eggs."

"You'd think the feds would be interested in keeping track of Pierce," said Sophie. "He was probably just as important as Decker to the Bratva case."

"That's why I don't think we'll find him," said Joshua. "Reading between the lines here, my guess is that Pierce gave everyone the slip after he cut a deal with the US attorney. He obviously gave them something, though, or they wouldn't have cut him loose for any period of time. They had to know he had the skills to disappear and cover his tracks."

"No other anomalies in the group?" said Harlow.

"None. I have certified death certificates for everyone else," he said. "The Russians really did a number on these people. It's too bad the case against them got torpedoed. At least someone finally punched Penkin's ticket."

"They haven't found him yet," said Harlow, avoiding Sophie's eyes.

"Based on the mess left at that club, I think it's fair to assume one of his rivals within the Bratva decided he was finished running the show—and breathing."

"Say hello to the new boss," said Sophie, looking at her. "Same as the old boss."

Not this time. Not if they could link Aegis to Meghan Steele and start a war between the US government and the traffickers.

CHAPTER THIRTY-THREE

Gunther Ross opened the passenger door and stepped into the hot morning sun. Barely eight in the morning and he could already tell the day would be a scorcher. He made his way across the parking lot to the small stand-alone warehouse that served as his area headquarters. Located in Glendale, the warehouse gave his direct-action teams quick access to San Fernando Valley or the Los Angeles Basin, wherever they were needed.

Disappointingly, these teams had spent much of the past twenty-four hours sitting on their collective asses, waiting for Decker and his very recently identified accomplice, Harlow Mackenzie, to resurface. Both of them, along with Mackenzie's entire investigative firm, had essentially disappeared after the close encounter with Decker at Ares Aviation. Surveillance teams watching the dozen or so properties owned by Mackenzie and members of her firm had reported zero activity at all locations.

He entered a six-digit code into the keypad next to the door and glanced upward at the closed-circuit camera pointed at his face. The door clicked a few moments later. He stepped into the air-conditioned, two-story space, closing the door behind him. By the time he'd turned around, a fit-looking, impeccably dressed man was headed in his direction. He recognized the guy from the file forwarded by Harcourt. Derek Green. His new assistant.

"Derek," he said, offering a handshake. "You come highly recommended."

"Mr. Ross. It's an honor to join your team."

Harcourt had taken Green off a domestic surveillance job in Tampa, where he'd been tracking a human-trafficking network that had recently decided to expand into arms dealing.

"Did you familiarize yourself with the overall operation?" said Gunther.

"I did. Find and neutralize Ryan Decker. Assess level of liability and exposure associated with Harlow Mackenzie and act to contain if necessary. Pretty straightforward job—if we could just find them. They're slippery as hell."

Gunther liked what he'd just heard. Green understood exactly what needed to be done and, from what Harcourt had indicated over the phone, wasn't the least bit squeamish about making it happen. That was the mistake he'd made with the last guy. Gunther had chosen a rising star with a flawless record from the field leadership pool for what he'd thought would be a straightforward mission. A few hours of fieldwork, culminating with the assassination of a "national security threat." Easy work. Easily justified with a healthy, tax-free mission bonus. Not a lot of time or room for moral compasses to start pointing in the wrong direction—or right direction, depending on your point of view. Of course, how could he have guessed that the operation would implode—to the point where his orders and judgment would be questioned by a subordinate? He wouldn't make the same mistake again.

"Very slippery," said Gunther. "And a few steps ahead of us at all times."

"According to the latest round of law enforcement reports, they've given everyone the slip. The FBI lost all contact with Decker and

Mackenzie's group last night. Everyone vanished within the span of an hour."

"They managed to find Decker yesterday?" said Gunther, walking toward the array of flat-screen monitors ahead of him.

"Not for very long," said Green, following him. "They tracked a vehicle supposedly carrying Decker and Mackenzie from an undisclosed location to LAX, somehow losing Decker on the way. When they got to the airport, Mackenzie pulled a Houdini while her passenger created a diversion."

"Her group is skilled," said Gunther. "I'll give them that."

He settled in directly behind Robert Cooper, the operation center's chief intelligence analyst.

"Morning, Bob."

"Morning, sir," said Cooper. "Sounds like Mr. Green has brought you up to speed on the status of our LA efforts."

"He has. Any idea where Decker was hiding when the FBI picked up his trail?"

"Negative," said Cooper. "We don't have a direct source within the Russian organized crime division. I pulled this from an LAX police department source."

"Was Special Agent Reeves mentioned?"

Reeves had been instrumental in bringing down Decker and World Recovery Group. An unlikely but useful pawn in the mess that had unfolded after Decker miraculously and most regrettably located Senator Steele's daughter. Reeves and Decker had previously clashed in Los Angeles, which had made it almost too easy for Gunther.

He'd progressively leaked information about Decker's investigation to the FBI, culminating in the perfectly timed FBI raid on the Hemet motel housing Decker's operations team. Timed to coincide with the explosion that vaporized fifteen children, including Meghan Steele, and focused nearly all of the public's outrage against Decker. More importantly, it directed Senator Steele's wrath away from the Russians and toward an easy public target, giving Gunther time to permanently sever any links between Aegis and the Steele kidnapping.

The diversion had worked, from what they could tell. Without any evidence directly linking the abduction and subsequent explosion to the Russians, the FBI had gone after Decker. Someone had to pay for the unmitigated disaster in Hemet, and Decker was a convenient target. The only target—by design.

"Supervisory Special Agent Reeves," said Cooper. "He was reportedly at the airport."

"I don't like the sound of that," said Gunther.

"Neither do I," said Cooper. "We've detected ongoing FBI surveillance at a number of the apartments linked to Mackenzie's group. In addition to some private surveillance."

"I assume you've pulled our people back? The last thing we need right now is FBI attention."

"Way back."

"And countersurveillance?" said Gunther. "Mackenzie's people?"

"No. Private investigators from several different firms," said Cooper. "I can't find any connections."

"Would it be worthwhile to grab one of them? See what they know?"

Cooper shook his head. "Mackenzie has been extremely cautious from the very start. I can't imagine she used anyone that could provide us with any actionable information."

"You're probably right," said Gunther, turning to Green. "What do you think?"

Green shook his head. "If I were them, I'd lie low and try to ride this out somehow—or leave the country. They're on everyone's shit list at this point. Ours. The FBI's. Probably the Bratva's. That's a lot of hard-hitting people roaming the streets."

"But it's a massive city," said Gunther.

"Which shrinks considerably when you link thousands of cameras to facial-recognition software," said Green.

"I'm sure Ms. Mackenzie is very aware of that risk," said Cooper.

"Decker is after something," said Gunther. "They won't stay off the radar for long."

"I hate to break it to you," said Cooper. "But she can avoid the camera zones using a privacy app available on the dark net."

"Then it's all about them making a mistake at this point," said Green. "Not exactly the most proactive plan."

"Very little about what we've done since day one has been proactive," said Gunther.

"Sounds like you could use some good news," said Cooper, looking over his shoulder with a grin.

"There's good news?" said Gunther.

"I can't say for certain"—Cooper clicked his mouse several times—"but we've pored over the information you provided, and I think we might have found *the one that got away*."

Gunther hadn't expected Cooper's team to find anything more than what the other Aegis analysts previously assigned to the task had uncovered. Learning that Decker hadn't been the only principal member of World Recovery Group to cheat death had been somewhat of a shock, but based on the contents of the file Harcourt had given him, he'd just assumed the information was a dead end. The lead was close to two years old and had been thoroughly investigated.

"You're kidding," he said. "Right?"

"Not kidding. Maybe," said Cooper.

"*Maybe* doesn't get me excited."

"How about this?" Another click of his mouse.

The massive screen in front of them displayed a satellite map image he'd seen before.

"That's what—a ten-thousand-square-mile area?" said Gunther.

"Fifteen thousand." Cooper zoomed in to a wide section of rural road. He'd already sifted through these images.

"Still looks like a lot of nothing."

"According to the file, that's what the ground teams reported. A whole bunch of nada. But they were working off some obsolete data." Cooper changed the screen again.

"That looks the same."

"Hold on," said Cooper. "There's a little story to this."

"Let's skip to the end."

"Of course," said Cooper. "The DEA had a string of mobile satellite interception stations operating in this area. During its heyday, this isolated stretch of inhospitable earth provided close to twenty percent of the nation's meth supply. The DEA intercepted thousands of satellite calls with those stations, most of them utter nonsense, but one of those calls got flagged and forwarded to Aegis through an agreement in place with the NSA."

"The search teams came back empty-handed," said Gunther.

"They didn't stray too far from the road. The assumption was that he had made the call en route to Mexico, and satellite imagery confirmed what they saw with their own eyes. There was nothing out there but a barren wasteland." Cooper paused to look back at him.

"But?"

"But very recent satellite imagery showed something unusual about five miles north of the transmission intercept point. Something that matched an unreferenced site description provided in the file. Check it out." Cooper zoomed in to a detailed ground-level image.

Gunther studied the picture. "Damn. That's in the middle of nowhere," he said.

"And virtually invisible, unless you know exactly what you're looking for," said Cooper. "It's actually quite brilliant, if it's what I think it is. Hard to tell with a two-dimensional image, but it would explain why the ground teams never saw it."

"I can take a team and check it out," said Green.

Gunther thought about it for a moment. As much as he wanted to tie up this loose end, it represented a distraction they couldn't afford at the moment. The chance of Decker piecing together these clues was nonexistent, given the resources available to him. Then again, Decker and his new allies had proven unexpectedly resourceful over the past forty-eight hours. Not only had their intelligence been unusually accurate, but they seemed to have anticipated his every move up to this point. Maybe sending Green wasn't a bad idea, in case Decker somehow showed up.

"I'll arrange for a separate team to meet you out there," said Gunther. "A team better equipped for this kind of mission. There's no way to sneak up on that site—and this guy won't go easy."

"Guys like that rarely do," said Green.

"I want you to watch from a distance for at least seventy-two hours before taking him down, unless Decker rears his ugly head again in LA," said Gunther. "If there's even an outside chance that Decker figured this out, I want to give him time to make a move. Neutralizing both of them at the same time would make my boss extremely happy, which would mean good things for all of us."

"What kind of good things?" said Cooper.

"The six-figure kind," said Gunther, purposefully deciding not to mention the bad things that could happen if the mission failed.

CHAPTER
THIRTY-FOUR

Decker drove into the motel parking lot, cringing at how dilapidated the place looked after he'd spent a few hours in what he'd thought was an equally run-down shopping area. Apparently, nothing held a candle to the Ucky Ass Motel. After parking in front of his room, he sat there for several moments, seriously considering a change of venue. The room's smell still lingered in his nostrils, despite having inhaled the smoky, griddle-burned air of a greasy diner.

Reluctantly, he got out of the SUV. Decker intended to check the room before off-loading the bounty of supplies and gear he had collected this morning. The motel was about as anonymous as any establishment could be, but Decker himself was a different story. He was utterly conspicuous here, drawing the wrong kind of attention from its few sketchy denizens. Not to mention from the motel staff, which probably consisted of one person, the owner, who undoubtedly had a copy of every room key. For that reason alone, he hadn't left anything behind when he'd gone shopping. His entire life was locked away in the SUV.

Decker had turned the dead bolt's lock halfway when the door two rooms down opened, disgorging a guy dressed in nothing but a pair of yellowish-white boxers. Decker couldn't tell if the yellow tinge was a stain or the actual color of the underwear and had no intention of examining them long enough to make a final determination. The man's gut hung over the front of the boxers, swinging sideways when he turned to face Decker, then settling again. A cigarette burned in his right hand, which he braced against the thick, pitted concrete column holding up the overhang.

"Hey, buddy," the guy said, revealing a tallboy in his other hand. "You headed out again? My car's deader than dead. I got a seat at a table. The dealer's gonna slide some action my way. Kind of need to get over there as soon as possible. I was thinking. You know."

Decker considered him for a moment, his initial revulsion softening just enough to engage the guy in a dead-end conversation. The guy had obviously hit rock bottom, a place Decker knew better than anyone.

"I really couldn't say when I'm leaving today. I'm not exactly working on my own schedule," said Decker. "I could spot you some cab fare, though. How far are you going?"

"Down to the strip. The old strip," said the man, stuffing the cigarette in his mouth and taking a few steps toward Decker. "I got a spot in one of the back-room games. Big money. It's a sure thing. Been playing there for years. My guy is going to hook me the hell up today. You could get in on this, too."

"That's okay. Thanks, though."

"You don't have to be there to get in on it," said the guy, trading the cigarette for the tallboy. "I've got the table locked down, man. Any money you give me gets doubled. Maybe tripled."

"I'm not a big gambler," said Decker, fishing for his wallet. "How much is a round trip to the old strip?"

"I have a better idea. I can get dressed really quick," said the guy. "You can check out the card game and see what you think. They bring in some whales, which drives up the stakes. That's when my guy is going to hook me up. He could hook you up, too."

Decker promised himself he wouldn't talk to anyone else, except himself, for the next twenty-four hours, unless his life depended on it. This guy was relentless—and already completely intoxicated. He was definitely moving to a new hotel this morning. This guy would be at his door all day talking about this once-in-a-lifetime opportunity.

"Sorry, man. I can't leave this room until my company calls. I'd be happy to pay for your cab fare," said Decker. "How much is a round trip?"

The guy took a few more steps forward, his body odor invading Decker's space.

"Fifty bucks should cover it."

Decker knew the old strip in downtown Las Vegas was just a few miles up Fremont Street, but he wasn't about to haggle with this guy. Anything he could do to get him out of here for the day was worth the money. He pulled three twenty-dollar bills from his wallet and offered them to the man.

"How does sixty sound?" said Decker, trying his best to feign a smile.

The guy plastered the fakest grimace on his face, sighing at the same time. "Wow. That's really generous of you," he said. "But I kind of have a confession to make."

Damn. He'd fallen for the oldest trick in the run-down-Las-Vegas-motel book. This guy was the Ucky Ass Motel's trapdoor spider, waiting around all day for something to walk by his lair.

"The thing is, I had to buy a seat at that table, which wasn't cheap. Emptied all the cash from my pockets," he said. "And then the damn ATM machine ate my card. Seriously. Barely had enough to get back here yesterday. It won't do me any good to take a cab over there without enough to throw around the table. I can pay you back with interest, as soon as I get back from the game. I have a briefcase in the room to carry all the cash. It's gonna be huge."

"All I can spare is sixty bucks," said Decker. "Seriously. I'm on a business trip."

"Here?" said the man, his pleading demeanor gone. "What kind of business?"

"None of your business," said Decker, pulling his shirt up far enough to expose part of his concealed holster.

"Must be serious business," the man said. "I don't want any trouble."

"You want the sixty bucks?"

The man scratched his groin and guzzled the rest of the tallboy. "I guess."

Decker tossed the money as far as he could and was back in the SUV, driving as fast as possible out of the motel parking lot, by the time the guy had retrieved the money. He turned right onto Fremont, headed toward the old strip, convinced that the quality of lodging would improve the closer he got to the downtown area.

A few minutes into the drive, his satellite phone chimed. He snatched it off the passenger seat, eager to hear Harlow's voice.

"Hello?"

"That's it?" Harlow's voice was completely soothing. "I expected some kind of smart-ass comment about your hotel. Katie said it was a one-of-a-kind place."

"She called it a hotel?"

Harlow laughed.

"Funny," said Decker. "I'm headed to a new . . . hotel."

"You don't have to relocate," said Harlow. "It's time to—"

"Yes. I have to relocate." He hurried through a recap of his encounter with his neighbor. "Believe me, this guy was going to be on me like white on rice unless I got out—"

"I was about to say it's time to check out of the motel. We may have found something," said Harlow. "Great you're making friends, though."

"Even funnier," said Decker. "What did you find?"

"I'm not exactly sure how to tell you without opening an old wound."

"The wounds are still very fresh," said Decker. "Just hit me with it."

"We suspect Brad Pierce cut some kind of deal with the feds."

"Pierce? He was killed with his family in Idaho. After serving a one-year sentence for a few bogus charges the US attorney was able to slap on him."

"They disappeared in Idaho. No bodies have been found. And there's no record of him in the Bureau of Prisons system, beyond a short stint in the Metropolitan Detention Center. Less than two weeks. We think he gave the feds enough to get released and promptly disappeared. He never testified in any of World Recovery Group's trials."

He didn't want to believe it. Brad had been like a brother to him for more than a decade. They had founded World Recovery Group after working together in the CIA and had grown the company from a contract investigative team to a global VIP-rescue powerhouse. Decker had shifted most of the blame and legal responsibility for the Hemet catastrophe onto himself to minimize Pierce's exposure. He hadn't seen or talked to Pierce since they were hauled away from the motel by the FBI.

Pierce's family had miraculously survived that fateful night, thanks to his wife's last-minute decision to drive the kids to their vacation home in the Outer Banks. According to the surveillance footage from Pierce's Annapolis home, the hit team sent to murder his family missed them by two hours.

"We ran a quick analysis of the media surrounding his release," said Harlow. "Coverage started out with a few dozen simultaneous news blurbs across the country in small to medium-size internet-based news outlets and spread from there. It very closely resembled the kind of strategy a publicist would employ to make a story go viral."

Decker didn't like the implications. Maybe the near miss at Pierce's Annapolis home hadn't been luck.

"I can't believe he would betray me."

"I pored through the court transcripts and listened to all of the media analysis. The US attorney didn't hit you with any surprises," said Harlow. "I don't see how he could have betrayed you to the feds, so to speak."

"Not after we were hauled in," said Decker, his face warming with anger. "Before."

"I don't see how— Why would— I can't see Pierce doing that."

"Neither can I, but someone tipped off the FBI. They hit us at precisely the same moment that my team hit the Bratva house. That's not a coincidence. I can believe that the Russians somehow detected my surveillance days before and set me up for a fall, but Reeves's simultaneous arrival at the motel in Hemet always bothered me. That would have required real-time intel, leading right up to the raid. And who's to say Pierce wasn't playing both sides? He could have tipped off the Russians and fed them information to save his own skin—and his family's. If your original theory is correct, he's the only member of WRG that got away unscathed."

"Aegis, or someone closely affiliated, had a drone flying over the house," said Harlow. "There's more to this than meets the eye."

"There's only one way to find out. Find Brad Pierce."

"I don't see how," said Harlow. "We haven't been able to find anything on him. He very thoroughly vanished the moment he walked out of the Metropolitan Detention Center. Not a single blip on the radar, except for the suspiciously timed media blitz about his release, which could have been planned months in advance, and the faked disappearance in Idaho."

"I know where to find him," said Decker.

"You're serious?"

"If he's not where I suspect he is, he's definitely gone—and we're back to square one."

"I can't see any harm in trying."

"Oh, there's plenty harm in trying. Especially with a guy like Pierce," said Decker. "He won't go quietly."

"Do you need backup?" she said. "I can hire a solid team to help you with this."

"No. I need to do this alone."

"This isn't the time for heroics," said Harlow. "And I don't mean to call your skills into question."

"I'm not being heroic. I'm being tactical. The location I have in mind is isolated. I'll have to approach it on foot, starting from miles away to avoid drawing his attention."

"I can put the team on a helicopter and keep them within quick ferry range if things get ugly."

"I guess I'd be a fool to turn that down."

"Yes. You would."

"How much lead time do you need for the helicopter and team?"

"Thirty-six to forty-eight hours—to do it right," said Harlow. "Depending on the location."

"It's pretty isolated. Have you ever heard of Aguilar, Colorado?"

"No."

"Ludlow?"

"Sorry," she said.

"There's a reason for that," said Decker. "Ludlow is a ghost town, and you'd miss Aguilar if you blinked while driving. They're in the eastern foothills of the Sangre de Cristo Mountains. Gorgeous country, but not much out there."

"Sounds like the perfect place to disappear."

"Or get swallowed up," said Decker. "I need you to pull up recent satellite imagery for the foothills west of Aguilar. As detailed as you can get it. I'll get my computer up and running when I stop for the night."

"I'll put together a package and get the ball rolling on your support team," said Harlow. "You plan on driving straight through?"

"I need to look at a map first, but I'm pretty sure I'd be driving long into the night to get there."

"Twelve and a half hours if you take Interstate 40 to Albuquerque and turn north on Interstate 25."

"That's right. Twenty-five runs right by Aguilar," said Decker, vaguely remembering the dusty little town. "I'll stop when the sun goes down—at a reputable-looking motel."

"Still reliving last night?"

"Still smelling last night," said Decker. "What else is going on with you and the crew?"

"Not much. We're holed up with my SCIF team in a very secure location, hoping to catch a break down in the city," she said. "I have third-party surveillance crews sitting on a few of my partners' apartments, hoping Gunther Ross's people show up."

"Careful with that guy," said Decker. "He's clever and sadistic. A pure psychopath. I can't say this strongly enough: do not underestimate him."

"I hear you. We're running the surveillance teams through a cutout, so there's no link back to us."

"Very few people in the world scare me, Harlow. Gunther Ross is one of them."

"We'll be careful. You do the same. I'm going to text you an email address. When you get your computer working, send us a quick email, and we'll get you connected to a secure site to share documents."

"Sounds good," said Decker. "I'll check in with you in a few hours, or you call me if anything earth-shattering occurs before then. My guess is everything will go really quiet while Aegis and the FBI try to reacquire us. Don't underestimate Reeves, either. He has some really sophisticated surveillance tools at his disposal."

CHAPTER THIRTY-FIVE

Reeves stood patiently in the security lobby of the Los Angeles Joint Regional Intelligence Center while the security officer inside a mostly transparent, bullet-resistant glass booth confirmed his identity. Even though Reeves had unrestricted access to every space in the JRIC, he still had to go through the same verification every time he stepped into the building.

"Supervisory Special Agent Reeves, please place your right thumb on the scanner," said the uniformed officer.

He complied, pressing his thumb against the biometric scanner on the counter in front of him. A few seconds later, the JRIC security officer passed his FBI badge through a thin slot in the glass.

"You're cleared," said the officer, smiling politely.

He got off easy today. The system randomly selected the authentication measures required for entry, sometimes requiring more than one and on occasion asking for all of them. Luckily, Reeves hadn't been subjected to the security triumvirate in over a month. The combination of retinal scan, multiple fingerprints, and voice recognition never went smoothly. He'd once spent ten minutes trying unsuccessfully to give a voice sample that the system would recognize, eventually requiring a supervisor override. It all felt like overkill, since everyone was cleared by facial recognition before they were even allowed into the lobby.

Reeves tucked the badge into his suit-coat pocket and stepped toward the gate in front of him. The sturdy glass-and-steel saloon doors swung inward, granting him entry to a small glass vestibule. When he was completely inside the tight chamber, the security officer pushed his temporary ID card and a lanyard-equipped badge holder toward him before motioning for Kincaid to approach the booth.

Reeves inserted the hard plastic ID card in the holder and looped the lanyard around his neck. Glancing back through the ballistic glass doors, he watched Kincaid place his right eye up to the retinal scanner. He really hoped Kincaid didn't get the special treatment this morning. They had already fallen far enough behind schedule. Reeves held his ID card up to a scanner next to a second set of swinging clear glass doors and continued into the JRIC when they opened. Kincaid joined him a minute later.

"One of these days they're going to add strip search to the menu," said Kincaid.

"That'll be the day you assume sole responsibility for coming here."

"I'll be sure to put in for a transfer," said Kincaid. "To Omaha."

"Omaha doesn't sound bad right now," said Reeves. "We're kind of back to square one now that Penkin's cabal has been cut off at the knees."

"More like at the neck."

"Right. The only silver lining to this whole mess is that it'll take the Russians a few weeks to fill the sudden void. It'll give us some time to find Decker."

"I'm not hopeful about finding Decker," said Kincaid. "Or Mackenzie. Her whole crew blinked out on us."

"Except for the lawyer."

"I don't expect her to vary from her routine," said Kincaid. "They're too savvy for that."

Reeves didn't disagree. After disappearing Decker right in front of them last night, Buzz Cut and the lawyer managed to ditch them three minutes out of the airport. They pulled their car off Century Boulevard into the snag-a-space parking lot next to the Los Angeles Airport Marriott and vanished. He'd held the pursuit vehicles back, since he could easily track the target vehicle remotely and simply hadn't expected them to pull another stunt on them so quickly. They found the lot completely full and the neatly parked vehicle in a space near the West Ninety-Eighth Street exit. The women had undoubtedly swapped into a vehicle that had been preparked long before Mackenzie and Decker left the safe house. He'd been grossly outmaneuvered, and it didn't feel good.

"I don't expect them to slip up, either," said Reeves. "So we're going to lean on technology."

"I thought you hated technology."

"I hate it when it doesn't work, or it's working against me," said Reeves, opening the door and entering the main JRIC hallway.

He headed straight for Surveillance, where he'd find everything he needed to rekindle the search for Decker. Halfway down the corridor, he passed the entrance to the two-story Crisis Tactical Operations Center. Contrary to television and the movies, the CTOC didn't run twenty-four hours a day, 365 days a year, sifting through surveillance data and tracking criminals. The CTOC was only activated in the event of a terrorist attack or a citywide law enforcement crisis requiring the coordinated response of multiple agencies and departments. Reeves couldn't remember the last time the vast space had been used.

Most of JRIC's day-to-day magic occurred in much smaller rooms, separated by section. Surveillance took up more than half of those rooms. He stopped at the JRIC's Fusion Center to check in before heading to the team responsible for facial-recognition operations. A woman with glasses peeked around her monitor when he entered.

"Angela," said Reeves.

She slid her chair over so the monitor didn't stand between them. "My favorite supervisory special agent," she said. "What can we do for you today?"

"More like what haven't you already done."

"Oh boy," she said, rolling her eyes. "I should have known this morning's request wasn't all of it."

"Maybe I'm just here to say hi to my favorite Fusion Center coordinator of all time."

"I'm the first and only coordinator," she pointed out.

"The words are still true."

"Special Agent Kincaid," she said, "I feel sorry for you."

"Me, too," said Kincaid.

Reeves shook his head while she and Kincaid shared a laugh. "This is going in your evaluation, Matt. Undermining a superior."

"Well, then," said Angela, straightening up in her chair. "We better get down to business before Mr. Fussy-pants writes us both up." She took off her glasses. "I disseminated your requests to the appropriate sections. I should have a fused workflow running by the afternoon, which will start producing data for you by tomorrow morning at the latest. Probably get it running tonight. We'll send you a secure log-in specifically for this data feed."

"Incredible. Thank you, Angela."

He really meant it. He'd dropped a load of requests on her lap this morning, representing a ton of work for the section. Last night's surveillance disaster had left him empty-handed, so he needed to start from scratch. He had agents watching most of Mackenzie's partners' apartments, but like Kincaid had said, it was highly unlikely that she would make that kind of a rookie mistake. On top of that, he'd have to divert most of his field resources back to the Russians within forty-eight hours, possibly sooner. The Solntsevskaya Bratva was his division's primary focus. Finding Decker would quickly fall to the wayside once new Russian leadership started to assert itself.

Thirty-six to forty-eight hours didn't give him a lot of time to pick up a cold trail, so he'd thrown everything feasible at the problem. He'd provided the Fusion Center with every byte of data available for Ryan Decker and the members of Mackenzie's investigative firm, which Angela's analysts would deconstruct and expand before creating custom search parameters for real-time, passive surveillance operations.

Facial-recognition software based in the JRIC scoured city-linked camera feeds, police vehicle cameras, and a network of private cameras that opted in to the LAPD system. The same software also analyzed millions of social media pictures for matches based on the parameters. License plate–reader software looked for tags linked to Mackenzie's group, their known associates and family, plotting their last known locations. Credit cards and cell phone numbers associated with the parameters would be tracked. His money was on facial recognition, which was why he wanted to have a chat with the team that ran the software.

"My pleasure," she said. "You're one of the few agents I don't mind hanging around the section. Kincaid, too, I guess."

"She's getting sassy in her old age," said Reeves.

"If I wasn't fifty-two creaky years old, I'd chase you out of the building for that crack," she said, standing up. "Now get out of here before I change my mind."

"What's her story?" said Kincaid on their way down the hallway to Facial Recognition.

"Angela and I go way back. She used to run the field office's IT group," said Reeves. "One of the FBI's IT integration pioneers. She put herself through UCLA in her thirties. Computer science bachelor's and master's degrees. They say she brought the LA office out of the dark ages. JRIC stole her about three years ago to run the Fusion Center. Stay on her good side."

"Will do," said Kincaid. "So who are we visiting in the Facial Recognition section?"

"Nicholas Watts. He's been working on something under the radar for a while now. Improved-range facial recognition."

Kincaid shrugged.

"I'll let Watts explain," said Reeves, knocking on the door. "It's kind of his baby."

"It's not on the market yet?"

"No. He's still working out some kinks in the system, but I think it might be useful to us, regardless of those issues."

The door buzzed before opening inward a few inches. Reeves pushed it the rest of the way, revealing a thin, middle-aged man in khaki pants and a red polo shirt sitting behind an expansive desk supporting four widescreen monitors.

"I was expecting you," said Watts.

"Really?" said Reeves.

"I watched you from the front entrance all the way to this door."

"Okay," said Reeves. "Am I on some kind of watch list here?"

"Yeah. The pain-in-my-ass watch list," said Watts, leaning back in his expensive-looking office chair. "I flagged your face when all those requests landed in my workflow. Figured you'd show up sooner or later to request the works."

"The works?" said Reeves.

"You're the only person that has expressed an interest in my special project."

"Am I that transparent?"

"Forward-thinking," said Watts. "Everyone else is satisfied with the status quo. Who's the sidekick?"

"The sidekick is Matt Kincaid, my deputy," said Reeves. "He doesn't know about your improved-range facial-recognition upgrade, and we would like to know a little more about it."

"Long or short version?"

"Short, please," said Reeves. "We have our hands full today."

"I've been practicing my elevator pitch."

Reeves turned to Kincaid. "The elevator used to stop at every floor."

"Funny secret agent man," said Watts. "Here we go. Current 3-D FR software measures the distances between eighty universally recognized nodal points on the human face, or as many as it can detect, comparing the captured face print to the face print we feed into the system. It's over ninety-five percent accurate within a fifteen-yard range, which isn't great, and its accuracy degrades exponentially beyond that. It's an image-resolution issue."

"I've read about using higher resolution or pan-tilt-zoom cameras to solve that," said Kincaid.

"Deputy Dog did his homework. Very nice," said Watts. "Coaxial-concentric PTZ cameras solve the problem, expanding that range to fifty yards, but now you're talking about a complete overhaul of a city-wide camera system the city didn't want to pay for in the first place."

"So you tweaked the software to improve the range?"

"*Tweaked* is kind of a crude word for essentially rewriting the program."

"Sorry," said Kincaid. "Your software enhances the image resolution?"

"I considered a variation of image resolution but scrapped the idea when something far simpler came to mind," said Watts. "My modification maps fewer nodal points per digital frame but randomly selects different nodal points for each frame analyzed. Current technology defaults to the same nodal points for every frame, which is great for static, close-up targets. My change should allow the current camera system to process moving targets at thirty yards, with a sixty to seventy percent accuracy."

"That's impressive," said Kincaid.

"I'd like to get that number to ninety percent. Then we'd have something special."

"Then you'd quit and go to work for yourself," said Reeves.

"It's all proprietary work on behalf of the JRIC," said Watts. "Though I'm sure I could recreate it if I had to."

"Are you ready to put it to the test on the streets?" said Reeves.

"I was hoping you'd ask," said Watts. "When your facial-recognition requests hit my desk this morning, I thought it would be a perfect match. And the timing is right. I don't have any major surveillance initiatives running at the moment. If anything higher priority comes in, which is pretty much anything other than what you submitted, I have to switch back to the current software package."

"I understand," said Reeves. "We're looking at forty-eight hours, maybe less, to pursue this."

"It's an interesting set of targets," said Watts. "Do you think they've mapped the camera zones?"

"That's why I'm here. They've proven to be a countersurveillance-savvy group."

"In other words, they ditched you guys."

"Twice," said Kincaid.

"Damn," said Watts.

"It wasn't the proudest moment of my career," said Reeves. "Which is why I really want to find them."

"You came to the right place. Even if they're using some kind of camera-zone mapping app, my modification will trip them up," said Watts. "The apps I've tested map safe passage around the detection zones by overestimating detection ranges. Double, sometimes triple the known effective ranges of our software."

"But not your modification," said Reeves.

"They'll pass right through the new detection ranges without suspecting it."

"What's the downside?" said Kincaid.

"Based on the accuracy percentages, you're going to see some false positives."

"I can live with a wild-goose chase or two," said Reeves. "Let's do it."

"*Excelente*, amigos," said Watts, sliding a piece of paper and a pen across the desk. "I'll need your signature authorizing the experimental use of the software in conjunction with your requests."

Reeves took the pen and quickly read the document, which had already been signed by Angela.

"Looks like you've been expecting me all morning."

"Angela has screened every facial-recognition request that has come into the JRIC over the past three weeks," said Watts. "She's really excited about the software."

"No wonder she was happy to see me," said Reeves, signing the document.

Watts stood up and shook their hands.

"What's your guess on how long it'll take?" said Reeves.

"If they're sneaking around the city right now, we'll start getting hits within the hour. The software modification doesn't leave much safe space in LA. If they're playing it smart and staying off the streets like I would? You know the deal."

"My guess is they'll think they're outsmarting the system."

"That's the whole point of the modification."

"What are the Fourth Amendment ramifications of the extended recognition range?" said Kincaid.

Watts smiled slyly. "There's a section in the document addressing that."

Kincaid glanced at Reeves and raised an eyebrow.

"The legality of this modification hasn't been explored yet," said Reeves. "In other words, we can't use any evidence spawned from this surveillance."

"You can use it," said Watts. "But any good lawyer will get it thrown out of court."

"And I'd get thrown out of the FBI," said Reeves. "Speaking of getting thrown out of the FBI, can you add another face to the list?"

"I assume you don't want anyone knowing about this face?"

"Just you and me."

"And him," said Watts, nodding at Kincaid.

"I suppose we don't have a choice," said Reeves, pulling out his phone. "I have his name and a few pictures. Is that enough?"

"Is the name real?"

"It appears to be real."

"And the pictures?"

"Driver's license and passport."

"That doesn't mean they're real."

"Good point," said Reeves. "I believe they're real."

"Then that's all I'll need. I'll call you with a link to access the special order. The rest you'll get in your FBI inbox," said Watts. "Anyone I know? If this is your boss or your wife, I'm kicking it out of the system."

"I've never heard of the guy before. Not many people have."

"Sounds intriguing," said Watts. "I won't ask any more questions. Curiosity killed the cat or something like that."

"Probably for the better," said Reeves. "I get the feeling this guy killed a few cats in his career."

CHAPTER THIRTY-SIX

Decker sat at the motel desk and studied the satellite images Harlow had emailed him, satisfied that he'd found Pierce's foothills hideout. Not bad for a little under an hour of searching, especially after having spent most of the day on the road. He could finally relax a little, grab a bite to eat, and knock off early for the night.

He'd decided to end the day's journey in Albuquerque after eight straight hours on the road. The sun had already dropped low on the horizon, appearing in the top of his side mirrors, when signs for Albuquerque started to appear.

By the time the sun vanished, Decker had settled in to the Day's Inn just east of the downtown area. The motel suited his purposes perfectly, offering tidy rooms in a safe part of town. He'd taken a room on the first floor so he could park right in front of his door and haul all of his gear inside without arousing suspicion. At Harlow's recommendation, he'd stopped at a nearby Walmart before checking in to the motel and purchased a large flat-screen monitor to help process the satellite imagery. She'd been right about the monitor. There was no way he could have properly scoured the detailed imagery she'd provided on the tiny laptop screen.

At least he hoped he'd found Pierce. Admittedly, the whole thing was a long shot, based on his recollection of several dozen conversations of varying length and detail with his former best friend and a single, spontaneously planned visit to the future site of the Pierce homestead after finishing a job in Denver.

He didn't remember too many details about the location, other than it was accessible by a jeep trail heading due west out of Aguilar and lay between two ridgelines in a shallow valley. The structure he'd identified on one of the satellite images matched the description perfectly and was the only house that deep in the foothills. It had to be his place. The only question was whether Pierce was still there. Decker suspected he was.

The Pierces hadn't started construction on their retirement getaway before Hemet. They'd still been in the early design phase. The presence of a house on that land could only mean one thing: Pierce had gone ahead with the project after vanishing.

It was the perfect hiding place. Pierce had paid for thirty-something acres of land with cash, in a transaction that had more than likely been sealed with a handshake and a simple deed transfer—the latter of the two likely recorded under an obscure corporation name or alias he'd never used before. Untraceable to anyone without knowledge of Pierce's original intent, which was why Decker was convinced he was there.

Hungry from the long trip, Decker briefly considered driving to one of the dozen or so chain restaurants within a few minutes of the motel. He scrapped the idea just as quickly after glancing at the gear arrayed on one of the beds. Pizza delivery might be the better option. The area around the motel felt safe enough, but he couldn't risk losing the rifles to a local thief staking out the hotel.

The gun shop outside Las Vegas had required him to produce a Nevada ID to purchase them, and Nevada had some of the most lenient gun laws on the books. If New Mexico had the same requirement, he'd have no choice but to drive the eight hours back to Nevada. Going after

Pierce without the rifles wasn't an option. If his former friend and colleague caught wind of Decker's approach before he settled into one of the ridges above Pierce's homestead, he'd need the range and firepower to get out of there in one piece.

The terrain provided plenty of opportunity for preplanned, static concealment, but little in the way of cover on the move. Without the long guns, a skilled operator like Pierce could pin him down quickly and move in for the kill—or wait for him to make a mistake. Actually, Pierce could nail him down even if he brought the rifles. Nothing was guaranteed out there. Not on Pierce's home turf. The thought of Pierce gaining the upper hand on unfamiliar ground gave him pause. Maybe he should consider using the helicopter team more proactively.

Decker wanted to take Pierce alive, which would require either catching him in the open and forcing his surrender or completely surprising him at the house. The likelihood of approaching the house unseen was nonexistent, leaving him with one option: drawing Pierce out, on Decker's terms. If he could sneak undetected into a well-concealed position on one of the ridges surrounding the house, he could direct the helicopter to land beyond the ridge. The sound of the helicopter would tempt Pierce to investigate—the most logical observation point being the ridge where Decker waited.

The plan wasn't perfect by any stretch of the imagination, but it was about as good as it would get without dropping a SEAL platoon down on Pierce's head. He leaned back in the flimsy desk chair and shook his head. It was hard to believe he was on the verge of hunting down and interrogating the man who had been his best friend for over twenty years.

A big part of him didn't want to believe that Pierce had sold him out, but the evidence, though indirectly circumstantial, told a different story. He wanted to give the friend he'd known since their Annapolis days a chance to explain how he had managed to emerge unscathed from the bloodbath unleashed on the rest of World Recovery Group.

If it turned out to be a simple matter of testifying against Decker in exchange for a deal, he'd leave Pierce alone, terminating their friendship. If it turned out to be more than that, he'd terminate Pierce for the suffering and misery he'd inflicted on everyone—after extracting every detail about the betrayal. He owed it to the men and women who'd lost everything in the wake of the Hemet disaster to take this all the way to the source. There would be no mercy.

Decker suddenly felt tired, almost light-headed. He needed to eat. In a hurry to get set up in Albuquerque, he had driven straight through, only stopping for gas. He still wasn't used to thinking about his basic needs. In prison, a strict schedule kept you fed, exercised, showered, and rested. Routine was the only thing he sort of missed about prison. Once you navigated the acute perils of prison life, the days spent locked up became somewhat meditative.

He'd felt the same way driving off the Naval Academy yard for the last time, after four years of military school life. Like he wasn't exactly sure what to do. His stomach growled, helping him with the decision. He searched the internet for pizza places, finding one that would also deliver cold beer. Decker hadn't known that was a thing. Pizza and beer delivered to your hotel room. Life on the outside had significantly improved over the past two years.

After ordering a large "kitchen-sink" pizza and a six-pack of Sierra Nevada Pale Ale, he checked the secure email Harlow had set up through a private web-hosting group used by one of the rescue organizations she trusted. A new message had been delivered less than five minutes ago. He clicked on the message, a thin smile forming as he read its contents. Harlow had found a group based out of Denver that could get a helicopter-borne support team to Aguilar by 10:00 a.m. tomorrow. Looked like he'd have to skip the beers. Or at least most of them.

He typed a reply, outlining the simple plan he'd conceived a few minutes earlier. Decker would leave the motel at three thirty in the morning, driving straight to Aguilar. A four-hour trip with a gas stop.

Once in Aguilar, he'd take the SUV a mile or so up one of the jeep trails leading west out of town and park about five miles from Pierce's homestead, where he'd continue on foot.

The helicopter support team should arrive at its staging area several miles east of Aguilar right around the time Decker settled into position on one of the ridges overlooking the target. He'd watch the site and initiate the final stage of the mission based on what he observed.

Harlow replied within seconds.

Sounds good. Call you later to finalize.

He could hardly wait.

CHAPTER THIRTY-SEVEN

Decker approached the outskirts of Aguilar along a two-lane country road, the foothills of the Sangre de Cristo Mountains barely peeking over the trees outlining the town. He was ahead of schedule, having involuntarily woken thirty minutes before his alarm, and could really use a proper cup of coffee. He'd left Albuquerque too early to hit a coffee shop on the way out, and the swill passed off on him at a gas station off the interstate was barely distinguishable from prison coffee.

Unfortunately, he didn't have high hopes of finding anything open in Aguilar. From what he remembered, the one-block downtown strip mostly consisted of shuttered storefronts, a few scattered taxidermy shops, and an abandoned-looking café. Maybe he'd get lucky. The road curved gently north, meeting Main Street at a four-way intersection that, peculiarly, didn't feature any stop signs.

He turned onto Main Street and drove through the downtown area, which turned out to be even smaller and more neglected than he remembered. His hopes rose when he saw the word *Bakery* written in a floral pattern on a storefront sign ahead but sank just as quickly when he pulled even with the establishment. The OUT OF BUSINESS sign was barely visible through the dust-caked window. So much for a good cup of coffee, or any coffee, for that matter.

His trip through downtown Aguilar ended less than a minute later at San Antonio Avenue, where Main Street turned into the hard-packed dirt road that would deposit him in the foothills. He drove for another minute until he reached the fork in the road he had identified on the satellite maps. Decker pulled over and opened the laptop on the passenger seat, matching a small retention pond near the split to the satellite image.

"This is it," he whispered, guiding the SUV left at the fork.

Decker drove into the draw between two ridges, the dirt road quickly giving way to a well-worn jeep trail. He stopped a few hundred yards later to activate the GPS unit mounted to the dashboard, studying his position relative to the displayed satellite map. After consulting the more detailed image on his laptop, he turned left, convinced he had made the right decision. The trail took him southwest for a quarter of a mile, through another draw. The ridges stood higher this time, making him wonder if he hadn't underestimated the topography. The farther west he traveled, the steeper the terrain he'd encounter.

Evenly dividing his attention between the thinning jeep trail ahead of the SUV and the GPS next to the steering wheel, Decker reached the end of the jeep trail fifteen minutes ahead of the original schedule. The poor trail conditions had eaten up half of the time he had gained on the drive up from Albuquerque.

Staring through the windshield at the rising hills to the west, he grimaced. His memory of this place differed significantly from the view in front of him. He'd have to haul some serious ass to get into position by ten. Eleven was more realistic, especially if he hoped to recover from what would undoubtedly be a strenuous hike. Under normal circumstances, the trek wouldn't give him pause, but at sixty-four hundred feet above sea level, four thousand more than he was accustomed to, he'd be wiped out after the five miles. Decker took the satellite phone out of the center console and called Harlow with the update.

"Are you there?" she said. "The helicopter launches in forty-five minutes."

"I'm at the first waypoint, but I need to push the timeline back," said Decker. "Sorry. I know that won't be cheap."

"This is already costing me an arm and a leg, so what's another leg, right?" said Harlow. "Don't answer that. What's the problem?"

"The hills are a lot higher than I remembered."

"You're kidding, right? I mean—you checked a topographic map?"

He didn't respond immediately, which may as well have been his answer.

"Dammit, Decker. How long of a delay are we talking?"

"One hour," he said. "Ninety minutes to be sure."

"Fine," she said, after a lengthy pause. "They'll arrive at their staging area by ten forty-five, in case you manage to gain some time back."

"Thank you. I don't mean to be a pain in the ass—or the pocketbook."

"It's really not a problem. I'm just a little nervous about this."

"I'll be fine. There's more cover and concealment out here than I remembered, too."

"That works both ways," she said. "Be careful out there."

"I'd say something like 'careful is my middle name,' but I think that ship has sailed."

"Way over the horizon," she said. "Make sure you check in every half hour. If you miss a check-in by more than ten minutes, I'm sending the helicopter directly to your last reported position."

"Understood," said Decker. "I better get moving. I'll call you at eight with the first check-in. I have a few things to do before I start."

"Eight o'clock sharp," she said, ending the call.

Decker pocketed the phone and shut off the vehicle, stepping into the cool, crisp mountain air. At least he wouldn't be hiking in the heat.

The temperature in Aguilar wasn't predicted to rise over seventy degrees before noon. It would be a few degrees cooler up here. He did a few dozen jumping jacks to loosen up from the long drive, taking a few minutes after that to stretch his legs. The hills would wreck his quads and calves if he wasn't careful.

After stretching, he made his way to the back of the SUV and opened the lift gate. It wouldn't take him long to gear up and go. Hungry from the drive, he started to rummage through a plastic shopping bag filled with snacks and power bars, suddenly remembering the two slices of leftover pizza in the cooler jammed in the passenger footwell. He tossed the bag of snacks back into the rear compartment and walked around the SUV to retrieve the cooler.

Cooler in hand, he shut the passenger door and turned toward the back of the vehicle, freezing in place when he looked up. Brad Pierce stood a few feet behind the SUV, pointing a suppressed M4-style rifle at his head. He wore a coyote-brown tactical ballistic-plate carrier over a gray T-shirt, unzipped khaki cargo pants and loosely tied hiking boots completing his outfit. Pierce looked like he had just rushed out of his house. Decker stared at him for a few seconds, careful not to move.

"If I hadn't known you for more than half of my life," said Pierce, glancing at the cargo compartment, "I'd say it looked like you had come here to kill me."

There was no point to sugarcoating this. Pierce had the upper hand, and he'd never been tolerant of bullshit.

"The thought had crossed my mind," said Decker.

Pierce lowered the barrel of his rifle a few inches to look over the magnified sight. "Why the hell would you want to kill me, Ryan?"

"I talked to Penkin."

"Sounds like you did more than just talk to him."

"He told me an interesting story."

"I bet he did."

"Meghan Steele was kidnapped by a group of American mercenaries and handed to him for disposal, but they figured out who she was and kept her for future leverage."

"It sort of explains why she was still alive and there were no ransom demands," said Pierce.

"We get hired to find her by Senator Steele after the FBI investigation hits a wall," said Decker, "and pull off a near miracle by locating her."

"It was pretty miraculous," said Pierce. "What's your point?"

"We were never meant to find her. Penkin told me that the mercenary group got back in touch with him a few days before the Hemet raid, furious that she was still alive. He claims the mercenaries were behind the explosion. That it was a deliberate trap."

Pierce lowered his rifle a few more inches. "How did they know we found her?"

"That's what I came here to ask you."

"Me?" said Pierce. "You think I ratted us out?"

"Somebody did."

"The Russians got the jump on us. Plain and simple," said Pierce. "They fed us intel about a new shipment of kids to buy enough time to rig the place with explosives. They outplayed us, and it sounds like Penkin continued to play you until the very end. A mystery mercenary group behind everything? I don't think so."

"I wouldn't have believed it, either, until about forty-eight hours ago," said Decker. "I'm pretty sure the mercenaries worked for Aegis Global."

Pierce studied him for a moment before slinging the rifle over his shoulder.

"I'm sorry about what happened to your wife and son, Ryan," said Pierce. "I can't even begin to tell you how sorry. But you're starting to sound a bit unhinged. I don't know how else to say it."

"I have evidence linking them to the Hemet explosion."

"Aegis Global's CEO recommended us to Senator Steele. We'd done work for them in the past," said Pierce. "They knew we were the best in the business. Why would they hire us if there was any chance we could find Steele's daughter?"

"Because they didn't know she was still alive when they hired us," said Decker. "As far as they knew, there was no chance we could find her."

Pierce sighed. "There's no conspiracy, and nobody ratted us out. The Russians just hammered us! Repeatedly."

"Then how did you make it out unscathed?" said Decker. "You're the only other survivor. It's hard to get past that. Everyone else lost family that night, and everyone else ended up murdered—or they took their own lives."

"Wait. You actually think I'd be okay with getting my friends and their families killed?" said Pierce. "What is wrong with you?"

"You never went to trial, and the Bureau of Prisons has no record of you outside the Municipal Detention Center. You vanished a few months after Hemet, reappearing once to fake your family's deaths. Oh yeah—and to publish a bunch of articles about your phony release from prison."

"I didn't betray you, Ryan," said Pierce, slowly shaking his head. "I gave our files on the Bratva to the Department of Justice in exchange for my release. I also promised to testify against the Russians in court."

"What? They would have obtained those files anyway through their investigation of our firm."

"Maybe. Maybe not," said Pierce. "They technically weren't germane to the charges filed against us, and the encrypted cloud service used to store the information wasn't subject to US laws."

"The cloud service was based in San Jose—wait, you totally suckered them," said Decker, unable to suppress a grin.

"I tried to wrap everyone into that deal, but the feds wouldn't bite. I had to take it. Nobody was protecting my family. It was only a matter of time before the Russians got to them."

"Can I put the cooler down?" said Decker.

"As long as you don't plan on shooting me."

Decker lowered the cooler to the ground, shaking his head. "I'm embarrassed that the thought even crossed my mind. Sorry, Brad. I don't know what I was thinking."

Pierce shook his head. "What the Russians did was unforgivable. But we have to move on."

"I can't move on. I have to finish this."

"Penkin is dead, right? I assume you kidnapped him," said Pierce. "What else is there?"

"They used Penkin like the rest of us. There's more to the Steele kidnapping than the Russians. A lot more."

"Who's *they*? Aegis? Mercenaries?" said Pierce. "Come on, man. It's over."

"Did you have breakfast yet?"

"No. You kind of interrupted my breakfast plans."

"Is there a place we can sit down and grab a bite to eat? I need to show you a few things," said Decker. "Somewhere with decent coffee, maybe?"

"My house is the only place within fifty miles where you can get a good cup of coffee."

"I don't want to stress out Anna and the kids," said Decker. "I'm probably the last person they need to see right now."

"They'd actually love to see you. But I sent them away as soon as I saw the news about Penkin. I figured a storm was brewing and that you'd show up eventually—possibly bringing it with you. I hope I was wrong."

"You're right about the storm, but I didn't bring it here. Nobody followed me," said Decker. "How did you know I'd take this route?"

"I didn't," said Pierce. "A retired gunnery sergeant owns the house at the end of Main Street, just past the retention pond. Vietnam vet. Crusty old guy with an even crustier wife. I've gotten to know them pretty well over the past year. He saw you stop in front of the fork in the road and pull out a laptop. Not many shiny new SUVs go left at that fork. ATVs and a few Jeeps, mostly. Especially at seven in the morning on a weekday. He called me right away and followed your dust trail."

"Your place is like five miles from here."

"Five point two miles over land. Eight point five miles over some hard-packed dirt roads that I know like the back of my hand," said Pierce. "I got here two minutes before you arrived."

"Sounds like good people."

"Really good people," said Pierce. "He has you covered with one of his hunting rifles right now."

"Then I'll keep this formal." Decker extended a hand. "So I don't get shot."

Pierce grabbed his hand and yanked him in for a hug. "It's great to see you, man!"

"I can't even tell you how good it is to see you again," said Decker, slapping his back a few times before ending the hug. He wanted to cry, letting some of the pent-up emotion flow, but he kept it together—sort of.

"Look at us," said Pierce. "Two grown-ass men holding back the floodgates."

"I've had a lot of practice. Opening those floodgates can get you killed in prison."

"I can't imagine. How the hell did you manage to get out early? I thought you got ten years. Five no matter what."

"That's all part of what I need to show you. A team of military contractor types tried to kill me less than an hour after I was released. They weren't Russian."

"I know I'm going to regret this," said Pierce. "Follow the gunny out of here. He'll bring you out to the county road and around the other side of this ridge. I'll drive you the rest of the way."

Pierce produced a handheld radio from one of his vest pockets.

"That reminds me," said Decker. "I need to call off the cavalry."

"Cavalry? I thought you said nobody followed you."

"I have a helicopter team standing by in Denver. They were going to stage somewhere east of Aguilar by ten forty-five, in case you got the drop on me. So much for that plan."

"Did you use one of our old contacts to arrange this?"

He understood why Pierce was worried. Any of World Recovery Group's prior business contacts would be required by the Department of Justice to report the interaction. The helicopter that arrived would more than likely read *FBI* on the fuselage, followed closely by an armada of government SUVs.

"Negative. A friend set it up. No names involved. She's the only one that knows the location of your house," said Decker. "You can trust her. She saved me from the group that tried to kill me right after my phony prison release."

"I don't trust anyone," said Pierce. "That's why I live off the grid, homeschooling my kids and constantly explaining why we live in the middle of freaking nowhere."

"She'd never betray us. I'd stake my life on that."

"I'll hold you to that if anyone uninvited shows up."

"I can leave now. The last thing I want is to bring any trouble to your doorstep."

Pierce stared at him for a moment before shaking his head. "I'll listen to whatever you have to say. But there's something you need to know before we go anywhere."

"Okay," said Decker, intrigued by the last-moment confession.

"Someone else survived that night."

"Not according to my research," said Decker. "You were the only anomaly on the list. No death certificates. Everyone else had one. It's the only reason I started to look into you. When I saw the house in the hills on recent satellite imagery, I knew it had to be you."

"I guess it's all a matter of perspective," said Pierce. "I didn't see myself as the biggest anomaly."

"I don't follow."

"When I ran the same list, I saw a different name," said Pierce. "Kurt Aleman and his family were killed inside the house they were renting in Tampico, Mexico. It's on the Gulf of Mexico side, about two hundred miles from the Texas border."

He'd heard the news from his attorney. Aleman, his wife, and their three elementary school–aged children were found chopped to pieces and thrown in the backyard hot tub. Decker had assumed that the Russians had reached out to the Gulf cartel for a favor. The Bratva had a long-standing alliance with them to smuggle cocaine into Europe and the US.

"You think he faked his death?" said Decker. "The police found their bodies."

"The police found *bodies*. I hired one of our more discreet Mexican private investigators to do a little digging, because Aleman was the only member of our team to escape the FBI dragnet and truly vanish."

Decker nodded. That much was true. Call sign GRAVEYARD, Kurt Aleman had been overwatch for the teams rescuing the children at the Bratva house. Nobody heard from him again after the house exploded. Oddly enough, Decker hadn't given it a second thought. He figured Aleman had quickly put two and two together on the ridge overlooking the destroyed house—and took his family on the run.

"Without getting himself killed, the investigator got a few police officers to talk off the record," said Pierce. "The Alemans didn't die in Mexico."

"How did he determine that?"

"Here's how he put it," said Pierce. "None of the heads floating around in the hot tub had blond hair."

"Jesus."

"Yeah," said Pierce. "Aleman took faking his death to the next level."

"How do we find him? If he went to that kind of trouble to throw everyone off his trail, he's long gone by now."

"Maybe not."

"Sounds like we have a lot to talk about over breakfast."

CHAPTER THIRTY-EIGHT

Harlow disconnected the call with Decker and turned to Sophie, who had listened to the conversation on speakerphone.

"What do you think?" said Harlow.

"We're not paying for a second helicopter," she said. "They're on their own with this."

"That was my first thought, but I'm glad it worked out the way it did. The thought of Pierce betraying him made me sick. The two of them go back to the Naval Academy, more than twenty years ago."

"Sounds like you did a term paper on them," said Sophie, smirking.

"Funny," said Harlow, opening her laptop to check for the incoming email promised by Pierce.

"I'm being serious—sort of. You seem a little too attached to this."

"It's hard not to get attached to a case like this," said Harlow. "It goes beyond Decker and his crew getting framed. Whoever was behind the Steele kidnapping crossed the line. Repeatedly. They moved fifteen kids into that house right before the raid, knowing they'd all be killed. Not to mention what they did to World Recovery Group's families."

"That's not what I'm talking about," said Sophie. "I think you're too attached to Decker, and I'm not the only one that feels that way."

"Is there something wrong with that?"

"What would you say if I got too attached to one of our clients?"

"Decker isn't a client."

"That's an entirely different conversation we'll need to have if this drags on any longer," said Sophie.

"Drags on?" said Harlow. "What's going on here?"

"Nothing. I'm just worried that you're sinking too much into this for the wrong reason."

"I'm doing this for the right reason," said Harlow. "I thought we were all on the same page with that."

"We are, as long as there's a path forward. Which it appears there is, but it's kind of out of our hands at this point—and we're trapped here until the situation is resolved. We're completely relying on Decker right now, which leaves me with an uncomfortable feeling. I thought it would be the other way around."

"I did, too, but things have changed," said Harlow. "We got him on his feet, running strong. If he convinces Pierce to join him, they'll be a force to be reckoned with on the ground, but they'll still need our support. Without it, Decker can only go so far. The team we've assembled here will be the deciding factor in the end. I'm convinced of it."

"It's just hard to see right now," said Sophie. "Decker is swinging from one loose thread to another. If this Texas lead doesn't pan out, I'm not sure where we go from here."

"True enough. The only idea I have left is to dangle him in public as bait to get the fish biting again. All we'd have to do is drive him around for a while. City cameras would do the rest of the work," said Harlow. "I imagine he wouldn't be very keen about painting a bull's-eye on his forehead."

"You might be surprised what he's willing to do to get at these people. It's actually not a bad idea."

"If we can control most of the variables," said Harlow. "Which we can't."

"I don't know. Katie is pretty good at stacking the deck in our favor."

"She is, but this Gunther Ross guy isn't going to make the same mistakes twice. We burned him pretty badly—both times. He won't underestimate us."

Sophie took a sip of her orange juice. "What else can we do?"

"Keep running surveillance. Hope Ross screws up."

"No. I mean . . . what haven't we looked into yet?" said Sophie. "So much has come to light over the past twenty-four hours. We need to work backward from what we know and connect some more dots. I guarantee we've missed something."

"I keep thinking about something we talked about yesterday," said Harlow. "How this is all tied to the kidnapping."

"Right. The big picture. Why kidnap Meghan Steele with no intention of returning her? We have enough pieces to start assembling the bigger picture. Assigning motivations to entities we haven't considered yet."

Pam and Sandra joined them in the great room, sitting around the glass coffee table.

"What's the plan?" said Pam. "Other than hiring a chef. I'm not eating any more of those frozen meals."

"I'm not cooking," said Sophie.

"I don't cook," said Pam.

"This is pretty much a takeout crew," said Sandra.

"We can't do takeout for twelve people every day for every meal," said Harlow. "It's too much exposure. I'll find a chef who can come in during the morning and prepare food for the day. The house is big enough to hide our SCIF team."

"Sounds kind of expensive," said Sandra, avoiding eye contact with her.

"I'll cover it," said Harlow. "Like I'll cover the house."

"We're all covering the house," said Sophie. "That's what we agreed."

"Anything past a week and I'm covering it. Seriously."

"You don't have to do that," said Pam. "It's not like we can go back to our normal lives with these people stalking us. We're not going anywhere until this is resolved."

"I can't promise it'll move very fast," said Harlow. "We just got off the phone with Decker and Brad Pierce. They've identified a possible third survivor of the World Recovery Group purge. They're convinced he's the mole that brought the whole thing down, but the information they're working off is thin. Lots of assumptions."

"Do they have a location?" said Sandra.

"Texas. In the middle of nowhere," said Harlow. "And that's purely based on an assumption. If this turns out to be a dead end, I'm not sure how we move forward."

"Harlow floated the possibility of using Decker as bait," said Sophie.

"And just when I thought she had a crush on him," said Pam.

"Nice," said Harlow. "He's a client."

"You just said he wasn't a client," said Sophie.

"Whatever. You all know what I mean."

"Using him as bait might be our only option. His only option," said Pam.

"That's what I was thinking," said Sophie. "He'd probably agree to it."

"Let's cross that bridge when we get there," said Harlow. "Right now, Sophie and I were thinking we could put our heads together and start from the beginning. From Meghan Steele's kidnapping. I'd lost sight of the fact that her kidnapping started all of this, and it somehow served a purpose for someone. If we can come up with some theories for who and why, we might be able to pursue this whole thing from a different angle."

"What variables do we have to work with?" said Sandra.

"Scratch the Russians," said Pam.

"Don't count them out completely," said Sophie. "They might link to one of the other variables in a way we didn't expect. Aegis, or whoever these mercenary types turn out to be working for, knew enough to hand Meghan Steele off to them."

Katie walked into the room from the kitchen. "Am I the only one working?"

"We're brainstorming," said Sophie.

Katie raised an eyebrow. "Like I said."

They all laughed.

"How is the countersurveillance going?" said Harlow.

"Not great," she said. "The FBI has teams at half of the locations, including our office, and Gunther Ross's crew is watching all of them—with off-duty cops or sheriff's deputies. I kind of want to knock on all of their car windows and explain how it's one big circular dead end."

"Except Ross's people would grab you off the street," said Pam.

"They can try. You know me, I don't go anywhere without a plan," said Katie. "So. What are we brainstorming? Lunch and dinner?"

Sophie pointed at Harlow. "She's getting us a chef."

"We're all not prima donnas here," said Katie. "I can cook for a dozen people. I just need to run into the valley to pick up supplies."

"I want to keep our exposure outside this house to a minimum," said Harlow.

"We can avoid facial recognition. Limit our trips out to one every three days or so, changing locations. We'll be fine."

"We'll have to plan it out in advance," said Harlow. "Take no chances."

"I think it's better than bringing someone in. You never know who or what you're getting in a situation like that."

"The more I think about it, the less sense bringing someone in makes to me," said Sophie. "If they caught a whiff of what was going on with the SCIF crew, they might call the police, which would put us on the radar. Ross obviously has local law enforcement connections.

It seems like half of the city's off-duty officers are working surveillance for him."

"Good point," said Harlow. "We'll plan a few trips into the valley to get supplies for a one- to two-week stay."

"I'll start working on a list," said Katie.

"There's no hurry," said Sandra. "We can eat the frozen stuff and order some pizzas for a few days. The longer we give the situation on the ground to settle, the better."

"Fair enough," said Katie, taking a seat on the leather couch next to Harlow. "So what's this brainstorming all about?"

"We're going back to Meghan Steele's kidnapping," said Harlow. "To try to figure out why she was taken."

"She wasn't kidnapped, from my perspective. She was murdered. Whoever grabbed Meghan Steele signed her death warrant. My guess is it's related to Aegis. Dig into Aegis first."

"But Jacob Harcourt recommended World Recovery Group to Senator Steele," said Harlow. "If Aegis is behind this, why would the CEO of Aegis run the risk of hiring the best in the business? Unless—"

"He knew she couldn't be found—because she was dead and buried," said Sophie. "Decker sounded crazy when he said that."

"It doesn't sound so crazy anymore," said Harlow, sitting back. "Let's get to work on this. Every angle. Every person. Every entity. We map it all out, starting with Aegis."

CHAPTER
THIRTY-NINE

Decker stood on Pierce's timber deck and took in the incredible view with his third cup of Bolivian coffee. He wasn't sure which he was enjoying more at the moment. Pierce's house faced west, situated at the bottom of a wide draw between east-west-running ridges. The arrangement gave him an unrestricted view of the Sangre de Cristos' twin snow-capped peaks, rising above a sea of deep-green pines. He'd vastly underappreciated this view when Pierce brought him out here a few years ago.

He looked at Pierce, who stared pensively up the gently sloping, pine tree–scattered valley.

"I thought you were crazy when you brought me out here," said Decker. "There was nothing but the view."

"That's all that matters," said Pierce.

"Which one—the view or nothing out here?"

"Both."

Decker laughed. "I guess you were on to something. I definitely missed the secret lair memo."

"I never meant this to be a permanent hideout," said Pierce. "Just a place to bring the family and get away from it all. There's some good hunting out here, too."

"I noticed the taxidermy shops. Looked like the only permanent businesses in town."

Pierce grinned. "The café has changed hands three times since we arrived. I think it's a bakery now."

"I hate to break it to you, but the bakery is out of business."

"Really? Crap. That was the only place within fifteen miles that served food, unless you count the gas station off the interstate."

"You guys get out at all?"

"We get groceries down in Trinidad twice a month," said Pierce. "There's a nice state park there on the lake, and a few decent Mexican restaurants."

"I don't want to drag you away from here," said Decker. "Anna would never forgive me if you didn't come back."

"She'll understand. I mean, how long can we actually stay here? The kids are growing up. It's only a matter of time before this place won't work for us anymore. It's barely working now. We have a chance to get out from under this."

"Maybe," said Decker. "The kids are almost in high school, right?"

"With the homeschooling, we have them taking a high school course load. There's not much out here to distract them. Nicki technically finished her sophomore year requirements in May. Thomas will be done with his freshman year in a month or so."

Thomas and Decker's son, Michael, had been friends. Not close friends, since they lived in different towns, but close enough for this conversation to hit Decker hard. Tears welled up in his eyes and he turned away, taking a deep breath.

"Not a day has gone by that I haven't thought about your family, Ryan," said Pierce. "Not a single day. I feel guilty every time I look at my family. This may sound stupid to you, or even insulting. I don't know. But the guilt can be crippling at times. Anna sees it, and I can tell she's getting worried."

"It's not stupid, or insulting," said Decker, staring off into the undisturbed valley. "It's the mess those assholes left us."

"Count me in."

"You should call Anna."

"I'll call her from the road," said Pierce. "We need to get moving."

"We should wait for Harlow's team to put together their package."

"It's a big camouflaged hole in the ground with a house in it. If we leave now, we can be in position before nightfall."

"You think we should do this at night?" said Decker.

"The nearest cover is two miles away to the east. I'm not crossing over flat ground during the day. If Kurt's watching, he'll pick us off before we can get a decent shot at him."

"Maybe we should consider a different approach," said Decker. "Something we can do during the day."

"Like what? It's flat on all sides."

"When was the last time you went skydiving?"

PART THREE

Chapter Forty

Decker sat facing aft on the floor of the Cessna 182, between the pilot and starboard-side door. Pierce sat across from him, his knees tucked into the drop bag attached to his chest. He shook his head with a grin.

"What?" said Decker.

"I'm just trying to figure out how I let you talk me into this," Pierce said over the steady buzz of the engine.

"You volunteered. Remember?"

"This is not one of your better plans."

Decker shrugged his shoulders through the skydiving rig. "At least it's not my worst."

The pilot tapped his shoulder. "We're about five miles out!"

He checked the Garmin Foretrex 601 attached to his right wrist. They were 5.3 miles from the drop zone, at an altitude of ten thousand feet. The plan was to jump one mile out and fall the rest of the way, deploying their parachutes around a thousand feet over the target. The tactic mimicked a military-style high-altitude low-opening (HALO) jump but took place at a lower altitude, so they would not require the use of oxygen.

Decker gave the pilot a thumbs-up and scooted closer to the door. At their current speed, they'd reach the jump mark in just under two minutes. Thirty seconds out, the pilot would cut the aircraft's speed in half, to seventy-five miles per hour, ensuring a smooth jump.

The pilot still looked unsure about the mission. He'd initially balked at the proposal, obviously uncomfortable dropping two strangers over private land, but a thick envelope of cash representing a sizable chunk of Decker's reserve money had gotten them off the runway. If the pilot backed out now, there wasn't much they could do, other than pull a gun on him—which was exactly what Decker would do to ensure the mission continued.

He'd stowed a pistol in one of his zippered cargo pockets; it would be the only weapon readily available to him until they hit the ground. They had broken down their rifles to fit inside the drop bags, along with the rest of the gear that would have ended in a 911 call by the pilot. Tactical vests. Drop holsters. Spare rifle magazines. Night-vision goggles. The kind of stuff you brought to a gunfight.

A minute later, the aircraft slowed significantly, and he opened the aircraft door, flooding the cabin with cool, mildly turbulent air. Below the exposed wingtip, a deep orange sunset lit the horizon. It would be considerably darker on the ground, the sun having already disappeared to anyone at ground level.

Decker kept his eyes on the stunning, distant view for now, not wanting to raise his heart rate any higher. Even though he had a few hundred free-fall jumps under his belt, it had been a while since his last drop, and he was well aware of the limitation imposed by that gap. Skydiving wasn't complicated, but he could have used a little more time going over the equipment and procedures. Pierce said it was like riding a bike, but a bike didn't go 120 miles per hour toward the ground. The margin of error would be minimal out there.

"Thirty seconds!" said the pilot.

He confirmed the pilot's announcement on his Garmin and edged forward until his legs dangled out of the fuselage. A glance between the Garmin and the altimeter on his left wrist verified that they read the same—for now. Once he stabilized in the air, he'd rely on the altimeter for altitude and the Garmin for directions. Pierce had insisted that they use both, since the GPS unit's altitude refresh rate was slower than the dedicated altimeter. It all circled back to margin of error.

"See you on the ground," said Pierce, slapping his shoulder.

"Not if I see you first," said Decker, mindlessly repeating one of the oldest, and possibly lamest, jokes in the military.

Decker took several deep breaths, focusing on the serenity of a sunset view few people would ever experience. He had mostly calmed his mind when the pilot tapped his helmet.

"We're over the mark! You're clear to jump!"

He nodded and pulled himself clear of the fuselage, where he was immediately whisked away from the aircraft. Decker tumbled a few times before somewhat steadying in a belly-to-earth position, the air rattling his body. Over the next few seconds, he wobbled like a newbie as he experimented with arm and leg positions. By the time Pierce appeared in his peripheral vision to the right, Decker had stabilized his descent.

His eyes drifted to the altimeter, noting that they'd already fallen two thousand feet. At this rate, without deploying his parachute, he'd hit the ground in under a minute. Ticktock. He glanced at the Garmin, the illuminated arrow telling him that he was pointed roughly ninety degrees in the wrong direction. A few minor upper-arm adjustments turned him toward the drop zone. Now for the hard part—gliding toward the drop zone.

During his skydiving heyday, he could track through the air with a one-to-one glide ratio, which meant for every foot dropped vertically, he glided the same distance laterally. Tonight, he'd be lucky to see a one-to-two ratio, which meant he needed to start tracking toward the drop zone immediately. Pierce simultaneously came to the same conclusion, sweeping his arms back and rocketing forward at an alarming rate. Decker hesitated, fully aware that every second he delayed would cost him distance on the ground.

"Screw it," he muttered, sweeping his arms back until his hands were by his thighs.

He instantly tracked forward, chasing Pierce, who continued to open the distance between them. The last vestiges of sunlight kept Pierce visible while Decker tweaked his body position to gain enough forward momentum to stop the rapid separation. He'd forgotten to check his Garmin before initiating the glide, so he was completely relying on his friend to guide them over the drop zone.

They tracked through the air for roughly thirty seconds before Pierce suddenly started to rise. Decker swept his arms forward, arresting the glide and meeting Pierce's altitude. His altimeter read seventeen hundred feet above ground level; the Garmin placed him just over twenty-five hundred feet from the drop zone due north of their target. He did some quick math and swept his arms back, counting to four before returning to a stable belly-to-earth position. One thousand feet above ground level. Two thousand feet from the DZ. Pierce was nowhere in sight.

Decker glanced along the right side of his body and located the bright-orange pilot-chute handle protruding from his skydiving rig. He pulled it out and to the right, extending his hand as far as it could reach—his body tugged violently, but most reassuringly, upward. The momentarily unforgiving thrashing meant one thing—your parachute had opened.

A few seconds later, he grabbed the toggles dangling from the main harness lines and took positive control of the parachute, using the back-lit Garmin to point him in the right direction. Settled on a course for the DZ, he searched the sky, locating another square shape above him. His last-second maneuver to get closer to the drop zone had put him back in the lead position.

Decker scanned the deep-rust-colored landscape, still unable to discern anything remotely resembling what they'd seen in the satellite images. They'd guessed it would be nearly impossible to spot from an angle at dusk, since it had barely been visible in the pictures taken from directly above, but Decker had hoped to see something. Even a flicker of light would give him hope that they hadn't dropped into the middle of Texas on a fool's errand.

At four hundred feet, the sun disappeared; the dark-blue twilight swallowed him. Decker checked his Garmin, making a final adjustment to his course by pulling the left toggle until the arrow pointed directly ahead. He took a moment to find the release handle for the drop bag attached to the front of his rig before settling in for the final approach. Pierce must have dumped air at some point during the descent, dropping in right next to him. His altimeter read one hundred feet above ground level.

At fifty feet AGL, Decker released the drop bag, which skimmed the hardscrabble ground, tugging gently on his harness. He pulled the toggles as the ground reached up for him, flaring the parachute and landing smoothly on his feet. The victory was short-lived, as a strong westerly gust filled his collapsing parachute and yanked him off his feet, dragging him nearly fifty yards before he finally slipped out of the harness.

Decker lay there dazed, convinced he had broken every bone in his body, until a dark figure materialized in the distance—headed his way. He sat up and unzipped the cargo pocket holding his pistol, scrambling to draw it. When he finally cleared the weapon from his pocket, a strong hand gripped his wrist, pressing the weapon down.

"Ryan. It's me," said a familiar voice. "Let go of the pistol. You look like you're going to shoot me."

Decker dropped the pistol onto his thigh. "Sorry. I'm a little messed up right now."

"Did you break anything?"

"I don't know," he said. "I don't think so."

"I'm pulling you up," said Pierce, grabbing both of his hands. "Ready?"

"Yep," said Decker, bracing for pain.

Pierce pulled him to his feet. "How does that feel?"

"Like hell," said Decker, testing his legs. "But nothing's broken."

"We need to get moving," said Pierce, pushing a nylon line into his hand. "Follow this to your drop bag and get prepped to move on the target."

"Which way is the target?" said Decker. "Sorry."

Pierce pointed to Decker's left. "About a hundred yards in that direction. Just past that slight rise."

"They shouldn't be able to see us," said Decker, his head starting to clear.

"Unless someone saw us land. Which is why we need to get moving."

"I'll meet you just below the rise."

While Pierce took off to find his drop bag, Decker tugged on the line, following it to the overstuffed duffel bag–shaped kit, which lay fifty feet away toward the orange-and-light-blue horizon. He unzipped the bag, removing the two rifle parts first. Priorities. He tore the packing tape off the back of the upper receiver, careful not to yank the bolt carrier or charging handle out with it. Satisfied that everything had survived the parachute drop, he connected the lower and upper receivers, securing them in place with the attached takedown pins.

He pulled the charging handle back and released it, then flipped the selector switch to "fire." Everything felt right so far. A quick trigger press yielded a definitive click inside the rifle. Perfect. Decker fished a loose thirty-round magazine out of his cargo pocket and inserted it into the rifle before yanking the charging handle back again. He engaged the safety and placed the weapon on the ground next to the bag.

His next order of business was the plate carrier. They'd agreed to leave the eight-pound metal ballistic plate behind, to reduce the chance of damaging the other gear in the drop, so the plate carrier was essentially an ammunition carrier at this point. With the vest fitted snuggly over his torso, he retrieved the final piece of gear from the bag. A pair of night-vision goggles.

Decker nestled the head mount into place and connected the chin strap, pulling it tight. He attached the PVS-14 night-vision monocular to the head mount and turned it on, assessing its functionality with a quick scan of his surroundings. Pierce had already started toward the target. Flipping the device up and out of his face, he set off for their rendezvous.

CHAPTER
FORTY-ONE

Gunther Ross reclined in one of the cheap, bulk office chairs that had been delivered to the warehouse with the operations center team's equipment. He glanced at the main screen above Robert Cooper's analyst team, wondering how much longer Harcourt would allow this to continue without results. Decker and Mackenzie's known business partners had vanished two nights ago, remaining effectively off the grid for the entire forty-eight-hour period. He had to admit it was an impressive feat given the resources put at his disposal. Ross wasn't sure even he could pull off that kind of a disappearing act.

Jessica Arnay, Mackenzie's firm's attorney and a suspected business partner, had remained in plain sight. He suspected her continued presence was most likely due to the time-sensitive and schedule-driven nature of her work on behalf of several rescue organizations that specialized in advocacy for trafficked or domestically abused victims. He'd contemplated grabbing her but decided against it. Arnay wouldn't know where the others had settled. She might be able to shed some light on a few links he hadn't discovered, but it wouldn't be worth the attention another high-profile kidnapping would generate. The attorney didn't go anywhere without a serious-looking security team that would require lethal means to neutralize. He'd only go there as a last resort.

He'd started to wonder if they'd left town. On the surface it made sense, but something told him that neither Mackenzie nor Decker would simply walk away. Ross had dispatched teams to check on Decker's estranged daughter in North Carolina and his parents in Minnesota after it became apparent that Decker was interested in more than vanishing without a trace. The teams reported that everyone had disappeared. Decker had somehow managed to remove them from the equation, probably with Mackenzie's help. He'd denied Ross leverage, which meant he wasn't done.

His phone rang; caller ID indicated it was Derek Green. He'd meant to call Green a little later and tell him to grab Kurt Aleman. There was no sense in keeping him out there another day. He answered the call.

"Hey. I want you to get Aleman in the morning," said Gunther.

"I don't think we can wait that long. Two parachutists just landed north of Aleman's location. You were right. Decker figured it out."

"Unbelievable," said Gunther, standing up. "How far away did they land?"

"My observers couldn't tell," said Green. "The parachutists disappeared right after they landed. It looked like a HALO jump. Very low-altitude opening. We never heard the plane."

"Could they have landed directly on the target and already breached?"

"I don't think—hold on," said Green. "Negative. They're up and moving again. What do you want us to do?"

"Were you able to get any further sense of potential escape routes?"

"I don't have a good sense of that place at all," said Green. "Other than some light escaping the ground at night, and some thermal irregularities, you wouldn't know it was here. That and the trail leading away from the road."

"All right. Hit the target. Stay connected at all times. I want a live feed. How long until the strike team hits?"

"Ten to fifteen minutes," said Green. "I have the vehicles staged behind a motel a few miles away. Then it's another five miles down the dirt trail to the target. We'll pick up the observation team on the way."

"Be careful," said Gunther. "We don't know who Decker brought along for the ride."

CHAPTER
FORTY-TWO

Decker canted his rifle and glanced at the Garmin on his wrist. Ten feet from the northern edge of the target, and all he saw in front of him was a completely flat expanse of central Texas hardscrabble. Kurt Aleman had done an exceptional job camouflaging this place, if he was indeed here. He took a few more steps before sinking to a knee and signaling Pierce. His friend moved up and settled in a foot away.

"Maybe I was wrong," whispered Pierce.

"There's definitely something out here," said Decker. "Has to be. The tire tracks in the satellite picture ended at the edge of the circle on the other side."

"Whatever we do, we need to do it fast," said Pierce. "We're awfully exposed right now."

Exposed was an understatement.

"Has to be a trapdoor or something on this side." Decker scanned left and right, still unable to find any indication that the ground ahead of him was fake.

"Maybe we should just walk around to the tire tracks," said Pierce.

"Hold on," said Decker, flipping the night-vision device in place over the left side of his face.

He panned back and forth, studying the green image. Nothing. He'd almost given up when he noticed a small crack of light toward the front of the target area, where he'd expect a larger door to exist to allow a vehicle in and out of the ground.

"I have something. A faint crack of light on the other side of the target," he said, rising off his knee. "This is crazy."

The longer he stared at the image, the more light he saw, until he could vaguely see the circular perimeter of Aleman's underground compound. From the satellite imagery, they calculated the diameter of the circle to be seventy-five feet, yielding roughly four thousand square feet. A tenth of an acre. All underground.

"I see it now," said Pierce. "If he hadn't run his mouth about this place, he could have kept it hidden forever."

"I get the impression he didn't expect anyone to survive long enough for that to be an issue."

"I still don't see any other hatches or openings."

"Neither do I, but there has to be something," said Decker.

"This could take all night."

"We don't have all night," said a voice behind them.

Decker tensed, his hand shifting slowly to his rifle's grips.

"No sudden movements. I have both of you covered."

"Aleman?" said Decker.

"Yes," he said. "I recognize Decker's voice, but I'm drawing a blank on . . ."

"Pierce."

"Makes sense. Your demise in Idaho wasn't very convincing," said Aleman.

"I wasn't willing to murder a family to cover my tracks."

"I didn't murder that family," said Aleman. "I paid the city coroner to keep an eye out for something useful. The Guzmans died of asphyxiation in their house. An accident. Gas fumes from a faulty pilot light. I would never do something like that."

"It didn't feel like a stretch for you."

Decker ran his options. He could drop and twist without warning, firing as he fell. Aleman's rifle would instinctively follow Decker. Possibly hitting him. Possibly not. Pierce's bullets would undoubtedly find their mark. He gave himself a fifty-fifty chance of coming out of it unscathed. Good odds given the alternative, but something kept him from moving—and it wasn't a sense of self-preservation.

"What did you mean by 'We don't have all night'?" said Decker.

"I'm pretty sure I've been under observation for the past few days," said Aleman. "Unless you're part of the group watching me, I suspect your dramatic entry will force their hand."

"We're on our own."

"Then we really don't have much time," said Aleman, walking past them with a rifle slung over his shoulder. "We need to get below."

Pierce and Decker raised their rifles at the same time. Aleman stared at them, his face washed out in the green image.

"I'll never forgive myself for what happened, and I don't expect you to, either," said Aleman. "But I would never have put you or your families in danger."

"Then why?" said Decker. "Why did you do it?"

"Can we get below?"

"Not until you answer the question."

"I did it because they threatened my family," said Aleman. "That's why I should have known they'd go further than they did."

"How far were they supposed to go?"

"They wanted up-to-date information on our rescue mission. That's it. I honestly thought it was a group of mercenaries hired by Aegis to make sure we didn't botch the mission. I figured they had their own strike team standing by in case ours failed. An insurance policy. It was their ass on the line, too. Right? Jacob Harcourt hired us. It was in his best interest to make sure we didn't miss something or botch the rescue."

"All Harcourt had to do was ask to put a liaison on the team to double-check our process," said Decker. "They threatened your family and you didn't think something was off?"

"How was I supposed to make the jump from a veiled threat to what happened?"

"Doesn't sound like much of a jump," said Decker. "You should have come to me. I would have shut them down immediately."

"I don't know what else to say, Decker, other than I'm sorry," said Aleman. "Can we go inside now?"

"No. I don't see any threats out here," said Decker. "You see anything, Brad?"

"Looks clear for miles."

"They're out there. To the south, where my property meets the road."

"I don't really care," said Decker. "What was your plan for dealing with the FBI?"

"I didn't have a plan. I was just as surprised as you," said Aleman. "Look, I'm sorry, Ryan. I should have come to you as soon as they showed up. I let it go too far." He sighed. "I don't expect any mercy from you."

"Mercy?"

"I assume you're here to kill me."

"This disaster has ruined enough families," said Decker. "I came here for information. I'm going to take the people responsible for all of this down."

"I have a file," said Aleman. "It's been an obsession of mine."

"Mine, too."

"I can imagine."

"No. You can't."

"Sorry. You're right," said Aleman. "We need to go below now."

"The Russians are behind this somehow," said Decker, testing him. He wasn't about to descend into Aleman's pit without some sense of what this traitor knew. If Decker detected the slightest hint of treachery, he wouldn't hesitate to go back on his words and kill him.

"The Russians were used—just like me."

"Why do you think Aegis is involved?" said Decker, glancing at Pierce. "It was Jacob Harcourt's idea to hire us in the first place."

"I don't know," said Aleman. "But I managed to identify the man that served as my go-between with whoever was behind all of this."

"Gunther Ross?"

"No," he said. "Who's Gunther Ross?"

"You better not be lying to me."

Aleman took a few steps toward him. There was no defiance to this gesture. Only surety, from what he could tell. "I've never heard the name Gunther Ross," he said. "My handler went by the name of Chris Barton, and they killed him with all the rest, from what I can tell."

"Killed the rest?"

"I counted thirty-one accidental deaths or unresolved disappearances. All people with some kind of past connection to an Aegis subsidiary company. My handler was one of them, which is why I started to look into it. Someone wanted all ties to the Steele disaster severed."

"That's too many people for just the Hemet operation," said Pierce.

"My guess is that a lot of them were involved in the rest of it," said Aleman.

"*The rest of it* being the family murders," said Decker.

"That's what I think. I just don't have any direct proof. Just two years of staring at this day in and day out, trying to make sense of the nightmare I unleashed."

"How much did they pay you?" said Pierce.

"I never asked for money. I told you, they threatened my family."

"You didn't answer the question," said Decker.

"It wasn't about the money."

"But you took money?" said Decker, his hands tightening on the rifle.

"They insisted. I didn't have a choice, and I knew they'd never pay."

"You didn't get paid?"

"They paid a hundred thousand up front," said Aleman.

"What did they promise on the back end?"

"One million," said Aleman. "I knew that number was BS."

"They never paid?"

"No," said Aleman. "They hit my house the same night as everyone else's."

"But you had already sent your family away," said Decker, lowering his rifle.

"Yeah."

"You know what happened to my family, right?"

Aleman nodded.

"Why you?" said Pierce. "Why did Aegis approach you?"

"I honestly don't know. I wish I did. Not that it would matter."

"You didn't have some kind of massive debt or bad investment hanging over you?" said Decker.

"No. Everything was—perfect," said Aleman, his voice cracking. "I don't know why they picked me. It never made sense."

As much as Decker wanted to hold Aleman responsible for everything, he couldn't. What he'd said so far made sense, and unless Aleman had always been a practiced liar, he sounded sincerely remorseful.

"I think I know why," said Decker. "They somehow knew you'd be on your own the night of the raid, watching over the rescue teams—and that you'd run when the house went up. They wanted you to escape the scene."

"So they could kill me right away," said Aleman. "Cutting the link to Aegis."

"You were the last person they wanted in FBI custody," said Decker.

A buzzing noise interrupted them.

"It's the phone in my vest," said Aleman. "Can I grab it?"

"You get a lot of calls out here?" said Decker.

"I manage the security system with a smartphone, using a wireless connection," said Aleman. "There's no cell coverage within ten miles of this place."

"Go ahead. Just keep your hands off the rifle," said Decker. "Actually. Brad. If you don't mind?"

Aleman lifted the rifle off his shoulder by the sling and let Pierce take it.

"Can I check the phone now without getting shot?"

"Go ahead," said Decker.

Aleman dug into a pouch mounted high on his plate carrier, retrieving the illuminated phone. He stared at the screen for a moment before pressing a few buttons.

"We have company," said Aleman. "Multiple vehicles just passed through the gate."

"How many?" said Decker.

"Eight."

"How long until they get here?"

"I won't know for sure until they hit the next sensor," said Aleman. "But it's five miles."

"Is the road sturdy?"

"Very sturdy. They can hit sixty miles per hour if the vehicles are solid."

"They'll be very solid—and armored," said Decker.

"That gives us five minutes tops," said Pierce.

"Five minutes to do what?" said Decker. "There's nowhere to go."

"That's not exactly true," said Pierce. "Looks can be deceiving out here."

"How deceiving?"

"Sneak-up-behind-you deceiving," said Aleman.

Pierce chuckled. "He's easy to sneak up on these days."

"Funny," said Decker. "A few tunnels isn't going to help us against thirty-plus armed mercenaries."

"Then we'll have to even the odds," said Aleman.

"How?" said Pierce.

"I said the road was sturdy, not safe," said Aleman, leaning down and opening a hatch. "We need to hurry."

Decker stared at the illuminated hole leading down into Aleman's lair, thinking this was a mistake. He didn't trust the guy any more now than he had when they hit the ground—despite Aleman's explanation and apology. Something told him that one of them wasn't coming out of that hole.

"Down the rabbit hole," said Pierce. "You first."

"There has to be another option," said Decker.

"There isn't," said Aleman. "We'll have a fighting chance down below."

Decker scanned the horizon around them, then shook his head. "Rabbit hole it is," he said, before climbing down the ladder.

Chapter Forty-Three

Decker hit the dusty ground hard, having jumped halfway down the ladder to clear the way. His knees took the brunt of the fall, crackling under the weight of his frame and gear. Probably not the best idea, but five minutes would go in a snap. Every second would count. Before he straightened up, Aleman landed a few feet away, rolling onto his side, followed immediately by Pierce, who landed like a cat.

Decker scanned his surroundings. They had landed at the back of a long patch of flattened dirt dividing smooth, ground-to-ceiling earthen walls. An aboveground pool and a swing set sat in the middle of the dirt strip, partially obscuring his view of two four-wheel-drive vehicles. A Jeep Wrangler and an SUV he couldn't identify sat parked in front of a steep ramp that terminated at the ceiling at the opposite side of the circle.

The timber ceiling, about twenty feet high, was held up by an extensive system of wood beams and reinforced metal supports. Light fixtures hung from the beams, flooding the open area with light. He was surprised by how little of the light actually escaped through the roof. Halfway down the ceiling, a garage door opener hung by metal support brackets, its track leading to a point just above the vehicles.

At first glance, he couldn't help being impressed with the structure, but the awe quickly faded to pity, his anger toward Aleman dropping another notch.

"You've lived down here for two years?" he said, turning to Aleman.

"Mostly. It isn't as bad as it looks," said Aleman, unconvincingly.

"I guess."

"What was your long-term plan?" said Pierce.

"Stay down here for five years," said Aleman. "And hope it all went away."

"Not much of a plan," said Decker. "Or life."

"I didn't think I deserved much more."

Decker turned to Aleman. "I'll never forgive you, but when this is all over, I want you to live a normal life with your family. They don't deserve this."

Aleman's phone buzzed again. "They're past the one-mile mark, moving seventy miles per hour."

"How do we defend this place?" said Decker.

"We don't."

"Fuck this," said Pierce, heading back to the ladder.

Decker started to follow.

"I have a plan," said Aleman. "But it doesn't involve turning this place into the Alamo. We buy some time."

"Time for what?" said Decker.

"Time for us to slip out of here."

"If we're going to use those vehicles to escape, I suggest we get moving," said Pierce.

"No. I have something better. Follow me," said Aleman, heading toward a doorway on the left side of the underground structure.

Pierce gave Decker a severely skeptical look.

"I know," said Decker, chasing after Aleman.

When Aleman reached the door, he grabbed the handle and paused.

"Watch your step. We built the structures a foot off the ground," he said. "It doesn't rain much here, but when it does, the pump system can't handle all of it. This whole space is a shallow pool when we get a big weather system. The kids love it."

Decker stepped over the high lip and into a high-ceilinged room that looked like any other family room you might walk into around the country—except it had no windows. Instead, basic Southwest landscape murals had been painted on the wall facing the central dirt patch. He followed Aleman through the expansive living space into an equally well-appointed kitchen. Once again, the outside wall featured a mural, but this time was a Caribbean water view with pastel rooftops and moored sailboats.

"Not your typical Texas view," said Aleman. "But that's where we hoped to end up someday."

"The air feels different in here," said Decker, hustling to keep up.

"Both houses are climate controlled. The other side is mainly used for supplies," said Aleman. "Mostly to maintain a normal humidity level. The space between them stays reasonably cool year-round due to the depth, and the houses are well insulated. Rammed-earth walls. But it's dry as hell out here year-round."

When Aleman disappeared through another doorway, Pierce whispered from behind, "It's like living on another planet."

Decker shrugged before entering a spacious office with several computer screens and a few shelves of blinking electronics. Aleman had already taken a seat and started typing in front of an expansive curved-screen monitor. By the time Decker and Pierce had piled into the room, the screen displayed a satellite map of the property with color-coded overlays and an array of symbols.

"Wow. This looks as *Star Wars* as your underground abode," said Pierce. "That's how I found you, by the way. That and about two thousand hours of staring at satellite images."

"I figured that's how you found me," said Aleman. "Probably the same for them. I loved to joke about how I was going to live like Uncle Owen."

"Who's Uncle Owen?" said Decker.

"Seriously?" said Pierce. "Even I know who Uncle Owen is. Luke Skywalker's uncle in the original *Star Wars* movie. They had that cool underground house on Tatooine."

"Must have missed that detail," said Decker, leaning over Aleman's shoulder. "What are we looking at here?"

"They triggered the sensor set to cover the access road," said Aleman. "Then hit the sensors at four miles out."

"What's all this other crap?" said Decker.

"More sensors."

"How many sensors do you have?"

"On the road?"

"On the property," said Decker. "Are we reasonably sure this is the only threat?"

"I have a ring of motion sensors a half mile out from the house, so we shouldn't be surprised, unless someone parachutes in again."

"How did you know we were coming?" said Decker.

"I was watching the sunset with my family," said Aleman. "I heard the plane and caught your chutes out of the corner of my eye."

"I knew we should have jumped after dark," said Pierce.

"Where's your family?"

"I sent them away as soon as I saw your parachutes."

"Did I miss something?" said Decker. "Like a *Star Wars* transporter?"

"Jesus, Decker," said Pierce. "That's *Star Trek*."

"There's a tunnel leading out of here, but we need to slow these assholes down first," said Aleman. "Or the plan won't work."

"We need the file," said Pierce.

"I almost forgot," said Decker.

Aleman swiped a thumb drive from the table under the monitor and held it over his shoulder. "Everything is on this."

Decker grabbed the plastic device. "No paper files?"

"I don't get out much, if you haven't noticed." Aleman pointed to a shelf on the wall next to the screen. "There's a copy on that shelf. You should probably split them up between you, just in case."

Pierce retrieved the drive and tucked it into a pocket under his vest. Decker did the same, turning all of his attention back to the screen. "They're getting close to the next sensor," he said. "Three-mile mark?"

"Right." Aleman clicked the mouse and highlighted what looked like a string of sensors past the two-mile mark.

"We can't track them to death," said Decker. "We need a standoff weapon system, like a fifty-caliber rifle."

"I have two of those."

"Do you plan to use them?"

"Not yet."

"We need to start engaging those vehicles at the one-mile mark, or we're not going to win this round."

Aleman ignored him and clicked the mouse a few more times, changing the sensor string's icon color from green to red. A box appeared in the corner of the screen, flashing, "2MILEARMED." The vehicles cruised by the three-mile marker, their icons speeding toward the next sensor.

"Armed?" said Decker, hoping it meant more than activated.

"IEDs spaced one hundred and fifty yards apart," said Aleman. "I can remote detonate them if necessary."

"Enough to destroy an armored SUV?"

"Destroy, no. Disable, most likely."

"They'll veer off the road after the first detonation," said Pierce.

"I have smaller IEDs buried in twenty-five-yard increments, moving diagonally away from the road between the first and third IEDs. My guess is they'll stop after a few detonations, assuming it's a minefield."

"What if they don't stop?" said Pierce. "I don't think this group takes no for an answer."

"Then we hit them with the fifty-caliber rifles until they get the message. I have tunnel-accessed gun ports covering three hundred and sixty degrees."

"How long did it take you to build this place?" said Decker.

"A long time. I sank most of the Marenkov kicker into this."

World Recovery Group's rescue of Boris Marenkov's son from Ukrainian nationalists had yielded an unexpected bonus—ten million dollars split evenly between the fifteen WRG operators involved in the rescue. Aleman had served as a Russian translator on the ground through the entire operation.

"Why?" said Decker.

"I was convinced that the country was on the verge of a collapse event."

"From what?" said Pierce.

"North Korean EMP. Russian cyberwarfare. Pandemic. Pick your poison," said Aleman. "Maybe I watched one too many episodes of *Doomsday Preppers*."

"Looks like it paid off," said Decker.

"I suppose it did," said Aleman, opening a new window on the screen. He expanded the grayscale picture to fit half of the monitor, bringing the scene into focus. They were watching the convoy approach on a live thermal feed.

"Where is the camera?" said Decker.

"Small boulder in the middle of the roof. Watch the screen. The first vehicle should hit in five seconds. Four. Three. Two. One. Boom."

Nothing happened.

"Time for the fifty—"

The screen flashed white for a second before returning to the original grayscale image. A "white-hot" vehicle slowed to a stop on the road, the SUVs behind it barreling past. Decker stared at the screen, transfixed by the surreal scene unfolding in the middle of Texas. The house vibrated briefly, a deep crunching sound penetrating the structure.

"Oh. That's a mistake. Should have stopped," said Aleman, widening the view. "The next one should go in— Three. Two. One."

Another whiteout filled the screen, the view immediately normalizing to show an SUV tumbling out of the camera feed. The convoy halted abruptly, most of them swerving wildly to avoid hitting the next vehicle in line. Another thump rattled the house.

"Now what?" said Pierce.

"We hope they go away," said Aleman, laughing uneasily.

Decker knew they wouldn't give up without more of a fight, his fears validated a few seconds later, when the eight remaining vehicles split into two groups of four SUVs—each turning off the road in different directions.

"Are the fifty-cals ready to go?" said Decker.

"One is in the south-facing tunnel. The other is in the armory."

"Where's the armory?"

"Go all the way to the back of this building, past the door we used to come in. You'll see a metal spiral staircase leading upstairs. The armory is up the stairs. First door on the left. Lights are motion activated. Door code is seven-five-one-three."

Decker started to leave, but his attention was drawn back to the screen. Another flash momentarily blinded the thermal camera, an ominous development revealing itself when the image returned.

"They're pushing through the smaller charges," said Aleman.

"At least they're moving slower," said Pierce.

"That'll buy us some time, but we really need them to stop," said Aleman, setting off the remaining charges simultaneously.

A discordance of rattling and distant explosions filled the air, Decker hoping they might be enough to at least give their attackers pause. The SUVs disappeared behind geysers of dirt and rock, emerging from the debris shower a few seconds later.

"It was worth a try," said Aleman, standing. "Grab the other fifty. You'll also find a night vision–equipped MK12."

"Got it," said Decker. "Where do we meet you?"

"No. You have to climb back up the ladder and engage from the roof."

"I don't like that," said Pierce. "For all we know he's going to leave and lock the door behind him."

"There's only one tunnel facing the road," said Aleman. "And it's barely wide enough for me to turn around."

"We'll be awfully exposed on the roof," said Pierce.

"It's the only way we can put three guns into action against them."

"Then how do we get out of this place if everything goes to hell?" said Decker.

"From the armory. You'll see the door when you get the weapons. It's the only one in there. Same code. Close the door behind you."

"I already forgot the code," said Pierce.

"Seven-five-one-three," said Decker.

"I'll get the weapons sorted," said Pierce, taking off.

"I'll be right behind you," said Decker, turning to Aleman. "How long is the tunnel?"

"About a quarter mile. You'll find flashlights hanging on the back of the door."

"Where is the tunnel you'll be using?"

"Near the top of the ramp, right in the middle. There's a wooden trapdoor."

"You built it into the ramp?"

"Goes straight out, giving me an unrestricted view of the approach road," said Aleman. "And I can wiggle out of the firing port, hitting them from behind if they drive onto the roof. That's how I snuck up on the two of you."

"I can't believe you built this place."

"Neither can I."

"Good luck," said Decker, putting a hand on his shoulder.

Aleman glanced uncomfortably at his hand before meeting his gaze. Decker withdrew his hand, not sure why he had done that.

"I'm sorry for what happened, Ryan," said Aleman. "I truly am. Nothing I can say or do will ever repair what happened."

Decker nodded, unable to find the words to respond. His rage against Aleman no longer burned as brightly.

"There's a file on the drive named THEORIES," said Aleman. "PRAETOR is my bet."

"What does that mean?"

"You'll know when you open the file," said Aleman, disappearing through the doorway.

CHAPTER FORTY-FOUR

By the time Decker and Pierce reached the metal ladder after grabbing the additional weapons, the deep boom of Aleman's 50-caliber rifle had started reverberating through the man-made cavern.

"We're late to the party," said Decker, grabbing the highest rung he could reach.

"Better late than never," said Pierce.

Decker stepped on the ladder and pulled himself up, straining from the extra weight of the Barrett Light Fifty and its ammunition. There was nothing light about the thirty-pound beast slung over his shoulder—especially on a ladder. Arms burning from the climb, he reached the ceiling and pushed the hatch open, well aware that he had just broadcast their position to anyone wearing night-vision goggles.

A bullet zipped overhead a moment later, followed immediately by several more. The fact that none of them had struck the upright hatch led him to assume the gunfire came from the speeding vehicles. He balanced his hands against the sides of the opening and walked up the rest of the rungs until he could slither onto the rocky ground. He had started to crawl away when a bullet splintered the top of the wooden hatch, knocking it onto Pierce's emerging head. The door struck his night-vision goggles, remaining a few inches above the frame before closing tightly.

Decker reacted instinctively, raising himself off the ground to open the door, but a tight series of cracks inches from his head pressed him flat against the ground. The gunfire was now too accurate for moving vehicles. Another salvo snapped by, the bullets still passing a few feet high. Convinced that the shooters didn't have the right angle to hit him while he lay prone, Decker rolled onto his back and grabbed the rope handle with an outstretched hand, yanking it open.

"You still there?" said Decker.

"If I say no, can I go home?"

"No," said Decker. "Stay very low when you climb out. I don't think they can hit us yet."

"Yet?"

Another bullet struck the top of the hatch, tugging the rope handle out of his grip. Pierce caught the solid door with a hand before it hit his night-vision device. "Enough of this," he said, heaving himself out of the hole.

Pierce crawled next to Decker and extended his MK12 sniper rifle's bipod, pushing the gun in front of them. Decker wouldn't bother to prepare the 50-caliber rifle until he was in position. The weapon would be an absolute nightmare to drag across the ground if it wasn't slung over his back. The distant crackle of gunfire mixed with the repeated pounding of Aleman's powerful rifle. He hoped it wasn't too late to buy them the time needed to escape.

"Ready?" said Decker.

"I guess," said Pierce.

They low-crawled across the stony earth, gradually drifting about twenty feet apart. Close enough to communicate in a gunfight, but far enough apart to force enemy shooters to make a conscious choice between targets. Muzzle flashes started to appear beyond the edge of the slightly raised roof soon after they separated, followed by a hail of bullets striking the ground in front of them. A few zipped right past Decker's head, reinforcing the obvious maxim, *If you can see them, they can see you.*

"You take the stationary shooters!" said Decker. "I'll hit the moving vehicles."

Rocks and sandy dirt kicked up between them as he lugged the 50-caliber rifle off his back. Decker extended the bipod and pushed the steel cannon in front of him until he could nestle his shoulder into the cushioned stock. He stared past the thick barrel at the horizon in front of him, grimacing at the situation.

A drastically uneven line of six vehicles sped toward them, the closest SUV no farther than a quarter of a mile away. The SUVs were too damn close. This would all be over in twenty seconds if they didn't get extremely lucky. As he reached for the cocking handle, the volume of incoming fire intensified, bullets snapping and cracking past Decker and pulverizing the ground around him. One of the bullets ricocheted off the rifle, grazing his shoulder.

Pierce's rifle started barking a moment later, yielding an immediate decrease to the intensity of incoming fire. *Much better.* A solid tug on the cocking handle chambered the first 50-caliber round in the ten-round magazine. Time to work the vehicles. He propped himself up with his left arm to bring the barrel even with the horizon and settled in behind the scope to find his first target.

Despite the increasing darkness, Decker easily found the lead SUV and centered the scope's illuminated reticle on the windshield. He pressed the stiff trigger until the rifle exploded into his shoulder. He pressed his eye back into the scope—the SUV was still speeding toward them. His shot had punched a softball-size hole through the glass on the passenger side. Not a mission kill.

Decker readjusted his aim and pressed the trigger again, placing a hole in the center of the windshield, which had the desired effect. The SUV careened to the right, freeing him to engage other vehicles. He took his face out of the scope to look for the next closest threat, finding it on the far-right side of the line. Before he could shift the rifle to line up a shot, the SUV screeched to a stop, after taking multiple hits from Aleman's semiautomatic cannon.

Taking a cue from Aleman, he quickly acquired the next SUV in his scope and rapidly fired three bullets at its black silhouette with the same result. The oversize vehicle veered out of control for a few seconds before stopping. With three targets neutralized in the span of several seconds, Decker started to feel confident about their odds.

He searched over the barrel of the rifle for the next target, and his hopes were instantly dashed. All of the approaching vehicles had stopped, the mercenaries inside jumping onto the ground to hide behind the armored SUVs. This couldn't be good. The sudden increase in bullets snapping overhead confirmed that assessment. They'd stopped the vehicle rush too close to Aleman's bunker—well within the mercenaries' accurate rifle range. At least they had stopped it. Things would have been far worse if they hadn't.

"I give this another five seconds!" said Pierce.

"Make it count!" said Decker, centering the reticle on a partially exposed shooter.

The half-inch-diameter projectile hit the man at close to three thousand feet per second, shearing an arm from his body and knocking him off his feet. The arm tumbled through the air past the man, hitting the ground and bouncing out of sight. Decker's next shot skimmed the hood of the same SUV, removing a head. Not surprisingly, he couldn't find any targets after that.

Decker was tempted to start firing at the vehicles, knowing the bullets would pass right through the armor, but his chances of hitting an unobserved target were slim. He'd just be drawing a lot of unnecessary attention to himself. The Barrett's muzzle blast lit up the ground like a spotlight.

"I don't have any good targets!" said Pierce. "A little movement here and there behind the vehicles, but nothing I can hit."

"They're up to something. Probably breaking out some sniper rifles," said Decker. "Let's pull back a little. We're easy targets here."

Decker squirmed backward, pulling the thirty-pound rifle with him, when he suddenly realized he hadn't heard Aleman's 50-cal in a while.

"When's the last time you heard Aleman?"

"Right around when we started firing," said Pierce.

If that son of a bitch had bailed on them, Decker would hunt him down and kill him. A bullet clipped his night-vision device, jerking his head sideways.

"Sniper!" said Decker.

"Third car from the left. Flash came from the ground on the front passenger side!" Pierce said before firing three rapid shots. "Suppressing!"

Decker swung his rifle toward the identified SUV, hastily firing at the front of the vehicle as soon as it appeared in his scope. The hood buckled from the impact, bending inward at the front. A muzzle flash erupted from the ground near the front tire, the poorly aimed bullet hissing overhead. Decker centered the green reticle on the space between the bumper and ground and pressed the trigger when he saw movement. The right front side of the SUV collapsed, his bullet blasting dirt beyond the vehicle.

"Target down!" said Pierce.

Sporadic rifle fire echoed across the gap between the vehicles and their position, most of the rounds sailing far above or thumping into the ground well in front of them. The mercenaries popped up and down, taking wild shots, nobody willing to risk losing a limb—or a head.

"I think we stopped them!" said Decker.

"Yeah! We did Aleman a big favor. He's probably halfway to Mexico by now," said Pierce. "You ready to get out of here?"

He was right. For all they knew, Aleman had lied about the escape tunnel door code. They could arrive in the armory, only to discover they had unknowingly climbed down into a seventy-five-foot-diameter grave.

"Crawl or run?" said Decker.

"Crawl. Unless you want to get shot in the ass," said Pierce, already turning around.

Decker abandoned the Barrett and started to work his way toward the back of the roof. When he reached the fake boulder, halfway across the roof, a series of hollow thumps reached his ears. He looked at Pierce, who had already stopped crawling and was staring at him.

"Is that—" started Pierce.

A grenade launcher? Yes.

"Run!" said Decker.

He pushed himself onto his feet and sprinted headlong with Pierce for the thin beams of light poking through the bullet-riddled hatch. They reached the door just as the first grenade exploded near their previous position. Decker grabbed the rope handle and pulled the door open, shoving Pierce toward the hole when the second struck several feet in front of the first. Pierce slid down the ladder, holding the sides, vanishing moments before Decker dived through the hole. He'd barely cleared the hatch when the rest of the grenades rained down on the roof, shredding the wooden door with shrapnel.

Decker frantically grabbed Pierce's vest straps as he plunged toward the ground, nearly pulling him off the ladder. His friend must have anticipated the desperate move, because he held tightly enough to stay in place for a few seconds, hanging by a single rung. They swung back and forth twice before Pierce let go, both of them falling feetfirst to the ground below.

He stood there for a moment, dazed by his luck. Jumping headfirst into a thirty-foot drop usually had consequences. Death, paralysis, or broken limbs, just to name a few. Somehow he'd landed on his feet, no worse off than the first time he jumped onto this ground.

Pierce just stood there with a disapproving look. "That was interesting. Can we go now?"

"I have to make sure Aleman isn't still in the tunnel."

"Are you crazy?" yelled Pierce. "He bailed! We'll be lucky if he didn't lock the damn door on us."

"It'll only take—"

Before he could finish, a second salvo of eight grenades hit the roof. Showers of dirt dropped from the ceiling as the ground shook from each successive impact. Decker and Pierce dashed for the closest door, piling inside moments before a grenade hit the hatch above the ladder, stitching the dusty ground with splinters and steel fragments. When the bombardment ended, they peered through the doorway at the ceiling, noticing that the roof had bowed inward at several points.

"We need to go," said Pierce. "Before this place drops on top of us."

"I have to check. You get out of here. I'll catch up."

Pierce shook his head. "That's not how it works. I'll be right here covering the giant hole in the roof. Just hurry the hell up. I don't want to die down here."

"Neither do I," said Decker, taking off for the ramp.

Tendrils of dirt streamed down from the timber ceiling, sprinkling his face as he ran. When he reached the vehicles parked at the base of the ramp, the third salvo of grenades hit, immediately dislodging one of the wooden support beams. The massive log thudded to the ground behind Decker, missing the Jeep Wrangler's rear bumper by a few feet.

He kept running, crouching instinctively each time another grenade pounded the roof. The last grenade in the cycle knocked another beam loose, Decker looking over his shoulder in time to see it cut the aboveground pool in half and empty several thousand gallons of water into the space at once.

He didn't slow until he reached the door, which lay flush against the earthen ramp. A quick examination revealed hinges at the bottom and a recessed handle at the top. He grabbed the handle and retreated down the ramp until gravity took over. The hatch slammed into the dirt at his feet, revealing Aleman's bloodied body at the mouth of the tunnel. Aleman lay on his back, blood streaming from a hole in the top of his left shoulder. Judging by the height of the tunnel, Decker guessed he had been lying flat when the bullet struck him—penetrating deep into his chest cavity. He was as good as dead if that was the case.

Decker knelt next to Aleman's head with the intention of making sure his assumption hadn't been faulty. The bullet could have ricocheted off the clavicle and exited his back a few inches lower, yielding a survivable wound. He doubted it based on the evident blood loss, but he wasn't going to leave Aleman behind, regardless of the past.

The moment Decker reached out to grab his vest, Aleman pushed a hand into him. His fingers clutched a smartphone.

"I need to turn you over and check for an exit wound," said Decker.

Aleman jammed the phone into his chest again, hoarsely whispering, "I'm not going anywhere."

"I can get you out."

"They stopped the grenades," said Aleman. "They're coming."

"It'll take them a while to—"

Aleman dropped the phone and coughed a mouthful of blood.

"Take the phone. Enter the same code for the armory on the screen and press the red button before you enter the tunnel. I have the place rigged to explode."

Decker put a hand on Aleman's forehead and nodded. "I forgive you, Kurt."

Aleman forced a thin smile but didn't respond. Tears formed in his half-closed eyes.

"What can we do for your family?" said Decker.

"They know what to do. They're expecting you. Go."

He picked up the phone and activated it, seeing the pass-code screen.

"Keep them busy down here," said Decker. "Take as many of those bastards with you as possible."

"That's the plan."

CHAPTER FORTY-FIVE

Derek Green descended the ladder, splashing down into a few inches of muddy water. He took in the underground structure with a mixture of amazement and pity. He'd seen places like this on those extreme survivalist shows but never thought anyone actually lived in one. This dude had lived down here with his family for two years! There had to be a better way to vanish than this. The guy had a wife and three kids. How the hell was this any kind of a life for them? Now he was starting to feel a little angry. This was one hell of a price to pay for whatever screwup this guy had perpetrated.

"He's over here!" said one the operatives clustered on the other side of the cavern.

He gave them a thumbs-up before glancing at two Aegis mercenaries conferring in the nearest doorway. One of them was the only surviving team leader. Aleman, Decker, and their mystery friend had pounded them unexpectedly with 50-caliber rifle fire. The IEDs had been bad enough, but the vehicle armor had done its job and protected the occupants. The 50-cals, though, sliced through the armor like it wasn't there.

"No sign of Decker and his accomplice?" said Green.

"Negative," said the team leader.

"Family?"

"Nothing. We've pretty much turned the place over."

"What about more tunnels like the one dug into the ramp? The openings are big enough to squeeze through."

"We haven't found any more yet," he said. "The only way they could have slipped away would be to head directly north."

"I was up there," said Green. "There's a small rise north of this place, about a hundred yards away, but the ground is nothing but flat after that. We'd see them on thermals, no matter what direction they took."

"Then they're in another tunnel," said the team leader.

"Find the tunnels," said Green, before walking over to the group gathered around the ramp.

He splashed through the water, stepping over the beam that had crushed the flimsy aluminum-framed pool. Now this was sad as hell. A cheap aboveground pool. Aleman had really screwed his family over big-time with this deal. The swing set was even more depressing. Made him want to pinch Aleman's nose shut and shove a rag down this throat, instead of putting a bullet through his head. When he reached the three operatives standing halfway up the ramp, he quickly determined that one of his snipers' bullets had robbed him of that satisfaction. Aleman was moments from dying.

"Has he said anything?"

"Not until a few seconds ago," said one of the men, glancing uneasily at Green.

"What's wrong?"

"He asked to speak with Gunther Ross."

"Interesting," said Green, kneeling next to Aleman. "How do you know Gunther Ross?"

A trickle of blood ran from the corner of Aleman's mouth, his eyes opening a few centimeters. "We go back a long way," he said.

"Like hell. Your paths never crossed," said Green. "Did Decker give you the name?"

Aleman barely shook his head. "I linked Gunther Ross and Aegis to this mess a long time ago. He'll want to hear what I have to say. There's more."

"Where did Decker go?" said Green. "Where's your family?"

"I'll tell Gunther."

He shook his head. "I can't get a satellite signal in here."

"Then pass this message along," said Aleman. "Praetor is finished."

"What the hell does that mean?"

"If you don't know, Gunther will probably kill you, too, when this is over," said Aleman. "Praetor."

Green took the satellite phone out of his vest and handed it to one of the operatives. "Go topside and call the first number on speed dial," he said. "Unplug the headset from your tactical comms rig and hold the radio up to the sat phone. It's the best we can do."

"Copy that," said the mercenary, taking off for the ladder.

Green unsnapped the pouch on his vest holding the tactical radio and pulled it out, unplugging the wire that ran through his body armor to his earpiece.

"It's only a matter of time before we find the other tunnels," said Green.

"I know," said Aleman.

"Save me the hassle of looking and I'll spare your family."

"After I talk to Gunther," whispered Aleman.

"We found a tunnel facing east," said a voice on the tactical net. "Second floor of the structure, hidden behind a wheeled shelving unit. Looks the same size as the one dug into the ramp."

"Can you see inside?" said Green.

"The night-vision image just washes out after a certain distance," he reported. "There's no way to see all the way to the end without climbing in."

"Do not climb inside. And stay clear of the tunnel opening. We're working on something out here." Green glanced down at Aleman. "When I find the rest of these tunnels, we're gonna start playing a little game called tunnel roulette."

His earpiece crackled. "Mr. Green. I have Mr. Ross."

"Thank you," said Green. "Mr. Ross, I have Kurt Aleman here. He wants to talk to you."

"What is this all about, Derek?" hissed Ross.

"We can't find Decker or anyone else. This place is unreal, with tunnels going everywhere. Aleman said he'd tell us where to find them if he got to talk to you."

"And you believed that?" said Ross. "Call me back when you've unfucked all of—"

"He told me Praetor is finished."

The line went silent for several seconds.

"Mr. Ross?"

"Is Aleman there?" said Ross.

"Right here," said Green, lowering the radio next to Aleman's head.

"Good evening, Gunther," said Aleman.

"You wanted to talk to me?" he said.

"About Praetor."

"I'm familiar with the Latin word," said Ross. "But I don't see how that applies here."

Aleman turned his head toward Green. "Have one of your men wake the computer in my office. Just shake the mouse. I have the whole Praetor file up. I was showing Decker when you interrupted."

"What did he say?" said Ross.

"He said the Praetor file is already up on the computer. He was going over it with Decker." Green motioned for one of the mercenaries to find the office. "I'm sending someone to verify it right now."

"Harcourt has been a bad boy," said Aleman.

"Sounds like you've been living underground too long," said Ross.

"Months and months of digging, I finally put the pieces together," said Aleman. "Decker showing up was a miracle."

"That must have been one hell of a Judas moment," said Ross.

"The enemy of my enemy is my friend," said Aleman.

"Just kill him," said Ross. "He's stringing us along."

Green stood up and pressed the barrel of his rifle into one of Aleman's eye sockets.

"Mr. Green," said a voice over the radio. "All the computer screen shows is a thermal camera feed."

"There's a small window in the upper left-hand corner," said Aleman. "What's that doing?"

"It's a countdown clock," said the operative.

"Get out of there!" yelled Ross over the net.

"How much time is left?" said Aleman.

"Eight seconds."

"Adios, fuckers," said Aleman, grinning.

Green took off down the ramp and sprinted to the right side of the vehicles, Aleman laughing the entire way. He stopped next to the swing set and sighed. At least a dozen Aegis operatives had swarmed the ladder, the closest to escaping not even halfway to the top. Resigned to his fate, Green sat in one of the swings and pushed back, lifting his feet to sway forward. He never felt gravity's pull.

CHAPTER
FORTY-SIX

Decker ran through the constricted tunnel, the light from his flashlight wobbling off the earthen walls ahead of him. He ducked every ten feet or so to dodge the protruding wood beams that had knocked his night-vision device and chin strap off his head at the very beginning of the trip. His shoulders rubbed the sides in places, slowing him down and forcing him to twist his gear-laden body through to keep going.

A muted light in the distance beckoned him forward, keeping him focused on getting as far away from Aleman's fireworks show as possible. He had no idea how big of a show he'd planned, but based on Aleman's final statement, he guessed it wouldn't disappoint.

He glanced over his shoulder obsessively, afraid to see the same light behind him. Getting shot in the back in this tunnel scared him more than being blown to bits back in Aleman's underground tomb. Parking that thought as deep as possible in the recesses of his mind, he checked the smartphone again and pushed forward. He still had plenty of time. The light at the end of the tunnel seemed to grow with every step until a head peeked into the tunnel, causing him to raise his rifle. It disappeared just as quickly.

Pierce's voice echoed off the walls of the tunnel. "Decker!"

"Pierce!" he replied, picking up the pace.

"Hurry up! Everyone's waiting!"

"I'm moving as fast as I can!" said Decker, his rifle catching on the framework and jamming against his chest.

He dislodged the rifle and slogged onward, reaching the end faster than he'd expected. Decker jumped down from the tunnel, landing next to the tail section of a single-propeller, Cessna-style airplane. He glanced around, once again impressed and a little taken aback by the scope of Aleman's preparations.

The aircraft sat in a rectangular underground hangar with little room to spare on any side. The tip of the left wing couldn't be more than two feet from the earthen wall, and the top of the tail rudder had about double that clearance from the wooden plank ceiling. Half of the roof appeared to be a warehouse-style sliding door attached to sturdy-looking tracks on both sides of the hangar. A shallow ramp sat in front of the aircraft, terminating at the far end of the roof-mounted door.

"Kurt?" said Pierce.

Decker shook his head as Pierce squeezed past him to check the tunnel. "As good as gone," Decker said. "He has the place rigged to blow. I triggered a timer before I entered the tunnel."

"For how long?" Pierce asked before swinging a heavy metal door off the wall and into place over the opening.

"Five minutes," said Decker, handing him the smartphone.

"How much time is left?"

"Ninety-three seconds."

"This is going to be close."

Pierce turned a heavy-duty dead bolt on the door and stepped away, nodding toward the Cessna. "Aleman's family is in the plane waiting."

"I can't fly that," said Decker.

"Neither can I," said Pierce, guiding him under the wing to the open pilot door.

"Any update on the aircraft?" she said.

"I haven't heard from the pilot. I expect them on station in a few minutes. I'll let you know the second they check in with me."

"Copy," she said. "Looks like we have some time. Murphy and Stack dragged three full carts out of Natural Foods. They haven't even started to load their car."

"Small miracles," said Reeves, ending the call.

"Should we alert the tactical section? Sounds like this could go sideways on us in a hurry," said Kincaid.

He shook his head. "No. Vale knows what she's doing, and we'll have aerial support in a few minutes. This is a standoff surveillance situation. Nothing more than that."

"What if this Spec Ops–level team drives right up to Decker's hideout and massacres everyone? Right in front of that surveillance bird."

Reeves ran his hand over his shaved head. "I have no idea. All we can do at this point is hope they have more discreet plans that give us a chance to locate their base of operations. We can surround the place and force a hostage rescue."

"Or you can call off the aircraft," said Kincaid, glancing at him. "And the ground surveillance. This was never our fight."

He considered Kincaid's suggestion, running all of the angles. Calling off the surveillance operation would effectively cut the cord between Decker and Reeves's division, insulating him from whatever happened next—but it didn't feel right. Gunther Ross had no reason to be tracking Decker or Mackenzie unless Reeves's instinct was right, and Ross was connected to the unseen part of the iceberg floating just beneath the surface of the Steele kidnapping.

"No. We have to see where this leads," said Reeves. "Something's not right about Gunther Ross. This might be our only chance to sniff that out."

"I was kind of hoping you'd say that," said Kincaid.

Reeves started to respond, but the satellite phone cut him off. JANA was on station and ready for tasking.

CHAPTER

FIFTY

Reeves jammed the satellite phone against his ear, listening intently to the information passed by JANA's sensor operator. JANA was the call sign for the heavily modified Cessna 182 circling high above the Hollywood Hills, one of two nearly identical aircraft flown by the FBI over the greater Los Angeles metropolitan area. To the untrained and unmagnified eye, JANA resembled any other private aircraft flying the busy paths from airport to airport in Southern California, but to the federal agents below, she was a skyborne treasure.

Equipped with steerable, fuselage-mounted high-resolution cameras capable of recording night vision and thermal imagery, JANA could lock on to a vehicle and automatically track it under any conditions. Flying between four to six thousand feet above the ground, and fitted with a noise-reducing exhaust muffler, JANA attracted little attention from the ground while on patrol. Reeves and Kincaid had yet to spot the aircraft, which had tracked both Murphy's sedan and Gunther's white Range Rover through the Hollywood Hills with pinpoint precision.

"Primary target turned left on Mulholland," said the operator onboard JANA.

Reeves turned to Kincaid, whispering rapidly. "Murphy turned left onto Mulholland."

Kincaid repeated his statement over the radio for Special Agent Vale, who was a quarter of a mile ahead of them on Beverly Glen Boulevard. Traffic heading into the hills was steady, putting several vehicles between Vale and the Range Rover, which effectively reduced the chance of counterdetection by Gunther to zero. When traffic thinned out, he'd pull Vale out of sight. With JANA circling high above, there was no need to take any risks.

"Secondary target turned left on Mulholland. Four-car separation from primary target," said JANA. "I think the black SUV directly behind the secondary target is connected. They ran a red light at the intersection to stay in position behind your secondary target."

"I concur," said Reeves. "We suspected more than one tail."

"Copy that. Redesignating targets in order. Targets one, two, and three," said the operator. "Be advised. Traffic is significantly lighter on Mulholland than Beverly Glen, and thins out even more to the east."

"Understand," said Reeves before covering the satellite-phone mouthpiece to talk to Kincaid. "They identified a second tail, and traffic is light on Mulholland," he said. "Gunther's people are gonna stick out."

"Maybe they don't care," said Kincaid.

The two-lane road wound uphill, past gated estates with sweeping views of the San Fernando Valley and surrounding hillsides. Mackenzie had either rented a house in the Hollywood Hills or had somehow managed to bury a real estate purchase using a shell corporation they hadn't linked to her. His bet was on the rental. Reeves had learned from two decades of investigative work that hidden assets rarely stayed hidden for long. Mackenzie would know this, too.

"Targets two and three have pulled off Mulholland onto a small dirt parking lot labeled THE NARROWS OVERLOOK on my screen overlay," said JANA.

"I know it," said Reeves. "It's a photo stop. One of the few stretches of Mulholland where you can see the valley and LA at the same time."

"Roger. Adding that to the system notes."

"I doubt they stopped to take pictures."

"That's probably a fair assessment. Occupants of both vehicles have dismounted."

"Can you get closeup pictures of their faces?"

"Not without breaking the track on target one," said JANA.

"How quickly can you take the pictures?"

"A few seconds. I just need to zoom in," said JANA. "But if target one pulls into a tree-covered driveway, we run the risk of losing it."

"Can you identify a stretch of road where that's unlikely?"

"Stand by," said the operator.

"Where's Vale?" said Reeves, nudging Kincaid, who asked Vale for her location.

"Just turned left on Mulholland," said Kincaid.

Reeves studied the map displayed on his tablet, gauging the distance from the intersection to the overlook.

"Tell Vale that Gunther just pulled off Mulholland at a scenic overlook a little more than a mile from the turn she just took. There's a dirt parking lot right off Mulholland with room for about a dozen vehicles, if I remember correctly. If there's room, I want her to stop at the overlook and pretend she's there for the view. When Gunther looks like he's leaving, I want her to get ahead of them on Mulholland. We might be able to use her to slow them down at the right moment to let Murphy slip away."

While Kincaid passed his order along, JANA's sensor operator responded.

"Target one will hit a good stretch in about a minute. I can get the closeup and get back to her."

"Let's go ahead and do that," said Reeves. "One of my trailing units is a mile from the overlook. I've ordered her to park and keep an eye on them while you reacquire target one."

"Copy. I'll let you know when I'm switching between targets."

Less than a minute later, Reeves and Kincaid arrived at the intersection of Beverly Glen Boulevard and Mulholland Drive, barely squeaking through the intersection on a yellow light. They had only driven a few hundred yards east on Mulholland before Jana's sensor operator spoke excitedly over the satellite phone.

"Targets two and three just gave birth to target four!" he said.

"Say again?" said Reeves, glancing at Kincaid with a puzzled look.

"They hand launched a drone when I zoomed in to get some high-res footage. Unbelievable! Did it right in front of a dozen or more civilians," said the operator.

"What kind of drone?"

"RQ-12 Wasp from what I could tell," said the operator. "Probably the solar model."

"What are we looking at in terms of capabilities?"

"Flight endurance of ninety minutes on a sunny day like today. High-res cameras capable of thermal imaging," said the operator. "Maximum speed forty miles per hour. Cruising speed around thirty."

"Basically, you're telling me they are not going to lose target one."

"Unless target one turns off Mulholland in the next fifteen seconds or so, I'd say that's a safe bet," said the operator. "Target four is climbing and banking east."

"Can they sit at the overlook and control the drone?"

"The RQ-12 link has a hard range of five kilometers, which is why they're getting back in their vehicles. They'll follow target one at a safe distance and observe from the vehicles. The ground control station is handheld. Smaller than a laptop."

Reeves elbowed Kincaid. "Where's Vale?"

"Coming up on the overlook."

"Have her keep going," said Reeves. "Gunther launched a military-grade drone. They're packing up and driving out. Just tell her to drive the speed limit and wait for instructions."

While Kincaid passed the word to Vale, Reeves analyzed the situation. Gunther's team was on equal footing now, until JANA departed, leaving Reeves blind. He figured if Gunther planned on moving against Mackenzie immediately, he'd do it while he had drone coverage. Reeves needed JANA to stay airborne for at least another hour. Once the drone was out of the picture, he could figure out a way to approach Mackenzie's hideout and warn her that she had bigger problems than the FBI. He couldn't do that with the Wasp overhead.

"Target four just overflew target one," said the operator. "There's no doubt they acquired that target."

"Understood," said Reeves, an idea hitting him. "Hey. Can you contact Tori Breene directly?"

"I can," said the operator.

"I'm going to call her and ask that JANA remains on station until they recover the drone," said Reeves. "I don't feel comfortable with target one under aerial surveillance. I can't approach without possibly setting off a dangerous chain reaction. I was hoping you might call her first and let her know about the drone. It might convince her to extend your trip."

"I'll call her right now. I don't know who these people are, but that's military technology. There's something seriously off here."

"That's an understatement," said Reeves. "I owe you one. Thank you."

"Don't thank me yet," he said. "Ms. Breene isn't exactly a pushover."

"Not at all. Let me know how it goes."

"Stand by."

Stand by. That was pretty much the extent of his authority right now. Stand by and watch.

CHAPTER
FIFTY-ONE

"Mr. Ross. They off-loaded the groceries, and I have two targets sitting around a table by the pool in the backyard," said Ramirez. "Positive ID on Harlow Mackenzie and Sophie Woods."

Gunther glanced over his shoulder at the operative, who held the drone's ground control station in his lap. "That's great news," he said. "How's the battery looking?"

"Looking good. We can stay up another forty-five minutes, but I seriously advise against it. The Wasp is pretty quiet, but with people hanging around outside the house, we run the risk of detection. I recommend we recover and recharge the drone immediately. If they leave the house, we'll have a fully charged drone to follow them."

"Can you park the drone in an aerial pattern far enough away to avoid detection? But still be able to tell if any of them are outside? Maybe zoom in if it's clear to get some detailed video of the property?"

"It might be tough up here," said Ramirez. "The drone will attract attention if it sits in one place for too long. This is the land of the rich and entitled. If someone calls the cops, we could be dealing with an LAPD helicopter."

"I'll defer to your judgment on this. Make one more pass and start thinking about recovery."

"Got it. We'll need to pick a side road somewhere down Mulholland. I saw a few on the map that would work."

"Sounds good," said Gunther before opening the door and walking toward the opposite side of an overlook parking area just a block away from Mackenzie's hideout.

The Barbara Fine Overlook was a bit of a buzzkill compared to the Narrows Overlook, where they'd launched the drone. Featuring little more than mansion rooftops nestled into dried-up hillsides, the supposed scenic vista completely underwhelmed. He took out his satellite phone and dialed Jacob Harcourt's direct line.

"Please tell me you found Mackenzie," said Harcourt.

"We've positively identified Harlow Mackenzie, Sophie Woods, and Kathleen Murphy. Pretty sure Pamela Stack was in the car with Murphy. We couldn't ID her when they got to the house."

"Any chance they made you?"

"No way. We put the drone up early. I took no chances during our ground surveillance."

"What about the FBI?"

"They pulled most of their surveillance off Mackenzie and her associates two days ago," said Gunther. "We didn't get a sniff of them around the Natural Foods parking lot. It all happened too fast for them to respond. I had units there in under twenty minutes."

Ramirez and Calvin had followed Gunther's SUV up Beverly Glen Boulevard, looking for possible surveillance. None of the vehicles behind them looked suspicious.

"Can you hit the house right now? I'd like to clean up this mess as soon as possible," said Harcourt. "I have Frist heading down here tonight. I do not want to spend the entire weekend with that cretin."

"I need to analyze the aerial surveillance to be sure, but I don't see that happening during daylight hours. The target house is in a gated community. One way in. One way out. Two guards at the gate."

"Two guards?" said Harcourt. "Sounds like a five-minute job."

"I know, but the house is deep inside the neighborhood, and cars are constantly coming in and out. Very high-end cars. It's too risky. One call to nine-one-one and we'll be in a world of hurt. Beverly Hills PD doesn't screw around up here."

"Fine. But I need this wrapped up as soon as possible. Have you read the after-action report from Aleman's place?"

"I have."

"Then you understand my concern. I don't need Decker, and whatever army he's scrounged up, parachuting onto my estate."

"I can't imagine he'd use the same tactic twice."

"You know what I mean!" said Harcourt. "The guy is resourceful. I need a bargaining chip in case he somehow manages to get to me. And I can't reiterate this enough—I do not want to spend the next two weeks locked down with Gerald Frist."

"Monday is the big vote, right? Does it really matter what happens to Frist after that?"

"You're kidding, right?"

"Sorry. Bad joke. We'll handle the Mackenzie side of the equation tonight, then focus on Decker. He's good, but he's not that good."

"That's what I wanted to hear," said Harcourt, pausing. "And as far as Mackenzie and her associates are concerned? No restrictions. No limits. You do whatever you have to do."

"With pleasure," said Gunther, the call ending.

He walked back to the Range Rover and hopped inside.

"Ramirez?"

"Yes, sir?"

"You mentioned a pool," said Gunther. "How big is the backyard?"

"It's one of the bigger lots in the neighborhood. Pool takes up about a quarter of the backyard. There's a big-ass stone patio with a fire pit next to it. The rest is green grass."

"Is the grassy area large enough to accommodate a helicopter?"

"Depends on the size of the helicopter."

"I'm thinking a Sikorsky S-76."

"Rotor diameter?"

He liked working with Ramirez. The guy was sharp and had embraced valuable skill sets ignored by most Aegis operators.

"Hold on," said Gunther, typing furiously on his laptop. "Forty-four feet. Fifty-two feet in length."

"How skilled is the pilot?"

"Night Stalker skilled," said Gunther.

"Then I'd say no problem," said Ramirez.

CHAPTER FIFTY-TWO

Harlow startled from a light sleep, a hard pinch to her shoulder launching her upright on the leather couch in the great room. Sophie loomed over her, a dead-serious look on her face.

"What the hell?" she said, rubbing her eyes.

"Pool guy," said Sophie. "Or not."

Katie and Pam piled into the room from the SCIF area, carrying compact P-90 submachine guns that were far from California compliant. Harlow took Sophie's hand and let her hoist her off the couch. Sandra appeared in the kitchen with a pistol, edging toward the slider leading to the patio.

"Pool guy?" said Harlow. "How many?"

"Just one. But the agent leasing this place swore this wouldn't happen."

"Well, there's a pool," said Harlow, still feeling groggy. "It's gotta get cleaned, I guess."

"Maybe," said Sophie, looking a bit uncomfortable. "There's something else."

"What?"

"I don't know. He just doesn't look like a pool guy."

"What does he look like?"

"Black guy with his head shaved bald."

"Like Reeves?"

"I don't know Reeves by sight," said Sophie. "But the description matches."

"Okay," said Harlow. "And he's alone?"

"I think," said Sophie. "He parked the pool van at the bottom of the driveway. It doesn't seem right."

"Why? Where should he park it?"

"Not blocking the driveway, from the street. If he's the regular pool guy, he'd just drive up to the house."

"Maybe he's trying to sell his pool-cleaning service?"

"It's a gated community," said Pam.

"There's a dozen service trucks in here at any given time," said Harlow. "Nobody in here does anything themselves. Lawns. Pools. Housecleaning. He's probably just trying to drum up business."

"You want me to get rid of him?" said Pam.

"Without waving that P-90 around," said Harlow. "In California—that's five to ten. No parole."

"Better than dead."

"I'll handle this," said Harlow, heading for the main entryway.

"You want us to stand down?" said Katie.

She shook her head. "No. Better safe than sorry."

They followed her to the door, taking partially hidden positions in the two-story foyer. Harlow touched the security panel next to the door, activating the screen and displaying the "pool guy's" face.

"What the hell?" she said, turning to her partners. "It is Reeves."

Pam reacted immediately. "Katie. Give me the P-90. I'll put it in the safe room."

"Stop. Just stay out of sight. I'm not letting him in," said Harlow, nodding at Sophie. "Time to find a new location."

"I have a few backups," she said. "Assuming we can shake them. I don't know how the hell they found this place."

"It worked for a week," said Harlow, gripping the door handle. "We'll make another place work."

When everyone had ducked out of sight, she opened the door. Reeves stood there holding a clipboard, dressed in khaki pants and a light-blue, short-sleeved oxford shirt.

"Supervisory Special Agent Joseph Reeves," she said. "I assume you're not here to clean the pool."

"I wouldn't know the first thing about pool cleaning," said Reeves. "But I do know something about surveillance."

"Congratulations," she said. "You found us."

"I'm not the only one that found you. Gunther Ross followed Ms. Murphy and Ms. Stack here from Natural Foods, too."

"Nope. No way," said Katie, poking her head around the corner of a doorway. "Nobody followed us."

"Nobody followed you by car to the house," said Reeves. "I had a surveillance bird track you from Sherman Oaks. Gunther Ross launched a drone at the Narrows Outlook, which circled over this house a few times before landing a mile or so south of here, in an ungated neighborhood just off Mulholland."

"Son of a bitch," said Katie.

"My sentiments exactly," said Reeves, looking directly into Harlow's eyes. "We need to talk."

"I'm not rolling on Decker," she said.

"I'm not asking you to. That's not why I'm here."

"Why are you here?"

"Can I come in? We're pretty sure Gunther's people left the area, but I don't want to take the chance." He glanced at the van down the driveway. "As you can see."

"Do you have a warrant?"

"No. I don't have a warrant, Ms. Mackenzie. I told you. That's not why I'm here."

"Then I'll ask you again. Why *are* you here?"

"To warn you about Gunther Ross," said Reeves.

"You could have sent someone else to do that."

"There's more to the Steele kidnapping than the Russians. Something big. I'm absolutely convinced of it," said Reeves. "But I don't have a shred of direct evidence to support this—gut feeling. I was hoping you might be able to help me with that, and help Senator Steele get to the bottom of her daughter's kidnapping."

Harlow motioned him inside, closing the door after he entered the foyer.

"I have some bad news, Special Agent Reeves," she said.

"Please call me Joe."

"Joe. I don't have the evidence you're looking for," she said. "We have one hell of a theory, and a ton of barely circumstantial evidence to support it. But in the end, it's just a wild theory."

"How wild?"

She gave him the broad strokes of their thinking about Harcourt's and Frist's roles in Meghan Steele's kidnapping and how it had all spiraled out of control when Decker found her.

"That's the abbreviated version," she said when she finished. "Write your email address and a secure phone number on one of those fake pool forms. I'll send you the file we've assembled and walk you through it over the phone. There's a ton of material in the file."

Reeves scribbled the information on one of the sheets and handed it to her.

"You should get out of here immediately," he said. "We've tracked Gunther to a warehouse in Glendale, but the parking lot is mostly empty. He's up to something, and I can guarantee it has everything to do with this house."

"We appreciate the heads-up," said Harlow, opening the front door. "I'll call you in about thirty minutes. Give you enough time to download the file and get far enough away from the cell towers servicing the area."

"I gave you a satellite number," said Reeves, walking through the door. "Can't be too careful."

Harlow started to close the door behind him but stopped. "How exactly did you find us?"

"I'll answer that question if you answer one of mine."

"Deal."

"I got a facial-recognition hit on Ms. Murphy," he said. "But it wasn't her fault. The camera had been moved a lot closer to the Natural Foods parking lot a few days earlier. The change must not have been updated in whatever app you use to avoid detection."

"And Gunther Ross has access to the same camera network?" she said, shaking her head. "We need to stop these people."

"Yes. We do," said Reeves. "My turn."

"Fire away."

"How is Mr. Decker these days?"

She laughed briefly. "Decker is Decker."

"That's not much of an answer," he said, smiling.

"It wasn't really much of a question," she said, shutting the door.

CHAPTER FIFTY-THREE

Senator Margaret Steele took Supervisory Special Agent Reeves's call in her office, mindful of the time. She was scheduled to speak at a cocktail reception in the Maryland State House building in Annapolis anytime between six and seven o'clock. Her hope had been to arrive early during that window so she could deliver her ten-minute speech and mingle for a half hour or so before escaping to join a few friends for a relaxed dinner in one of their homes overlooking the Severn River.

After spending a week worried about Decker, she had been looking forward to unwinding with friends and putting a few drinks between the sour news and her weekend. Getting a call from Reeves this late in the afternoon didn't bode well for her plans.

"Joe. Shouldn't you be knocking off early to enjoy the weekend?" said Steele, hoping he got the hint.

"Ma'am. I stumbled onto something we need to discuss. It's serious."

"How serious?" she said. "I'm headed out in five minutes for a speaking engagement in Annapolis."

"Serious enough to cancel the engagement. I have evidence linking Aegis Global to your daughter's kidnapping."

A woman with a blonde ponytail protruding from the back of her olive-green ball cap leaned out of the door as they approached.

"Ms. Aleman is our pilot," said Pierce.

"It's Larissa," she said. "How much time is on the clock?"

Decker checked the phone. "Sixty-seven seconds."

"I need the two of you to open the hangar door," she said. "There's a locking bolt behind the door on each side of the track. Pull those out and walk the door open with the rope lines attached to the back of the door. It'll get tight back there, but you have to pull the door all the way to the back of the track or the tail rudder won't make it out."

"Got it," said Decker.

"Once I start the engine, I need you to push the plane up the ramp," she said. "I can't build up enough momentum to pull the plane up the ramp without help."

"Where do we grab it to push?" said Pierce.

"Use the support struts under the wing," she said. "Between the propeller and the two of you, we'll be fine."

Decker nodded, wanting to say a few words about Kurt, but she'd already pulled her head back inside the plane. There'd be plenty of time for that later. He whispered to Pierce before they split up, "You think she'll leave us here?"

"I sure hope not. I don't feel like walking back to the motel."

"I wouldn't blame her," said Decker before crawling under the rear fuselage. "I'm not sure this thing can take off with all of us."

He located the bolt and yanked it out, dropping it to the ground. A knotted rope lay over the top of the wing, which he grabbed and walked back a few feet.

"You ready?" said Decker.

"Yep!" said Pierce.

The Cessna's engine roared to life, startling him to the point where he almost dropped the rope. The propeller noise was deafening inside the enclosure, the prop wash kicking up a cloud of dust that filled the space almost instantly.

Decker pulled the rope, easily moving the door along the track. Careful not to stumble into the tail elevator, he kept heaving until his back hit the rear of the underground hangar. From there, he adjusted his grip on a higher knot and pulled again, repeating the process until the back of the door hit the end of the track. He glanced at Pierce, who gave him a thumbs-up, and they dashed forward to push the plane out of the hangar. Before grabbing the strut extending from the wing to the fuselage, he checked the countdown timer. Twenty-nine seconds.

The aircraft rocked back and forth, trying to roll up the ramp under its own power, but without distance to build up speed, it would never make it without help. He dug into the ground with his boots and leaned a shoulder into the strut, straining against the impossible weight of the aircraft. The Cessna inched forward, leaving Decker with serious doubts about getting it up the ramp. He pushed harder, but the aircraft barely made any progress.

He was particularly concerned because the noise of opening the hangar door had undoubtedly attracted the attention of any mercenaries that hadn't descended into Aleman's underground lair. Just when he was about to suggest they go topside and engage any responding targets, the propeller sound intensified, and the plane started to pick up speed.

Decker pushed against the strut with renewed energy, the aircraft now easily moving up the ramp. The plane tipped forward when its wheels reached level ground beyond the ramp, the movement taking Decker by surprise. He let go of the wing and turned as the tail swung up and out of the underground hangar, missing the edge of the hangar door by no more than a foot.

The door next to him opened, and two young kids beckoned him inside. As he climbed into the cabin, Pierce rolled under the fuselage and starting jogging alongside the moving aircraft. Decker gripped the back of the front passenger seat and extended a hand to Pierce, who took it eagerly and swung inside. He reached up and pulled the door shut, making sure it latched securely before turning to find a place to sit.

From what he could tell, they were in the same-model Cessna that had dropped them fewer than thirty minutes earlier, except the front passenger seat remained in place.

"Can we take off with this many onboard?" Decker asked, twisting in the cramped cargo compartment.

"You volunteering to jump out?" said Larissa.

"Only if I have to."

"We'll be fine," she said, pushing the throttle forward.

Decker held on to the passenger seat as the Cessna raced forward. He took the phone out of his vest and checked the timer.

"Three seconds!" he called out.

She nodded but didn't turn to look. He glanced to his left in time to see a brilliant flash, followed by a billowing fireball that rose a few hundred feet into the night sky. The plane yawed to the left a few seconds later as the shock wave hit them. Their pilot easily corrected the nudge, pointing them directly at the dark-blue line on the horizon. Fortunately, most of the explosive force had been directed upward due to the depth of the underground structure.

The plane rumbled across the flat ground for several more seconds before Decker felt it leave the ground and hang in the air, almost like it couldn't climb any higher.

"Hang on!" said Aleman's wife.

Decker tightened his grip on the passenger seat a moment before the plane pitched skyward, picking up speed. If he'd let go at that moment, he would have undoubtedly flown back into Pierce, who was pressed against the back of the cargo area. His two-handed grip on the passenger seat back started to loosen as the aircraft continued to climb above the Texas landscape. He risked a quick look through the portside window, the ground below them flickering orange from the tower of flames a short distance away. He couldn't imagine what was going through the children's minds right now. Nobody said a word until the Alemans' homestead was a bright-orange speck behind them.

"Where are you taking us?" said Decker.

"Avenger Field in Sweetwater," she said. "Unless you brought passports."

Decker had mixed feelings about the destination. They had flown out of Avenger Field for the jump, which presented a risk. If their pilot had decided it was in his best interest to report the jump to the police, they could face a precarious situation upon landing. Then again, the pilot would never expect them to return this quickly. The skydive destination was over fifty miles away, and they'd taken a taxi to the airfield, hopefully giving the pilot the impression that they weren't returning. He glanced at Pierce, who shrugged and gave him a why-not look.

"No passports," said Decker. "Thank you for flying us out of there."

She barely nodded and kept her attention on the dark-blue sky in front of them.

The young girl in the passenger seat turned to him with tears streaming down her face. "Is our daddy gone?" she said.

"Leah," said her mother. "Don't."

"It's okay," said Decker. "I'll tell you all about your dad when we land. I want to let your mom pay attention to the flight. Deal?"

"Deal," she said, sniffling.

Larissa looked at him and nodded a thank-you. A few minutes later, she eased the Cessna into a lazy left turn, straightening on a course aimed at the largest gathering of distant ground lights visible in any direction. "We'll be on the ground in twenty minutes," she said.

"What should we do about the weapons?"

"How did you get to the airfield?"

"Taxi from our hotel."

"Have a taxi wait for you at the VFW lodge at the south end of the airfield, on Route 170," said Larissa. "I'll bring you as far south as I can on the runway and you can make a run for it. It'll be so dark on the field nobody will see you. Tell the taxi driver you're DEA. They're always up to stuff around here."

"Sounds like a solid plan," said Decker, looking back at Pierce, who nodded.

Once the taxi was arranged, he settled in for the rest of the flight. The twenty minutes passed quickly, his mind racing with ideas about how they would proceed once they got clear of Sweetwater. He guessed the plan would very likely depend on the contents of Aleman's thumb drives.

Larissa executed a flawless, near featherlight landing at Avenger Field, taxiing them to the opposite side of the runway, where she turned the Cessna so the cargo door faced the southern boundary of the field. Decker opened the door, pushing it up against the bottom of the wing. He nodded at Pierce, who scooted along the metal floor and pulled himself out of the cabin, landing on the concrete runway.

Decker did the same but leaned back into the aircraft as soon as his feet hit the tarmac. The two boys crammed against the opposite side of the cargo compartment expanded to fill it now that they were gone, and Leah peered over the passenger seat headrest. They were obviously expecting him to say a few words about their dad. He glanced at Larissa and found her eyes welling with tears.

"I need to tell you guys something before I leave," said Decker. "I served with your dad for many years, and he was the bravest person I ever met. He helped rescue dozens of kids, just like you, so they could see their families again. He risked his life over and over again to do it, because he couldn't bear the thought of parents like your mom never seeing their kids again. Your dad was a hero in every sense of the word. Don't ever forget that."

Larissa wiped the tears from her face and took a deep breath before extending a hand between the seats. He took her hand, squeezing it tight.

"Where will you go?" she said. "What will you do now?"

"Whatever it takes to make sure you and your kids can live a normal life. That we can all live normal lives again."

"Kurt always said you were one of the best things to happen to him," she said.

"Second to you, I hope!"

She laughed. "That goes without saying!"

"Keep your eye on the news. We're going to take this thing down, whatever it is. My guess is it's bigger than any of us ever figured."

She squeezed his hand and let go. "I better get out of here. I didn't call ahead to make this landing."

Decker nodded, giving each kid a thumbs-up. "Remember! Your dad is a hero!"

Larissa's daughter, clearly the oldest of the three, rose in her seat. "Is he gone?"

"He's gone," said Decker. "Unfortunately, that's the risk of being a hero."

He shut the door and saluted them before racing to catch up with Pierce, who had already taken off for the waiting taxi.

"That was nice of you," said Pierce, when Decker finally caught up.

"What was I supposed to say?"

"I didn't mean it that way. They just lost their dad. And the way they've been living?"

"I know," said Decker. "I hit the ground wanting to kill Kurt—in front of his family. When I saw how they've been living for the past two years, everything changed. He was just as much of a victim of this as everyone else."

"I'm still pissed at him."

"Not me," said Decker. "Not anymore. I'm refocusing all of my rage."

"Where?"

"I won't know until we access Kurt's files," he said, reaching under his vest to retrieve the thumb drive. When his fingers gripped the plastic drive, he stopped in the middle of the open ground between the departing aircraft and the fence.

"This isn't a good place to stop," said Pierce.

Decker showed him the thumb drive, which crumbled in his hand. Pierce scrambled to produce the copy from his vest, which appeared to be intact when he opened his fist.

CHAPTER FORTY-SEVEN

Gunther Ross paced the warehouse, pointlessly checking his phone every several seconds. Green was gone. There was little doubt about that. Aleman had sacrificed himself so his family and Decker could escape. A last-moment transmission over the radio suggested that an aircraft had emerged from an underground bunker north of the Alemans' homestead seconds before the explosion. He hadn't heard from anyone assigned to the mission since the call disconnected, leading him to conclude that the blast had consumed everyone.

Given the shape and size of Aleman's bunker, it was conceivable that Green's entire team could have been underground or standing on top of the seventy-five-foot-diameter roof when the place exploded. Gunther's night had gone from a stunning triumph to a disaster in the span of minutes.

Not only did Decker slip through his grasp, but Aleman had also somehow pieced together the Praetor connection, undoubtedly passing that knowledge along to the one man they could least afford to possess it. Decker was no longer a loose cannon. He was a ticking time bomb—headed right in Jacob Harcourt's direction.

He wandered over to the array of screens that had so far yielded nothing useful over the past forty-eight hours. He woke Cooper with a tap to the shoulder. Cooper's head shot forward off the back of the seat, his hands finding their place on the keyboard in front of him.

"Sorry," he said, rubbing his face.

"Anything?"

"Nothing. Not a single hit on LAPD's facial-recognition network, and our surveillance teams report all quiet. Even the FBI has pulled most of their stakeout teams. Mackenzie and her team have gone dark. My guess is they skipped town."

"They're just as aware of the facial-recognition zones as we are," said Gunther. "We can't discount that."

Cooper nodded. "I agree, but we don't have any active measures to pursue. We're locked in passive mode, waiting for them to make a mistake. Statistically, they can't keep this up forever, but I get the sense that time isn't on our side."

"It isn't."

Gunther's phone buzzed, ringing a moment later. A quick look at the phone's screen confirmed the worst—Harcourt wanted an update that he couldn't provide.

"I'll be back in a few," said Gunther, already headed for the one door leading out of the warehouse.

Halfway to the exit, he accepted the call. "Mr. Harcourt. I still haven't heard from Green's team."

"That's funny, because I just intercepted a call patched through the Aegis twenty-four-hour crisis desk—from one of Green's operatives!" said Harcourt. "Are you aware of what happened out there?"

"I have some details. They suffered heavy casualties approaching Aleman's bunker. A combination of IEDs and fifty-caliber rifle fire. Then there was some kind of explosion and I lost communications."

"Some kind of explosion? That's a bit of a whitewash, Gunther! Only eight members of the thirty-three-man team survived! The operative I talked to said the explosion was bigger than anything he'd ever seen. The only reason he survived was because a few of them had been ordered to help the wounded."

"Aleman was ready for this," said Gunther, opening the warehouse door and stepping outside. "Green's team said his bunker was like something out of a postapocalyptic movie."

The parking lot enclosed in razor-wire fencing was quiet, glowing orange from the perimeter's inward-facing sodium-vapor lights.

"The operative I spoke with said an airplane took off from a nearby bunker, headed west," said Harcourt. "Were you planning on sharing that information with me?"

"I've been collecting and analyzing all available information, which has been spotty at best. I didn't want to bother you until I had something concrete."

"From what I can tell, we have a concrete fuckup on our hands. So now's the time to bring me up to speed."

"Aleman set off a massive explosion, which killed most of Green's team. I was on the phone with Aleman, communicating through Green, when a countdown timer was discovered on one of Aleman's computers. Everyone panicked after that, and I lost the connection."

"Son of a bitch. Did you confirm Decker's presence?"

"Yes. Decker was there. Green reported three shooters. Two using fifty-cal rifles. Decker and his accomplice stuck around long enough to stop Green's advance."

"I was really hoping we could wrap this up tonight," said Harcourt. "Well. At least Aleman's gone. One less liability out there."

Gunther started to reply but cut himself off, unsure how to proceed.

"What's the problem?" said Harcourt. "You're rarely at a loss for words."

"I don't know how to say this without just saying it."

"I can already tell I don't want to hear this."

"Aleman referenced Praetor," said Gunther.

"What?"

"He said he had a file on Praetor. And that he showed it to Decker."

"No way," said Harcourt. "Praetor is buried. It's mentioned once in an *Atlantic* article, and that's not an official reference. Lucky guess by a journalist that died in a skydiving accident."

"He used the word repeatedly. What if he did more than show it to Decker? What if he passed on some kind of file?"

"A file on what? A bunch of paranoid theories?"

"The timing might raise the wrong eyebrows," said Gunther, knowing he probably overstepped his authority with the observation.

"What do you mean?"

"Nothing. We'll triple up our efforts to find Decker and his associates."

"No. I want to know what you meant by that," said Harcourt. "I pay you to think, Gunther. What did you mean?"

"I'm thinking about the legislation initiated around the time of Meghan Steele's kidnapping," said Gunther. "And its relation to Praetor."

A long pause ensued before Harcourt responded. "Point taken."

"We need to assume that Decker will connect the same dots."

"Which lead back to me," said Harcourt.

"And Senator Frist? I wonder how he might react to these new developments."

"Another point well taken. I imagine he won't respond well."

"And if Decker connects him to Praetor . . . ," said Gunther, intentionally pausing to let Harcourt finish.

"We need to make sure the two of them never cross paths."

"Is this something you'd like me to take care of?" said Gunther. "I'm woefully unengaged at the moment."

"No. I can handle Frist and whatever Decker throws our way. I need you to focus on Mackenzie. We have to assume that Decker will share everything with her and that she'll pass the information to her associates."

"We'll bury them all. No trace."

"That's what I like to hear. You have no restrictions when it comes to dealing with this. Take whatever action is required, and I'll deal with the fallout. Understood?"

"Understood."

CHAPTER FORTY-EIGHT

Decker stared though the windshield at the dark nothingness ahead of them. Beyond the barely visible dashed line separating the two eastbound lanes, their headlights reflected nothing but the occasional bush that grew too close to the interstate's shoulder. It was enough to lull you to sleep within minutes without a cup of coffee or a Red Bull.

The original plan was to drive through Dallas to Texarkana, six hours away, and stop for the night, but neither of them seemed up to it. Less than an hour outside Sweetwater, Pierce was already grumbling, and Decker agreed. They'd be lucky to reach Dallas before calling it a night. Ideally, they'd get through the Dallas–Fort Worth area, putting a little more distance between themselves and the mess they left behind outside Sweetwater.

Then again, why should they worry? There was no way the authorities could link them to what happened on the Alemans' property. The pilot might put two and two together, but he wouldn't be able to provide any useful information. They'd paid him with cash and hadn't driven their own car to the airfield, not to mention the fact that the pilot had dropped them over private land—which was illegal. Decker figured the pilot would keep his mouth shut once word got out about what had transpired at the Alemans'. He had nothing to gain by bringing it to anyone's attention.

Their only real concern was Aegis, and judging by the fireball that rose from Aleman's bunker, he didn't think Aegis had the resources to make anything happen in Texas tonight, or anytime soon. Between the IEDs, the 50-caliber sniper fire, and the explosion, Decker couldn't imagine more than a handful of mercenaries surviving. The survivors would have the same priorities as Decker and Pierce: get as far away as quickly as possible. The only way he and Pierce could run into trouble tonight was if they booked a room in the same motel as the surviving mercenaries.

Decker turned his attention back to the laptop. The Praetor file was comprehensive, to say the least, filled with several hundred PDF copies of newspaper articles, government filings, and congressional testimony. He'd sifted through it for the past hour, searching for concrete support of Aleman's five-page, single-spaced conspiracy theory, which was admittedly light on factual connections, from what Decker could determine. That said, he was working at night on a laptop, in a moving vehicle—hardly the most focused setting.

He needed to get the contents of the thumb drive to Harlow, who had a team assembled in the right setting to parse the voluminous information and make sense of its greater connection to Aleman's premise. They'd need more than a conspiracy theory to bring these allegations to light. They were just as outrageous as they were damning—unthinkable on every level.

On the surface, the word *Praetor* didn't sound menacing. Its early-Roman context was equally innocuous, most commonly associated with an elected magistrate given broad authority and power over a jurisdiction, answerable only to the consuls that outranked him. Over time, the expected duties of a praetor expanded beyond judicial and civil responsibility to encompass military command. The result was a permanent military class of praetors, wielding considerable power within their jurisdictions and Rome itself.

With their positions under constant threat from political enemies, the praetor generals formed elite guard units to enforce their judgments and protect them against the constant plotting by their rivals. Comprised of veteran soldiers loyal only to the praetor's gold, the Praetorian Guard model gained enough popularity to inspire Augustus, the Roman Republic's first emperor, to form his own Praetorian Guard, numbering in the thousands—beginning a notorious tradition that would plague Rome for another four hundred years.

By the early second century AD, Praetorian Guard units had grown in strength and size under each successive emperor to rival even the most robust armies fielded by the Roman Empire. Based in and around Rome, where regular armies were forbidden, the guard became the dominating force of the Roman life—influencing policy, instigating mutinies, and assassinating public officials. At the apex of its power, the Praetorian Guard had assassinated close to a dozen emperors and raised several of their own choosing to power.

Kurt Aleman had stumbled on an article Jacob Harcourt wrote five years ago in which Harcourt made a case for the appointment of a "viceroy in Afghanistan" to lead a "Praetorian Guard to victory in the Afghanistan war." He proposed an arrangement where the United States would hire a private army, commanded by a viceroy-like leader— presumably Harcourt—who would report directly to the president or whomever the president appointed.

The arrangement would keep US soldiers out of harm's way, an attractive premise after close to twenty years of fighting in Afghanistan, but an equally dangerous one. This modern-day Praetorian Guard would not answer to Congress or be held accountable for its actions. Like the Praetorian armies of ancient Rome, it would be beholden to nothing but money and power, with Harcourt at the reins—feeding Aegis Global's bottom line.

Decker closed the laptop and shut his eyes for a few moments, trying to clear his head. He needed a complete reboot after the past few days. He'd lost the ability to focus, his brain racing in any of a dozen different directions. Unfortunately, other than a short stretch of sleep tonight, he didn't foresee them taking a meaningful break anytime soon. Success would rely on continuing the rapid tempo that had kept Gunther Ross and Aegis off balance so far.

He opened his eyes and rubbed his face. "I could use a coffee. Anything with caffeine."

"Are we stopping outside Dallas?"

"I think that's the best call," said Decker. "Somewhere off the beaten path."

"Then coffee isn't a good idea. We're only two hours away, and you need a solid night of sleep."

"What are you, my mother?"

"If I were, we'd still be sitting in Colorado—plotting a way to smuggle you into a country that doesn't extradite."

"The thought had crossed my mind," said Decker.

"I doubt it. Running away isn't your style."

"Has to be easier than this."

"Running from this might seem like the easier path, but it's just a short-term solution," said Pierce. "You don't want to spend the rest of your life looking over your shoulder."

"Sage advice coming from a guy hiding in the mountains."

"Touché."

"What was your plan?" said Decker.

"Wait for all of this to blow over."

"That's not much of a plan."

"No. It isn't. That's why I was hopeful when I heard about Penkin. We all were. My wife especially. She knew our situation had a limited shelf life."

"Then we better make this count," said Decker. "Take our time and drive a stake through the heart of it."

"Jacob Harcourt?"

"Aleman seemed to think so. It's no secret that Aegis has its hand in every conflict and shady government around the world, but I don't see a nexus to the Steele kidnapping. If it exists, I don't think it's on this thumb drive. Aleman would have highlighted it in his summary."

"Sounds like it's time to put Ms. Mackenzie to work on this."

"I was just about to call her."

"Don't let me get in the way," said Pierce. "Unless you need some privacy."

"What's that supposed to mean?"

"Nothing. Just—you seem pretty attached to her."

"She saved my life," said Decker. "She's gone above and beyond for me."

"I'm not saying she didn't."

"What are you saying?"

"I guess I'm saying it's good to hear you talking about something other than the business at hand."

"She's a critical aspect of *the business at hand*," said Decker. "As you call it."

"Forget what I said. Give her a call."

"I think I will," said Decker, his face feeling flushed. He dialed her with the satellite phone. "You want me to put this on speakerphone?"

"Sorry, Mr. Touchy," said Pierce, moments before Harlow answered.

"What took you so long?" said Harlow, her voice clearly audible throughout the vehicle. "I thought something happened."

Pierce winked at him and grinned.

"We're fine. I started sifting through Aleman's file and got carried away."

"Am I on speakerphone?"

"No. But apparently the eavesdropper can hear everything anyway."

"May as well put it on speaker," said Harlow. "I have Sophie and Pam with me."

"Hi, Pam," said Decker. "I still owe you for that motel."

"No need," said Pam. "It wasn't that expensive."

"I can't imagine why," said Decker, laughing.

Harlow got down to business. "Did you find anything useful in the file?"

"I need to get this to you as soon as possible. Aleman thinks Harcourt is behind the kidnapping, but I don't see how or why. Aleman doesn't connect those dots as far as I can tell, but there's a lot here to digest. There's no doubt that Aegis is involved somehow, but my guess is we're dealing with someone under him in the organization. Someone with the authority to run operations without Harcourt's permission."

"Maybe not," said Harlow. "We've been studying the bigger picture, trying to make connections between everyone we know or suspect is involved, and I think we found a plausible motive for kidnapping Meghan Steele."

Someone in the background on Harlow's end of the call spoke, but Decker couldn't understand what was said.

"For murdering Meghan Steele. The Russians were told to dispose of her," said Harlow. "If we're to believe Viktor Penkin's dying confession."

"I think we have to believe him," said Decker.

"That's the general consensus here, too. Which leads us to the motive."

"Go ahead."

"We think Meghan Steele was taken as a distraction, and possibly—"

"A distraction? From what?" interrupted Decker. "You don't kidnap and murder someone to create a distraction."

"You do if billions of dollars are at stake. And an influential US senator stands in the way of those billions."

"I just can't—" said Decker, barely able to continue. "I can't see why they would kill her."

"To create a long-term distraction for Senator Steele, and to earn her trust."

"What?" whispered Pierce, shaking his head.

"Earn her trust?" said Decker. "The whole thing literally blew up in our face, killing her daughter."

"Do you recall Senator Gerald Frist being involved when you were hired to recover Senator Steele's daughter?"

Pierce shook his head, which corresponded with Decker's recollection of events.

"No. I heard Senator Steele mention him a few times, but I wasn't aware that he played any role in hiring us," said Decker. "Jacob Harcourt approached us directly, on behalf of Senator Steele. She wanted to keep our involvement a secret for as long as possible, for legal reasons."

"I think Senator Frist may have played a bigger role in all of this," said Harlow. "Frist owns a substantial stake in Aegis Global."

"How substantial?"

"Substantial enough for him to have a vested interest in removing any obstacles to Aegis Global's continued domination of the private military industry," said Harlow. "Senator Steele and Senator Frist have been friends for years, but they never saw eye to eye on the use of contract military forces. She had a consistent record of voting against expanding their use—right up until her daughter was taken."

"You think they flipped her?"

"*Flipped* isn't the right term. She understandably missed a key vote five days after the kidnapping. I say *key* in that it laid the groundwork to expand the authority and discretion of private military units hired directly by the top US commander in Afghanistan. Mostly support and logistics missions, with some security functions included. Guess who sponsored that authorization?"

"Frist," said Decker.

"Correct. She was absent from another vote a month later that authorized the US commander in Afghanistan to use private military units to support and augment combat operations. The number of Aegis Global employees assigned to Afghanistan quadrupled overnight. The running joke in Kabul was that the US commander had finally replaced the NATO-led security mission."

"Why did she miss the second vote?" said Decker. "I thought she had made it a point to continue her work."

"She did," said Harlow. "But it fell on the same day as the only ransom threat deemed credible by the FBI."

"Quite the coincidence."

"Given Senator Steele's waning support for the Afghanistan war, these votes would have very likely gone the other way," said Harlow. "And that's not all. Frist snuck another authorization through the day after the Hemet disaster—this one allowing the US commander in Afghanistan to give tactical control of private military forces to a provisional combat commander, under circumstances where no coordination or conflict between regular military forces and private forces exists. The definition of *provisional combat commander* in the authorization is nebulous. This represents the first instance of a private military force conducting independent and direct combat missions for a US military-theater commander."

"It's like the start of a Praetorian Guard," said Decker. "Aleman's theory centers around a concept Jacob Harcourt wrote about a few years ago. Privatizing the war in Afghanistan."

"We read the same article, and the pattern fits. Frist has been slowly removing the roadblocks, mostly while Senator Steele has been distracted—but now it appears she's giving Frist her full support. She's even cosponsored a few bills and authorizations indirectly supporting his agenda."

"Harcourt's agenda," said Decker. "I have no doubt he fashions himself as the future viceroy of Afghanistan."

"There'll be no shortage of well-compensated, high-ranking positions under Viceroy Harcourt. I'm sure Frist will come out of this an extremely wealthy man, given his stake in the company."

"How did you determine his stake? Aegis Global is privately held," said Decker.

"You really don't want to know."

"Ah. How I miss being able to say that."

"So what's next, Decker?" said Harlow. "As you can imagine, we're getting a little antsy here. Everyone is itching to do more than come up with theories."

"Before we talk about a plan, let me go over this one more time, to make sure I have it right. Harcourt and Frist orchestrated the kidnap/murder of Meghan Steele to distract Senator Steele and eventually work their way into her good graces by offering World Recovery Group's services—all the while assuming our efforts would yield no results."

"Right."

"Their ultimate goal was to distract the senator from their slow-burn plan to stack the deck in favor of this Praetorian Guard concept, which Harcourt would be the obvious benefactor of, since he would likely be appointed viceroy of Afghanistan, with Frist benefiting financially and possibly with a powerful position," said Decker. "I have to stop here and say how fucked this is."

"Really fucked," said Pierce.

"Agreed on both accounts," said Harlow.

"The plan almost went south when we located Meghan Steele," said Decker, "even though I don't see why they couldn't have let us rescue her. They would have been even bigger heroes in Senator Steele's eyes, accomplishing their second goal of making her an ally."

"She wasn't their ally yet, so I think they used the Hemet bombing to create another opportunity to slip a key authorization past her," said Harlow.

Decker's next question would be uncomfortable for all of them, particularly for him.

"Then why the rest of the mess? Why kill all the families?" he said, pausing to swallow. "Why send the FBI after us? They could have left us alone and blamed the Russians."

The car remained silent for several seconds.

"I know you don't want to hear this, Decker," said Harlow, pausing. "But I think they did it to maximize the distraction and confusion. Special Agent Reeves focused all of his energy on building a case against you. Senator Steele became obsessed with the details of the case. Nobody was paying attention to Frist and Harcourt, who took full advantage of the chaos that ensued. I'm sorry to put this all so bluntly."

Decker gave it a moment before responding. "It is what it is. The only question in my mind is, Who do we go after first?"

"Frist kind of rhymes with *first*," said Pierce.

"He'd be the softer target," said Decker. "We could probably snatch him right off the street in DC."

"You don't grab a US senator without inviting severe consequences—especially when you have little more than theories backing you up," said Harlow. "You'll bring the entire law enforcement establishment down on your head, and you'll instantly alienate every politician and Beltway insider that might have become an ally. Harcourt is the harder target, but nobody—except for Frist—will shed a tear if that self-serving asshole vanishes."

"We're going to need one hell of a plan to grab Harcourt," said Pierce. "He's guarded by a private army."

"I have a better idea," said Decker.

"Harlow," Pierce cut in, "we barely know each other, but this is where I usually hang up on him. Nothing good comes after 'I have a better idea.'"

"I've heard 'You're not going to like this' a few times already," she said. "I'm not sure how much worse it can get."

302

"Trust me," said Pierce. "Whatever you've seen from him so far—it gets way worse."

"She doesn't scare off easy," said Decker.

"She doesn't scare off at all," said Pam.

"What's your idea, Decker?" said Harlow.

"We grab them both, at the same time."

"And how do you propose we pull that off?"

"I don't know. That's your job, Harlow. You get the two of them in one place, and we'll grab both of them."

"Sure. I'll just give them a call and suggest a meet-up," said Harlow.

"Might be that easy," said Pam.

"We'll see," said Harlow. "Anything else we can do for you? Maybe get Harcourt and Frist to turn themselves in?"

"One thing," said Decker. "How is my daughter doing? And my parents?"

A long pause ensued. "I'm told they're doing fine, under the circumstances. Most importantly—they're safe."

"Thank you," said Decker, ending the call.

Pierce turned to him. "They're going to be fine. Sounds like they're in the best hands possible."

"I know," said Decker, rubbing his face. "I just couldn't live with myself if something happened to them."

"Nothing's going to happen to them," said Pierce. "I'm going to change the subject now."

"Please."

"I was serious about Harcourt and the private-army thing. I can see us getting to Harcourt, barely, but I can't picture escaping with him."

"Remember the Delgado case?"

"I do."

"Remember how we got his son out?"

Pierce sat quietly for a few moments, staring at the road ahead. "It could work, but that's a trip for two."

"I've heard they've modified it for three."

"Still leaves one of us behind," said Pierce.

"I'd be happy to volunteer," said Decker.

"You against an army?"

"I keep beating the odds. No reason to bet against me yet," said Decker. "Do you know how to find Bernstein?"

"I've very carefully kept in touch with a few of our most trusted, unadvertised contacts."

"Good. Let's reach out to him in the morning. Check on his availability."

"There's only one problem," said Pierce.

"What?"

"Bernie doesn't take IOUs."

"Not a problem," said Decker. "I have some money stashed in banks outside the US."

"I figured the FBI didn't find all of it."

"They didn't find half of it," said Decker. "International wire transfers aren't a problem. ATM withdrawals are another story. We can pay Bernie and whoever else we need to pull this off."

"And here you had me thinking you were poor."

"I am poor," said Decker. "In the United States."

CHAPTER FORTY-NINE

Supervisory Special Agent Reeves scrolled through his backlog of emails, figuring he'd better start tackling them. The power vacuum left by Viktor Penkin's kidnapping and murder had attracted a few contenders, who would undoubtedly start littering the greater Los Angeles metropolitan area with bodies. Reeves had witnessed this cycle before and knew that there was little for his division to do until the new power structure emerged and the situation settled, but he'd focused the bulk of his crew's resources on Decker for close to a week. It was time to let Decker go.

There was little chance he remained in the LA area, and the Bureau of Prisons still hadn't declared him an escaped prisoner. He remained a person of interest connected to Penkin's murder, but Reeves had no evidence linking him to the scene. The same applied to Mackenzie, who had done a masterful job disappearing within the city, if she hadn't already left. He was starting to have serious doubts whether either of them had stuck around.

Senator Steele wouldn't be happy, but Reeves wasn't a miracle worker, and he certainly didn't have the authority to expand the scope of his interest in Decker beyond Los Angeles. He'd stretched the Russian connection as thin as possible without drawing attention from his superiors, who would not be happy to learn that he had diverted resources from the Russian organized crime division during one of the biggest events to transpire on his watch. With that thought in mind, he picked up the phone to call Special Agent Kincaid and pull the rest of the surveillance off Harlow Mackenzie's associates.

He didn't want to give up on finding Decker altogether, but the trail had disappeared and what little momentum they had managed to generate had stalled. Someone else could worry about Decker and the odd links to Aegis. He'd package what he'd collected on Decker, Gunther Ross, and Rich Hyde and pass it up the chain of command within the criminal investigative division, where it would most likely get deep-sixed.

He dialed Kincaid's number, hearing the phone ring a few offices down, when his cell phone chimed a text alert. While the office phone rang, he checked the text alert, nearly hanging up when he read the message.

"Special Agent Matt Kincaid," he heard before the receiver hit the phone cradle.

Reeves put the phone back to his ear. "Matt. We have a hit on Kathleen Murphy, a.k.a. Katie Murphy, one of Mackenzie's primary business partners. I'm pulling up the details right now."

He found the corresponding email, which had arrived at the same time as the text, and clicked the attached link. A few seconds later, he was logged in to a JRIC facial-recognition activity register customized with his search requests. He clicked on the only facial-recognition hit registered to his targets.

"She was tagged less than a minute ago by a camera across from the Natural Foods on Sepulveda in Sherman Oaks. Distance and direction puts her in the parking lot," said Reeves. "There's a note in the register indicating that the camera was moved less than a week ago from the 405/101 on-ramp sign to the traffic signal on Sepulveda, right next to the Natural Foods. I think she got nailed by a camera she didn't expect."

"LAPD is always moving the cameras around and adding new ones to screw with the zone-mapping apps," said Kincaid.

"She won't have any idea she's been made. She could lead us right back to Mackenzie."

"I thought we were throttling back on this one."

"We were," said Reeves. "But if Mackenzie's still in town, Decker might be around, too."

Reeves knew he should let this go, but the opportunity was too tempting. He could wrap this up in under an hour, delivering Decker's location to CID and the federal marshals. A quick call to Senator Steele, and Decker was gone for good.

"What's our move?" said Kincaid.

"I want every agent we have in the valley on this. I'll review the camera footage on the way so we can identify her car. The first agents to arrive will plant a GPS tracker and observe from a distance."

"You might want to consider aerial surveillance. Mackenzie's crew is pretty adept at ditching us on the ground."

"I'll call Tori in CID to see if they have a bird airborne," said Reeves, standing up. "And if they're willing to let us borrow it."

"Give me a few minutes to send out a message to our teams in the valley. Meet you at the elevator," said Kincaid, hanging up.

Reeves grabbed his field tablet from its charging station and stuffed it in a brown leather briefcase, along with a satellite phone. He'd need the phone to communicate with the plane. Before walking out of his office, he patted his coat, feeling his cell phone and his badge holder nestled inside the pocket. It wouldn't be the first time he rushed out of here without one of those.

He met Kincaid at the elevator lobby, Reeves checking his watch the entire way down. It would take them longer to get out of the Wilshire Federal Building's parking garage than it would to drive up the 405 to their destination—assuming the northbound traffic was clear. The Natural Foods on Sepulveda Boulevard in Sherman Oaks was just north of the hills separating the Los Angeles Basin from the San Fernando

Valley, a route normally clear this late in the morning, unless there was an accident.

They could be on scene in under a half hour, which should leave them plenty of time to coordinate an effective surveillance effort, assuming Ms. Murphy hadn't ducked inside Natural Foods for a snack. He suspected she was there to resupply the crew hiding somewhere nearby. She didn't own property in the valley and could have chosen to stop at a dozen less crowded spots for a coffee or bite to eat. He expected her to be inside for a while.

When they pulled onto Wilshire Boulevard, he called Tori Breene, who had the unenviable task of authorizing and coordinating the use of the field office's more controversial surveillance tools. Aircraft, drones, and cell-site simulators made the public's A-list of protested assets—and she was responsible for all of them.

"Supervisory Special Agent Breene," she answered.

"Tori. It's Joe Reeves from Organized Crime," he said. "I need a favor, if possible."

"I thought you might have taken a vacation after the Penkin thing. Your division has been awfully quiet."

"The past week has been one big game of musical chairs," said Decker. "Except in this game, you end up with your throat cut from ear to ear if you don't have a seat when the music stops."

"Charming."

"It actually hasn't been that bad yet, which is why I need a quick favor."

"Now it's a *quick* favor?"

"I need to follow a car for about an hour. The target is parked at the Natural Foods in Sherman Oaks on Sepulveda."

"That's all you're going to tell me?"

"The less you know about it, the better."

"You mean the less your boss, who also happens to be my boss, knows about it, the better."

"It's related to Penkin," said Reeves. "I've been chasing down a possible suspect in his murder, who may not be connected to the Russian mob at all."

"Cartel?"

"No. Possibly a personal grudge."

"That's one hell of a grudge."

"It's a bit of a stretch," said Reeves. "Which is why I want to keep this as informal as possible. I just need an hour. This crew ran circles around my ground surveillance teams recently."

"This better be legit."

"It's completely legitimate—just such a long shot I'd rather not have it cross the SAC's desk. All I'm asking for is a handoff once the target stops. My division will take over from there."

"One hour. Everything will be logged as usual."

"Understood. Like I said, this is completely legit."

"It better be," she said. "Do you have a satellite phone?"

"Yes," said Reeves, scrambling to pull it out of his briefcase.

"Give me the number. They'll call you when they're over the target area."

Reeves read the number off the back of the phone. "I owe you one, Tori."

"If I had a dollar for every time I heard that here," she said. "Jana is their call sign. Give them about fifteen minutes to get on station. They're circling east of the city right now."

"Thank you, Tori," he said, but the call had already ended.

Reeves switched to his handheld radio, checking whether any of his units were in range. He got a few squawks in reply but knew radio communications with agents in the valley would be spotty at best on this side of the hills. His phone rang, caller ID identifying Sarah Vale, an agent on stakeout in Van Nuys. He answered the call.

"Agent Vale," he said. "How far out are you?"

"A minute. I heard your call on the radio, but most of it was garbled."

"Has anyone arrived ahead of you?"

"Negative. The next closest agent is Gaines, and he's about five minutes away."

"Do you have a GPS tracker unit?"

"I do not," she said. "Neither does Gaines. Simonetti has one, but she's a few minutes farther out than Gaines."

"That's fine," said Reeves. "I have one of our surveillance aircraft on the way over. ETA fifteen minutes."

"You don't trust us not to lose them again?" she said, and he couldn't tell if she was serious or joking.

"No offense, but I wouldn't be too surprised if they were capable of ditching the aerial surveillance, too."

"None taken," said Vale. "That was a first for me."

"You and me both," said Reeves. "I'll resend the photos of Kathleen Murphy and try to pinpoint the target vehicle with the facial-recognition shots. She's parked in the Natural Foods parking lot."

"That's not a big lot. Kind of odd-shaped. There's a lot of ways out of there."

"That's why I called in a surveillance bird. We'll have it for an hour. Should be long enough to get a solid fix on wherever they're hiding out."

"I'll park in the lot and wait," said Vale. "How far away are you?"

"At least fifteen minutes."

"No worries. We'll have three vehicles here within ten. Another three by the time you arrive. We won't lose them this time."

"Perfect. Coordinate with the other units until I arrive." An idea suddenly hit him. "Hey. Are you dressed for street surveillance?"

"Yeah. I'm casual."

"Good. I'll probably send you inside when Gaines gets there. To make sure she hasn't already given us the slip."

"I'll be ready," she said.

He ended the call and went to work on his tablet, disseminating Kathleen Murphy's photos to the inbound team and studying the traffic-cam photos. From what he could tell, Murphy had parked a red four-door sedan, face in, on the inside of the row directly across from the store's entrance. He navigated to Google Maps and zoomed in on the store, taking a screenshot of the image. A few seconds later, he'd used an embedded graphics tool to draw a red circle around the spaces, adding RED 4DOOR SEDAN to the image. He sent the package to Vale, with instructions to forward it to the responding agents.

When she acknowledged the message, he leaned his head back and let Kincaid guide them north through the mercifully light traffic on Interstate 405. Reeves spent the time strategizing what he'd do with Mackenzie's location when the aircraft finally marked it. Continue surveillance? Keep it under wraps until Decker was declared a fugitive and then turn it over to CID? Hand it over to Senator Steele and let her deal with it?

He knew the right answer was to call the whole thing off and get back to work on the Russians, but something deep inside refused to let it go. A persistent gut feeling that the Decker-and-Mackenzie angle was just the tip of the iceberg. That he'd be derelict in his duty to Senator Steele if he ignored it. Reeves turned to Kincaid.

"What am I forgetting?" said Reeves.

"That we're skating on thin ice with this?"

Reeves stifled a laugh. "Very thin ice."

"More like slush."

"If this doesn't pan out, that's the end of it. No more Decker."

Kincaid gave him a friendly but skeptical look.

"Seriously," said Reeves.

"I didn't say anything."

"You didn't have to," he said, his phone and tablet chiming at the same time.

He checked the tablet in his lap, expecting to see a response from Special Agent Vale but instead finding another automated message from

JRIC's facial-recognition division. The system had registered another hit on the same camera, but this one at a much farther distance.

"Murphy's on the move already," said Reeves, clicking the link.

He grabbed his phone to warn Vale, glancing at the screen again. *What the hell?* The system had flagged Gunther Ross. How was that even possible, unless—*oh, shit!* He dialed Vale.

"Come on. Come on," he said, waiting for her to pick up.

"Good timing," she said. "I have Kathleen Murphy and Pamela Stack in sight. I couldn't believe it when both—"

"Agent Vale! Sorry to interrupt, but I need you to listen carefully."

"I'm listening."

"I don't have time to explain, but there's another group interested in locating Decker, and we just got a facial recognition hit on their presumed leader from the same camera that caught Murphy. This group is extremely dangerous. Spec Ops–level mercenaries. I need you to back off as far as possible. It's your call how many vehicles to keep on the surveillance. New target vehicle is a white Range Rover. Three occupants. Looks like they entered the parking lot from—"

"Saugus Avenue. I see it," she said. "Crap. They just cruised a few feet behind Murphy and Stack. Still moving. Looks like a surveillance pass."

"They're after the same thing we're after—Decker's location. Did you put a tracker on Murphy's vehicle?"

"No. Simonetti got held up in traffic. I guess that's a good thing."

"Yeah. They probably had people there soon after you arrived," said Reeves. "Dammit. I should have seen this coming."

"This group has access to the city's cameras?"

"I don't see any other way to explain this," said Reeves. "Pass the word to your teams."

Gunther Ross's conservative approach to navigating the parking lot suggested he thought he was safe from the newly installed camera. He hadn't come within standard facial-recognition range. Watts's experimental software upgrade had paid off.

"Joe," she said. "I don't know what kind of wild thinking you're indulging in, but—"

"Senator Steele!" he cut in. "I would never bring something like this to you if I didn't think it warranted your immediate attention."

Steele was taken aback by his tone. Reeves had always been one of the most respectful and thoughtful law enforcement agents she'd known.

"What's going on, Joe? You sound upset."

"I don't know how to say this, so I'm just going to say it. I strongly suspect your daughter was murdered by Aegis Global."

For a moment, she couldn't form a thought, much less a response.

"Joe," she said at last, "I consider Jacob Harcourt, the CEO of Aegis Global, a close friend. When Senator Frist called on him for help, he didn't hesitate. I know you always resented the outside involvement, but I had to take every measure conceivable to get my daughter back."

"Ma'am. It pains me to say this, but I think Frist was involved, too. There was nothing anyone could have done to bring your daughter back after they grabbed her."

"I don't believe that," she hissed. "Decker found her. She died in that house because he waited too long!"

"She was never supposed to be in that house," said Reeves. "She was supposed to be dead and vanished shortly after her abduction. The Russians kept her for leverage when they realized she was your daughter. Decker was never meant to find her."

"Reeves," she said firmly, abandoning his first name on purpose.

"Yes, ma'am?"

"I'm going to hang up and forget you called. I owe you that much," she said. "But I don't ever want to hear from you again. Is that clear? You're so far out of line here, my head is spinning."

"I made this call, understanding perfectly well that we may never speak again. But I firmly believe you've been betrayed, and I'm willing to risk our friendship to warn you."

Steele took a deep breath and exhaled, forcing herself to think about the lunacy he'd just shared with her, rather than simply ending the call. Based on her numerous interactions with Reeves, she believed that he wouldn't do something like this to her unless he felt sure he had enough evidence to support his allegations. She'd give him a chance to explain himself.

"Joe. You have five minutes."

Forty minutes later, she ended the call—her hands shaking. Senator Steele felt her world collapsing again. She didn't want to believe anything Reeves had told her, but deep down, she knew it was true. Despite the rage building inside, she had no intention of accepting his allegations without concrete proof, which he admittedly did not possess. She'd sift through the documents he'd emailed to her government account and decide how far she was willing to go along with Reeves's plan to learn the truth.

Steele wiped the tears from her face and dialed Julie Ragan, her chief of staff.

"I was just about to call you," said Julie. "The car is ready. I let our point of contact at tonight's event know that we're running—"

"Julie?" said Steele. "We have to cancel tonight's engagement. The whole night, actually. Something has come up."

"Not a problem. I'll let them know," said Julie. "Is there something I can do for you? Is everything all right?"

"I need you in my office right away."

Ten seconds later, Julie Ragan opened the door and stepped inside, closing it behind her. Steele stared at the family portrait mounted to the wall behind her desk, finally acknowledging Ragan's arrival with a nod. She stood up and approached Julie, who looked alarmed.

"Sorry. I didn't mean to scare you," said Steele.

"No worries at all. I just know you were really looking forward to getting together with your friends for dinner."

"I was, but . . ." She trailed off. "I need you to do me an unusual favor."

"Absolutely," said Ragan. "Whatever you need."

"I need to know where Senator Frist is headed this weekend. He said he was going out of town, but that's all I know."

"I'll look into it and get right back to you. Anything else?"

She shook her head. As Ragan started for the door, Steele stopped her.

"And Julie?" said Steele. "I don't care what you have to do to get this information."

PART FOUR

CHAPTER FIFTY-FOUR

Gunther Ross tightened his grip on the strap hanging above him as the tactically modified Sikorsky S-76D banked west and dived for the Santa Monica Hills. His stomach pitched until the pilot leveled the helicopter and straightened on their final course to the target.

"One minute!" yelled the copilot.

Gunther scanned the Sikorsky S-76D's passenger compartment. His seven-operator team wore basic plate carriers over comfortable civilian clothes, emphasizing speed and mobility over restrictive protection. He expected the team to be in and out of the house in less than two minutes, encountering little to no resistance.

If the shock of a helicopter landing wore off and the occupants resisted, his team would respond accordingly. Gunther had created strict rules of engagement (ROE) for the team to follow, which would hopefully keep key targets alive if the use of lethal force became necessary. Key targets included Mackenzie and her partners, with the primary emphasis placed on taking Mackenzie alive.

Only Gunther could authorize a lethal response against her, no matter what the situation. Without her, they'd have no leverage against Decker. All efforts to locate Decker's daughter and parents had failed.

Lethal force was authorized against her firm partners only as a last resort, and anyone *not* falling into either of the previous categories was fair game.

The first thirty seconds after the helicopter landed would set the tone for the rest of the mission. If Mackenzie's crew took up weapons and tried to engage his team, there wasn't much he could do to prevent her team from being massacred. Each Aegis commando carried a suppressed HK416C assault rifle and six spare magazines. Whatever Mackenzie started would end just as quickly—hopefully she'd survive.

To prevent this combative scenario from unfolding, the first three men out of the helicopter had been tasked with immediately securing the master bedroom, which mission planners back at the operations center had managed to pinpoint using images of the house from an online rental ad.

Thermal imagery from the drone indicated that the master bedroom's ambient temperature was higher than the rest of the house, suggesting a concentration of computer equipment and warm bodies. If the team reached the master bedroom before Mackenzie and her partners panicked, Gunther could defuse the situation with hostages.

"Thirty seconds!" yelled the copilot.

Gunther triggered his tactical radio. "Remember your ROE. We need Mackenzie alive."

The operators nodded and checked their weapons while Gunther requested a final situational report from Ramirez, who sat in an SUV down the street from the Summit Estates entrance gate, controlling the drone high above.

"Watchtower. We're twenty seconds out," said Gunther. "Request final SITREP."

"This is Watchtower," said Ramirez. "Blinds are drawn, so I have no visible contact. Still showing a significant heat signature from the master bedroom. I'm getting a little more heat from the two-story great room, so you may have targets gathered in that space. Happy hunting."

"Keep an eye on the neighborhood for us," said Gunther.

He grabbed the door latch and nodded at the operative on the other side to do the same. All of the men shifted their bodies, pointing toward the door they would use to exit the helicopter. Gunther would be the first out of the starboard-side door, leading Bravo team to the patio slider, where they would breach the house and take a hard right into the great room.

"Doors open!" barked the copilot.

Gunther lifted the latch with one hand and pushed the heavy door outward with the other, using both of them to slide it toward the back of the helicopter. Warm wind rushed into the cabin as house lights from the hillside neighborhood rose to meet them. They passed over a lighted tennis court on the right, Gunther able to read the shocked expressions on the players' faces before they vanished in the dust storm raised by the helicopter's powerful rotor wash.

The tennis court disappeared, momentarily replaced by a steep rise of wind-scattered bushes until a glowing blue pool rushed into view. When the helicopter's wheels gently impacted the ground, Gunther jumped onto the lawn, never hearing the copilot give them the green light to disembark.

Gunther sprinted across the short stretch of tightly mowed grass, hitting the well-lit patio and heading straight for the wide slider underneath the deep pergola attached to the house. He slowed his pace to let the team's breacher get in front of him as they closed the remaining twenty feet to their entry point.

"Bravo Three. Shotgun the glass," said Gunther, not wanting anything slowing their momentum.

The operator tasked with forcing an entry raised his semiautomatic shotgun while running and fired repeatedly at the glass in front of him. Designed specifically to shatter glass, the shotgun slugs instantly disintegrated the massive glass plate, a cascade of broken fragments showering the hardwood inside the house.

"Bravo team is in," said Gunther. "No sign of resistance. We caught them with their pants down."

CHAPTER

FIFTY-FIVE

Harry Bernstein gently tugged the yoke left, nudging the ancient aircraft back on course. A glance at the flip-down computer monitor installed above the center control panel showed them flying down the center of the drop corridor, on target to pass directly over the drop zone. The digital readout underneath the glide-path image indicated a distance of one and a half miles to the drop.

Bernie had been doing this for so long, he didn't have to read the time to drop zone to know that the thirty-second warning wasn't far away. Before he took his eyes off the screen, the readout flashed "30SEC." He reached above his head and flipped the parachute warning light switch to "STBY," which activated a small red light next to the rear cargo ramp, alerting his flight crew that the aircraft was on final approach to the drop zone.

He had to keep playing with the yoke to keep the C-123 centered over the drop corridor, the Vietnam-era aircraft giving him a little more hassle than usual tonight. Nothing out of the ordinary for a fifty-two-year-old hunk of flying metal that had changed hands more than a dozen times in her lifetime.

He'd owned the retired military transport for close to a decade, having purchased her from a flying club in Arizona that couldn't afford her maintenance. On top of its significant cargo-carrying capacity and a rear-loading ramp, the costly purchase had added a unique capability to his sky fleet, which his client had specifically requested tonight.

Bernie checked the screen again, correctly guessing that five seconds remained until they crossed a three-dimensional point five thousand feet directly over the drop zone. Keeping the yoke steady with his left hand, he raised the other and toggled the standby switch, flashing the red light next to the ramp until his internal stopwatch told him five seconds had expired. Instinctively, his finger flipped the adjacent switch.

A few seconds later, his headset activated. "Three packages delivered. Setting up for recovery."

"I'm going to climb to ten thousand feet and start a lazy circle," said Bernie.

"How long can we circle around up here?" said his flight crew leader.

"I really don't know," said Bernie. "We're well outside DC's updated air defense identification zone, but all it will take is one jumpy air traffic controller to ruin our night."

CHAPTER FIFTY-SIX

Jacob Harcourt read the text on his phone and glanced up at Senator Frist, who had plopped down on the seventeenth-century Scottish Caquetoire armchair that nobody but Harcourt himself had ever sat in. Two hours into Frist's weekend stay, the text couldn't have made him happier.

"So? Do we have them?" said Frist.

"Yes. *We* have them," said Harcourt, feigning his warmest smile. He motioned toward the exquisitely stocked built-in cocktail cabinet next to his desk, at the other end of the cherrywood study, hoping to dislodge Frist from the two-hundred-thousand-dollar Highland clan antique. "Shall we celebrate? I think you'll find my selection of spirits worthy of the moment."

"I'll have what you're having," said Frist, shifting in the seat. "This is damn uncomfortable for a throne."

Harcourt saw his opportunity. "Oh, it's not a throne. Quite the opposite, in fact. It's a common chair of its era. Seventeenth century."

"No wonder. The moment I sat in it, I could tell it was essentially junk. Expensive junk. No offense."

"None taken," said Harcourt. "How does a Dalmore fifty-year-old Highland single malt sound?"

Frist stood up, frowning at the antique like he'd been seated in a folding chair.

"I was thinking more along the lines of Johnnie Walker Blue," said Frist, making his way to the deep leather chairs facing the room's cathedral ceiling windows. "Celebrate in style."

He wasn't about to tell Frist that he'd downgraded his choice from a seventy-thousand-dollar bottle of scotch to a one-hundred-and-eight-dollar bottle. Why ruin one of the few moments of happiness Harcourt would experience all weekend? While Frist settled into one of the chairs, facing the other direction, Harcourt opened the cabinet below the lacquered-cherry counter and removed one of ten unopened boxes of Johnnie Walker Blue Label he kept on hand to give out as gifts.

Quietly opening the box, he tore away the bottle's seal and lifted the cork. The smooth aroma reminded him that he was holding a damn fine bottle of scotch, just not the most expensive. That said, he had no intention of lowering his standards this early in the game. He had an entire weekend with Frist ahead of him, which was guaranteed to present more opportunities.

"Two fingers?" he asked.

"Make it a double. With Decker still on the loose, I can use the shot of courage," said Frist, laughing.

"A double it is." Harcourt filled the fine crystal tumbler. "You have nothing to worry about here. I have more than sixty highly trained Aegis contractors on the estate, not to mention a state-of-the-art security system. You saw the security room. Every square inch of the estate is covered with sensors, and we're watching the sky in case he's stupid enough to skydive in again."

"I know. I know," said Frist. "We're just so goddamn close to the finish line, and I can't stop thinking about him. I was scared out of my mind flying out here! I got in the helicopter half expecting Decker to turn around in the copilot seat and blow my brains out!"

"Gerry. You've been watching too much TV. Decker is a very resourceful man, but he's just one man."

"He apparently found an equally skilled friend. The Aleman thing was a disaster."

"Two men," said Harcourt, pouring two fingers of the Dalmore—then adding another. "And we have the ultimate bargaining chip."

"If we had his daughter, we'd have the ultimate bargaining chip. It worries me that she disappeared that quickly."

"Mackenzie beat us to her," said Harcourt, walking the drinks over.

"At least Mackenzie's out of the picture. If she could find Aleman, God knows what else she could have pieced together." Drinks in hand, the senator proposed a toast. "To killing Decker."

Frist's single-mindedness got tiresome at times, especially when you were on the cusp of sealing a deal to make billions of dollars.

"To Monday's vote," said Harcourt. "May we carry the day."

"Sorry. I'm having trouble focusing on the big picture," said Frist, before clinking Harcourt's glass. "To Monday."

"Hear, hear," said Harcourt, taking a generous sip of the fifty-year-old spirit.

He barely had time to savor the scotch's initial palate of tangy marmalade, roasted coffee, and chocolate before the handheld radio on his desk crackled to life.

"Mr. Harcourt! Rooftop spotters report three parachutes descending toward the southern end of the estate."

Frist downed his drink in one massive gulp, slamming the tumbler down on the marble coffee table.

"This isn't a problem," said Harcourt, taking his drink with him to the desk. He took a quick sip and swiped the radio from the desk. "What are we looking at, Dutch?"

"Two parachutists and one package," said his security chief. "They opened their chutes low as hell. They'll be on the ground in ten seconds."

"A package?" said Harcourt.

"It's definitely not a person," said Dutch. "It's about the size of a Pelican transport case."

"They must be using an airborne guidance unit. GPS guided."

"It might be a bomb!" said Frist, grabbing his glass before scrambling away from the floor-to-ceiling window.

"It's not a bomb," said Harcourt before lowering his voice and turning away from Frist. "Dutch. Any way that package can get to the house?"

"Negative. It's already in the trees," he said. "About six hundred feet from the southern fence line. One of the spotters hit it with a range finder."

"And the parachutists?"

"They landed a lot farther back."

"I want every single man available out there," said Harcourt. "I don't want them getting anywhere near me."

"How many do you want to keep back?"

"Just you," said Harcourt. "Lock the house down hard. Nobody comes back inside until Decker and his associate are dead."

"Sir. I don't know if that's a good idea," said Dutch. "I'd feel more comfortable with a small team. Just in case."

"Four men, plus yourself. Keep them in one place. I don't need a bunch of yahoos running around."

"Understood, sir."

"What's your plan to keep them from reaching us?" said Harcourt.

"I have four ATVs on the way, three men each," said Dutch. "I want to get to that package before Decker does. I'll bring the rest up in a skirmish line spanning the estate with teams in reserve."

"Sounds like you could hold off a battalion."

"As long as we get to that package first. God knows what they brought with them."

"Make it happen, Dutch," said Harcourt. "I'll be in the study."

"I'd be happier if you retreated to the safe room."

"I have complete confidence in you and the team assembled. Keep me posted," said Harcourt, placing the radio on the desk.

"Copy that, sir," squawked the radio.

Frist was already at the bar, pouring another drink. "I'd feel happier if we retreated to the safe room, too," he said, his glass filled to the rim with scotch.

"Gerry. Before you guzzle enough scotch to kill an elephant, set the glass down and follow me. I want to show you something." Harcourt walked toward the back of the study. "I promise you'll get back to your drink."

Frist reluctantly set his precariously overfilled glass on the bar counter and joined him. Harcourt pressed his palm against a hand-size rectangular wood panel, and a standard door–size section of the wall swung inward, revealing a short hallway that ended with an original Picasso. A stolen work beyond value.

"Safe room to the left," said Harcourt. "Picasso to the front."

"I never really got what people saw in Picasso," said Frist, heading for the open doorway.

"He's an acquired taste," said Harcourt, trailing Frist. "Like the Dalmore."

Frist glanced around the luxuriously appointed room. "Looks more like a sitting room."

"That's the point. You sit in here and wait for help to arrive. The walls are blastproof on all sides. Separate ventilation. Two weeks of food and water for four people. Bathroom. Secure communications. Weapons."

"And you don't want to wait this out in here?"

"The study windows are bullet resistant," said Harcourt. "I'd rather not hide in here like a rat on the eve of a great victory. The house is secure. My study is secure. And we can be in here within seconds. Let's finish our drinks while Aegis Global finishes Decker."

CHAPTER FIFTY-SEVEN

Decker lay hidden in the thick forest, waiting for any indication that Harcourt had taken the bait. Glancing at his watch, he shook his head. They should have reacted by now. Pierce's voice broke the quiet, whispering through his wireless earpiece.

"Do you think we need to force this?"

"Give it thirty more seconds," said Decker.

"We should have landed already. Unless Harcourt's security missed the parachutes."

"If they missed the parachutes, we're screwed," said Decker.

A car engine rumbled to life directly ahead of him.

"I'm on the move," said Decker, lifting himself off the ground.

"Covering," said Pierce.

Decker sprinted through the trees, shoving the barrel of his suppressed rifle through the open passenger window of the concealed SUV. He triggered the six-hundred-lumen light attached to the rifle, causing both occupants to shield their eyes with both hands.

"If this vehicle moves one inch, I'll kill both of you," said Decker. "If those hands move downward—at all—I will kill both of you. Nod if you understand."

They both nodded.

"Nod if you want to see your families again," said Decker, getting another round of nods. "Is the vehicle in park?"

The driver nodded.

"We're in business."

Pierce emerged from the trees on the opposite side of the road, his rifle pointed east, in the direction of Harcourt's estate.

"Looks clear," said Pierce, crossing the two-lane rural road.

"I still say we ice these two and move on," said Decker.

Pierce arrived at the driver's window a moment later, pressing the barrel of his rifle against the driver's head. "It'll be worth the thirty seconds to stow them away. I'm sure these two would like to walk out of here alive."

"Worth it for *them*," said Decker before opening the door and pulling the body armor–clad operative onto the shoulder of the road.

Twenty seconds later, the two men were zip-tied by their wrists and ankles to separate trees, duct tape covering their mouths. Decker jumped in the front passenger seat and removed his mask before placing the communications rig he'd ripped off the guard on the dashboard. He reconnected the earpiece set to the radio and inserted the translucent earbud, triggering the transmit mechanism to test the connection. He heard a click through the earpiece, followed by faint static.

Pierce got behind the wheel a moment later. "Anything on the net?"

"All quiet. They must have already responded."

"Perfect," said Pierce, putting the SUV in gear and taking off.

As they sped toward Harcourt's estate, Decker turned to Pierce. "No more mercy when we hit the estate."

"Yep."

"Just so we're on the same page."

"We are," said Pierce, suddenly slowing the SUV.

Headlights appeared briefly on the road ahead of them, disappearing as the vehicle turned onto the private drive leading to the main gate to Harcourt's estate. Pierce eased their SUV onto the smooth, tree-lined drive and followed the taillights to a well-lit guard shack a few hundred yards away.

"I'll do all the talking," said Pierce.

"You might want to take your mask off first," said Decker.

Pierce pulled the black mask off and tossed it on the dashboard. Decker drew a suppressed pistol from his thigh holster and placed it in his lap.

"In case the talking doesn't work."

"Just don't shoot me by accident," said Pierce, pulling into place behind the SUV in front of them.

"Keep your head back. You know the rules."

"Funny," said Pierce, easing them forward as close to the other SUV's bumper as possible.

Decker studied the guards at the gate, watching how they handled the other SUV. He assumed the identical vehicle had come from a similar position observing the eastern approach to the estate. Harcourt had responded predictably by recalling them and throwing all of his manpower at the parachute threat on the opposite side of the estate.

"They're waving them through," said Pierce.

"Follow them as close as possible. Don't stop."

Pierce accelerated with the lead SUV, driving so close that the slightest unanticipated change in speed would result in bumper-to-bumper contact. One of the guards on Pierce's side raised his hand to stop them, but the guard standing next to him waved them on. Halfway to the plantation-style white mansion in the distance, the radio chatter started.

"ROADKILL. This is WARHAMMER. Proceed to the service entrance. I'll let you in once you secure the area around the entrance. Report to the security office for tasking."

"ROADKILL One copies."

Decker pulled the microphone clip up to his mouth and pressed the transmit button. "ROADKILL Two copies," he said.

"Don't loiter on the driveway. Get to the service entrance immediately so I can let you inside. WARHAMMER out."

Decker released the transmitter and dropped it in his lap.

"ROADKILL?" said Pierce.

"The other guy was WARHAMMER."

"These call sign heroes spend a little too much time picking out cool names."

"I kind of like ROADKILL," said Decker.

"What did the god of war have to say?"

"WARHAMMER wants us inside the house," said Decker. "Sounds like they sent everyone south to check out the parachutes."

"Perfect."

"The guys in the other SUV got the same invitation."

"Nothing we can't handle," said Pierce.

Pierce rolled up his tinted window and donned his mask. Decker did the same. WARHAMMER would no doubt be watching the vehicles closely when they pulled up to the service entrance. The tinted side windows would give them a few extra seconds of anonymity before Decker spoiled the surprise.

Decker holstered the suppressed pistol and slipped the earpiece wire under his rifle so it wouldn't get snagged. The SUV ahead of them pulled off the main drive, turning onto a stone driveway that wrapped around the home's four-bay garage and continued behind the house. He knew from studying Google Maps satellite imagery and dozens of pictures featured in a *Virginia Mansions* digital spread that the driveway opened to an enormous stone parking area behind the house, which was connected to a glass showcase garage filled with Harcourt's luxury sports cars.

The lead vehicle drove past the four-bay garage, passing a neatly parked fleet of Suburbans before stopping at a covered entrance. Easy enough. Now for the hard part. Decker pulled the earpiece out and tossed it in the footwell before bringing the rifle even with the top of the dashboard. He took his hand off the trigger, keeping the rifle level, and grabbed the door handle as Pierce slowed the SUV.

CHAPTER FIFTY-EIGHT

Dutch Garraty watched the two SUVs pull up to the service entrance, panning the camera away as soon as the two vehicles stopped. He focused on the far-right corner of the showcase garage, the closest point of approach to the service entrance. The camera mounted to the roof of the floor-to-ceiling glass structure didn't depress far enough to give him a view of the south-facing wall. If Decker had somehow slipped through his dragnet of guards and avoided all the estate cameras, this would be his most logical point of approach.

"WARHAMMER. This is QUEBEC ROMEO One," said his quick-reaction team leader. "I've reached the package. It landed in the center of the clearing next to the eastern pond. Had one of those airborne guidance units. Very high-end. I sent two ATVs ahead to recon the other drop site. I could have sworn I caught a glimpse of a parachute in the trees."

"Careful, John," said Dutch. "These guys are good."

"I haven't picked up anything on thermals."

"They could be hiding out. Waiting for a ride back to the house."

"They wouldn't get very far. I have the heavy-weapons support team watching over us."

Dutch muttered to himself, "I don't see what his play is here." Landing that far away from the house might have worked if Decker hadn't used the same tactic a few days ago, but under the current circumstances, Dutch didn't see how they expected to reach the house undetected. Grabbing one of the ATVs would get them only so far, as John said. Dutch had more than fifty trained operatives sweeping the estate. Decker certainly had skills, but there was no way he was getting to the house, and even if he did, the house was virtually impenetrable.

"The package is a square plastic transport case. A big one. It doesn't look locked," said the team leader. "Do you want us to open it?"

"Negative. Just keep Decker from reaching it."

He scanned the wall-size bank of monitors displaying the camera feeds that covered the grounds adjacent to the fourteen-thousand-square-foot house. Because of the mansion's ridiculous size, Dutch had installed digital cameras capable of tracking movement and locking on to targets. Sophisticated software analyzed all the feeds, and none of the feeds indicated movement around the house.

"WARHAMMER! This is QUEBEC ROMEO One. Recon elements report dummy parachutes!"

"Say again?" said Dutch.

"They dropped mannequins!" said the team leader.

"Oh fuck!" he hissed, panning the service entrance camera back to the SUVs.

Two figures lay sprawled on the ground behind the lead Suburban, blood pooling around their heads.

CHAPTER FIFTY-NINE

Decker pressed "Start" on the timer attached to the ball of C-4 and sprinted away from it toward Pierce, who lay pressed against the back of the house twenty feet away. He hit the ground next to Pierce and covered his ears right before the quarter-pound plastic explosive charge detonated, obliterating the reinforced service door and instantly shattering the vehicles' bullet-resistant windows. He took his hands off his ears and peered through the intensifying haze at the flaming mess.

"Might have been overkill," said Decker.

"You think?" said Pierce.

They moved in unison toward the blasted entryway, their rifles pointed toward the patio in case WARHAMMER had left a few sentries on the patio or pool deck. When they reached the scorched hole, Decker peered inside through the smoke, or tried to.

"I can't see a thing," he said.

"Just go," said Pierce. "We don't have a lot of time."

"Hold on," said Decker, pulling another racquetball-size piece of C-4 from his vest.

"What the hell are you doing?"

"I bet WARHAMMER's office isn't too far away." Decker programmed the charge's timer. "He's part of the help, right?"

"Good point," said Pierce, crouching on the other side of the smoldering doorway.

Decker side-armed the ball of C-4 into the darkness and slid out of the way along the side of the house. The charge detonated a moment later, a shock wave of fire and fragments blasting out of the doorway and peppering the adjacent SUV.

CHAPTER

SIXTY

Jacob Harcourt started walking toward the safe room after a second blast shook the house. Frist already stood in front of the hidden door, the bottle of Johnnie Walker Blue Label shaking in his hand.

"Dutch," said Harcourt into his radio, "what the hell is going on out there?" No reply. "Goddamn it, Dutch. I demand a SITREP."

"Can we get in the damn safe room now?" said Frist.

"Where do you think I'm headed? To fix a snack in the kitchen?"

"Watch it, Jacob," said the senator. "You said this place would be safe."

"It is safe," growled Harcourt, switching his radio to the emergency frequency. "Any call sign. This is Jacob Harcourt. I've lost contact with WARHAMMER."

"Mr. Harcourt. This is QUEBEC ROMEO One. I spoke with Mr. Garraty less than a minute ago. He recalled the entire security force to the house right before the explosions. I lost contact with him after that."

"Why would he recall the entire security force?"

"The parachutes were decoys. Mannequins."

"How far out are you?" said Harcourt.

"The ATVs are a minute from the house," he said. "I piled as many as I could fit on the vehicles. Close to thirty men."

"That's good to hear. I'll be in the safe room with the senator. Have your men proceed directly to the study. I'm calling the police and the FBI as soon as I get situated—"

"And the goddamn Secret Service!" interrupted Frist.

"Please," said Harcourt, giving Frist an exasperated look.

"I'm serious," said Frist.

"I just need you to secure the study and wait for law enforcement to arrive," said Harcourt into his radio. "If you run into Decker or his accomplice on the way, you are authorized to use lethal force."

"Kill them!" yelled Frist.

"Kill them on sight," said Harcourt, placing his hand on the camouflaged biometric panel.

"Understood, sir. We'll be there in a few minutes."

Frist slipped into the safe room hallway the moment it cracked open far enough to admit his body, the bottle of scotch catching on the cherrywood doorframe and tumbling to the hardwood behind him. The senator dropped to his knees and groped for the bottle, knocking it several feet into the study. For a brief moment, Harcourt thought Frist might crawl after it.

"There's plenty of booze in the safe room," said Harcourt, pulling the senator to his feet by the collar of his blazer. "We'll break out another bottle as soon as the door locks. We can break out ten bottles for all I care."

"You have Blue Label in there?" said Frist, glancing back into the study.

"No!" said Harcourt, finally losing it. "I have bottles that cost twenty times as much!"

Instead of looking insulted, Frist's eyes widened, and his feet started moving. When both of them stood inside the safe room, clear of the doorway, Harcourt hit the panic button mounted to the wall next to the entry. In the blink of an eye, a titanium door slid out of the wall, sealing the entrance. A loud hiss immediately followed.

"What was that?" said Frist.

"The positive-pressure air system just activated. They can't smoke us out, use poison gas, or anything like that. No air can be forced into the room."

"Then how do we breathe?"

"Gerry. I'm not going to explain every intricacy of this room to you," said Harcourt. "Suffice it to say, the room is self-contained and impervious to explosives."

"How big of an explosion?" said Frist. "And I don't think that qualifies as an 'intricacy,' given what we heard out there."

"That sounds more like the Gerry Frist I've come to admire," said Harcourt, sucking up a little to keep him calm. "The walls can withstand more than anyone would use to breach a room without bringing the entire house down with it."

"I don't think he cares about demolishing your house."

"Fair enough. Which is why we took out an insurance policy. I just need to keep him occupied long enough for our small army to arrive."

"I hope you're right," said Frist. "I don't want to die in here."

"Then let me introduce you to an old friend of mine," said Harcourt, tapping a screen embedded in the wall next to the stainless-steel panic button.

A cherrywood panel on the opposite side of the room slid open to reveal a recessed alcove stocked with expensive-looking bottles. Harcourt reached inside and removed a bottle he'd sampled only twice since he'd purchased it. One of sixty-eight bottles ever produced. He reckoned a few glasses of the rare spirit were a worthy sacrifice, if it might distract this panicmonger. Actually, he'd be happy to give up the entire bottle if it shut him up.

"The Balvenie forty-six-year-old," said Harcourt, cradling it in his hands like a priceless relic.

"How much is that per bottle?"

"About thirty thousand dollars."

"Now that sounds like the kind of friend I'd like to meet," said Frist.

"Gerry. After Monday's vote, you'll be well on your way to meeting more friends like this," said Harcourt. "We just need to wait this out and let the professionals take care of Decker."

Chapter Sixty-One

Decker and Pierce raced through the floating ash until they reached the epicenter of the second blast. The hallway was barely passable at that point; the plastic explosive's high-order detonation had collapsed part of the ceiling. After pushing through a tangle of scorched lumber and fallen drywall chunks, Decker located the security hub—easily identifiable by a thick blood trail leading from the hallway into the glowing room.

Decker crouched next to the splintered frame, taking a quick peek inside. A man lay motionless on the floor in front of a bank of flickering screens, his right leg missing from the knee down. Blood pumped out of the stump at a steady rate. Pierce settled in next to Decker, aiming down the smoke-filled hallway.

"Give me your tourniquet," said Decker, sliding into the room.

The man on the ground came to life, twisting onto his back and swinging a pistol in Decker's direction. Decker grabbed the man's wrist and pounded the butt of his rifle into his solar plexus. The pistol fired once, striking the ceiling above Decker's head, before the man's grip loosened and the pistol fell to the floor. He kicked the pistol across the room and placed the barrel of his rifle against the man's head.

"WARHAMMER?" said Decker.

The mercenary just stared at him with contempt.

"Tourniquet," said Pierce, tossing the nylon device on the man's stomach.

"Today's your lucky day," Decker told him, slowly backing out of the room. "Make sure Harcourt and the good senator know we're coming. I assume they're in the safe room already?"

"You'll never get them out of that room," said the man. "It's impenetrable."

"They're exactly where I want them," said Decker, stepping into the hallway.

He found Pierce crouched in front of a short stairwell leading into the house, tying the end of a spooled wire to the eye hook he'd screwed into the wall two feet above the first step.

"Hurry up," said Pierce, waving him on. "Watch the leg."

Decker stepped over WARHAMMER's mangled leg and proceeded up the stairs. He crouched in the doorway, aiming down a short hallway that led into the kitchen. Pierce stood on the top stair and jammed the claymore mine into the drywall high on the right side of the stairwell. He spent the next few seconds connecting the tightened wire to the mine's modified trigger.

The first team to barrel headlong up the stairs would get hit by seven hundred one-eighth-inch-diameter steel balls traveling at four thousand feet per second. The effect would be devastating at close range in an enclosed space, hopefully discouraging any further attempts to enter the house.

"Ready," said Pierce, tapping his shoulder. "You sure you know where we're going? This place is bigger than Buckingham Palace."

"Senator Steele drew us a nice map."

They moved rapidly through the luxuriously appointed rooms, confident they were alone inside the cavernous house. Decker slowed the pace when they reached the mansion's pièce de résistance, a three-story, windowed great hall overlooking the estate's gardens. The entrance to Harcourt's private study was at the opposite side of the ballroom-size space, and Decker couldn't discount the possibility that the warped tycoon might stick around long enough to fire off a few shots before retreating to the safe room. Sweeping the space with their rifles, Decker and Pierce cautiously made their way across the parquet floor, studying the nooks and crannies of the great hall. When they reached the open study door, he glanced through the window next to him. Lights flickered wildly in the distant tree line.

"We need to pick up the pace," whispered Pierce, nodding at the light show.

"Concur," said Decker, removing a flash-bang grenade from a pouch on his vest and pulling the pin.

He tossed the grenade into the study and crouched next to the door, the room exploding with light a moment later. Decker slipped into the room and turned left, searching for targets, while Pierce did the same with the other half of the room. They trusted each other to clear their assigned sectors, an instinct born from thousands of hours of training and live operations.

"Clear," they said at the same time.

Decker headed right for the hidden door leading to the safe room hallway. Senator Steele had provided Special Agent Reeves with the general location of the door based on the tour Harcourt had given her when she visited the estate with Senator Frist. All part of the con job the two of those assholes had run on her, which Decker planned to make right—in the next few minutes.

"I'm going to step outside to play that beautiful piano for a minute, unless you need me in here," said Pierce.

"This shouldn't take long," said Decker, pulling out a cell phone–size block of C-4.

"Good. I've always wanted to play on a Steinway." Pierce stepped out of the room.

"It's a Steinway D-Two-Seventy-Four, to be precise," said a voice from a hidden intercom speaker. "Custom designed for this house."

"I'll be gentle," Pierce yelled from the grand hall.

"What got your attention? Someone sitting at your half-million-dollar piano?" said Decker. "Or the block of C-4?"

"The piano, Mr. Decker. I bought it as a gift for my wife. It means a lot to her. The charge you're holding is barely enough to get through the outer door."

Decker unsnapped the drop pouch attached to his left leg and removed a one-pound block of C-4, holding it up for Harcourt to see. "How about this?" he said. "And call me Decker."

When Harcourt responded, he heard a frantic voice in the background.

"Still not enough to get through," said Harcourt. "The room is a layered titanium box that can withstand a shaped charge."

Decker laughed. "I don't need to blast through the walls to accomplish my mission. Can you imagine what's going to happen when I detonate a one-pound block of C-4 against one of those walls?"

"I've read the literature, Mr. . . . Decker," said Harcourt. "We'll be fine. It'll ring our bell, but that's about it."

"I was thinking it would collapse the floor and bring the entire house down on you. Probably start a fire, which I would help along by tossing a few incendiary grenades on the rubble. Nothing tastier than that slow-cooked, low-country BBQ taste, right, Senator Frist?"

When several seconds passed without a reply, Decker guessed that Frist was having a meltdown and Harcourt was having serious reservations about his future prospects in the safe room. He was also aware that the clock was ticking. The flickering lights visible through the study window were getting closer.

"Decker. I think there's been a big misunderstanding," said Harcourt.

"Seriously?" Decker shook his head. "I have to admit, I was not expecting you to grovel."

"I believe you've been fed some very erroneous information. Probably by the Russians, or possibly one of my competitors. Whatever you've been told—"

"Stop. Just stop. You know why I'm here, and it's not the vote on Monday—though I can pretty much guarantee that's not going to happen." Decker pulled out a second one-pound block of C-4.

The intercom activated for a second, Frist yelling, "How does he know about the goddamned vote?" before cutting out. Decker had them right about where he wanted them. Just a little farther and he'd seal this deal. He set the first block of C-4 on the desk and held the second up for the hidden camera.

"I'm pretty sure this is enough to fragment the titanium walls and shred your bodies like pulled pork. When they finally get the fire under control and cut through the walls with a plasma torch, Senator Frist's shredded, slow-cooked remains are sure to make North Carolina proud."

"Decker. You're a smart man. I have close to sixty men headed back to the house. You'll never get out of here alive. If you leave now, I'll call them off."

A sharp crack ripped through the study, and the walls rattled for a moment.

"That must have been the quick-reaction force coming through the service entrance," said Decker. "I can't imagine the next team using the same access point. Not after seeing the mess left behind by a point-blank claymore explosion. By the way, WARHAMMER said hello. Well, he didn't actually say hello. He was too busy with the missing leg and all."

Pierce stepped inside the study a moment later, tossing a fist-size object into the room and closing the door behind him.

"Never got to the Steinway. Blew all my time setting up my grand claymore opus. I hope it's appreciated," said Pierce, taking a smartphone-size, touch-screen controller out of the pouch on his vest and checking the screen. "We're in business."

The touch-screen controller was wirelessly connected to the camera grenade Pierce had just thrown into the room. Shaped like an egg, the impact-resistant device was self-righting and contained a 360-degree, maneuverable, night vision–capable camera. Pierce could pan the camera around the room and view the feed from the handheld controller.

"Neither of you will get out of here alive," said Harcourt, cutting all pretenses. "It's not too late to make a deal. Leave now, and my security teams stand down."

"I'll take my chances against your third-rate army," said Decker, turning to Pierce. "Lock the study door and help me prep the C-4."

Precious seconds passed while Pierce locked the door and Decker affixed the smaller C-4 charge to the cherrywood panel he guessed would access the hallway outside the safe room.

"Decker," said Harcourt, "it pains me to do this, but I need you to open the laptop on my desk and click the link in the email on the screen."

"I'll take a pass on the YouTube video."

"You'll want to see this video," said Harcourt. "Harlow Mackenzie and her partners have their own channel. You really should check it out."

CHAPTER

SIXTY-TWO

Jacob Harcourt studied Decker on the fifty-inch, wide-screen monitor mounted to the wall, anxious to see his reaction to the live video feed. Decker's threat to bring the entire house down on the safe room and cook them alive under the wreckage seemed awfully plausible at this point. Everything depended on Gunther Ross's insurance policy, which was ready and waiting.

Harcourt's security team was moving cautiously through the house, checking for trip wires. Pierce had been too far away from the service hallway to remotely detonate the claymore mine. Likewise, with the study door closed, he couldn't electrically detonate anything he had planted while pretending to admire Harcourt's Steinway. Harcourt just needed to keep Decker and Pierce occupied until the team could breach the study door and put an end to this annoying and costly distraction.

"Can you put it up on the screen?" said Frist, holding at least two thousand dollars' worth of rare scotch in his trembling hands.

Harcourt played with the tablet in his lap until the monitor's screen split in half, one side displaying the static picture of his study, the other mostly occupied by Harlow Mackenzie's bloodied and bruised face. A silver strip of duct tape reached from ear to ear, a line of dried blood running down her chin.

"How does that look?" said Harcourt, motioning for him to take a seat.

Frist drained half of his glass with an uncertain look before surrendering to the seat next to him. "This better work," he said, downing the rest of the scotch and glancing at the bar.

"We can polish off the bottle when this is over," said Harcourt, taking a sip of the Balvenie, Frist's desperate eyes watching his glass.

He leaned back in the rich-smelling leather chair and connected to the videoconference.

"Mr. Ross. I trust you understand the stakes here?" said Harcourt.

The camera zoomed out to reveal a masked figure holding a pistol to Mackenzie's head. The rest of Mackenzie's partners knelt in the background with duct tape over their mouths.

"I understand the stakes," said Gunther, his voice muffled by the mask. "Just say the word." He pressed the pistol into Mackenzie's temple.

"Decker. Can you hear me?" said Harcourt.

Decker nodded, staring vacantly at the computer. *Checkmate.*

"You can speak into the computer," said Harcourt. "We're on videoconference."

"I can hear you, but I can't see you."

"You don't need to see me. As long as you and Ms. Mackenzie can see each other, this meeting will be productive."

"What the hell is this?" said Decker.

"Come on, Decker. Don't play dumb. You have exactly ten seconds to walk out of this room before my associate blasts Ms. Mackenzie's brains onto the wall next to her."

"She has nothing to do with this."

"Wrong. She has everything to do with this right now, and only you can save her."

"I don't care what you do with her," said Decker, grabbing the block of C-4 on the desk.

"I'll kill them all, Decker!" said Harcourt. "Harlow Mackenzie. Her partners. I'll even go after their families, like I did before. Did you hear that, Mr. Ross? If anything happens to me, you don't stop until their family lines are erased! Same with Decker's daughter. Same with Decker's parents. Kill every single one of them. Finish the job. Are you starting to get the picture, Decker? Walk away right now, or all of those deaths are on you!"

"I know a bluff when I hear one," said Decker, sounding very unsure of himself.

Harcourt muted his end of the teleconference and turned on the handheld radio, contacting the team leader that had assumed command of the quick-reaction team. "How are we doing out there?"

"We just reached the great hall," whispered the team leader. "Give me two minutes."

"You have one," said Harcourt. "The next time I talk to you, it'll be face-to-face, inside my study—standing over two dead bodies. Click the transmitter twice when you're set up on the door. If I click three times, you breach the door and kill anyone inside. There might be a chance of resolving this without blowing up my office."

"Understood, sir. Radio silence except for the clicks."

He unmuted the teleconference. Time to up the stakes.

"Mr. Ross. Kill Kathleen Murphy," said Harcourt. "Right now."

Gunther Ross turned and nodded at one of the masked men guarding the women, who grabbed Kathleen Murphy by the hair and yanked her forward onto her stomach. A second gunman stepped into view and fired his rifle twice, the woman going slack on the ground.

Decker didn't react to the slaughter. He just sat at the desk, looking defeated, his eyes fixed on the screen like he didn't understand what he'd just seen.

"Now imagine Kathleen Murphy's only sister, Hanna, waking up to find her husband and three children hanging from a tree in their backyard, right before being skinned alive and dissolved in a barrel of acid in her own garage. This is what will happen to everyone connected with you—Harlow Mackenzie, her partners, and Brad Pierce. Add him to the list, too. Why not? Do you see how far I'm willing to take this?"

"I don't understand," said Decker.

"What don't you understand? And make it quick. The clock is still ticking. I'm giving you another ten seconds until I execute the rest of them, except for Ms. Mackenzie. My associate has something special planned for her."

Decker shook his head, still staring at the screen, which zoomed back in on Harlow Mackenzie's terrified face. Harcourt was starting to think that he wouldn't need the team to blast their way into the room. Decker wore the pathetic look of a man who had been solidly outmaneuvered. Beaten so badly—he was unable to react. When he finally spoke, Harcourt almost took pity on him.

"I thought it was the Russians," said Decker, rubbing his face. "I just—I figured it had to be them. Why would anyone else go after the families like that? I can't believe—why would you do that?"

"You just figured it out?" said Harcourt. "Jesus, Decker. And here I was the whole time worried you'd already pieced it together. I mean—you found Meghan Steele against all odds. Take away the fact that she should have been dissolved and poured into a drain three months earlier, and you performed a near miracle. I knew you were good, but that was something else. Impressive. I struggled with that."

"Struggled?" said Decker.

"I didn't want to throw you and your whole group away. But at the end of the day, I figured a group that sharp would sniff me out eventually. I had to bring the entire world down on you—permanently."

The handheld radio clicked twice.

"Time's up, Decker," said Harcourt, gripping the radio. "Surrender now, and the killing ends with the current audience. If my men have to breach that door, I'll make good on the promise to murder every family member I can track down, no matter how remotely they're related. Those deaths will be on you."

"Not much of a choice," said Decker, glancing at Pierce, who held the phone in one hand and a second device in the other.

When Decker nodded, Harcourt knew something was wrong. An explosive crack blasted from the radio, but the screen remained the same. Cries for help and frantic orders followed over the handheld radio as Pierce slowly approached the completely intact study door.

"That was just a warning," said Decker. "The next one will be lethal. I promise."

"Team leader, what's your status?"

"They detonated a claymore on the far side of the hall right as I was about to breach the door. Most of my men are injured, but nothing life threatening. We're pulling back. Who knows what the hell else they have waiting for us in there."

"Get back on the door. They didn't carry a hundred claymores in with them."

Decker's voice interrupted them. "Three more, to be precise. The rest of them placed in a lethal arrangement near the door. I'll let you withdraw your men, but if you return to that door, I'll have no choice but to kill you."

"Do as he says," said Harcourt, turning off the radio and setting it on the table next to his drink.

Decker remained seated at his desk, petting the block of C-4 like it was a cat. For the first time tonight, Harcourt seriously doubted he'd get out of this alive. Decker had completely lost it!

"This is insanity," said Frist. "He can see and hear into the other room."

"Not now," said Harcourt, giving Frist a severe look. "Decker? I thought I had made the consequences clear."

"You did. Crystal clear—for me. I'm not sure about the rest. Special Agent Reeves. Do you need Mr. Harcourt to clarify anything?"

What did he just say? The camera panned left to a razor-bald black man holding up a badge.

"Supervisory Special Agent Reeves," said the man. "I think I've heard and seen more than enough to have a very interesting discussion with the Department of Justice regarding the Steele case."

"What is going on here?" said Frist. "Where's Ross?"

The camera panned back to "Ross," who pulled the balaclava off his head, revealing someone Harcourt had never seen before.

"Who the hell are you?" said Harcourt.

"Just some computer dude you tried to kill today, bro," he said in a surfer accent.

Applause broke out in the room behind the twenty-something kid. Murphy rose from the dead to take a bow toward the camera.

"Decker. I don't know what is happening, but I'm done with the games. You just signed a bunch of death warrants. I don't need Ross. I have other people who can fulfill that contract. I'll have two different groups working on it by the time you blast through the first door. Irrevocable."

"Time to go," said Pierce.

"I'm being told there's a small army hunting us down," said Decker. "Sorry to cut your time short, Senator. Do you have any questions for these two?"

Surely he didn't mean—

"No. Unfortunately, I've heard everything I need to hear," said Margaret Steele. "Upon the wicked he shall rain snares, fire and brimstone, and a horrible tempest: this shall be the portion of their cup."

"Margaret," said Frist. "This is some kind of setup. Harcourt brought me here. I don't know what the hell is going on!"

The line remained quiet.

"Margaret?" pleaded Frist. "Margaret?"

The feed focused on Harlow, who stared at the screen with a neutral expression, slowly shaking her head.

"I predict tough times ahead, Senator Frist," said Harlow. "You might want to start making a mental list of the dirty deeds you've done for Jacob Harcourt over the years. Might come in handy when you're going head-to-head with Gunther Ross in the US attorney's office."

"Head-to-head with Ross? What are you talking about?" said Frist. "Why would I do that?"

"From what I've been told," she said, "there's only one plea deal on the table."

"You just killed everyone you ever knew," said Harcourt. "All of you are dead."

"Yeah? Good luck with that," said Harlow, before nodding at the screen. "Don't do anything I wouldn't do, Decker. We'd like to see you in one piece again."

The videoconference screen went blank, and Decker got up from the desk, holding one of the C-4 blocks in his hand. Harcourt reactivated the intercom system connecting the safe room to the study, ready to plead with him, but Decker just stood there for a moment before opening one of the desk drawers and dropping the C-4 inside. He slid the second block in the drawer and shut it.

"Looks like I won't be needing any of that. Not with Senator Steele quoting Scripture," said Decker before pointing his rifle at the hidden camera. "The only question now is, which one of you is Judas? My money's on the good senator."

The video feed cut out after a single gunshot.

"Decker!" said Harcourt. "Decker!"

A second shot killed the audio.

"What the hell just happened here?" said Frist. "None of this was real. Right?"

Harcourt lifted his glass of scotch off the table, ignoring the ridiculous question. Of course it was real. They were finished. Actually, they were destroyed. Destined to spend the rest of their lives in jail, if they lived long enough to see the arraignment.

"What did he mean by, Which one of us is Judas?" said Frist.

He took a generous pull of his drink, marveling at the velvety-smooth honey and vanilla notes. "Did you tell Margaret you'd be here?"

"Of course not!" said Frist, eyeing his drink.

"Who did you tell?" said Harcourt, downing the rest of the scotch.

"I could use one of those, too," said Frist, staring at him like he was some kind of errand boy.

Harcourt returned the glass to the table and reached down the side of his leg, lifting the cuff of his wool trouser and drawing a compact pistol from a hidden ankle holster. Without pausing, he pointed the pistol at Frist's forehead and pressed the trigger, finally erasing that stupid look from his face.

"I'll get right on it," said Harcourt, sinking into the chair.

He briefly considered blowing his own brains out but quickly dismissed the notion. He had enough money to buy a small country—not to mention the army to defend it. Nobody put Jacob Harcourt out of business that easily.

CHAPTER

SIXTY-THREE

Decker raced over to Pierce, who was leaned up against the wall next to the study door.

"What do you think?" said Decker, crouching next to him.

"I think I have hurt feelings," said Pierce. "Harlow forgot all about me."

"Very funny," said Decker. "What about our breakout plan? Do we need to modify?"

"Negative. There's only one way in the house right now, and every one of those mercs is headed for it. Take a peek," said Pierce, nodding at the window. "We also have a dozen or so injured men surrounding the great hall."

Decker glanced out of the window, careful to stay hidden. A platoon-size group of dark figures swarmed across the patio, headed in the direction of the service entrance. Beyond the seemingly endless patio, six four-seat ATVs sat parked in the grass, offering an irresistible temptation.

"I assume you saw the ATVs?"

"I did," said Pierce. "And I suddenly don't feel like running ten football fields to get out of here."

"Set the charge. We'll let them fill up the great hall before making our move."

"Got it," said Pierce, producing a small block of C-4. "Think it's enough for these windows?"

"There's more in the desk if you need it."

"I still say we level this place."

"Trust me," said Decker. "I want nothing more than to bury those two assholes alive and burn this house down on top of them—but this was part of the deal."

A minute later, with the charge set on the window and the lights turned off, they waited in the dark behind Harcourt's overturned desk. Pierce watched the handheld screen for signs of activity in the great hall, while Decker kept his rifle pointed at the safe room door, on the off chance Harcourt got a crazy idea.

"I'm starting to get movement around the great hall."

"Hit the window," said Decker.

Pierce ducked below the top of the desk and activated the personal locator beacon attached to the shoulder strap of his vest. The room exploded a second later, glass and wood fragments snapping against the thick wooden slab in front of them and generally shredding the rest of the room.

Pierce peeked over the splintered edge of the desk. "We're in business."

The entire floor-to-ceiling window was gone, along with half of the wall.

"I guess that was enough," said Decker.

"Ready for round two?" said Pierce, switching frequencies on the digital detonator.

"Please tell me it's the Steinway."

"It's the Steinway." Pierce clicked the trigger three times.

The study door rattled from a bizarrely resonant explosion that Decker hoped would keep the rest of Harcourt's security team away from the study. They moved quickly to the scorched windowsill, climbing through and hopping ten feet down into the mulch beds next to the eastern edge of the patio.

A waist-high stone wall bordering most of the patio kept them concealed from the house until they reached the ATVs. The house was oddly quiet given the level of havoc and destruction they had wreaked inside. Maybe Harcourt's security team had finally decided enough was enough. Decker peeked over the top of the wall, scanning the driveway zone for guards, while Pierce searched for an ATV with the keys left behind.

Two figures dashed out of the service entrance, taking cover behind the closest SUV.

Decker sighted in on the hood, preparing to fire if they exposed their heads, when a bullet cracked into the top of the wall next to his left shoulder, pelting him with stone fragments. He shifted his aim to the study window, not finding a target. A second bullet snapped inches from his head, striking one of the ATVs. The guards behind the SUV started firing on full automatic, driving Decker below the wall.

"How are we doing with my ride?" he yelled.

"They took the keys with them!" said Pierce, moving between ATVs in a crouch.

"Careful! There's a sharpshooter out there! I can't find him."

Pierce scrambled behind the closest ATV, a bullet flattening its tire at the same time. "Thanks for the warning!" he yelled. "Rooftop. Eastern chimney."

Decker moved several feet down the wall to throw the sharpshooter off target and eased his rifle upward until the top of the chimney appeared in the illuminated reticle of the ACOG sight. He rose less than an inch and started pressing the trigger repeatedly, hitting the base of the chimney with half of the magazine. Without assessing the impact of his bullets on the sharpshooter, he shifted back to the SUV and fired the remaining fifteen rounds.

After a quick magazine swap, he moved back to his original position on the wall and checked the chimney in time to see a dark figure tumble off the roof and hit the ground near the study.

"I found one with keys!" Pierce called.

Decker emptied most of the second magazine in a five-second fusillade directed at the SUV, hammering the hood and peppering its bullet-resistant windshield. When an ATV engine started up behind him, he fired the last few rounds and took off, looking for Pierce. Jumping into the passenger seat, he reloaded his rifle as Pierce floored the engine, and the ATV struggled forward.

"What's wrong?" said Decker.

"Front tire is shot out. It was the only one with a key."

"Stop for a second. We need to take out the rest of the ATVs."

It was unlikely they'd find the other keys in the tangle of limbs and guts left behind, but he didn't want to take the chance. Their ATV barely moved faster than a golf cart at this point. They fired until all of the ATVs sat on at least two flats, then resumed their agonizingly slow trip to the pond near the southeastern corner of the estate.

CHAPTER
SIXTY-FOUR

The moment Pierce turned off the ATV's engine, the steady hum of an aircraft washed over the clearing. Decker jumped off the ATV and glanced back in the direction of the house. Powerful headlights bounced up and down somewhere beyond the trees. The ATV path had narrowed significantly about a hundred yards back, preventing the Suburbans from driving straight to the clearing, but he wanted to be long gone before they got that close. One hundred yards of forest was hardly a buffer for a patient shooter.

"I got the package," said Pierce. "You contact Bernie. We need to move fast."

Decker took out his satellite phone and dialed the pilot circling above as he followed Pierce to the Pelican transport case in the middle of the clearing.

"Which one of you was driving? My mother drives faster than that," answered Bernie.

"Talk to Pierce about it," said Decker.

"What are we looking at?" said the pilot.

Decker glanced at the headlights again. "Pickup in thirty seconds."

"That's pushing it," said Pierce, already unsnapping the oversize crate.

"Dammit, Decker! You could have given me a heads-up," said Bernie. "That's cutting it really close."

"We made a lot of new friends down here."

"I bet you did. Be there in *around* thirty seconds. This isn't a performance jet, you know."

"See you shortly," said Decker, pocketing the phone.

Pierce opened the crate, and they started separating the components. Bernie had promised no assembly required, and he'd kept his word. His version of the Fulton Recovery ground package consisted of a three-man harness connected by a braided nylon rope to a large suitcase-size sack inside the case. The hardest part would be figuring out the harness within the next twenty seconds or so. The rest was up to Bernie.

Decker cracked two chem lights and dropped them on the ground next to the harness, relieved to see that Bernie had upgraded his design. Decker and Pierce stepped into the side-by-side leg holes and simultaneously yanked the harness snug between their legs before pulling the shoulder straps over their arms. With the sound of the C-123 bearing down on them, they methodically snapped and tightened each strap, starting from the waist and working their way up. Missing a single strap, on either harness, could be catastrophic for both of them.

Normally, they would inspect each other's harnesses, but they didn't have time. The headlights had stopped moving, their beams poking into the clearing through the trees, and the pickup was imminent. They sat on the ground, and Pierce pulled the yellow rip cord on the side of the nylon bag, activating a compressed helium bottle and launching an SUV-size balloon. The near-instantaneously filled balloon raced skyward, a strobe light flashing beneath it.

The same nylon line connected to their harness rapidly unraveled from the bag, pulled tight by the balloon, until its four-hundred-foot journey ended, tugging on their harness.

"I hate this part," said Decker.

"I hate all of it," said Pierce.

The C-123's massive dark shape appeared over the eastern edge of the clearing, passing directly overhead a few seconds later, the balloon's strobe light vanishing above it. Without warning, they were yanked off the ground, rising smoothly above the clearing. For a few more seconds, they continued straight up like a rocket, until the aircraft had flown far enough to start pulling them sideways. The trip up was surprisingly gentle until they steadied behind the aircraft about a hundred feet off the ground. The lights from Harcourt's mansion rapidly faded into the distance as the crew started to winch them toward the plane.

They started to spin until they extended their arms and legs, stabilizing their 125-mile-per-hour flight through the darkness as they edged closer to the ramp underneath the aircraft's tail. After five minutes of "flying" behind the C-123, they reached the edge of the ramp, where the flight crew yanked them inside. When the ramp sealed shut, the plane banked sharply to the right and climbed to a normal altitude for an aircraft this size.

When they leveled off, Decker and Pierce removed the Fulton harness and sat down on the bench lining the cargo compartment, both of them staring into space for a few minutes. Decker felt exhausted, more emotionally than physically. Leaving Harcourt and Frist behind had been the hardest promise he'd ever kept. The two of them were responsible for murdering his wife and son, among countless others. Leaving them to the system—or "the wolves," as Harlow had put it—didn't sit well with him.

"Deep thoughts?"

Decker shrugged. "No. Just zoning out."

"If anyone's earned the right, it's you."

"I guess."

"No guessing about it," said Pierce. "Those two would still be walking around like Godzilla, stomping on the little people, if it wasn't for you."

"We'll see," said Decker, feeling himself spiraling into darkness.

The cargo bay's intercom broke Decker's thoughts.

"That's the thanks I get?" said Bernie. "You just sit back there like passengers on Delta Airlines? Get the hell up here, pronto."

Decker yelled at the open door leading to the cockpit, "You need to hire a damn copilot! I'm too tired to move."

"Did you say *copilot*?" said Bernie over the intercom. "I can't afford to hire a copilot hauling your sorry ass around."

The flight crew chief shook her head. "Bernie's full of crap. He's never given up the controls. Ever. Ain't no copilot in Bernie's past or future."

"I heard that!" said Bernie. "I had the intercom rigged so I can remote activate—"

"Yeah. Yeah," interrupted the flight crew chief. "Five months ago. On a Monday afternoon."

"Really? You all knew?"

"Did you think we were just quiet all the time back here?"

"At least you're not plotting against me anymore."

"Yeah. That's what we spent every moment of our time in the air doing before. Plotting against the only pilot on the plane."

Decker laughed. "And for your information, I'm a fully paying customer. I'm not keeping you from hiring a copilot. The second half of your fee will be transferred as soon as I get to my laptop."

"The second half is on me," said Bernie. "Good to have you back, Decker."

"I'm not back. This was a onetime deal."

"You're back, or I'll charge you double for the trouble."

"We're back," said Pierce.

He gave Pierce a skeptical look. "I'm not back," he said.

"I said *we're* back. Unless you have better plans," said Pierce. "No rush. It'll take a little while to build up our client base again."

Decker laughed. "Not a lot of demand for taking down rogue CEOs and unscrupulous senators."

"Sounds like our new mission statement," said Pierce.

"I'd invest in a firm like that," said Bernie.

"We'll see," said Decker, his thoughts suddenly far away. "We'll see."

CHAPTER SIXTY-FIVE

The walk from his hotel next to the Annapolis City Dock to St. Mary's Cemetery measured 1.3 miles on his phone, but it may as well have been fifty. Maybe it was the oppressive midsummer Annapolis heat that made it feel that long, or maybe it was the fact that it had taken him a full day to work up the nerve to make the trip.

Decker had meant to walk the mile or so yesterday but had found himself unable to leave the hotel. He ate dinner in his room and spoke with Harlow for almost an hour, which felt good for him at the time but came back to haunt him in the morning. He liked Harlow a lot, which was a little too much at the moment. It had taken him all morning and another solitary lunch in his room to reach the point where he could leave the hotel. Halfway to the cemetery, he wished he'd taken a cab.

When he reached Westgate Circle, orderly rows of white grave markers appeared beyond an old stone wall bordering Annapolis National Cemetery. After walking around the traffic circle and continuing up West Street, the tidy white lines yielded to trees, bushes, and a scattering of timeworn gravestones that formed the historic Brewer Hill Cemetery.

He kept going until he caught a glimpse of a gravestone beyond the homes lining the south side of West Street, where he stopped for a moment to take a few deep breaths. When Decker started up again, he didn't stop until he reached the wrought-iron entrance, pausing in the shade of a lone tree growing just beyond the fence. Now what? All he knew for sure was that they had been buried in this cemetery. He hadn't been allowed to attend the service.

Across the cemetery, a black Suburban pulled up to the vehicle entrance on Spa Road and blocked it. A few seconds later, he heard a vehicle pull up behind him and turned around to face another black SUV. He walked slowly backward until he stood a few feet inside the cemetery. At least he'd die on the same patch of ground as his wife and son. The SUV pulled forward, making room for a black Town Car. Now he was confused. There was no way Harcourt would make a public appearance after what had transpired two days ago.

The rear window rolled down, revealing one of the last faces he expected to see this Sunday afternoon.

"Mind if I join you?" said Margaret Steele.

"I don't really know where I'm going."

"I'll show you," she said, getting out of the car with a large bouquet of colorful daisies.

Decker instantly regretted not bringing flowers himself, which must have shown on his face.

"I brought two," she said, splitting the bouquet in half.

"How did you know I'd be here?"

"I had you followed."

"Seriously?"

"Not really," said Steele. "Mr. Pierce told me you were headed here. I did hire someone to watch the hotel."

"I almost didn't make it here today, either."

"I would have waited as long as it took," she said, her eyes watering. "I'm really sorry for keeping you from them. I had no right to do that."

"I don't blame you. I'm sorry I couldn't do more to save your daughter."

"There was nothing you could do."

"I played it back thousands of times in my head."

"Ryan—may I call you Ryan?"

He nodded.

"Ryan. My daughter was dead the moment she was taken, and everyone else? They were dead the moment I agreed to hire you. They didn't think you'd find her, and when you did—"

"This kind of thinking makes my head spin."

"I wish I could say it gets better." She offered her arm. "Shall we?"

She guided them to a single elegant gravestone engraved with the names of his wife and son.

"I'll leave you alone," she said, stepping away with her bouquet.

"Thank you for this," he said, kneeling in the grass in front of the stone.

He placed the flowers on the ground in front of the grave next to an old bouquet—and closed his eyes, vividly recalling the last time he had seen them together. The scene had faded from his mind so much over the past two years, he was afraid he'd lose it completely. He cried without holding back, something he hadn't done since he learned they had been killed.

After he'd stopped crying and wiped his eyes on his sleeve, he glanced to his left and saw Senator Steele kneeling in prayer in front of a gravestone only a row over. He kissed his hand and touched the stone in front of him before getting up and walking over to her. When he saw the names on the gravestone in front of her, he fell to his knees, crying again.

DAVID THOMAS STEELE
MEGHAN MARGARET STEELE

Margaret Steele held him until he was done, helping him up onto unsteady legs. Decker dried his eyes again and took a deep breath.

"Are you okay?" she said.

"I feel better than I did about ten minutes ago," he said in what was left of his voice. "It was good seeing them again, if you know what I mean."

"I know exactly what you mean," said Steele, regarding him kindly. "And I don't want to rush you out of here."

"I think that's all for me right now. I'll probably stick around town for a few days and visit some more." He glanced over at his family's plot, then turned back to Steele. "I saw the bouquet. Thank you for leaving flowers while I couldn't. That means more to me than you know."

"I think about our families a lot," she said. "Can I give you a ride back to your hotel? I'd like to discuss something with you. Something I've been thinking about quite seriously since Friday night."

"I might walk around for a little while," he said. "This town holds a lot of memories for me. I'm afraid if I go back to the hotel, I'll lock myself inside again."

"I doubt that very much, but I understand. Do you mind if we talk on the way back to my car?"

"Sure," he said, intrigued by her persistence.

"I'm not someone to mince words, so I'm going to lay this on the table and get your first impression. Just so you understand, I won't take no for an answer today. I really need you to think about this."

Now he was really intrigued.

"We got lucky with Harcourt," said Steele.

"Lucky?"

"I've withdrawn the bill that I cosponsored with Gerald Frist," said Steele. "Apparently, he was accidentally shot by one of Harcourt's guards during the confused rescue that ensued after your escape. My guess is it wasn't so accidental."

"I should have brought the house down on him," said Decker. "Please tell me he's in custody."

"Unfortunately, Harcourt's nowhere to be found."

"And you want me to find him."

"Not yet," said Steele. "My point is that Harcourt would have pulled off this Praetor agenda if you hadn't intervened."

"I don't understand what you're suggesting."

"Aegis Global is just one of far too many criminal enterprises masquerading as legitimate businesses. Some don't even pretend, like the Solntsevskaya Bratva and drug cartels. Getting lucky isn't a legitimate strategy for dealing with known and emerging threats of this scale. I need someone willing to work with me to expose and ultimately stick a dagger through the heart of these threats."

"Mr. Pierce and I won't be able to solve the drug cartel problem in a week," said Decker. "I don't want to set your expectations too high."

She laughed. "I have significant private financial resources that I'm not squeamish to spend, and a considerable network of contacts, government and private, domestic and international. And I have access to information that you could only dream of at World Recovery Group. The only thing I lack is an utterly reliable and effective group of associates to channel these resources against these threats to humanity."

"I feel like you're working up to a job offer."

"More like a side business," she said. "One that will never be directly connected to me in any way."

"I don't even have a primary business. And there's still the somewhat showstopping issue of my prison status."

"I'll take care of that, either way."

When they reached the gate, she led them into the shade to get a slight reprieve from the blazing sun.

"So. Does this sound like something you're interested in?"

"You told me I can't say no yet."

"I was being dramatic," said Steele. "Yes or no. First impression."

"Yes. As long as I get to finish the job with Harcourt."

She shook her head. "No. I'm going to let the system take care of Harcourt, unless he becomes a threat again. I don't suspect he will. Within a few days, he'll be one of the most wanted people on the planet and all of his assets will be frozen. Aegis Global will collapse shortly after that. I'll make sure of it."

Decker stared at his shoes for a time, then took a breath. "I can live with that—for now."

"I won't hold you up any longer," said Steele. "I'm not in a rush to get anything off the ground, so I'll be in touch once you start building the foundation for a new firm."

"I might be a little more discreet with the scale this time."

"Not a bad idea," she said. "In the meantime, if there's anything I can do for you, don't hesitate to reach out. I'll send you my private number."

"Thank you."

Senator Steele had stepped away and almost reached her car when Decker thought of something she could do for him immediately.

"Senator Steele!" he said, heading toward her.

Her bodyguards reacted instinctively, moving to cut him off.

"It's fine," she said, waving them away.

"I thought of something you might do that would mean everything to me."

"Whatever it is, Ryan," said Steele, "I'll do what I can."

"I haven't spoken with my daughter, Riley, in over two years," said Decker. "She blamed me for her mother and brother's deaths, and I haven't seen or heard from her since everything fell apart in Hemet. My wife's sister shielded her from me, which I guess I can understand, given what the papers and the prosecutors said. I know there's no way to magically undo all of that, but a visit from you personally explaining what really happened might start the process. I know this is a big ask."

"Consider it done," she said. "I'll figure out how to do it right. You don't have to worry about a thing. I just need to know how to get in touch with her."

"I can put you in touch with someone that knows where to find her," said Decker. "Oh. There's one more thing, which is kind of related."

"You have my undivided attention," said Steele, standing partly behind the car door.

"I'm not sure I should risk getting on a commercial flight to Los Angeles until my status with the Bureau of Prisons is resolved."

"LA?"

"I have some unfinished business there. Possible partners in this venture you're suggesting."

"Harlow Mackenzie's firm?"

"Yes. She's the one protecting my daughter."

"Let me know when you want to fly back. I'll arrange a flight. Make sure you give me a private number for Ms. Mackenzie. I'd like to thank her personally."

"And make her a job offer?"

"I'll let you take care of that," she said. "Welcome back, Ryan. Three days ago, I couldn't have conceived of saying that."

"Me, neither," said Decker. "But I'm finally starting to feel like it's good to be back."

ACKNOWLEDGMENTS

This is the toughest part of the book. So many hands touch every book I write. Some far more than others—but in the end, the story wouldn't be the same without every hand or fingerprint.

First and foremost, I have to thank the readers who have stuck with me for close to a decade. Without all of you, my wife wouldn't have let me quit my day job five years ago. Seriously. Thank you for your continued readership and support.

To the entire Thomas & Mercer team. They kept left-brain Steve centered throughout the entire process. Not an easy task!

A special thank-you to Gracie Doyle for reading and handing my somewhat unorthodox synopsis to Megha Parekh, who took the Ryan Decker series concept and ran with it! When I say "ran with it," I mean she really got into the characters, the story, and the series. Megha's editorial direction has been nothing short of insightful and incredible. No Thomas & Mercer thank-you would be complete without a Sarah Shaw shout-out—for creating a perpetually welcoming and fun environment for authors!

To David Downing, who has been my developmental editor for three Thomas & Mercer books. Always a pleasure to go back and forth with you over the bigger-picture concepts in my manuscripts. I don't think we've disagreed on anything consequential yet! Or maybe I'm just being too easy on you. There's always the next novel.

To Matthew Fitzsimmons, a perfect sounding board for my early draft. He found no flaws! (I wish.) Thank you for the ninth-inning changes to my lineup. They made a huge difference. Harlow owes you a drink.

Last but not least (well aware of the cliché, David!), to my wife—for her story- and character-building guidance throughout my career. As my first reader, she's kept me from circling the drain more times than I can count. *The Rescue* wouldn't be the same book without her. Did I mention her unwavering support?

About the Author

Steven Konkoly is the *USA Today* bestselling author of more than twenty novels and short stories, including the speculative postapocalyptic thrillers *The Jakarta Pandemic* and *The Perseid Collapse*, the Fractured State series, and the Zulu Virus Chronicles. A graduate of the US Naval Academy and a veteran of several regular and elite US Navy and Marine Corps units, he brings his in-depth military experience to bear in his fiction. Konkoly lives in central Indiana with his family, where he still wakes up at "zero dark thirty" to write. For more information, visit www.stevenkonkoly.com.